Don Ayotte
2018

HORIZON OF FEAR

Action adventure novel

DONALD RALEIGH AYOTTE

© 2017 Donald Raleigh Ayotte
All rights reserved.

ISBN: 1548859060
ISBN 13: 9781548859060

Disclaimer

With the exception of historical and current public figures, no character in this book is intended to portray any private character, living or dead. Any resemblance to same is purely coincidental.

DEDICATION

*This novel is dedicated to the many military men women
and law enforcement agencies from the many nations who
have fought and paid the ultimate price to keep their citizens
safe from terrorism. My hat is off to all of you.*

INTRODUCTION

This novel discusses the threat of Global Islamic Terrorism at its worst and the affects of religious extremism on the world's population. Although Jihadism is not a sovereign state and cannot be dealt with as a nation, the problem of rogue non-state actors must be dealt with greater intensity than Jihadism presents itself.

Acknowledgements

I would like to thank my wife, Sue for putting up with me while changing careers from Journalism, to become a novel writer.Family is the most important thing in my life. I would like to acknowledge my friend and ally, Wolfgang von Baumgart for his skill in editing and offering very helpful suggestions in the final manuscript.

I would also acknowledge Maribeth Fischer and the Rehoboth Beach Writers Guild for good times we had during the "Free Writes", where I first started this novel. It is a place for creative writers to gather to practice their chosen craft.

Chapter 1

Nate awoke from a sound sleep with the alarm blaring and bright sunlight entering the bedroom window after being filtered by the leaves of an enormous maple tree. The early morning sunshine warmed the misty cool Delaware air, evaporating the damp haze that hung across the fields like low-lying clouds.

It was just before Memorial Day weekend and tourists hadn't yet descended on the beach area like a swarm of locusts on a wheat field. The weather was warm and the sun baked the lingering coolness of winter from Nate's body.

He thought of packing his reliable beach chair into his second hand car and driving to Dewey Beach for a relaxing morning of doing nothing or maybe taking his twenty-three foot cuddy cabin cruiser out of the Indian River Inlet into the ocean for a little fishing.

"No," he thought, "today was a day for relaxing." Taking the boat out seemed like too much work, so he decided to go with the beach chair.

He heard the vibrating sound of his cell phone as he looked over to the nightstand where it sat slowly undulating toward the edge of the stand.

He grabbed at it and missed. The phone tumbled to the floor and rolled under the bed. By the time he had retrieved it the vibrating had stopped. He quickly checked the number of the last incoming call. It was a 996 area code. That number was faintly familiar and Nate scoured his memories.

He was still half-asleep and a little groggy from a late night, but he knew it would come to him as soon as he took his mind off it. He wandered into the kitchen, grabbed a cup of coffee from the batch made the day before and jammed it into the microwave.

It finally hit him like a sledgehammer striking an anvil, 996 was the area code for Saudi Arabia and the only person he knew that would call his cell phone from there was his old friend, Omar al-Douri.

He quickly dialed back. Omar answered on the first ring. "Nate, I don't have much time to talk and I'm not sure this line is secure," he said, speaking quickly. "I've received information that a terrorist plot on several cities in Europe could include a tactical nuclear weapon. I've already spoken to *Global News Weekly* in Zurich where you used to work. Karl is on his way to talk to you," he said.

Karl was an old associate and friend from *Global News Weekly*. They had worked together on many assignments and although Nate hadn't seen him in years, he frequently kept in touch.

"I'm in danger and I have to get my family out of Saudi Arabia," Omar blurted, sounding fearful. Nate heard a couple of clicks, then no signal. He thought of calling Global, but decided to wait to see what Karl had to say when he arrived from Europe.

Nate had known Omar for nearly twelve years and it wasn't his nature to become unhinged about anything. He had always admired his friend's ability to stay completely calm under pressure. It's what had made him a successful businessman in a country like Saudi Arabia. He had many connections and his family was well respected by the Royal House. Nate was troubled, but decided to wait for Karl to arrive and wondered why *Global News Weekly* would be sending Karl to speak to him. Parting three years earlier with the publication had not been exactly the most pleasant experience in his memories.

He shed the thoughts from his mind as he sipped his coffee and thought about spending the day in the sun. It was supposed to be warm today and he was eager to feel the sun on his face as he read and relaxed.

The late morning and early afternoon time Nate spent sitting on Dewey Beach before the tourist season began was exactly what he needed to recharge his life batteries and keep his sense of balance. He enjoyed watching the gentle waves roll onto the beach, spotting an occasional tanker offshore as it entered the mouth of the Delaware River at Lewes on its journey to either the Port of Wilmington or Philadelphia or perhaps on their way out into the ocean to faraway places like Africa, Asia or South America.

Nate stood at the water's edge looking south toward the Indian River Inlet until the beach became a thin tan line blurring into the horizon. Occasionally, seagulls fought over scraps of discarded food left by beachgoers or slyly stalked the bait buckets of surf fishermen while they were busy pulling in bluefish.

Expensive beach homes, most of them three stories tall, lined the beach as far as the horizon to the south. Only two miles north was Cape Henlopen and the mouth of the Delaware Bay.

The breeze was gentle and cool today with just a hint of the hot summer that was yet to come. The brown sand was warm, but not hot enough to burn the soles of your feet and the water had not yet warmed enough, except for the bravest of souls to swim in. It was quiet, peaceful and nothing seemed to break the peace of the moment.

Nate's watch displayed 10:20 and the sun was already high in the sky, as the days were lengthening in late May before summer began with a vengeance. The summer had been in the mid 90's and very humid and the beach sand at the peak of the season was hot enough to burn a person's bare feet.

Time on the beach hung suspended in limbo waiting for Memorial Day weekend and the arrival of multitudes of recently released kids from universities mostly on the East Coast and tourists that had booked the beach homes a year in advance, paying exorbitant fees.

He sighed and lay back in his canvas all-purpose blue beach chair, breathing in the fresh cool breeze, thinking of *Global News Weekly* and his old job. The ringing of his cell phone broke the silence and the intensity of his thoughts just as the sun was warming his body.

Glancing down at the number on the display window, he picked it up and said, "Hello, Ken." Ken Miller was his current managing editor. Although Ken wouldn't hire him fulltime, he was certainly willing to buy everything Nate wrote for him.

"It must be nice," he thought, "having an experienced journalist who was between jobs, writing for peanuts, just to maintain a portfolio of published pieces."

"Hi Nate, I was wondering if you could do me a favor," he asked.

"Sure Ken," Nate said, in his nicest butt-kissing voice, "what've you got for me?"

"I've got a town meeting in Bethany Beach that will discuss the possibility of constructing an offshore wind farm that will generate electricity," Ken said, with just a hint of begging in his voice.

The mere mention of offshore wind farms vividly triggered Nate's journalistic memory.

A brilliant inventor and his colleague tried to share an innovative sustainable / renewable energy proposal with the local sport fishing community, in which a series of floating tidal hydrokinetic electric generators would have been anchored to the bottom of the Indian River Inlet. The plan was designed to harness its rapidly moving waters to generate enough clean power to light up half of Delaware at a cost cheaper than conventional coal fired plants.

They were greeted with catcalls, vulgarities and threats, despite all of the environmental, job creation and other economic benefits the project would have created for "Lower Slower Delaware", as Sussex County came to be known.

Some state and local politicians were also present, but they added nothing of substance to the discussion, so as not to offend the unruly mob.

"So much for politicians…" thought Nate, as he snapped back to the task at hand.

Nate knew the one thing Ken disliked about his job was covering meetings. He would do nearly anything to avoid it including hiring a stringer to do it for him.

"Oh well," Nate thought, at least it keeps my writing hand busy and that's important for a writer.

"Sure Ken," he said, "what time does it start?" "Seven o'clock, but be there a little early and get some quotes and e-mail me the story Monday morning," Ken replied, sounding hurried as usual.

Ken always looked and sounded hurried and stressed, unless you happened to catch him on a Monday morning after a weekend of fishing. He often arrived at the newsroom after a weekend of fishing, still wearing his ancient fishing hat with hooks and lures embedded in a clustered fashion.

Ken was in his early fifties and a little out of shape, probably from sitting behind a desk doing the ulcer-forming job of meeting publishing deadlines. He was good at his job and was easy to work for. He had given Nate the opportunity to keep his writing hand busy by allowing him to freelance for his weekly paper, "*The Sentinel*," which wasn't bad as far as weekly papers go. With Ken at the helm, it seemed to be doing a lot better than it had done under the inexpert tutelage of the previous editor.

Ken seemed to have an eye for news and was always trying to improve the quality of the paper's coverage. He had more ability than this position offered and Nate often wondered why Ken had settled for working there. "Oh well, better him than me," Nate thought, almost audibly.

Nate glanced at his watch, it was only eleven-thirty and he had plenty of time. He always carried his laptop with him locked in the trunk of his old beater in a padded carrying case. He knew that he could easily leave at six-thirty and drive the eight miles to the town hall, cover the meeting and send the piece in as a word document by e-mail. There were plenty of hot spots for him around in the area to get up on-line and he knew where most of them were.

"Nope," he thought. "I've got plenty of time to relax and nothing will come between relaxation and me today." The sun was like a shot of adrenaline to his system and he welcomed it.

Time had always been the most valuable commodity for him. Even a trivial assignment as this one excited him and it would make relaxing in the sun for the rest of the day even more soothing.

The late spring sun was warm, but not unbearably hot. Early summer was not his best season at the Delaware Beaches. He liked autumn for several reasons by far, but mainly because the temperature was still warm while the humidity was low and the water was still warm enough for swimming. If a stray hurricane didn't wipe out the beaches, fall had it, "hands down."

Nate was restless for the fast life of reporting and the adventure it brought into his life. He closed his eyes, briefly envisioning the good times in Zurich when he was on the cutting edge of his profession.

He glanced up wiping the sweat from his forehead and thought for an instant that he had spotted Karl Schroeder, but the walking silhouette was still too far down the beach to recognize and his glasses were in the car.

"Anyway, Karl couldn't have possibility have made it here this quickly," he thought.

"Buying a sailboat to travel up and down the East Coast wouldn't be a bad idea," he daydreamed, pondering his options.

The only problem with that idea was, although he lived well, Nate was cash poor. He had bought the cuddy cabin cruiser as a fixer-up special from a neighbor who needed the money and had just finished repairing everything on it. With the fresh paint, she looked new.

Just as he started to drift off to sleep, a clear unmistakable voice interrupted the calm of his thoughts. "It's been a long time Nate," the voice said. He looked up to see his old friend and colleague Karl Schroeder looking remarkably the same in the three years since he had last seen him.

Karl was still working for Global and in better days they had worked together on many assignments in the Middle East, Africa and other trouble spots that happened to pop up. They were generally assigned to the kind of stories that were in isolated parts of the world that could result in kidnapping for ransom or political gain or even death if they weren't careful. In spite of being dangerous, the work was always exciting, the pay was good. They were young and hooked on journalism, convinced that it was the best job in the world.

Karl was an American citizen by birth. His parents were successful and wealthy and had emigrated from Germany just before he was born. He spoke both German and English without an accent and felt comfortable in both countries. At six-one, with blond hair, blue eyes and a ready smile for almost anyone, Karl looked every part of the German heritage that was his.

He had been Nate's friend for eleven years, ever since their college days at the University of Delaware. Nate hadn't seen him in the eight years since he had been forced to resign from Global by a ruthless young editor on his way up.

"What brings you back to the Western Hemisphere," he asked, surprised that he had arrived so quickly. He knew that Karl enjoyed living in Europe far more than the United States, but he also knew Karl very well and knew that he wasn't here without a good reason.

"It's good to see you again, Nate. The magazine sent me to see if they could get you to come back," he said, with an encouraging grin. A source in Saudi Arabia has informed us of a terrorist plot, that involves the probable use of tactical nuclear weapons in Europe and perhaps the Middle East," Karl said, without drawing a second breath.

Nate liked that about Karl. Always articulate, he had probably practiced what he would say on the way down the beach or even on the plane trip from Zurich.

Nate got the distinct feeling he was being baited like a trout by a shiny lure, with just enough information to set the hook. It wasn't a bad feeling, but Karl was withholding information just to set the hook.

He decided to keep Omar's call a secret for now or at least until he found out how much Karl knew about the terrorist plot. He wondered how Omar had gotten his cell phone number, not that he minded. Omar had been a good friend and it would be good to see him and catch up on old times.

"How'd you find me," Nate asked, thinking of his isolated spot on the beach.

"It wasn't hard," Karl replied, "I just googled your name. I knew you would be writing for someone and it only took about five minutes to find this small paper in Bethany Beach. Your editor told me about your favorite spot on the beach."

"Well, you're a sight for sore eyes. It has been hard for me to get good work after they blackballed me for mouthing off to that pipsqueak," Nate said, a bit angry even now.

"After the tongue-lashing I had given him, it didn't matter how good a correspondent I was, as long as Jack Warren was there, I assumed that I wouldn't be going back," he thought.

Karl saw the look on Nate's face and quickly realized what he was thinking. "Nate, Jack has been demoted -- matter of fact, he's damn lucky he wasn't fired," Karl said, with a bit of amusement in his voice. "He got into an argument with Hans Schuler at the Christmas party after he had one too many."

Schuler was the CEO of *Global News Weekly* and to him his opinion was the only one that counted. Global never fired anyone. They just made it unbearable to work there and Hans figured Jack would just fire himself. Being demoted to correspondent was quite a humiliation for Jack.

"He hasn't written anything yet worth printing," Karl said, dismissing the subject as if it were old business.

Karl was one of those rich kids, whose parents were jet setters. He spent nearly all of his childhood and teen years in boarding schools. It wasn't that his parents didn't love him. They both had careers and came from old money. It was simply the way they were raised..

Karl had given up trying to spend more time with his parents when he was twelve and his childhood was gone before his parents were barely aware that he was their son. When he had opted to stay in America and attend the University of Delaware, they figured their responsibilities, as parents were finished. Although he and Nate had very different beginnings, they had become fast friends in college had co-written many assignments for Global.

Karl and Nate were both people watchers. You had to be able to read people or you would never be on the cutting edge of your profession. You had to have a nose for a story and a good knowledge of how to ask questions, as well as what questions to ask to get the story behind the story.

Everybody has a story on the surface, but if you know how to ask questions, the real story is locked inside. It was evident by the nearly imperceptible grin on his face that Karl knew Nate was hooked and would be returning to Zurich with him. He also knew that Nate had been given a raw deal when Jack forced him to resign from Global and he had told him as much.

"Can you work for eighty-five thousand plus bonuses," asked Karl, knowing damn well it was more than he was making when he resigned. Nate had a hunch that something big was in the air and the high offer confirmed it and he wanted in on it.

"I've got no problem with the money, but you need to tell me what's going on here Karl," Nate said, looking him in the eye. "We'll talk on the plane. Nate, can you pack tonight? Our plane leaves Dulles airport tomorrow afternoon at two." It was just like Karl, always assuming, never asking; but, he was used to that and there was never any offense taken. "I'll be ready. I have some business to finish today, but packing won't take long," Nate said, as Karl started scrawling something on a piece of paper.

While walking along the mostly deserted beach, he looked at the piece of paper Karl had handed him. On it were hastily scrawled a motel and room number as well as his cell number and at the bottom of the paper, "Rusty Rudder 10 p.m." He tucked the scrap of paper in the pocket of his swimming trunks and leaned back in his favorite beach chair to relax and think. His mind didn't want to process the events of the morning that had steamrolled their way into his life. Nate smiled at the thought of returning to Europe and the excitement that international journalism presented.

Telling his roommate, Andrea, would be the easy part. He knew that he would be leaving, when Karl's plane left for Zurich the following day. He knew as soon as Karl had made the offer, that he had been taking it easy far too long and Karl knew it, too. This was exactly the chance Nate had been waiting for.

He had met Andrea two years before at the beach just after she had finished with a nasty divorce. She had been a reporter in desperate need of a place to stay and he had offered to rent her a room in his house with free run of the place. She had been skeptical at first, but soon realized that he wasn't interested in a relationship at that particular time and had gladly accepted his offer. They had become great friends in the last two years and he trusted her completely. Nate knew that he wouldn't have to worry about his house while he was in Zurich, with Andrea living there. With all the excitement, he had almost forgotten his assignment for Ken.

Nate's first instinct was call him and beg off, but Ken was a friend and it wouldn't take but two hours to write this one up and e-mail it in after the meeting at seven p.m.

The meeting went easy and he started work on the short piece. Nate's mind drifted to his meeting with Karl at the Rusty Rudder. He was sure there was something more to the offer that Karl wasn't disclosing. He knew that for Hans Schuler to send Karl to Delaware to offer him his job back, for the kind of money that Global was offering that something important must be in the air.

The Rusty Rudder was the largest complex in Dewey Beach and the bar itself in the summer after Memorial Day weekend was so packed that there was usually standing room only. The band blares out rock and roll music with liquor and beer flowing as freely as a waterfall after a thunderstorm. It was Karl's nature to manage adding some fun into the mix after business was accomplished and he never missed an opportunity. If there was a lively spot to spend free time, he would find it. Nate smiled, recalling the days he and Karl had worked assignments and scheduled nighttime fun in some of the best spots Europe had to offer.

Nate sighed after finishing the story for Ken; all six hundred and fifty-three words of it, sending it and bagging up his laptop. He glanced at his watch as it read 10:32 p.m. and knew where Karl would be. Nate found him just where he thought Karl would be, doing what he was best at doing. He parked across the way in front of the Books and Coffee restaurant and strode quickly to the front doors of the Rusty Rudder.

Beside Karl at a table close to the band, was an elegant Asian girl in her mid-twenties, sipping an exotic drink. It usually didn't take long for Karl to connect with someone interesting. His ability to flow naturally into interesting conversations gave him the extraordinary ability as a journalist that had led him to the top of his profession.

Karl was the ultimate bachelor with a long history of short romances. Nothing was more important to him than his work and he was at the top of his game and intended to stay there. It wasn't as if he wouldn't entertain the thought of a permanent relationship, if he thought he could fit it in. Karl was married to his job and any woman would have to fit herself in, if she wanted a relationship with him.

Nate was surprised that he even took the time for short romances. Karl spotted him across the bar and broke into a toothy grin. "Hey Nate, have a seat. This is Julie," he said exuberantly.

"Hi Julie," he said, politely shaking her hand.

"Hi Nate… Karl has been bragging about you," she said with a beautiful smile.

Julie was tall for an Asian girl, with long black hair just touching her tan shoulders. Her midnight dark almond eyes twinkled as she sized him up. Her summer dress was a captivating aqua floral print with a subtle hint of the Caribbean Islands. It exposed just enough of her ample breasts to be tantalizing. She smiled, revealing a perfect set of white teeth that contrasted beautifully against her lightly tanned skin. She wore an emerald ring set off in gold that revealed class more than wealth. She sat poised, with her backed slightly arched, giving the impression of a modeling background.

"Well, Karl sure knows how to pick 'em," he thought, wondering how he would get his friend alone to pick his brain. He needed to get a clear picture of just what was going on and his reporter's brain was working overtime trying to figure it out.

"Julie was just leaving to meet with her friend," said Karl, immediately solving Nate's dilemma.

Nate took a refreshing sip out of the Samuel Adams lager that Karl had ordered for him as Julie said her good-byes and promised to return with her friend in about an hour. The cold beer refreshed him after a warm muggy day on the beach and Nate started to relax.

Karl had his famous scotch and water in front of him, but he was known to sip on just one all evening while staying focused on his objective. He drank just to socialize and kept the alcohol to minimum. Nate couldn't recall the last time he had seen Karl drunk.

With Julie gone, Karl's manner quickly became serious. "I'm glad you were able to come early," he said, "We need to talk and I'll tell you why the company sent me to get you," he added, handing him a neatly folded check.

"Time is of the essence on this one Nate," Karl said with one of his rarely used serious looks.

Nate took the check, looking at him inquisitively. "It's an advance to cover you 'til your paychecks start," Karl said. Opening the check, he knew that his eyes registered surprise at the amount that appeared. Twenty-five thousand dollars sure covered a lot of expenses, he thought. He slipped the check in his wallet, knowing as soon as the bank opened he would deposit the entire amount in his account and give Andréa access to cover household expenses while he was gone.

"Well, Schuler has handpicked you and me as a team because of our established contacts and resources in the Middle East, especially Saudi Arabia," Karl said. Nate just listened while taking a large sip of his beer. He knew that Hans Schuler didn't give anything away unless he received every penny of value from his investment.

Karl received Nate's rapt attention when he had mentioned the Middle East. He knew Karl would only reveal enough to keep him placated and get on that airplane to Zurich in the morning. Time had somewhat eroded their once close relationship and he sensed Karl's reluctance to reveal the full picture as he viewed it.

It had taken Nate years to build up those contacts and the trust between these sources and himself and most of them were his sources. "That must be it," he thought. "Omar wouldn't trust anybody else and this was too big to let slip from Global's hands."

Karl and Nate could not easily be replaced, or perhaps not at all. "One of contacts came to me last week with some important information when I was on assignment in Saudi Arabia," Karl said.

"He informed me that terrorists linked to Al-Qaeda had obtained a number of tactical nuclear weapons, small enough to be carried in a large suitcase, but powerful enough to completely devastate a one-mile radius from the blast's epicenter if detonated," he added. Instinctively, Karl looked around to make sure they were not overheard, but there was no chance of that since the band's music blasted everything else out of existence.

Nate sat there for a moment, caught in complete silence. It's not often that he was left speechless, but this was overwhelming and he needed a chance to absorb the enormity of the information. Then, he asked the first question any journalist would ask after hearing a story like this.

"How reliable is your source? Were you able to get a second source," he asked, already sensing the answer. "The answer to both of those questions is: my source has been very reliable in the past and another inside source has actually seen the weapons," Karl said, looking more serious than he had ever seen him.

"There's more," Karl continued. "It is also confirmed that Al-Qaeda intends to use the weapon somewhere in Spain, the day before Christmas to gain maximum terror, impact and political chaos."

Nate was stunned and sat in silence, thinking of the surreal set of circumstances that Global was inviting him back into, but at that moment, he knew he was hooked. He knew that he had been included back in the loop. This is what he'd been born to do and Karl knew it, too.

"I'm sure you remember Omar al-Douri, our major source for almost everything in Saudi Arabia," Karl said, knowing that his name would bring back memories of the times that Omar and Nate had experienced before Omar had moved back to Riyadh from Washington, DC.

Omar was more than a reliable source. He was a friend. They had a lifelong agreement with him to protect him and his family if his life or safety were in danger due to their professional relationship. Nate had decided against his better judgment to keep the phone call from Saudi Arabia to himself for a while. He ordered another beer and listened, as Karl began once more.

"These details must remain confidential. I know your ethics Nate, but it's something I have to put emphasis on."

With business out of the way, Karl's broad smile appeared and he looked up to the door and spotted Julie returning with that radiant smile that seemed to be a permanent part of her character. With her was her friend, a stunning woman in her mid-twenties, also smiling.

She wore a casual peach colored evening dress that seemed to flow with her body as she glided effortlessly toward the table. She strode directly to his chair with a smile and said, "Hi Nate, I'm Julie's friend, Abbey. It's good to meet you," while grabbing the chair next to him, just as the waitress appeared to take drink orders.

"Hi Julie," Nate managed, taken a bit aback at her beauty.

Abbey was breathtaking, not beautiful in the usual sense, but attractive with dark brown hair framing her face, making her beautifully shaped blue eyes the most important feature of her face. Her eyes devoured him in a way that excited and energized every fiber of his being. There was a sensuality surrounding her that went beyond beauty and created a chemistry of its own. Nate disengaged his mind from the present topic and smiled, things were looking up, he thought.

Karl was already heavily engaged in conversation with Julie, so it appeared that he was on his own with Abbey. She grabbed Nate's hand and guided him to the dance floor. Fortunately, the band was playing a slow song and he could think of no other place he'd rather be. The music flowed, becoming vivid background entertainment that gave encouragement when their bodies met blending and flowing with the beat of the band.

Abbey gently folded into his arms, "Julie tells me you're a writer, Nate. What kind?" He really didn't want to talk about work, but he could keep it light. "I'm flying to Zurich with Karl in the morning to start working for *Global News Weekly*, but let's not talk about work Abbey," he said, hoping she would take the cue. She did. Abbey circled her arms around his neck, pressed her cheek into his chest and just danced.

She was a few inches shorter than his six-foot one-inch height and followed his lead effortlessly. "That was the thing about Karl," he thought, "this kind of thing followed him."

It seemed like they danced for an hour, but when he glanced at his watch, he realized only twenty-five minutes had passed. Nate glanced at the table Karl and Julie had been sitting at and it was empty. Karl and Julie were nowhere to be found. As they sat down, the waitress handed him a note. He opened it and Karl had written, "My room at 9 a.m., be packed and ready, Karl."

"It looks like we've been abandoned," Abbey said with a slight smile. It was just as well. Nate wanted to be alone with her and she pulled her chair up against his. They sat and talked awhile. He gave her his e-mail address and they both decided to go to his house. Nate lived only ten miles from the beach, but it took about twenty-five minutes to drive there from the Rusty Rudder.

The couple arrived at his house to find Andrea watching TV. He had already called her from the beach earlier and told her he would be flying to Zurich in the morning and she had two suitcases out and ready.

Andrea was the most organized person he had ever been around and she was excited that he had been offered his old job back. She smiled, gave him a hug and a kiss on the cheek, said hi to Abbey, and went back to watching her movie.

She didn't know how long he'd be in Europe, but Andrea was all ears when he told her she could stay in the house rent-free and long as she kept the place in livable condition. She gave Nate a disapproving look that said it all. Before she had rented the room, the house had been a mess. She had organized the whole place and slowly deep cleaned every nook and cranny.

He and Abbey disappeared into his bedroom, while Andrea gave them a knowing look and turned back to watching a movie on television.

Abbey was everything he knew she would be and more. "Why did I have to wait until my last night in town to meet her," he thought. "Well, if it hadn't been for Karl, I probably would have never met her."

He couldn't remember ever meeting someone in a bar and spending the same night with her but this seemed natural, like it was meant to happen. The night went by much too quickly and between breathless erotic interludes, she helped him pack while they talked each other's ears off. They talked about everything and nothing; and when the morning sun peeked through the window, its rays diffused by the leaves of the maple tree that shaded the house from the intense heat of the summer lit the room with its warm radiance.

Andrea dropped them off at the Rusty Rudder to pick up Abbey's car. "I'll e-mail you Nate," she said, as she started her car to meet Karl.

Andrea drove him a mile north of the Rusty Rudder to the Econo Lodge where Karl was staying. When they came to a stop in the parking lot, she became uncharacteristically silent. Nate leaned over and kissed her on the cheek. "Take care of yourself, Andrea. Call me on my cell phone anytime."

"I'll e-mail you," she said, kissing him on the lips. "Now, go before I start crying."

Within seconds, as Nate was about to knock on Karl's door, his cell phone rang. He looked at the display window and recognized the number.

"Hello ... Nate Adams," he answered. "Nate, I thank Allah that I have reached you," the voice that could only be Omar's said excitedly.

"Omar, is that you, Where are you," he asked.

"I'm in Zurich. Nobody knows that I'm here, not even my wife, Nate. Where are you," he asked.

"I'm still in Delaware, but Karl and I are flying to Zurich today. We'll be there at three in the morning, Zurich time," Nate told him.

"I don't want anybody to know that I'm here -- not even Karl, until I talk to you," Omar replied.

It wasn't until after he gave Nate his cell number and location, making him promise not to say anything until they met and talked, did Omar calm down.

This was completely out of character for Omar. He was one of the calmest and most organized people that Nate knew. "Just relax and wait for my call, Omar. If things change, don't hesitate to call me immediately," he said, before hanging up.

⋏

Fatima, Fatima," her mother called.

"I'm here mom," she yelled, jumping off the new blue swing set in the backyard of their home in Alexandria, Virginia that her father had bought for her after returning from Iraq on one of his frequent business trips.

Her dad was back from Iraq and she ran breathlessly to the house. Her mother had promised to call her just as soon as her father walked through the front door.

She had been named for her mother, Fatima. Her father, Immad loved her and showered her with hugs and kisses every time he returned from a trip.

Her parents were born in Iraq, and grew up on the outskirts of Baghdad and had moved to America before she was born ten years ago in 1980. She loved America and it was her home. Except for speaking Arabic, she considered herself a product of American culture.

Life in Virginia was great. She had two girls near her age that always seemed to be at her house. She was glad they had gone to a movie tonight with their mother. She wanted her father all to herself.

Her father had arranged for her to receive training at the mosque twice a week, so she could read the Koran in Arabic.

"It's the only language it should be read in," he told her.

When she attended classes at the mosque, she had to conform to religious tradition and wear a special scarf that covered her hair and face, only leaving her eyes uncovered, much to her consternation.

Her dad was her hero. He never neglected to bring her a gift from wherever he visited while he was on one of his overseas ventures.

She had secretly guessed that her dad worked for the CIA and knew better than to even suggest that he did anything but other than conducting business in Iraq.

He had told his mother one night at dinner that it was only a matter of time before that madman Saddam Hussein would invade Kuwait. "Hussein considers Kuwait one of Iraq's provinces and is insane enough to invade." Her father had told her just how cruel of a dictator this man had become and that Iraq was on a collision course with the West because of him.

Men came to the house occasionally who weren't businessmen. Her father and the men would retire after dinner to the back yard just out of earshot and speak in hushed tones. It was usually just after one of these meetings that her father would leave on another trip.

In the last year, her father's trips to Iraq had been more and more frequent with fewer days in Virginia between trips.

"I want to be just like dad when I grow up," she told her mother one day, in the spring of 1991. She was eleven years old and loved life here. She would study hard in school to make the best grades. Her father had promised to send her to American University, close to Washington, DC if she studied hard.

He told her how women were treated in Iraq and other Arab countries. Most women weren't allowed to attend a college or drive a car and they were strictly compelled, by Sharia law to wear clothing that hid their faces. She was happy that her parents had moved to America before she was born.

Just as her father had predicted, in 1990, Iraq invaded Kuwait. She watched it on American TV in horror as they described how people were murdered in the streets, houses, and even hospitals. She heard how all the riches of Kuwait were plundered and people were butchered in the name of Saddam Hussein.

She gasped when she learned of other details from her father later. He had been on his cell phone with one of his friends in Kuwait who barely escaped with his family when tanks and ruthless shock troops came across the unguarded border with Iraq and seized the oil fields while butchering everything in sight, even the dogs.

When she asked for more details, her father told her, "No, my little one. It is only enough for you to know of the evil in the world and never forget it."

At eighteen, Fatima stood at her graduation giving her valedictorian speech, while her father and mother sat proudly in the front row in a seat especially reserved for the top student's parents. "She is a special girl, Fatima," Immad told his wife, as his face shone with pride.

That fall, she was a freshman at American University, just as her father had promised; and her eyes were firmly set upon entering the CIA and following in his footsteps.

Now, at age thirty-six, she was on a flight to Zurich with two other agents to ascertain if there was credibility to intelligence reports of a terrorist plot to explode tactical nuclear weapons in Europe. They faced a diabolical attempt to regain territory for Islam and create a new caliphate in Southern and Western Europe to replace the old caliphate, finally driven out of Spain in 1492.

Now, sitting in the aircraft halfway across the Atlantic Ocean, she stared at the intelligence reports concerning an influential weekly news magazine and one of their correspondents, Nate Adams. Her eyes rapidly scanned the data, not missing even the slightest detail.

She looked across the aisle at the other two agents assigned to this mission and wondered if she would work well with them. Her stake in this matter was much greater than theirs.

Chapter 2

On the plane, Nate's mind drifted to memories of his college days and the time he had met Omar and vividly recalled the day they had met.

Omar, attending Georgetown University, was from Riyadh and was then twenty-two, a year older than Nate. He was majoring in business with a minor in political science and was as energetic a young man as Nate had ever recalled meeting. Omar loved everything American and Nate knew the instant he had met him in a bar near Georgetown University, partying with some of his friends, that they would build a lasting friendship.

Omar flew back to Riyadh after graduating, married and went into his family's business. He had become an important source of information for stories all over the Middle East and Nate valued their enduring friendship to this day.

Nate knew that Riyadh had changed and grown substantially in the nine years since he had been there. Today, the city had a population of more than four million people and covered six hundred square miles. Riyadh means, "Place of the Gardens" in Arabic and it was truly a beautiful city and a quintessential mixing pot of Arab culture.

Nate reflected back to landing at King Khalid International Airport for the first time and how he marveled at the mixture of contemporary and traditional Arab architectural brilliance.

In 1891, Ibn Saud conquered Riyadh by defeating the Rashid clan and in 1932, formed Saudi Arabia with Riyadh as its capital. Riyadh is a mixed bag politically.

Most Americans didn't have a clue how popular of a folk hero, Osama bin Laden is and his name still lives on, in much of the Islamic World. Since the attack on the twin towers, many Arabs and others see him as a military genius for attacking America, "The Great Satan." He did so without a sovereign country of his own to launch an attack. The most popular name for Arab women to name a newborn son is "Osama".

He was an exiled Saudi citizen, who sought sanctuary in any country that provided it, from the desolate Sub-Saharan wastelands of Sudan to the lofty, rugged and barely accessible mountain caves of Afghanistan. In his twilight, he lingered in a ramshackle compound near Billal Town, Abbottabad, Pakistan until his death on May 2, 2011 at the hands of a US Navy SEAL Team. Even the twenty-five million dollar bounty that America had placed on his head had not broken the terrorist leader's hold on his people.

Nate could easily view the beautiful lights of Zurich as they neared the city and the airliner prepared for its landing approach. After eight years, he still recognized many of the old landmarks. When he looked at his watch, it was nearly three in the morning, Zurich time.

Landing and customs seemed effortless or maybe it was just that he was excited to be in Zurich again. Karl retrieved his car from the parking lot and they were on their way to downtown Zurich and the Swissotel.

Nate stopped before entering and looked at the clear star-filled sky, filling his lungs with the fresh unpolluted air. "It was good to be back," he thought. Mixed feelings of excitement and resentment for Global coursed through his body as he stepped into the Swissotel.

Global had a permanent lease on a suite at the Swissotel in Am Marktplatz, near the center of the city. It felt good to be back on the payroll, he thought. The Swissotel had all the luxuries, including sauna, Jacuzzi and breakfast in bed. "I'm not going to miss the quiet comfortable pace at the Delaware Beaches," he thought. Nostalgia is fine, but the excitement of chasing a breaking story is always the ultimate thrill for a journalist who wanted to stay at the top of his game. At this precise paradigmatic moment, the broader world seemingly beckoned him to greater challenges and adventure from the relative routine and spiritual confines of tiny Delaware.

"Some things have changed at the office Nate. We'll talk after we check in and get some early breakfast," Karl said, with a warning edge to his voice, breaking into Nate's line of thought.

Fatigue had finally set in, along with jet lag. Nate knew that he would be asleep as soon as his head touched the pillow. Karl was slowly bringing him up to speed on office politics at Global after they had retrieved his Mercedes at the airport. Karl was a true blue Mercedes guy. Nate had never cared for them that much himself, but Karl swore by them.

"Schuler hadn't appointed a new managing editor for the Middle East department yet. Matter of fact, he doesn't seem to be in any hurry to replace Jack," Karl said. "He hasn't changed since you left and he still keeps people guessing."

"Only two things motivated Hans: money or power. It must be power this time because Hans would be slow to swallow his pride for money; but, he certainly would if it was enough," Nate thought. One thing Nate knew for sure was that there was a lot more to this than met the eye.

Nate knew that Karl hadn't told him everything as he often did, so he would form his own opinion and contribute to the accumulated known facts. That was fine with him; and as soon as he could, he would meet and talk to Omar. With Nate's shrewdness, he would probably know more than Hans or Karl combined. Nate knew from experience that, with Hans Schuler, it was always fortuitous to hold a trump card or two.

Omar's voice on the phone had been one of distrust for Global. He instinctively didn't trust reporters or the CIA, but he knew Nate would not betray their friendship. He simply wanted to talk to someone with whom he had a shared track record. Nate understood his position and would honor that trust as everything that Omar held dear to him was now suddenly on the line.

Monday morning came quickly and he awoke with the nagging intuition to return Omar's call as quickly as possible. He wasn't pleased with the idea of keeping his conversation with Omar from Karl, but for now, it was necessary. They had always trusted one another implicitly but after all it had been eight years and those bonds of trust would have to be somewhat renewed. "A promise is a promise and Omar sounded as if his life was in danger," he thought.

Global had brought him back and one thing Nate had learned in life that was usually true, if something sounded too good to be true, it usually was. That didn't mean that going back to work for Global was a bad thing; it just would be wise to approach it with a healthy caution.

It was already eleven o'clock and there was not a chance that Nate was going into the office until he had spoken to Omar and understood exactly why he didn't implicitly trust Karl. "Perhaps trust wasn't the right word," he thought. "Maybe Karl had good reason to hide part of the total package, but many questions had to be answered."

Why had Omar fled Riyadh for the relative safety of Zurich and just why was Hans willing to shell out twenty five thousand dollars up front? He sorely needed the answers to these questions.

"Karl, we need to call the office and postpone going in until at least four o'clock; I'm not up to speed and need to do some shopping," he said, knowing that was a shallow excuse. He gave Nate a cynical glance and nodded, while he kept reading the file he had taken from his briefcase.

Nate quickly took a shower, dressed and strolled down to the gift shop. He dialed Omar and he must have waiting for the call, because he answered on the first ring, "Nate, thanks for calling back," he said anxiously. I just called my wife and she is with friends out of the country. I'll tell you more when we meet, I don't trust the security of cell phones."

"I'll meet you at eight tonight at the Bierhall Kropf in Gassen 16," Nate said. "Do you mind if I bring Karl. Do you have any reason to distrust him Omar?" After a brief silence, he said, "No, I'm just being cautious. Karl's alright." Nate was thrilled to hear Omar say that because he must have been frightened to want him to keep their conversations from Karl.

He knew that Omar's life and the safety of his family must be in jeopardy. If Al-Qaeda had knowledge that Omar knew about any of the details of their plan, they would certainly eliminate his whole family. Nate knew all too well that was the way in the Middle East.

He looked out the window and realized just how beautiful Zurich was. It was a pleasant city where the climate is mild in the summer, while the rest of Europe roasted with over ninety degree temperatures. The high in Zurich would be only seventy-five today, while Madrid would be sweltering with over ninety-four degrees. He liked Europe, perhaps because of the diverse charm of its rich history and the way it blended with its vibrant ultra-modernity. Like many European cities, Zurich was a blend of the old and new.

Since its beginnings as a Roman customs post established at Lindenhof in 15 BC, it had flourished and grown. Near the cobblestone streets of old town were quaint walking paths on either side of the Limmat River. The older part of the town had been built on the western bank of the river. Two striking buildings were the Fraumünster and Grossmünster churches which appeared to act as sentinels situated on either side of the river, eternally guarding the city's people. The crowning touch, however, was Lake Zurich with a breathtaking panorama of mountains in the background. Europe had a rich history that America with all its wonders had not yet had the time to develop.

As he ambled along the corridors of the hotel, he could not shed Omar from his thoughts and sensed the terror that must have enveloped him to send his wife and daughter into hiding. He seemed to arrive at the room all too soon. Karl was reading one of his files and looked up as Nate entered the room.

"Omar has been in touch with me," Nate said abruptly. "He's terrified for his family's safety and has sent them into hiding. We're going to meet with him at the Bierhalle Kropf at eight tonight."

Nate waited a moment and got no response so he continued, "when we meet with Schuler, I think we should keep this to ourselves for now."

Karl's mind must have been reeling. It's not often that he'd seen him speechless. He didn't say anything for a full ten minutes, but Nate could sense the wheels his of mind turning.

He finally answered, "We'll play this one your way, Nate," he said cautiously. "I have a feeling on this one."

Nate sensed danger, far more danger than any previous assignment and he wasn't sure Karl was picking it up yet.

When it came to danger, Nate had a sixth sense that was rarely wrong. Right now, all the alarms in that sixth sense were going off.

Like a pair of prima donnas, they decided to get to the office about three in the afternoon. He knew that secrets were difficult to keep in a newsroom. Office staff had heard through the grapevine that Nate Adams had been resurrected from the East Coast of America for an important assignment. There had been much speculation about the assignment, but nobody's guess was even close.

Greta Doerhing was the first to ferret out the news of Nate's impending return. Although one could never detect it by her behavior or facial expression, she was ecstatic at Jack Warren's downfall from grace and hoped that it was only a matter of time until Nate returned with his usual flair. She had been his silent champion when he had resigned eight years before.

"Nate will never change," thought Greta, as she walked over to his new desk with a vase of fresh spring flowers, cut from her garden early this morning. "He was incorrigible, stubborn and a little insubordinate," she reflected privately and a bit nostalgically. Nate's rugged good looks was not all that excited Greta, it was a sense of being the best at what he did. His piercing blue eyes and sandy brown hair belied his sure manner and gave him a presence that couldn't be ignored. "Fortunately for me, Nate can't read my thoughts," Greta's mind imagined before racing back to reality.

Nate had stayed physically fit, "How did he do it," she almost said aloud. She was his strongest ally and was excited at the prospect of his return, although she deduced it was only a matter of time before he was in the hot seat once again.

Greta was one of those girl fridays that had the ability to arrange almost anything at the drop of a hat. She knew people everywhere and everybody in the office seemed to owe her favors. No one else knew what her salary was except Hans and she liked it that way. It kept people in the office wondering and a little off balance.

Greta walked over to Nate's new desk and put a new phone on it with a satisfied look on her face. "It would be great to have him around again, even if he hardly ever came into the office," she thought, as she walked away from the newly installed desk.

Greta looked Swiss, and she was a bit taller than most women at five-eleven, with natural blonde hair, sparkling blue eyes and a breathtakingly great athletic body. No one in the office knew how old she was; some guessed as low as twenty-five and others as high as forty, but Greta kept them guessing. Around the office, she kept her hair out of her face in a professional bob at the nape of neck, but Nate had seen her at an office Christmas party with her golden hair down, in a captivating aqua colored evening gown that revealed just the right amount of cleavage. The transformational effect was stunning, almost magical and Nate wondered what she was like inside.

Karl and Nate entered the office and Greta spotted them instantly and flew into Nate's arms giving him a warm hug. He was glad to see her too, but before he could open his mouth to tell her so, he heard Hans' voice behind him. "Nate, it's good to have you back, come in the conference room as soon as you're finished here," he said with one of his rare smiles.

"I'll be done in about fifteen minutes Hans," Nate said, smiling and shaking his hand. "It's good to be back," he added, remembering Hans' total lack of support in the incident with Jack Warren that had caused him to resign.

Hans was already in the conference room with four other people when Karl and Nate entered. Nate looked around the room briefly to acclimate himself to the room's setup and get a read on the people.

The two men Hans was speaking with wore telltale suits that had American Government Issue appearance written all over them. Their aggressive stance and overall body language betrayed their CIA operative demeanor.

Hans hadn't changed much in the last eight years. He still wore sunglasses to hide a wandering left eye he had received from an injury earlier in life. Distinctly European, he was tall at six foot, with a slender build and if you saw him on the street, you could easily mistake him for an accountant. It was on that assumption that many people had underestimated Hans. He always played his hand well with intricately laid plans. It was the only secret of his success and he loved the game. Ever since Nate knew him, Karl never came to a meeting unprepared.

The other two people in the room were women. Greta was there and she apparently had become Hans' most trusted employee, but he was still surprised to see her there. The other woman was more difficult to read. She was dressed in American clothing, but bore a distinct Middle Eastern flavor in her movements and body language. Although she made movements that indicated self-assurance, she also had the subtle submissive posture of Middle Eastern women who were accustomed to male dominance. She was in her mid-thirties, with light brown skin and black hair. She was breathtakingly beautiful with dark mahogany almond shaped eyes. Her shiny black hair framed an exquisitely sculptured aristocratic face and she seemed to be exceptionally aware of her surroundings.

Nate caught her returning the favor by subtly analyzing him. There seemed to be something he was missing about her. She displayed the ability to project herself as she wished to be perceived by others, ability usually found in very highly trained operatives.

Hans opened the conference, "Nate, I assume Karl has brought you up to speed." "Thanks Hans," he said, looking directly at the three people who were definitely not journalists. "Why is the American CIA being briefed on the details of a Swiss magazine news story," he asked. "If my guess is correct and I'm betting that it is, they are CIA operatives, aren't they," Nate asked, seeking a confirmation.

The look in Karl's eye told him that he'd hit the nail directly on the head. Karl interrupted the conversation in a difficult and awkward moment, "I thought you wanted to keep this a very limited operation as far as people who needed to know, Hans," he said.

Karl and Nate both instinctively knew that if their assignment was compromised, their lives wouldn't be worth a plugged nickel. "The situation changed while you were in America, Karl," Hans blurted out, trying to keep the situation from deteriorating any further.

Nate had an edgy feeling that Karl had been intentionally kept out of the informational loop. Hans had played this one with his usual touch of finesse. He had successfully used Karl's long-term friendship with Nate to his ultimate advantage.

Karl and Nate looked at one another simultaneously and realized Hans had violated one of the most important rules of journalism by asking an intelligence agency of another country to interfere in the business of his news magazine.

"This is Mark Gordon and James Hammel," Hans said, introducing the two operatives, but neglecting to mention the woman. "They will be following the story, to gain intelligence only, and the story will be our scoop," Hans said, trying to sound convincing.

Karl and Nate both understood that America was in serious danger if tactical nuclear weapons had found their way into the hands of Al-Qaeda, but Hans couldn't be naïve enough to believe anything CIA told him. Nate knew from experience that the Agency always had its own agenda.

"Look, Hans ... This assignment is dangerous enough without these two guys watching our every move," Nate said. You can't believe they will actually step in and help us if they compromise our safety, do you? They have their own agenda, Hans." Hans didn't reply to Nate's rebuke, but instead went on with introductions.

"Nate, this is Fatima al-Zaidi. She is an Iraqi-American and she will be going with you undercover as a journalist," Hans said, "She will be using the codename of Jennifer Martinez."

This was the last straw, as far as Nate was concerned. He didn't know what Karl was thinking, but it must be similar to his own reasoning.

He smiled and said, "Hi Fatima, I mean Jennifer, there is no way you're going to trail along with us as a reporter -- no offense, but no thanks!"

Karl was becoming more edgy by the minute and as Nate looked at him, he suddenly blurted out, "Hans, Nate and I haven't even eaten lunch yet. Do you mind if we pick it up again at six?"

"Be here at nine in the morning," Hans replied, looking a little upset.

"Touchy, touchy," Nate thought, as he and Karl sought the quickest exit to a very bad situation. He knew as he strode through the door that they were in trouble on this one.

Chapter 3

Nate was not relieved as he left the offices of Global. With a sigh, he glanced around briefly, but he couldn't ascertain whether they were being followed or not.

"What do you think Nate," Karl asked, giving him a questioning glance. "Just how in the hell do we get into these situations, Karl," Nate replied, already knowing the answer.

Let's get over to the Bierhalle Kropf, it's a little early to meet Omar, but we'll have late lunch and a beer," Karl said, motioning to his car.

⋏

Abdullah Jasim had just turned nineteen and was living in Zurich with his friend, Muhammad Qudama. It had become very lonely for them here; all their friends were in Riyadh and it felt like they were halfway around the world.

He felt proud today because he had finally been given the privilege of serving Allah. His leader, Umar Badawi, had told him just this morning that his training was over. He and Muhammad would have the ultimate joy of killing the infidel Nate Adams and the traitor Fatima al-Zaidi. If they were successful, they would surely be given much responsibility for Allah. They waited silently with their weapons in a car just down the street from the Bierhalle Kropf, eagerly anticipating the glory they would receive.

Abdullah was the first to spot them, but did not see Fatima with them. The infidel Nate Adams and his friend were both about to die and they could get Fatima later. Adrenaline pumped through his veins as he slowly got out of the car with the reassuring bulge of his weapon in his pocket.

⁂

After eight years, Nate remembered even the little details of their favorite hangout when they were working in Zurich. Zurich has some of the best food and nightlife the world has to offer, and he was in the mood for a great steak and some good dark Swiss lager.

As they walked through the front door, Nate spotted Frederick still behind the bar. He was the only man I knew that looked good with a handlebar mustache. He was about five-ten, with light brown hair and blue eyes. He spotted Nate about halfway to the bar and broke out into a broad grin. "Nate," he chuckled with a loud guffaw, "I heard you've been in America in exile and the Bierhalle hasn't been the same without you."

Nate grabbed Frederick's hand to shake and at that instant, a clear loud crack sounding distinctly like a gunshot broke through the music of the bar.

Nate felt something tear through the sleeve of his shirt, burning his right upper arm. Frederick's hand was torn from Nate's grip as he was thrown back instantly by the bullet that had only grazed Nate's arm caught Frederick fully in his left arm.

Nate instinctively fell back and onto the floor. Straining to look up from his prone position, he saw two more rounds slam into the mirror behind the bar approximately where he had been standing.

He crawled to the end of the bar to search for a weapon, anything he could use, looking up in time to observe their new acquaintance Jenny who must have been following them, pump two rounds into the chest of a Middle Eastern looking man in his late teens or early twenties.

Jenny was holding a Glock 9mm handgun, checking the area for a second assailant. She had dropped to one knee with her long black hair tied in a ponytail looking at the dead man on the floor. Instinctively, she swiveled her body around the room minutely surveying her surroundings for any trace of remaining danger with the Glock held level for immediate action.

Everybody in the bar was lying on the floor to avoid being hit by gunfire. Nate looked for Karl and saw him behind an overturned table with a Glock 9mm, ready for action. Nate seemed to be the only one who wasn't armed here and he would remedy that situation as quickly as he could.

Nate jumped behind the bar to check on Frederick's condition. He found him lying on the floor bleeding profusely from a wound in his upper left arm. The bone seemed to be broken, observing the strange angle in which the upper arm was bent. He grabbed a bar towel and made a tourniquet to stop the bleeding while an employee was calling for the police and an ambulance.

After feeling assured that the second assailant was long gone and had successfully escaped for now, Jenny appeared at his side helping with Frederick. The bleeding in his arm was subsiding as the tourniquet accomplished its job. "Sorry Frederick," Nate said. "Welcome back Nate," he replied, with a sheepish grin.

"You seem to be a popular guy, since you were obviously the target," Jenny said, indicating the two holes in the mirror exactly where he had been standing. She had apparently followed us from the office, fortunately for him.

"Thanks Jenny, I guess I'll have to re-evaluate the matter of you tagging along," he said gratefully, with the sincerest look he could muster.

"Jenny, we're supposed to meet with Omar, our source from Riyadh at eight o'clock and we'd be happy to have you present," he said, just as Karl walked up. Nate looked at him, pointing directly at his Glock, "I want one of those and don't give me any shit about it, Karl."

"I'll see what I can do," he replied

Karl was calling Hans to report in. They decided not to inform Hans of their meeting with Omar later, so he was under the impression they were still flying to Riyadh at the end of the week.

Nate wasn't sure exactly what Hans' angle on this was, but he knew Hans' professional record as far as journalistic ethics went. Jenny broke into his thoughts, "Nate is your arm alright," she asked, sounding a bit concerned. He looked at the area that was burning on his arm where the bullet had grazed him. There was a burn mark that would take perhaps a week to heal.

"I'm fine, Jenny. By the way, do you know anything about journalism," he asked jokingly. She laughed and it was contagious, "I'm afraid not, Nate but I have a lot of other qualities," she managed to get out, between her chuckles.

Looking up from their laughter, Nate spotted an athletic looking man with brown hair and a matching mustache on his way over to the table they were sitting at. He reached them with an outstretched hand.

"Detective Ernst Klinestuber," he said pleasantly, in passable English. Mr. Adams, I remember you from some time ago. It appears that you have brought a piece of American violence with you."

"No, Detective. I'm afraid that this violence was brewed in the Middle East and they've carried it around the world with them, as fear has no sovereign nation," Nate told him.

The detective changed his attitude after interviewing several people in the Bierhalle, several whom he knew; and by the time he returned to their table, his manner had changed considerably.

"We rarely have this type of imported violence in Zurich, Mr. Adams," he offered with an apologetic look. "I apologize for my harsh words."

"No apology is necessary, Detective. You can bet that these guys were not alone," Nate said.

"That is all I need from the two of you, Mr. Adams and Ms. Martinez ... take care," the detective said, excusing himself.

Eight o'clock came before they expected it. There was nothing further to discuss until they spoke with Omar and obtained specific information. Nothing could be said on his cell phone of any importance, because it just wasn't secure.

They all agreed that the assassins had probably gotten their information about the meeting at the Bierhalle Kropf from Omar's call to Nate on his cell phone. "Where the hell was Omar," he thought, as he got up and walked toward the bathroom. He reached reassuringly inside his coat and felt the bulge that concealed the new Glock 9mm handgun that Karl had provided for him with no explanation. In the bathroom, a man walked toward him, "Nate, it's been a long time," the voice could only be Omar's.

Nate stared at his friend for a few seconds. "Omar, it's good to see you. I hope you didn't reveal the location of your wife and children to anyone," he said, concerned about their safety.

"We were attacked in here earlier and one the assailants was shot and killed by one of my associates. It was an assassination attempt on my life," he explained. "Fortunately for me, they missed."

"I'm sorry I brought you into this, Nate. I can't stay in Riyadh right now, once these terrorists had knowledge that I knew about the tactical nuclear weapons and their location," Omar started to explain, when Nate cut him off.

"We go back a long way, Omar and I owe you; Global made a deal with you, to protect you and your family if you were ever in danger because of our professional relationship and I'm going to make sure they honor that deal. Besides, I'm a big boy and can take care of myself," he added secretly, thanking whoever was looking out for him.

After brief introductions at the table, they decided to go to Nate's suite at the Swissotel. The Bierhalle had become too dangerous for Omar and they were easy targets at the bar. Omar had changed in the eight years since that he'd seen him. There were lines of seriousness and much more wisdom in and around his eyes. He had silver streaks of gray starting to lace through his once jet black hair.

Nate had briefed Jenny on Omar's reliability as a source. Jenny analyzed Omar for a few moments before deciding that he was probably correct about him, and then she got right to the point. Nate reached behind a bookcase where he had hidden a digital recorder earlier and silently pushed the play/record button.

According to Omar, Al-Qaeda's plan was in advanced stages and the weapon had been moved to Brussels for safekeeping. He told us of rumors of more than one tactical nuclear weapon, but could not confirm them. Jenny's phone rang, interrupting them briefly, as she ducked into the bathroom to answer it. Karl had gone to the mini-bar and was fixing himself a scotch and water. When he returned, he brought Nate a dark lager from the small refrigerator in the suite's kitchen. The cool rich lager tasted great and went down smoothly. Nate was extremely fond of the dark lager that this region produced.

Jenny came out of the bathroom smiling broadly, as if she had won the lottery, "Nate, the assailant was a local resident alien named Abdullah Jasim and the Swiss police believe they have apprehended the second assailant. They are roommates. His name is Muhammad Qudama," she beamed, giving them their first break.

She started explaining that the Agency had a *quid pro quo* arrangement with the Swiss police on this case and the other two agents along with herself would intensively interrogate the would-be assassin.

"Okay Jenny," Nate said, still just getting used to the idea of the new limited partnership with her. "This is where the reciprocal relationship starts. I want to be at that interrogation if we're to share fully."

"Alright," she said, stopping him. "I don't mind, but it seems we're after the same thing here."

Nate let her last statement stand, but he wasn't sure it was completely true; however, it would work for now. There would be plenty of time to work the details out later.

"We're going to interrogate him at nine in the morning. I'll pick you up, Nate. You should be armed," Jenny said, checking the bulge under his coat, "but, just a little less conspicuous would be better," she added, smiling.

Nate smiled, "I could start to like this girl," he thought. "After all, she is quick with a Glock and not bad to look at either."

It had been a busy day for him both mentally and physically and jet lag had not only caught up with him, but had passed him by. Karl could take a hint, and he picked up his suitcase and said, "I'm headed to my condo, Nate. See you in the morning after the interview. Call me on my cell."

He didn't look happy at the prospect of not being in on the interview. "Oh well," Nate thought. "Too many people there would ruin any chances of getting the information they needed, that is, if this guy knew anything." Nate would probably be behind a two-way mirror with the local police and one of the agents. The only people in the room with the prisoner would be Mark Gordon and our own new partner, Jenny.

Nate took another long cold drink from his lager and sat back in the chair after Karl left. He reached behind the bookcase and turn off the digital recorder. Omar's safety was the greatest immediate concern. They had all decided it would be better for Omar to have Agency protection for the time being. Omar had been the first to agree that his family would fare much better in America, for now.

After Omar and Jenny left for another pair of connected suites on the floor above, Nate sank back into the chair, very exhausted. He started to drift into a deep sleep on the chair, when there came a soft knock at the door.

"Who the hell could it be," he thought, as he reached under his coat for the Glock. Nobody he could think of would be coming here and he had been given a harsh wake-up call earlier this afternoon. He wouldn't be giving anybody a clean target a second time.

Nate looked through the peephole in the door and saw Greta waiting impatiently. He hurriedly opened the door. She stepped inside; shutting the door behind her and without saying a word flew into his arms. She felt good. Nate had always avoided this with her in the past because of Global's intricate inner office politics, but something within him said "To hell with politics." Now, under the circumstances, he didn't really care much about office politics. Things had changed for the better for him and he knew it.

Nate knew why she had come no matter what she said, so he didn't ask. They were both thinking the same thing and all he said was, "Are you sure, Greta".

"No," she replied, "but, I don't care. Life is too short." She was right about that. Life was too short. He was tired and needed her.

"You're not getting away this time, Nate," she whispered as he unzipped her aqua summer dress, allowing it to slip from her shoulders and fall to the carpet with only a hint of sound. He caught his breath as he reached behind and released the catch of bra, relinquishing it of its burden. She was even more beautiful than he thought.

Nate knew she was beautiful, but she was more than that. He wondered why it had taken this long but knew the answer to that question. The fatigue seemed to leave his body as they fell back onto the bed. He smelled her essence as he nuzzled and kissed her white breasts and belly. He didn't turn out the light; he wanted to see every inch of her so there would be no regrets later.

She slept peacefully as the gray of dawn ended the night's blackness and the fresh orange rays of sunlight reached the bed though the open curtains. His mind was racing and, although he should've been tired, the adrenaline coursing through his body would not let him sleep. He couldn't even start to define the relationship between the two of them, except to say that it had become much more complicated. He wasn't quite certain, but knew it was good.

When Jenny arrived, Greta's dress was still lying in a crumpled heap on the floor of the entrance hallway of the suite. She looked at the dress. "Who's the lucky lady," she asked with a curious smile.

He didn't answer, but it sounded like a rhetorical question anyway. It was nine by his watch and Greta would be late for work. "We stayed up late," Nate whispered as Jenny glanced at Greta's sleeping form, rolled in a generous portion of blanket, sleeping soundly. Nate rolled out of bed silently, telling her to meet him in the café downstairs after he showered.

They arrived at the Zurich police station about thirty minutes later. Muhammad Qudama was in an interrogation room alone and looked anxious, very unsure and scared. Mark and Jenny entered the room as the other agent James, along with Nate monitored the interrogation through the observation glass.

Jenny started with what seemed to be a traditional greeting in Arabic, which seemed to surprise the prisoner. The young Saudi seemed overwhelmed by the circumstances of his roommate's death.

"Damn," Nate thought, "The kid couldn't be more than eighteen or nineteen. He hadn't even tasted life yet."

After several hours of interrogation, he revealed that they had received their orders from a fellow Saudi in the Al-Qaeda chain, known only as Ahmad, who lived in Brussels. He had met Ahmad only once and was giving a description of him to the composite artists. Nate turned to Jenny, she smiled and said, "And this one is just a scared youngster that should be working a job somewhere. He's probably told us everything he knows, and I think we've got a couple of good leads."

Nate's cell phone rang he picked it up already knowing who was on the other end. "Hi Greta, are you at work yet", he asked. "Nate, I called in and took a day off, god knows I have enough coming," she replied. "When you're finished, maybe we can get some late lunch or an early dinner," she asked hopefully.

"I'll call you in about an hour, I've got to finish some details with Jenny," he said. "Nate, before you hang up, I have something to tell you. They reassigned Karl to the Tel Aviv office, effective today," she stated.

"Nothing surprises me anymore, it doesn't change the assignment. Look, I'll be back as quickly as I can. We'll talk and have lunch," he replied.

Jenny gave him a naughty look as she waited until he broke the connection. He returned an innocent stare, while she gave him that "Men will be men" look.

"It's not smart to have inter-office romances Nate," she chided, with an impish look in her eyes. He didn't feel like discussing it and changed the subject to Omar and his family's safety.

Jenny informed him that the Agency had arranged to have Omar's family meet him at the airport in Billings, Montana where they would stay at a small ranch about five miles outside of town. Things were already in motion for Omar. New passports and driver's licenses were being produced with new identities, complete with résumés and credit histories. Omar would even get a new cell phone number.

Omar had done his part in the war on terrorism and it had cost him dearly. Even if they got the terrorists and retrieved the nukes, Al-Qaeda was a large organization with a very long memory and multiple branches worldwide, coupled with a blood thirst for vengeance.

According to the Agency, when this thing was over, Omar could regain his true identity and live happily ever after. Of course, he knew Omar was used to living in the real world and naturally wanted to talk to Nate before they whisked him off. He was well aware that there would be a price on his head and his life had forever changed.

Nate took a cab to his suite and on the way back, immediately dialed Omar. Omar had been in contact with his wife and seemed relieved that the Agency was relocating them.

Nate perceived that Omar didn't trust the CIA to keep their word much beyond their initial move to Montana. He had every right to suspect just that. The Agency didn't have a good record and most Americans suspected them of shady dealings.

Greta hummed a tune while she made a short breakfast in the small kitchen. He wasn't hungry, but sat to have coffee while she finished munching her toast.

"How long can I keep the suite," he asked. "This is a leased rental by Global, Nate. Keep it until they tell you to make other arrangements," she said, standing and wrapping her arms around his neck. She was wearing a white T-shirt with *Global News Weekly* printed on the front with no bra and just a skimpy pair of panties. Her faint perfume made his senses reel. The overall effect was overwhelming. He wanted to discuss Karl with her, but that would have to wait until later.

Nate awoke to the phone ringing, "Hello," he heard Greta saying, as he jumped out of bed and headed for the shower. When he came out thirty minutes later, Greta informed him that Hans and Christine decided that he alone would be enough to cover this story.

"After the assassination attempt, they probably don't want to risk two correspondents," he told her sarcastically. "Hans was a mastermind at orchestrating people and things had gone exactly like he was writing a script," he thought. He had played it right and Nate could see that Hans' actions were calculated with one goal in mind.

The last time Nate had seen Hans' daughter Christine, she was eighteen, full of life and a cute young Ingénue. Hans sent her to New York's Columbia University rather than a European college.

According to Greta, Christine was being styled by Hans to relieve him of the day-to-day pressure of running Global. She had been conspicuously absent at their first meeting with Hans. At eighteen, she had been tall and thin with long auburn hair, a little curious about her dad's business and a little mischievous.

He looked curiously at Greta and wondered if she knew details of the office politics that could help give him a much-needed edge, but decided not to ask. Even though the relationship seemed real, she was still a player in a larger game and he didn't completely trust her.

Nate rode with her to the office, but she entered about ten minutes ahead of him. She didn't want office gossip and speculation. It was bad enough that Hans and Christine knew that she had stayed over last night.

Walking into the office, he spotted an exquisitely beautiful young woman of perhaps twenty-six, standing by his new desk, glancing in his direction; she smiled and immediately started walking toward him. He was stunned that she had changed so drastically in eight years, but he recognized her immediately. Christine closed the gap quickly and he put his hand out as she strode past it with the biggest smile on her face. Her radiant smile could warm anyone to the bones.

"That's no way to greet an old friend," she said, smiling and hugging him and placing a wet kiss on his cheek. She had changed and now displayed a new air of sophistication, assurance, and maturity that wasn't there before. Her stunning attractiveness was sensational and completed her total feminine package.

She walked with him to his new desk. "Why don't you brief me on what's happening with your story," she asked, pointing toward her office, where they would have more privacy.

"Did your dad give you the responsibility for the Middle East," he asked.

"This is my first big story Nate and I begged my dad to call you back on this one. You know the area and the people; and besides, I thought you got a raw deal from Global," she told him.

They talked for about an hour. Nate revealed everything to her and told her he would be leaving for Brussels with Jenny and the other two agents as early as tomorrow, but those plans weren't detailed yet. She handed him a large brown envelope. In it was a company credit card, Euros with the bank wrapper still on them and a permit to carry a weapon. How Hans got his hands on a permit, he didn't know, but he wasn't arguing. "There's ten-thousand in there Nate," she said. Nate thanked her and she just dismissed it as if it were nothing.

"This will help and cash cuts through a lot of red tape," he said.

"Nate, get this one for me. This is the first big one that dad has let me handle on my own, that's why I wanted you on it," she said, repeating her earlier statement with a more serious look on her face. He nodded and said, "you can bank on it Christine, I want this one, too. It will be the biggest one of my career."

"Now that business is over Nate, how have you been doing in the states? You know I was at Columbia and I almost called you so many times," she beamed, genuinely excited that he was back. "Well, maybe this would work out since, he would be working with Christine on this one, and he just felt that a certain trust that Global had extended might take the edge off of the distrust he felt for Hans," Nate thought.

"The day was getting better already," he thought. Greta had already booted up the new computer at his desk and he decided to check his e-mail account.

Abbey had already e-mailed him asking if she could visit on her and Julie's vacation to Europe in August. Nate returned her message telling her that he would be glad to have her. He was always getting himself into trouble. Well, as far as he was concerned, he was a single man with no commitments. August was still three months away and situations had a way of changing.

When he called the hospital to check on his old friend Frederick the bartender, they told him that he had been released with a cast on his left arm where the bullet had passed through, breaking the bone. They had given him some antibiotics and sent him home after a short observation period.

Nate was finally to get on the keyboard, typing some preliminary notes for the story, when the phone on his desk rang. It was Jenny, "Nate, are you ready for a trip to Brussels?"

"I'm all set Jenny. When are we scheduled to leave," he asked. "I thought tomorrow at noon would give you enough time to organize yourself in the office, Nate," she responded. "I don't want to say anything else on an open landline. We'll be at your room in the morning at eleven-thirty,"

After Jenny hung up, he started typing some notes on the story again. He smelled Christine's perfume and looked up. "You want to go and have some dinner and catch up on old times," she asked with a winning smile.

He looked at his watch, it couldn't be four-thirty already," he thought.

"Sure, let's make it something light, I'm not very hungry," he said with a tired sigh. Boy was he going to sleep in tomorrow morning! He wanted and needed to be well rested and at the top of his game.

As they walked out and down to her Mercedes, she suggested, "I know a little café near here where we can get an American style sub and great Swiss lager." "Sounds good to me … I really don't want anything fancy tonight," Nate replied gratefully.

Christine ordered her favorite sandwich and while they waited for the food, Nate told her he would be going to Brussels tomorrow to follow a couple of leads that just might lead them to the tactical nuclear weapon.

"Don't reveal our destination to anyone in the office other than Greta. There might be leak in the office and I might not be so lucky next time," he told her. She just nodded, smiled and mumbled, "Of course, Nate."

Journalists had become targets for the terrorists and he would always carry a weapon when he could. It makes a big difference when you can shoot back and they know it.

Ever since Africa and the Middle East, terrorists and thugs had been targeting foreign journalists for murder, kidnapping, or political gain, most journalists wanted to be armed in dangerous situations if they could. The world of journalism was changing as the world became more violent. As a reporter, Nate was exceptionally observant, but lately he had become constantly aware of the people around him, reading body language as second nature.

Christine's voice snapped him back to reality, "Nate, you look tired. Can I give you a ride back to the suite?" He looked at her gratefully, and nodded. Tomorrow would be a full day and he could feel the wheels turning. Whenever that feeling came over him and the adrenalin started pumping through his body, things started happening and he was certain this was no exception.

He was relieved when Christine dropped him off and didn't want to come up to the room. That could get tricky. He was keenly aware as he walked into the lobby, noting there was a sprinkling of American tourists and a couple of Middle Eastern looking businessmen in suits.

He decided to give them a closer look. One had scuffed dirty shoes and his suit was an ill-fitting rack suit. He looked to be in his early thirties. His hair wasn't neatly clipped like so many other Middle Eastern businessmen.

Nate got into the elevator, pushed number three and was on his floor in seconds. He had only walked about ten steps toward his suite when he heard the sound of the other elevator reaching the third floor. He took another couple of steps and turned to look just in time to catch the bad haircut guy reaching under his rack suit for a gun. By the time Nate got to his Glock 9mm, the guy was already aiming.

Nate hit the floor like a hundred-pound sack of potatoes as two shots passed over where he had just been standing. Aiming from a prone position, he drew a bead on the terrorist and fired twice. Both rounds caught him in the chest, violently propelling him backward about six feet.

He scanned the area looked for the guy's friend, but he was nowhere in sight, he dialed Jenny's cell phone. She answered immediately and after hearing what had just taken place, she told him to go to his room and she would call the police. Instead, he walked over to the assailant and he could see that he was still breathing, but not moving.

Jenny must have been in her room because she bounced out of the staircase door within fifteen seconds. She immediately went to the assailant and kicked the gun from his hand, giving Nate a disapproving look. Bad haircut guy gave a final gasp and his eyes went blank

"Nice shooting," she said. "There's another one around somewhere. They were in the lobby together," he told her. "What tipped you off," she asked. "Look at his haircut and shoes. Most Middle Eastern businessmen are not wearing ill-fitting rack suits, sporting bad haircuts, and dirty shoes. She smiled and said, "There's hope for you yet."

Within minutes, the Zurich police were on the scene. A different detective than the one who supervised the incident at the Bierhalle Kropf, looked at him and glanced at the Glock lying by the body. Nate remembered him from the police station.

"Oh, not you again, Mr. Adams… You seem to be an unpopular guy," he said in reasonably good English. Detective Klinger was a competent and tidy looking man of five-nine or so, about forty, with glasses that seemed to slip down his nose as he took notes. He wore casual clothes but looked well dressed in them. "This guy didn't have a chance." Nice shooting, Mr. Adams," Klinger said, while examining the body.

After Nate explained what happened, Klinger asked for his Glock and permit. He scrutinized both for a couple of minutes before returning them. "Thank you, Mr. Adams," he said politely. Klinger didn't seem to be concerned about the dead Arab. He was probably glad to have a vicious killer off the streets.

The police were an efficient team, as they worked with the ambulance driver and paramedic to remove the body. Klinger directed them to take the corpse directly to the hospital to get a death certificate.

Once inside his suite, he sighed, wanting to get some of events of the last day documented while it was fresh in his mind. Exhaustion hit him like a locomotive traveling downhill from a mountain curve. He lay on the bed for a short nap and was asleep almost instantly.

He awoke many hours later with a gentle nudge to his shoulder, opening his eyes he saw Jenny standing over him.

She was dressed for comfort and action, wearing designer blue jeans tightly hugging her hips and buttocks and a red cotton shirt with a neatly tied knot at her midriff. On her feet were the latest Nikes with ankle length socks. Her hair was neatly pulled back into a ponytail, tied with a ribbon the same color as her shirt.

He could see by her muscle tone that she was in incredible shape. He looked at his watch; it was only nine-thirty in the morning. Breakfast came in hot steaming covered dishes for both of them. He savored the eggs, bacon and hash browns as they poured their energy into his depleted body. After taking a shower, he felt like a million dollars.

"How'd you get into my room," he finally asked her. "I told the maid I was your girlfriend and wanted to surprise you," she said, laughing. He inspected his Glock; made sure the clip was reloaded and checked the extra two clips, bagged his laptop and watched as she finished her breakfast.

"Jim and Mark left in a different car about an hour ago," Jenny told him. His mind had been preoccupied thinking about what she had just said. There had to be a leak in either the office at Global or one of the agents on the team. He excluded Jenny immediately from suspicion because even though she was an Arab, she was a loyal American who had shot the terrorist trying to assassinate him at the Bierhalle Kropf.

He had a bad feeling about Jim Hammel, but couldn't put his finger on it. The man was secretive and quiet, and his demeanor revealed nothing about him. His behavior indicated he was hiding something and didn't want to be close to any of them.

He couldn't remember being wrong when he got this type of gut reaction about something. Nate didn't really believe in premonition, but from experience he had learned to trust his gut reactions and when his intuition was this strong, alarms went off in his head and the hair bristled at the nape of his neck.

"What's on your mind Nate," Jenny asked amiably. He looked at her. She was in a good mood and seemed to be a bundle of energy. "Whose idea was it for Mark and Jim to go on ahead," he asked.

Jenny didn't say anything for about a minute, and then asked, "Why, Nate?"

"Think about it, each time there's been an attempt on my life, Mark and Jim weren't there, just you and I. These people are getting information from somewhere, either your team -- you excluded of course, or my office," he told her.

Jenny's thoughtful look turned serious very quickly. She seemed to be recalling small details that might give her a clue. "We're going to be about two hours behind them," she said.

He checked the map and the trip seemed like it was a little less than four hundred miles, about seven hours.

They loaded the trunk of the Mercedes 480-SL Roadster that she had rented for the trip. Nate looked at her, "You've got good taste, Jenny," he told her, as he slammed the trunk lid and slid into the passenger's seat.

The air was cool and they had the top down. Jenny had a lead foot on the gas pedal and the beautiful countryside flew by. They were traveling through the western part of France and for a little while, it seemed like a vacation instead of a dangerous assignment. Nate shut his eyes with his head leaning back against the headrest, the wind hitting his face with a refreshing briskness.

It was sunny, with a few billowy clouds hanging in the sky like giant cotton balls. They passed a small stream where a family was picnicking under an enormous tree. Traffic was light and they filled their lungs with the vital Alpine air.

Jenny had an urgent look on her face that soon changed to a look of anger, as she thought about what Nate had said. "What's up Jen? You look like your boyfriend left you and your dog bit you," he asked, trying to keep the conversation light.

"Jim Hammel asked to be assigned to this case. Mark and I were already assigned to it. If what you suspect is true, he is not only trying to assassinate you, but me also," she said, with fire in her eyes. "By the way, Jim made the suggestion that we proceed forward in two teams," she said. "Do you think Mark is in league with Hammel," he asked.

Jenny's face turned thoughtful and after a long pause, she said, "I'm fairly certain that, if Jim is dirty on this one, then Mark doesn't know anything about it," Jenny said emphatically. "I've known Mark a long time and he is a straight shooter and all CIA", Jenny said, looking him in the eye.

"I hope that this is one time that I'm not right on this one," he replied, believing in all probability that he was right on the money. By the sound of her voice, it sounded like Hammel had forced his way on the team with his own nefarious agenda.

They decided not to follow the route that Mark and Jim had taken two hours earlier. Instead, they followed the famous Route du Vin, or Wine Road in Northeastern France's Alsace region. This route follows closely to France's eastern borders with Germany and Luxembourg.

They were not far from Strasbourg, the region's largest city located on the border with Germany. They would enter Belgium from the south and it was only a short jaunt to Brussels. As they passed through the Ville de Colmar, he recalled this was the birthplace of the builder of New York City's Statue of Liberty, Frédéric Auguste Bartholdi. Jenny seemed to enjoy driving and he was content to lie back in the seat and take in the breathtaking panorama that lay before him.

He appreciated history and was impressed with the mixture of old and new that nearly every city in Europe offered. This particular region of France had a winemaking tradition that dated from centuries earlier. Some of the finest wines in the world were made in the Alsace Region of France. He was sorely tempted to ask Jenny to stop so he could pick up a couple of bottles of fine wine. The best wine in the world was made at out of the way smaller family vineyards and wineries.

They stopped in Strasbourg in an attempt to call Mark, but couldn't raise him. They were both hungry and decided to eat at a small café. Strasbourg is a large city with a population of near three hundred thousand and like most European cities, is a mixture of old and new architecture. Jenny returned from the bathroom and put her cell phone in her blue jeans pocket. She had called the Agency headquarters and voiced her concerns.

"The Agency tried to call both Mark and Jim's cell phones while she was on the line and couldn't reach either one," she said.

They decided to drive through to Brussels. On the outskirts of the town of Metz, Jenny's cell phone rang it was the Agency. After answering it, she listened for about two minutes without saying anything. Before she broke the connection, her only words were, "Alright, thanks."

She drove for about a minute or two obviously thinking. Suddenly, she looked at me and said, "Mark has been killed. He was shot in the side of the head. The French police found his body in a ditch by the road just this side of the Belgian border. There's been no communication from Jim. I think you might have been right about Hammel, Nate," she said, in a hurt but approving voice. I've been told to get us to Brussels as quickly as possible to a safe house I know about and pick up a package. In it are intelligence reports about this guy Ahmad and many of his associates the Belgian police have been investigating for some time," she said.

As Nate thought it over, something didn't make sense. What did Jim have to gain by killing his partner? Why would Jim kill Mark at this particular time? Mark could have suspected that Jim's motives were not what they should be and confronted him. The outcome would be obvious. Nate was relieved that Jenny had decided to accept his role in this operation, even though their goals were different. "Or were they," he thought. He concluded that when it came down to the bottom line, their goals were very similar.

They both wanted to stop the terrorists from exploding a nuclear device in a heavily populated area of Europe and they both wanted to stay alive. That's might be where any similarity in their goals ended, but that was enough. Nate fought hard in his mind to remember that his primary objective was to get the story for *Global News Weekly*. He knew that the greater goal was to stop these terrorists from their ultimate goal of murdering millions of people and imposing their will and extreme sect of religion on all of Europe.

He had been recording details of their trek to track down these maniacs. If Jim Hammel had killed Mark Gordon, that could be in the story also. He had to be careful, as any over reporting on this one could very well give the terrorists an advantage at their peril.

The CIA wouldn't care for any feature story he would write. However, one thing certain: every detail in the story would be true. He was sure Jenny was aware of his job and wondered what her orders were concerning him.

Right now, he was in the middle of a very important assignment and he needed her expertise and contacts. It appeared that the Belgian police were already watching Ahmad and his terrorist cohorts. If he was the next step up in the Al-Qaeda chain, it would have taken him a long time to get this lead on his own.

Jenny was in a good mood with the wind whipping her ponytail as she bounced to the music on the radio. "We'll be there in an hour and a half," she stated amiably. It took the pressure off to have her in a good mood and back to normal.

He chuckled at that last thought, "What was normal for her," he thought.

"If Hammel has gone to the other side, he would have given away the location of the safe house," Nate said, watching for a reaction.

She looked at him and said, "Yeah, I thought about that. We'll stop and call the Agency when we reach Brussels. I'm sure that the Agency has already called and warned them.

Nate knew he needed to call Christine and give her an update, if he could get to a hotspot for his laptop to send her an e-mail with an attachment, giving her more detail of his upcoming story. He opened his laptop and started writing from his notes and vivid memory. About forty-five minutes later, he had enough finished to pique her interest. He would send it a soon as he could.

The top of the laptop had barely clicked shut when his cell phone rang. It was Christine. "You've sure got a knack for knowing when to call," he told her. "I was just about to dial your number."

"Nate, our reporter in Brussels told us the French police found Mark Gordon's body in a ditch beside the road. Are you alright," she asked.

"I'm fine, Christine, I've got something to send you as soon as I get up online," he said nonchalantly. He wrote down her e-mail address at Global and told her he would call as soon as they reached their destination.

When he looked up at the road sign, it read "**Namur 2 Km**". Traffic was heavy and their Roadster had slowed considerably. Jenny seemed to know right where she was going, "We'll be there in twenty-five minutes," she said.

They pulled up in front of a three-story brick-faced apartment building in an affluent neighborhood about a half an hour later. He put his valuables in the trunk and walked to the door of the lower apartment.

Jenny knocked twice, waited then knocked twice again. They heard the latch being unbolted and one knock on the other side of the door. Jenny opened the door and said, "Thank god Bill," as she hugged him fiercely like a long lost brother.

After they were introduced, Nate sized Bill Trenton up. His six-two muscular frame was well proportioned. He had dark hair, cropped close to his skull like the younger men these days. His whole look was reminiscent of military training. His fierce no-nonsense appearance emanated a sense of strength.

"Here's the package, do you know how long you're staying," he asked, getting right down to business. "Thanks, we're not sure, but we would like to use this place to get organized," she said, with an uncertain tone to her voice.

They exchanged looks and immediately went to the table to open the package that they were hoping was loaded with information. Within minutes, she had the information spread out on the table. Nate grabbed the first page and looked at the picture of Ahmad immediately recognizing him.

"This guy Ahmad was with the bad haircut guy in the lobby of the Swissotel just before he tried to gun me down," Nate told Jenny. "It's going to be hard to track him down because he knows what we look like."

"By the look of the information in this package, the Belgian State Security Service has concerns that if the terrorists can't deliver to their primary target, they may settle for Brussels. We should be able to rely on cooperation from them," Nate commented as he flipped a page.

Bill looked over at them with a questioning glance, "I'm curious what the terrorists offered Hammel to turn on his own country. He hasn't turned up yet and we're all assuming he's guilty. I know it looks bad, but something else could've happened to him," he said.

Chapter 4

Brussels is a large city, located right in the center of Belgium. The metropolitan area has nearly two million people. It has been referred to as the *de facto* capital of Europe. It is a busy city with a diverse population. Belgium is primarily bilingual with the northern half, speaking Flemish and the southern majority speaking French, with some German spoken along the eastern border areas.

The Brussels Capital District is the site of NATO Headquarters, key offices and institutions of the European Union and the Secretariat of the Benelux Union, making it a major strategic target for terrorists; and there already were suspected Islamic terrorist cells and radical clerics in the Molenbeeck area, known to Belgian authorities.

Except for the tragedy of Mark Gordon's murder, the trip had been scenic and relaxing. Bill Trenton had installed secure high-speed wireless Internet in the safe house and Nate made haste with his laptop, sending Christine an upgraded version of details of the upcoming story that he had completed.

Christine attempted to assign another reporter to assist him when he called her, but he declined. This mission had quickly become dangerous, but he had realized the impact of that fact back in Delaware when he had decided to fly to Zurich to take the assignment. He certainly didn't want to play nursemaid to another reporter when terrorists were shooting at him. Nate was very happy with the situation and for the time being, there would be no changes.

"I've got a pleasant surprise for you Jen," Bill said. "We have acquired some new surveillance equipment from headquarters. They outfitted a utility van and have the bad guys under surveillance right now. If the bomb is here, they have it securely hidden, we've gone over everything we can with radiation detectors and haven't come up with anything yet."

Jenny and Nate had been scouring through the information from their own both people and reliable Belgian sources. They knew there were clues that they must have passed over, or not made a neural connection, tying them together.

"It was all here -- it had to be," Nate thought, as he leafed through the mountain of material. Some of the information was very detailed, but most of it was of a general nature.

"Jen, look at this guy right here, named Immad Janabi, he must be their courier. He seems to travel an awful lot, using the Brussels Euro Star Midi Station. It shows here that he's gone to London five times in the last six months. Immad could be the advance man to transport the weapon to London. Al-Qaeda may consider it much easier to transport to France and Spain form London than Brussels," he said.

"Doesn't make much sense, but maybe they have a greater infrastructure in England than Brussels," she replied.

By the looks of Immad's background, he had only been in Brussels for about a year. Before that, he lived in Riyadh for six years, after that the trail went cold. "I can't believe they didn't shadow him to London and check his contacts," he said incredulously.

"Calm down Nate, our interest in Immad just increased when we learned about this plot," Jenny said, while she scrutinized the available intelligence on Immad.

"Let's check out these other five clowns that hang out with him, it's obvious they all work together in a cell."

They worked the rest of the evening and through most of the night, gleaning every bit of information they thought would help them. Nate fell asleep, his head resting on a pile of paperwork and was awakened by Jenny's gentle nudge and a cup of steaming coffee.

After a couple of cups, he felt completely refreshed and rested. When he looked at his watch, it was already ten-thirty on Friday morning. The week had flown by rapidly. If anyone had told him last Friday morning that he would be in Brussels in a week's time chasing terrorists, he would have told them they were crazy. Jenny was already up and he wanted to see Brussels and get some breakfast.

They walked down to Jenny's rented Roadster and drove to the Eurostar Midi Station. He figured they would eat breakfast and he wanted to check the storage lockers. Criminals were known to stash items in them for safekeeping, so, why not terrorists? When he spotted the lockers, he said," Jenny we need to get an agent over here with a radiation detector right now and check these lockers for the nuclear device." She opened her cell phone and called Bill. He thought it was a good idea and worth a shot.

Nate and Jenny were just finishing breakfast when he looked over by the ticket counter and spotted Immad at the ticket counter. He didn't have to tell Jenny, she looked immediately where he had been staring.

"What luck," he thought, as Immad walked away from the counter with a ticket in his hand. Nate waited until Immad was out of sight of the ticket counter and asked the girl at the counter where the gentleman was traveling. She looked at him for a moment and said, "London, Monsieur."

Without hesitating, he bought two tickets for London on the two o'clock train, smiling at his blind luck. "I swear Nate, you must be the luckiest person I've ever seen," Jenny chuckled. Nate knew it wasn't luck. He had always had a knack of being in the right place at the right time. It's what had made him a successful reporter and correspondent.

"Thank god for the money that Christine had given him," he thought. They went to the waiting area adjacent to the one Immad was sitting in to keep an eye on him. Jenny called Bill at the safe house and updated him on our change of plans and he wasn't surprised at anything the two did after hearing about their last three days.

Immad appeared to be about thirty, with neatly cut hair, about five-ten. He had an intelligent look as he carried himself with confidence. This man bore all the traits of an extreme fanatic on a mission from Allah. His body language betrayed no nervousness or hesitation in his ultimate goal.

This man was the type that would have to be killed, to be stopped. He was a part of the new breed of Jihadi Muslims who were taught from their early years in school that non-Muslims were infidel monkeys and pigs to be butchered. Nate knew for a certainty that if the Western Powers didn't change their strategy in their dealings with this extreme type of blind hatred, they were fighting a losing battle.

While Nate was keeping an eye on him from behind a newspaper, another man about the same age, of Middle Eastern decent walked up and sat at the chair next to him. The newcomer placed a briefcase he was carrying down and folded his hands in his lap. Immad appeared not to notice as the young man slowly stood up and walked away, leaving the briefcase behind.

This briefcase was much too small and the wrong type to be a tactical nuclear weapon, but it could easily be filled with plastic explosives and a timer. Jenny and Nate must have been thinking the same thing.

There was still a half hour before the train to London boarded. Jenny walked to an area where two Belgian police officers were standing while Nate kept an eye on the young terrorist. He saw the look on the officer's faces as she showed them some identification.

One of the officers immediately spoke into a portable radio and then they both walked to where Immad was sitting, approaching from his left side while he was glancing in the opposite direction. The young Arab didn't see them until the last second, by that time it was too late. He reached under his jacket for a gun but Jenny was quicker. This guy would not be taken. He drew his weapon while staring down the barrel of Jenny's Glock. Jenny fired once slamming him back into the seat from a standing position, while Nate ran to cover her.

He hadn't seen where the other Arab had gone and wasn't taking any chances. Suddenly, there were police everywhere with guns drawn. The officer on the scene called the bomb squad and nobody went near the briefcase.

Jenny swiftly approached Immad, wrestling the gun from his limp hand. He stared at her with complete hatred as she spoke to him in Arabic. His wound didn't look lethal, but the young terrorist would always know he had been shot. Nate had seen his kind of hatred before. It was the kind of hatred that would overcame pain and make a Jihadi wish only for martyrdom an Paradise, complete with seventy-two virgins that he believed was his true reward for killing the infidel.

A man in his early forties with slightly graying dark hair approached Jenny and Nate, offering his outstretched hand. "I am Pierre LaDuc, Chief of Detectives for City of Brussels," he said. Nate introduced himself as a correspondent for *Global News Weekly* out of Zurich and decided to let Jenny introduce herself. He remained silent as she introduced herself as Jenny Martinez, assigned with a special anti-terrorist investigation team from America. She immediately produced authentic identification to prove it.

"I believe we may owe you two a rather large debt of gratitude," Pierre said. "If this is indeed a bomb, it would have killed many people if it had not been for you two."

By then, the bomb-sniffing dogs were on the scene. The dogs were quick and they wasted no time going directly toward the suitcase. Their actions gave an immediate indication that the briefcase contained plastic explosives. Most probably, it was Semtex, wired to a cell phone for remote detonation. Fortunately, Immad was still alive and paramedics were on the scene, putting him on a stretcher.

"Make sure they keep him alive. I'm sure we can get something out of him when we question him," Jenny said.

Pierre walked over to the paramedics, looking over the suspect. The round had entered his upper chest closer to the shoulder. When the medic told him he would survive, Immad replied with a blank stare.

"I need to speak with both of you privately," LaDuc said. After we had found a much quieter place to talk that afforded the privacy they needed, he started. "We've been tracking this guy for a week, but we lost him the other day. How did you find him," he asked with a questioning look.

"We just got lucky. After reading the intelligence, we realized that this guy had been to London five times in the last six months. Quite frankly, we were looking for something a little different when another courier dropped this briefcase off with him and walked away," Jenny told him.

"I'm aware of what you're looking for and if there is any way I can be of help, here is my card with my cell phone number written on it," he replied. "Mr. Adams, I'm familiar with your news magazine, you are American, yes," he asked.

Nate nodded but by now, he had realized the trip to London was off. He stood there with the tickets in his hand. "Allow me to get you a refund Mr. Adams, it is the least I can do," Pierre said. Nate gave him a grateful look as he walked toward the ticket counter.

We decided to visit the lounge for some light lunch and a couple of drinks. "I'm going to keep you around for the luck factor if nothing else Nate. America got the credit for saving a lot of lives on this one and we can use the good will, believe me," she said. She was right. America's reputation in Europe could use a boost. It felt great to be the good guy for a change.

Nate dialed Christine's cell phone. Within seconds, he heard her cheery voice, "Nate, how's it goin'," she asked. Christine listened as he related the day's events and told her he would write the story tonight and e-mail it to her.

"You didn't waste any time earning that advance did you," she asked with a slight chuckle. Global's next edition would carry an in-depth story, but Belgian and other European TV and radio were already carrying the news flash.

"We avoided one tragedy, but are still working on the main objective," he said. "Christine, don't let anyone take me off this assignment. This one is mine." "I wouldn't worry about that Nate," she replied, before breaking the connection.

He sat back sighing, taking a long cool drink from a dark Belgian lager. He needed to relax and think. There was a lot of good intelligence in that package and they were missing something. It was too bad that they had taken Immad down when they did. His intuition told him that Immad would have eventually led them to the weapon. It was a small price to pay and much had been accomplished to furthering the unification of Europe with America on their war on international terrorism. It had become a global problem and they must work together with other nations in Europe to win.

Jenny had brought the intelligence package with her and they decided to sit and mull it over. They scanned the information on this guy Ahmad one more time to see if and where he had been traveling other than Zurich. According to the Belgian reports, he had been to Paris three times in the last six months.

Nate scanned the dates and compared them with dates that Immad had traveled. The three dates that Ahmad had traveled to Paris corresponded with three of the dates Immad had traveled to London. They were coordinating something big, but what? "Hey Jen, look at the travel pattern of these two," he said to her, looking perplexed. She quickly grabbed the information on the other four and zeroed in on travel dates and destinations.

They found that two more of these clowns had traveled on these same dates, one to Marseilles and one to Madrid. They would both have to update our superiors on these new revelations. His intuition told him that this was a well-organized and well-funded plot, probably time coordinated for maximum international affect.

"This plot appears to be far reaching and much more sophisticated than we suspected Jenny," Nate told her, still looking down at the material.

Immad had been taken to Erasme Hospital on Lennik Road. When Nate and Jenny entered the second floor, uniformed police were heavily guarding Immad. Nate spotted Pierre LaDuc and strode over to where he was giving instructions to his uniformed officers.

He saw them coming with a very warm look in his eyes. "Monsieur Adams and Mademoiselle Martinez, it's good to see you. Your superiors have already been in touch with me. The Commissioner of Police has already instructed me to cooperate with you fully," he beamed.

They found a place to sit and updated him on the information they had pieced together from their reports. "London, Paris, Marseilles and Madrid … Mon Dieu! We never suspected. Whatever Brussels can do to help, anything," he added.

"Don't forget, Monsieur LaDuc, this cell is based in Brussels and there is a good chance that Brussels could be a target also," Nate emphasized.

The truth of the situation was that if the terrorists felt they were getting too close and there was a chance they would lose the bomb, then they might decide to detonate it immediately at their current location. "We will have to play this one close and leave nothing to chance," said Nate.

The elevator on the second floor and the door opened for riders getting on. When Nate glanced up toward the open door, he spotted Ahmad speaking to a young nurse at the station. Nate tapped Jenny on the arm. She looked up and instantly spotted him carrying a briefcase. The door closed and when it opened, they jumped out into the lobby.

Nate dialed Pierre LaDuc's cell phone then yelled into the phone that Ahmad was on his way up to the fifth floor carrying a briefcase. Nate and Jenny hit the second floor just in time to see the door close with Ahmad inside.

His eyes grew wide when he spotted him. Nate was glad LaDuc was still there.

He could imagine the furor right now on the fifth floor. They didn't wait for the elevator, but instead flew into the staircase flying up the stairs two and three steps at a time. Jenny was in great shape. Nate glanced at her as she passed him on the fourth floor without using a turn signal.

He tried not to imagine the damage Ahmad could inflict if he managed to detonate plastic explosives on the fifth floor of this crowded hospital.

"Jen, stop before you get to the door," he said. Nate had noticed each staircase door had a small window, four by twelve inches and he didn't want to jump into a firefight without first peeking. He crowded ahead of her and looked through the small window into the area in front of the elevator. Nate spotted Ahmad standing in front of the elevator he had just exited. In front of him were Pierre and four uniformed officers with drawn weapons.

Ahmad had placed the briefcase by his feet and was punching numbers on his cell phone. He was using the phone as a detonator for the explosives. Nate flung the door open violently to startle him and yelled, "Drop the cell phone, Ahmad if you want to live."

He started to press buttons again and Nate fired once, catching him in the back of the head. He dropped like a sack of potatoes, hitting the floor. He grabbed the phone the terrorist still clutched in his lifeless hand. The display window showed that if he had pressed another two numbers and the send button, it would have been over for many people on this floor.

"I'm sorry ... there was no time to explain. He was using the cell phone as a detonator for the explosives in the briefcase," Nate explained to Pierre with the most sincere a look as he could muster.

He handed Pierre the cell phone and as the detective looked at the display window, his eyes growing wide. He wondered who the hell this guy would be calling when five people had their guns trained on him.

The entire fifth floor of the hospital was in an uproar and chaos had replaced the sanity and orderliness that usually ruled. A nurse approached Amhad's lifeless corpse and muttered, "Sacre Bleu."

All Nate could think was, "There had better be explosives in that damn briefcase. I just shot an unarmed man in the back of the head."

Jenny peered at Ahmad and the large pool of blood on the floor by his head and speculated, "I thought you were just a writer, Nate... nice shooting."

Even LaDuc looked awestruck, but quickly recovered, directing his men and other security personnel arriving on the scene. Police and security personnel were clearing all non-essential personnel from the fifth floor and were checking everyone entering the hospital. The hospital was in a near state of lockdown.

The same bomb-sniffing dogs emerged from the elevator quickly confirming his intuition of another bomb in the briefcase. Nate breathed an extended sigh of relief. He couldn't believe that he was actually happy about the explosives being in the briefcase. The bomb squad technician even confirmed that the explosive charge was Semtex, after he disarmed the device. "It would have taken out most of this floor", he said, wiping the sweat from his brow.

"These guys had to come up with another *modus operandi*," he thought. "After two failed attempts, one would think the rest of the crew would find a new line of work."

"Where's Immad," he asked LaDuc. "In room five twenty-four," he replied, looking at him while shaking his head. The perplexed look on his face conveyed more than words could say at this point. "Monsieur Adams, either you are the luckiest man I've known or you are in the wrong profession. Either way you have earned my respect," he said.

Jenny and Nate entered room five twenty-four and found Immad wide-awake. "How could anyone be asleep on this floor," he thought.

"Your partner Ahmad is visiting Allah trying to collect his seventy-two virgins," Nate told him. "By now, I'm sure he's realized that myth isn't even close to being true," he added with a grin.

Jenny decided to conduct the interview with a kinder tact. She spoke in Arabic to him for a couple of minutes and his face visibly softened. They exchanged glances and Nate decided it was best for him to leave. Obviously, Jenny could get more out of him using honey than he could with vinegar.

Immad must be made to realize that he had forfeited the next twenty years of his life and the only thing that would help him was cooperation. As he turned to close the door behind him, Jenny was speaking Arabic to the young terrorist.

He gazed down the hallway to watch a heavily padded bomb squad remove the briefcase, when he spotted a man of about thirty walking briskly toward him with an extended hand. "Phil Connors," he said. "Nate Adams," he returned.

"I figured I'd see you here," said Phil. Phil Connors was the correspondent for Global, his office was in Brussels but he freely roamed around this region of Europe. Although Nate didn't know him by face, he had read pieces Connors had written for Global. Connors was an energetic affable young man with a full head of light brown hair who had a reputation for being competent and dependable.

"Christine told me to cover the story, I hope you don't mind," Phil said. Well it made sense, since he was smack dab in the middle of the story and couldn't be expected to be objective.

Connors looked down at his notepad and Nate noted that he had already scribbled a half of tablet of notes.

"Christine told me that she wanted you to be free to write your own feature story, anything you want to say for the record," he asked. Nate just nodded, knowing it was better at this point to say nothing.

Nate decided to call Greta and see if she would like to come up for the weekend. She picked up on the second ring, "Hi Nate, I wondered when you'd call. I hoped that I had made an impression on you," she joked, with a devilish chuckle.

"She had made an impression, alright," he thought. "You want to come to Brussels for two or three days," he asked.

"I'll leave today, take the rest of the weekend and some vacation time I have coming. It will be wonderful," she mused. "Christine gave me some expense money and I'll get a suite at the Scandic Hotel over on Rue d'Arenberg," he told her.

She sounded surprised, "Nate, isn't that place a bit expensive."

"Probably, but who cares! We'll have a great time," he shot back. "We made arrangements to meet at the Scandic Hotel at midnight in the lounge."

He hadn't been excited about anyone for a long time, but he was excited at the thought of seeing her. Nate wasn't quite sure if it was a relationship or not but what they had was good and he wasn't sure that he wanted anything as permanent as a relationship now. Then again, there was Abbey, too.

He walked to the nurses coffee station. The coffee was a little burnt, but he didn't care and after a few minutes, he calmed down. He slowly sipped the coffee and stood for a few minutes thinking about midnight at the Scandic. It wouldn't exactly be a vacation, but Greta was the one woman who would understand. She knew what deadlines were, how deadly serious this assignment was and she didn't seem like the complaining type.

Jenny's voice startled him, snapping his mind back to reality. Glancing at his watch, he realized that thirty minutes had passed. "He started talking to me about the nukes", she quietly mentioned, after scanning the area and finally feeling comfortable that they were alone and weren't being overheard.

"They've got the nuke in a safe location at a rented farmhouse outside the city. He is just a courier and doesn't know many details. He thinks it will be moved to London by tomorrow and I've got to find a secure place to call in," she said.

"Greta's coming to meet me at midnight and I'm getting a suite at the Scandic Hotel over on Rue d'Arenberg for a few days, our schedule permitting. Why don't we drive over? You can call on the way, unless it's more private," Nate trailed off, with a questioning glance.

"Great idea Nate," she said, smiling tiredly at him. Nate drove silently, lost in his own thoughts while she gave directions to the hotel.

She called the safe house before calling Washington and relating to them more than she had told Nate. It was her guess that the nukes were in transit to London, but she had the names of two recipients of packages that Immad had delivered.

They seemed to be getting a lot of information from these young agents and Nate wondered just what kind of creative interrogation techniques they were using.

If Christmas Eve were the date, these people were getting their assets in place much too early. Many details didn't make sense or connect with one another, leaving his mind unsettled.

This wouldn't be the first time a source had gotten details wrong. Along with the information, they deduced from the Al-Qaeda cell and their travels, that this was a well-detailed comprehensive international plan that could and would strike a major blow to the Western World.

The devastating horror of multiple nuclear explosions destroying several European cities as well as New York City or Washington, DC was nearly unthinkable, but the naked facts that were coming to light, revealed that scenario was quickly becoming a distinct possibility.

When they reached Rue d'Arenberg, the Scandic Hotel Grand Palace was truly a majestic place. Nate could see it would be well worth every penny paid. He looked at Jenny and she seemed preoccupied, "Why don't you get an adjoining room," he asked her nonchalantly. "You certainly don't need to stay in the safe house any longer and you might be safer at the Scandic," said Nate. "That's a great idea Nate, I think we're going to work fine together," replied Jenny.

It was already five o'clock when they reached the registration desk. He was in luck; one of the girls spoke great English. He was about to pay three hundred and fifty Euros for a suite with an adjoining room, when the hotel manager appeared at the girl's side and asked, "Excuse me Monsieur, are you the Nate Adams who is on the television?"

Nate looked at the TV in the lobby. "My god, where did they get that awful picture of me," he thought.

Jenny, on the other hand, looked great. The lobby TV was blasting away about their exploits of the last two days on a local French language channel. The manager was explaining to him that they could accept no money for their accommodations.

"It would be our pleasure Mr. Adams," he finished. Everyone in the lobby seemed to be staring in their direction and he was a bit tired and definitely hungry. A young man brought their luggage and his laptop to the room a few minutes after they got there and in another thirty minutes, they were in the restaurant eating porterhouse steaks.

"My treat, Jen… This beats the safe house all to hell, doesn't it," he asked.

"What about you, Jen I'm sure you have someone special," Nate asked, between bites of the delicious steak. A slight sadness, gave her away briefly and her silence spoke volumes. Finally, she stopped eating and picked up her glass of wine. "My fiancé is in Iraq with my brother, fighting for a free Iraq. "We are not able to see one another very often," she spoke softly.

People in the restaurant had recognized them and a girl of perhaps sixteen had appeared at their table, asking for an autograph in heavily accented English. Nate hastily scribbled his autograph for the eager girl, handed the waitress a hundred Euros and he and Jenny headed in the direction of the lounge to relax.

They talked and took the time to unwind from the day until about eleven o'clock when Jenny started to yawn. She excused herself and went to her adjoining room catch up on some sleep while he moved to the bar. Nate asked Stephen the bartender for another dark lager. Jenny was quickly becoming a friend and Tuesday they would be going to London to track the nuke, if indeed, there was only one.

It had been well documented that when the Soviet Union disintegrated, about eighty of these relatively small, but devastatingly lethal tactical nuclear weapons or "suitcase nukes" as they were referred to in popular American parlance, came up missing before the dust settled.

The December 26, 1991 break-up of the Soviet Union created a cash crisis for Russia and its former satellite states. To make matters worse, many powerful and unscrupulous men sought to enrich themselves by using their political or military positions, regardless of the ultimate consequences of their reckless actions.

Consequently, many different types of weapons were clandestinely sold to terrorist organizations and countries, including tactical nuclear weapons. "If a terrorist group was well-connected and well-funded enough to buy one 'tac nuke,' then why not four or five or more," Nate thought. "There were probably enough tactical nuclear weapons in existence to devastate the Western World," he concluded.

"Hey there big boy," a voice behind him, that could only be Greta's purred. He turned, while she grabbed him and planted a passionate kiss on his lips that left him catching his breath. He hugged her so tightly that he thought she would break, but she didnt seem to mind.

"You want to take this into the room," she purred in his ear. No answer on Nate's part was necessary, as they moved toward the door, still holding hands.

"The only one in the office that has figured it out was Christine and maybe Hans," she said laughingly.

They were still awake at two in the morning. "We're leaving for London on Tuesday morning. According to new information, the terrorists had probably transported the bomb there, yesterday afternoon," Nate said to her.

"Can you stay until Tuesday," he asked. Greta gave him a smile and nodded. She was tired from driving and soon fell asleep. He couldn't close his eyes. His mind was racing and he got out of bed, opened his laptop, and started writing. It was always like this with Nate. When his mind was racing, he had to get it out of his system. He wrote until five-thirty in the morning.

After e-mailing a copy to Christine, he finally fell into a deep dreamless sleep.

When he awoke at eleven o'clock, both Jenny and Greta were gone, probably in the restaurant eating lunch or shopping. There was a note on the pillow, "Nate, we went to the hotel café. See you there, Greta."

Seeing the two of them in the restaurant eating and laughing together, they looked as if they had been friends for life. "I hope they've got hamburgers and fries," he said, as he picked up a copy of the French newspaper, "*Le Monde*."

Plastered on the front page was a better picture of Jenny and Nate walking towards her rented Roadster. It had been taken the day before, apparently with a telephoto lens.

"Just what we need," Nate thought cynically. Ironically, we were caught on the wrong end of the camera and laptop. Now, they would be easily recognizable targets for any trigger-happy Al-Qaeda up-and-comer's pot shots.

"Good morning sleepyhead," Greta said, looking very cheerful. I ordered you large cheeseburger, fries and a glass of water. He had swallowed enough coffee to last a lifetime and water was fine with him. It seemed like ages since he had had a good cheeseburger, and he dug in with gusto, after lavishing it with specialty mustard.

"These two days are the only vacation I will get. You two have a good time," Jenny said, as she got up and went to the cashier. Greta was still eating while Nate literally inhaled his hamburger and fries and ordered a second helping.

Jenny was just leaving the cash register when he got up and caught her at the door. "Look, I don't mean to give advice Jenny, but we've become very visible because of the media. It makes us a target for every Islamic extremist, whether they are with Al-Qaeda or not." Nate said, with a concerned look.

"Calm down Nate, I'm just going to do some shopping and give you two some space, but thanks for caring," she said, chuckling to herself.

"Just like a woman," he thought.

She was a valuable asset to have around and was quickly becoming a friend. She knew what to look for and certainly knew how to take care of herself.

He decided to wear a ball cap and sunglasses in a half-hearted attempt at appearing incognito. They decided to stay in the hotel and use the two days to their advantage.

The shops contained many items that appealed to tourists and they bought a few frivolous items. Nate recognized a couple in their late twenties who had obviously been following them. The couple had been in two of the shops they had gone into and he had spotted them walking at a distance, but definitely following them. They were too inept at this to be professionals.

The man was about thirty, five-eleven with dark brown hair and about as average looking as they come. The woman was about five-seven, wore designer glasses that accented her slightly attractive features that were shaped by an abundant full shock of brown hair. She wore form-fitting blue jeans with a peach colored top that showed her abundant cleavage. The couple moved to the other side of the store to browse through magazines at an attempt at nonchalance.

He heard Jenny's voice and looked up to see her hurrying towards me, "Nate, have you noticed anyone following you?"

"As a matter of fact, I was about ready to call you," he answered. He looked over at the magazine where the couple had been standing, but they had vanished. "There was a young couple about thirty or so following us from shop to shop," he explained to her, still staring at the spot they had been standing.

"Your suggestion might be a good idea, Nate. We should stick together for now," Jenny admitted. "I don't want to lose you along with that uncanny intuition of yours," she chided.

"Jenny, I think we should leave for London today," he blurted suddenly.

"Let's go the suite where we can talk," she replied. The cable news coverage was just too intense and people began to recognize them just walking to the restaurant.

"We are just too visible in Brussels and I don't believe these people following us were paparazzi.

"They disappeared quickly enough when we teamed up in the shop and this tells me that these people are not curiosity or autograph seekers," he told her, once they were in the suite. "I knew it was too good to be true. I haven't had two days off in a row in three months but, I think you're right, Nate. Let's go to London," Jenny sighed.

They bought two first class tickets to London on the Eurostar train via Paris through the Chunnel after dropping off Jenny's rented Roadster and being assured of another one in London.

They left Brussels at six o'clock after Nate arranged for Greta to keep the suite free until Wednesday afternoon. Before he left, Nate handed her a disk with instructions to place it in Christine's hands, personally. On it were his notes and the first twenty-five hundred words of his story, for a backup of what he had e-mailed her.

She smiled and gave him a passionate kiss, "Stay until Wednesday and have some fun," he told her, as they were walking out the door.

Jenny had obtained intelligence reports on the two Saudis in London to whom Immad had delivered packages. As they scanned the two terrorists' information and background, they could see that these two were seasoned terrorists. The reports indicated that they had been linked to the 2000 attack on the *USS Cole* in Yemen.

Nate was tired and dozed off with the reports still in his hand. When he awoke, they were rolling into Paris and Jenny had already ordered dinner for them. Starving, Nate wolfed down his dinner and told her to wake him when they arrived in London.

They left the train station in London in a better version of Roadster than they had driven in Brussels and checked into London's Novotel Euston, where two of Jenny's colleagues were waiting.

"Nate Adams," he said, offering one of them his hand. "Mike Phillips and my partner Sam Baker," he replied. "I've heard a lot about you lately," he added.

These two guys appeared to be cast from the same general mold. They looked to be in their mid-thirties, close-cropped hair, around six feet tall, with college degrees. They all sported a serious military no-nonsense appearance and this was their only drawback. They were easily recognizable as exactly what they were and would be close to useless as undercover agents in a covert operation.

Jen and Nate checked into adjoining rooms and were busy reading the additional data that Mike and Sam had been able to gather.

Information from the intelligence reports indicated that, the two new terrorists appeared to be more fanatic and hardened than the two they had dealt with in Brussels. They were part of a five-man cell group and all lived in the same apartment building. They were also a little older, in their mid-forties if this information were correct. This guy Umar Badawi could be Jamal Badawi's brother.

Jamal was the reputed mastermind of the *USS Cole* bombing in Yemen. The other one was an Egyptian named Muntasir al-Mashad. They were older than the other three in the group and obviously played a leadership role.

Al-Mashad had a scar and red burn marks on the left side of his face, indicating previous action. Nate was sure the same last name of Badawi was no coincidence and his intuition told him that the extent of the plot was far more than met the eye.

Lately, he had become more of an anti-terrorist agent than a correspondent on a story for a global news magazine. The two seemed to blend on this assignment to the point where it was hard to ascertain where one role ended and the other began. The home office was pleased. They were getting good press throughout the world on this one.

Jim Hammel had literally dropped from the radar screen since the body of Mark Gordon had been found. "There must be a connection with the people following Jen and him and the timely disappearance of Hammel," Nate thought. All the dots were there, but he couldn't connect them. Jenny had assured him that everything was being done to locate Hammel. Once found, professionals would tail him.

Nate wouldn't want to be his shoes when they caught up with him. It was common knowledge that nobody trusted a traitor, especially the enemy. It would be difficult to gain trust from either side after killing his partner.

He related his concerns and suspicions about Hammel and a much larger terrorist strike to Jen. She admitted that the Agency was concerned his suspicions could be correct, but stopped short of adding any additional information.

"Jen, let's go do some surveillance on this cell," he said. She just shook her head and told him there were undercover agents from the Agency and MI-6 British intelligence already living in the same apartment building.

"They will have much better access to what's going on Nate," she said.

As Nate began think about her, he realized that he knew very little about Jenny except that her brother and fiancé were fighting to improve the conditions in Iraq. He had nearly forgotten about her Arab background until she had interviewed Immad in the hospital with such ease that the interrogators at Guantanamo Bay would be envious. Jenny was well suited for her job and worked hard to ensure the safety of America.

"What are you thinking about Nate," she asked.

"I was just thinking about how little I know about you Jen," he replied thoughtfully.

"Why did you decide to become a journalist," she asked.

"I've always loved to write and having an adventurous spirit, this is the perfect job until the next perfect job comes along. What I'm wondering is how long the Agency will keep us paired up," he asked inquisitively. Her face changed moods four times in as many seconds, finally settling on the first pensive look that she had started with. It looked good on her. She took life too seriously, but suddenly it occurred to him that he was fortunate to have her help.

"You should learn to have fun and live a little Jen," he told her. She had changed into shorts and a T-shirt without a bra, her casual at home look. Working with her, he had forgotten just how beautiful she was. Her face was almost the perfect re-creation of the Persian princess you see in movies about the Persian Empire and Alexander the Great.

"That guy in Iraq was lucky to have her," he thought. Nate could see by the look on her face when she brought him up in conversation, she was a woman in love.

He walked to the refrigerator behind the mini-bar, extracted two bottles of icy cold stout ale and offered her one. "We're in London, let's enjoy a little of it," he told her. He took a long cold drink of the ale and looked at the two photos wondering if these guys really believed they would immediately go to heaven and receive seventy-two virgins for being a martyr. Whatever their motive, they had to be stopped, he thought.

"C'mon Jenny, get dressed, we'll go out to Ronnie Scott's Club," he said excitedly. Ronnie Scott's was a club near Piccadilly Circus on Shaftesbury Avenue. In the main part of the club, you could sit at a table or at the bar and order dinner while watching the show. Celebrities and die-hard fans frequented the place at the most unexpected times. If you liked Latino music, the disco upstairs was the place to be. Nate had been there before and had enjoyed that the club catered to a wide diversity of people.

Jenny disappeared into her room via the adjoining door. Knowing women as he did, he figured on at least an hour before she would reappear. He quickly took a shower, dressed into the only sports coat he had brought with him, and sat down to take another look at these two characters who wanted so badly to destroy western civilization.

Forty-five minutes later, Jenny stood in front of him in an aqua evening gown that highlighted her creamy brown skin and dark eyes. He would be the envy of every man in Ronnie Scott's Club. The only thing he could find to say was, "Where the hell did you hide your gun?" She simply smiled and lifted her gown. Strapped to her inner thigh was a smaller version of the weapon she usually carried.

They decided to take a taxi over to the club to avoid parking problems. The taxi driver looked in the mirror and studied them intently. He picked up a newspaper and looked at it then looked back at them.

"Mr. Adams and Miss Martinez, what brings you to London, not the same topic as Brussels, I trust," he asked."

"No, of course not, just a little relaxation" Nate replied, "We're taking a little getaway from work for a couple of days," he lied, convincingly.

"You're a man that stays abreast of the news," he said to the taxi driver.

"I recognized the beautiful lady. Her picture is all over Europe, but your photograph is nearly as well known. Ronnie Scott's Club is a good choice. Many celebrities frequent this place and you won't be bothered," the taxi driver offered.

He hadn't darkened the doors of a club this famous and exclusive for eons, or perhaps since the last time he was here, but the taxi driver had greased the wheels for them by speaking to the doorman. Nate watched as the doorman spoke into a walkie-talkie while checking them out. The driver came back and told them to go to the front of the line.

"Mr. Adams, Miss Martinez, please go right in. We have a table waiting for you," said the doorman. The inside was magnificent and the show had started. If you liked modern jazz, Ronnie Scott's was the best in London and perhaps in all of Europe. Although he knew it by reputation, it had been long on his list of places to visit and sample again, when it came to London's nightlife and besides, he knew that Jenny would enjoy a night out.

They sat at a secluded table. When the waiter came over, they asked for menus and a couple of glasses of ale. He informed them that Mick Jagger was known to frequent the place and was here tonight.

Jenny was looking intently at the set menu. "Money is no object tonight," he told her. They decided on green lentil soup to start, followed by crab risotto, with rhubarb crumble for dessert.

Jenny was beaming, "Thanks for getting us out of the hotel tonight," she said, gratefully.

"We both needed a treat Jen. Relaxing is nourishment for the soul. I wouldn't miss the opportunity to dine at this club anyway," he replied. After taking a long drink from his glass of ale, he started on his green lentil soup.

As his fork deftly slid into his rhubarb crumble, his cell phone rang. Nate reached into his shirt pocket with one hand to grab the phone while stuffing another delicious bite of dessert into his mouth. The phone's display window showed him Karl's number.

"Hello Karl. What's up," he asked. "Where the heck are you, Nate? You're a hard man to track," Karl replied.

"I'm in London and right now I'm at Ronnie Scott's Jazz Club finishing my dessert. I didn't know anyone was tracking me," he told Karl.

"Jesus... Your photograph is all over the front page of every newspaper in Europe, after shooting that terrorist in the Brussels hospital," he shot back.

"Damn," he said, "I've got to try to be a little more low-key."

Nate decided to change the subject. "Where you at now," he asked

"When you started sending information indicating multiple attacks that are to be coordinated with tactical nuclear weapons, the office decided to assign me on this after all. I'm in Marseilles, following the best other solid leads they have," Karl said.

"Don't say anything else over this open line, it's not secure," Nate told him.

"Okay, I'll be on the next train to London and talk to you there," he replied. Nate gave him the details of where they were staying and got off the phone.

Jenny didn't say anything for a couple of minutes. "When's Karl getting here," she suddenly asked.

"Don't let this ruin your evening, Jen. He won't be here until about noon tomorrow. Let's relax and enjoy the evening," he told her. She was still eating her crab risotto with a look of pure joy on her face.

"You've never eaten crab before," he asked her. She just shook her head and he could see she was enjoying every bite.

The club was packed with a waiting line outside. Nobody seemed to notice them. Nate looked around and didn't see anybody famous that he recognized but, if a person liked to watch people, this was the place to come.

"Would you rather listen to Latin music after dinner," he asked. She shook her head and said, "No, I like jazz and it's nice here," she replied.

They talked the night away and she laughed and started to unwind. Suddenly, she changed the subject and her face took on a serious tone, changing the mood at their table.

"My fiancé was shot by terrorists last week and they don't know if he will live," she suddenly blurted, as tears welled up in her eyes.

"Jenny, I'm sorry. I don't understand why they wouldn't let you go to Iraq to be with him," he said. At this moment, the trained agent disappeared and he could only see the vulnerable young woman inside her. Tears slid from her eyes tumbling down her cheeks like raindrops. After a few seconds, she caught herself, acting almost embarrassed.

"Finish your dinner Jenny," he told her gently. "It will make you feel better."

"Would you like to go back to the hotel," he asked.

"No. I'll be all right in a few minutes. She ordered a double scotch and water on the rocks.

Nate thought about her life, but couldn't understand the commitment it must take to change a country that had never known the concept of a democratic government. It gave him a new respect for her.

"Whether Iraq made it or not, they at least deserved the chance that America was giving them," he thought.

He awoke to a pounding on the door. "Nate, get up. It's noon," Karl's voice boomed outside the door.

"Damn! I was hoping for another couple of hours sleep. Just a minute Karl," he yelled back. When he turned over to get out of bed, he saw Jenny's black hair peeking from under the blanket.

He peeked under the blanket. She was naked except for aqua panties. "Shit, I hope we didn't do anything," he thought. "No, I would sure remember if we did."

He remembered that he had to help her into her room. She must have come in after he went to sleep. She probably didn't want to be alone.

No matter what he told Karl, he probably wouldn't believe it. He shook Jenny but she was groggy, so he picked her up and carried her through the open adjoining door to her suite.

When he finally opened the door, Karl looked dog-tired, "What took you so long, have a tough night," he said, attempting to grin through the exhausted look on his face.

"C'mon in and have a cold ale. You look bushed," Nate told him.

"I've got to get some sleep," he said, looking at the unused spare bed in the suite. "Two Arabs have been following me all over Marseilles and I've been on my guard for twelve hours. After what happened to you at the Bierhalle Kropf, I figured I was a target as well," he replied.

"I think there's an informant in our office. I don't see how they could have known you were in Marseilles," he told Karl, "From now on, we should work together."

"As far as I know, Christine sent me on this assignment and the only other person with a need to know is Hans himself," Karl blurted. This was another scrap of proof that someone close to them was feeding information to the enemy.

Neither of them said a word after that, but the silence told Nate they were on the same track. Karl was asleep as soon as his head hit the pillow. He slept peacefully with the knowledge that he was secure in the fact that someone was watching his back.

Maybe they were jumping to conclusions, but an attempt had been made on his life and Karl wasn't simply imagining the two Arabs following him all over Marseilles.

If it were Hans, the terrorists would have their cell phone numbers and might have the technology to listen to their conversations.

Nate decided to wait for more information to include Christine in the loop about their suspicions of a mole being in very close at the office.

Jenny appeared in the doorway, interrupting Nate's thoughts, yawning and stretching. She was wearing her famous T-shirt without a bra and aqua panties. He quickly put his finger to his lips, giving her a shhhhh sound and pointed at Karl asleep on the bed.

She smiled, disappearing into her connecting suite, casting a sheepish giggle in his direction. When she reappeared, she had changed into a sweatshirt and blue jeans.

"You're a real gentleman, Nate. I'm glad we went out last night but my head is pounding," she moaned. "You don't have any aspirin, do you," she asked, attempting to smile.

He returned from his bag with a bottle of generic brand aspirin that he knew would do the job. She smiled gratefully as she swallowed three of them chased by a glass of water from the mini-bar.

"Jen, let's go into your room and let Karl get some sleep. He's had a rough trip," he said.

"No. Let's go down to the café and get some breakfast and coffee," she sighed. "Maybe a little breakfast will help shake this hangover."

He brought Jenny up to speed on the latest suspicions that he and Karl had developed. He knew it was more than a suspicion. When his intuition was this strong, he knew he should give credence to the sense of danger that was burning within him like a branding iron.

"The trouble is, how I will tell my boss that I suspect him of endangering our lives, or worse, outright collaboration with an enemy sworn to destroy us," he told Jenny.

If he were wrong, he would be searching for a new line of work. It could be anyone in the office that had access to the information. God, he was jumping to conclusions without facts -- a bad habit for a journalist. They finished looking at the material on Umar Badawi and Muntasir al-Mashad. When they finished talking, it was five in the afternoon.

They entered the door to their joint suite and realized that Karl had risen from the dead and was just coming out of the shower. "All I needed was a little sleep to feel like a new man," Karl beamed at them, still toweling his hair.

"I've briefed Jenny on our suspicions Karl, but I think we may be a bit premature in our assumptions. Let's get some good old journalistic verification before we take any action," he cautioned Karl.

He gave them both a momentary serious look and nodded his approval. "Ok Karl, let's start. What did you find in Marseilles," Nate asked.

"What I was able to ascertain, Nate backs up everything you suspected. In other words, we all pretty much agree that five or perhaps six tactical nuclear weapons exist and are now in the hands of Al-Qaeda operatives," Karl said.

"I noticed that you called them operatives and not terrorists," he said questioningly.

"Yeah, those guys are operatives, Nate. They aren't the ones that will die … and hell, they may not even believe in Islam. The one thing I'm certain of is that they hate America and the West with a passion that I've never seen or experienced before," he said.

The office did research on these operatives here in London. Umar Badawi and Muntasir al-Mashad were both educated in American Ivy League schools. If there were a Ph.D. in terrorism available, both of these guys would have it. Believe me Nate, these guys are both sharp and mean and they probably have no intention of dying for the cause," Karl drilled his point home.

That's what Nate liked about Karl. He was sharp and to the point and didn't pull any punches. That's what made him a great correspondent.

Nate laughed and said, "That's what I like about you Karl; you're always so positive, but I can tell you, these two killers are going down."

"What makes you think London is the coordination point Karl," asked Jenny.

"I don't have a solid reason to assume that is the case Jenny, but all trails so far lead back to London. These guys won't crack if we pick them up for questioning and I'm sure they're looking out for us," Karl explained.

"We aren't the only ones on this, are we Jenny? Hell, the French and Belgian police aren't stupid and I wonder how many deep cover CIA operatives are also assigned to this case," Nate asked. "Not to mention: MI-5, the Bundesnachrictdienst, DGSI, Russian GRU and 12th Directorate; Mossad, ISI and the Iranian VAJA.

"Hell, they're all probably watching and waiting to see what our next move is," he said after thinking about it for a while.

"I'm sure Scotland Yard is monitoring any travel done by this group." Jenny said. I'm going into my suite and call headquarters get any information they can give us," she offered.

She walked into her suite closing the door behind her with the cell phone in her hand. As soon as the door closed behind Jenny, Karl turned to him. "Nate, do you trust this girl," he asked.

"With my life," he shot back. "Look Karl, she shot my would-be assassin at our favorite watering hole in Zurich," he added. "Okay Nate, that's good enough for me," Karl conceded.

Jenny came out with her purse," I'll be back in a couple of hours," she said, without even stopping to explain.

Nate's cell phone rang, "Nate is Karl there yet," Christine asked. "He arrived today Christine, everything's fine," he answered. "Christine, are you too busy to come to London, we're staying at the Euston Novotel. We need to speak where there is no chance of being overheard," he told her.

"Nate, you just read my mind, I'm booked on the next train to London on the Euro Star," she said. He could see that she was excited by the tone of her voice.

Christine and Nate went back a long way, to the time she was just a teenager following him around the office asking endless questions about everything. She was the best thing Hans had ever accomplished. He dearly hoped that their suspicions about him were not true.

Jenny entered the flat used by Sam Baker and Mike Phillips, the two agents from the special ops section. Phillips spotted her as she entered.

"Mike, here is our little reporter now," he bellowed, as Jenny walked up to him.

"Don't give me any of your chauvinistic crap, Phillips. Just give me the rest of the information that headquarters sent you," Jenny said, with a cold businesslike stare. Baker knew Jenny and knew better than to challenge her, but Phillips made a bad choice in doing so and he just couldn't help smiling at what he knew would be coming.

"We gave you the whole package al-Zaidi," he said to her. Jenny's eyes became slits as Phillips began smiling at her. With lightning speed, Jenny drove her open palm in Mike Phillips solar plexus. He took an awkward step backwards and collapsed holding his chest. He gasped for air with a mixed look of surprise and fear on his face.

While Phillips was recovering, Sam Baker handed her the rest of the information. "Good to see you again, Fatima. Mike has had this one coming for a long time," he chortled, barely able to keep from laughing.

"Good to see you again Sam, it's been a long time," she replied. "You didn't have to do that, I'd have given it to you," said Mike, finally recovering enough to talk.

"If you had intended to give it to me, I would already have had it," Jenny countered.

Jenny quickly opened the rest of the info and found detailed information for follow-ups. "You must be trying to steal the glory for yourself Mike," Jenny accused. "Remember you're here to support me. I'll let this one slide, but try it again and you'll be out of a job," she added.

"There's sensitive information in there -- too sensitive for civilians," Mike said. "Look, Nate's source gave us the start on this case and he's proved to be a valuable asset; so I'll decide who views this," Jenny asserted.

"Jackass," Jenny muttered, as she walked out the door. Guys like Phillips were worse than the Arab religious extremists where women rights were concerned," she thought, as she walked to her car.

Jenny spotted Nate and Karl as she walked by the lounge and ducked in for a quick drink with them. Karl was talking about girls, his favorite subject, when Jenny approached them. She tossed the manila envelope on the table in front of Nate.

"You'll find some interesting new material in there Nate," she said. "Now's not the time to look at this Jen," Nate said. Let's finish our drinks and take a look upstairs."

Nate finally turned his attention to the new information. These guys were certainly at the train station a lot. He could be almost certain by the photographs taken that Umar Badawi had rented a locker at the station. He had a strong hunch that the "package" might be in this locker awaiting transport to America.

Nate took his time flipping through the thirty some pictures that had been taken at various intervals in the last month. Badawi seemed to be using a large rented locker at the end of the second group of lockers along this wall. He studied the photograph and thought he detected the furtive look on Badawi's face. Nate had spotted this look on many people he had interviewed in his professional life. It was clearly the look of someone trying to hide something.

"What'd you find Nate," Jenny asked. "Take a look at this. I'll bet they're hiding it right in this locker, under our noses, in plain sight," he said showing Jenny the picture.

"Is it your intuition again Nate," she asked. "Well, we couldn't go wrong taking a look," Karl interjected.

"No, this time it's better than that," he said. "It's an educated guess."

"We had better call Scotland Yard on this one for support," said Jenny, I'll arrange it immediately. "We've been ordered to work closely with them on this one," she said. Nate checked his Glock 9mm while Jenny called.

She had seemed to know just who to ask for, and they talked for a minute. "Let's go," she finally said, "It's all set up and they'll meet us there.

They arrived at the station to find undercover agents from England's finest already in place. "Hello, you must be the Nate Adams Europe has been talking about. I'm Archibald Tice, Chief of Detectives," he said vigorously pumping Nate's hand.

Tice was a swarthy-skinned man of about fifty with powerful beefy arms that matched the gravelly tone of his voice. His undercover baggy blue jeans and blue T-shirt that read "Swiss Alps" gave the impression of a construction worker rather than Scotland's Yards Chief of Detectives. Under that swarthy construction look, his movements were those of a competent highly trained detective.

Detective Tice got right to the point, "Let's see that photograph and we'll locate the locker," he said. If the weapon is in there, we're ready to arrest the entire Al-Qaeda cell – the whole bloody lot of them," he added. "I've got the master key to the lockers," Tice said, while carefully scrutinizing the pictures. "Let's go," he said, while walking quickly toward the second set of lockers.

Tice suddenly stopped in front of a locker that looked large enough to house a tactical nuclear weapon as well as other items. Undercover detectives ringed him in a semicircle as he inserted the key. Nate stood beside him as he opened the locker door revealing a large aluminum suitcase as well as other common bomb-making materials.

"Voila, we've struck pay dirt on this one, detective," Nate said smiling broadly

Nate grabbed the suitcase and it was far heavier than it appeared but he lifted it carefully out of the locker and placed it on the floor. At that moment, at least ten camera flashes exploded at various intervals.

"Damn," Nate thought, "who the hell tipped off the press?"

Tice used his handheld radio to call the undercover team to move in on the Al-Qaeda cell.

"Is this what I think it is," he asked.

"Yeah, I'm pretty sure. It looks like the ones I've seen in photographs," Nate told him. "This is the first time I've seen the genuine article, if that's what it is."

Suddenly all hell seemed to break loose as technicians from the UK's Ministry of Defence Nuclear Tactical Support Group showed up and surrounded the large aluminum suitcase. Nate overheard the lead technician talk about some unspecified Russian markings, as he snapped a few photos.

Jenny grabbed him, "Let's get out of here," she shouted over the confusion. They looked for the door fleeing the scene that had become a media madhouse free-for-all. Photographers, reporters, police, state security agents and nuclear technicians, each with personal agenda, quickly filled the area vying for the limited space as Nate and Jenny fought their way to the nearest exit.

They started running with Karl close on their heels but when Nate turned to look, he wasn't there. "Did you see Karl," he asked Jenny. "He went back inside. He knows where to find us," Jenny screamed over the din.

"We'll send the photos directly to 'Company HQ' for further analysis," said Jenny, excitedly. "… and Global, of course," said Nate, calmly.

Nate knew that this news bombshell, would be broadcast worldwide in a matter of minutes as the cable news picked it up and anything this big would be in print the next edition. He was giving no interviews, but Global would have the story for this week's edition. "Other media may have the headlines but, we have the in-depth story", he thought.

"C'mon Nate, you're a journalist. Give us and interview," one reporter yelled as a full gaggle of newshounds caught up with them at the car, snapping endless pictures. Jenny was the more photogenic and they swarmed her without shame, fawning over her like schoolboys over a cheerleader.

He decided to call Christine and catch her before she boarded the Euro Star for London. He caught her just as she was leaving the office and told her they would meet her in Zurich. When he turned to Jenny, she was just tearing herself loose from the reporters and photographers.

"We're done here, Jenny. Let's get back to the hotel and pack, and then hop a train to Zurich. Karl is just going to have to catch up," he told her.

Their cell phones rang nearly simultaneously," Hello Karl," he said, 'what's up Nate? I'm here with Archie Tice. The sweep on the Al-Qaeda cell didn't go exactly as planned. It looks like Badawi and al-Mashad slipped through the net and got away," he said.

"It doesn't matter, Karl. We're headed to Zurich to figure out what we have as far as information on the other four cities involved. He could see by the look on Jenny's face that she was hearing essentially the same information on her end.

On the train, they relaxed and poured over the growing folders of the information they had accumulated, as they sipped coffee. It appeared that Badawi had traveled to Madrid several times and there was a good chance that it might be where he was headed.

Nate was sure we would cross paths with these two again and he knew that the next encounter meant certain elimination for them or us. There was no middle ground and the die had been cast.

Jen's eyes were closed and she was resting peacefully, sleeping with the assurance that someone was watching over her. She turned slightly, brushing her thick black hair from her face, while she sought a better position for her nap.

Sleep was catching Nate as he daydreamed about sailing the Mediterranean near the Greek Isles. Suddenly, his cell phone rang and Abbey's voice caught up with him from across the Atlantic. "Nate, this is Abbey. I've been thinking about you. Julie and I are flying to Paris today. What are you doing," she asked, forcing it out in one breath. "The news had to have gotten to American networks," he thought.

We've been very busy, Abbey. This is a bad time for me," he said.

"We've been watching the news, Nate. You've been a busy boy," she said, with an attempt at humor. She wouldn't be brushed off that easily. "We'll be in Zurich later tonight, but situations have been changing rapidly for me lately," he said.

Where are you now," he asked her. "We're actually close to the French coast now. We'll be landing in Paris in an hour-and-a-half," she answered. He gave her his suite number at the Swissotel and told her to call him.

Chapter 5

Jenny walked right into his suite. They were bushed even though they had been able to sleep a little on the train. The events of the last few days had exhausted them. Jenny didn't bother to stop at the desk and get her own room, but instead immediately passed out on the other king sized bed in the suite.

Nate awoke to a loud pounding at the door and his cell phone ringing. He looked at his cell's display window and saw Hans Schuler's number on the screen.

"Hans, what's up," he asked, wondering why Hans would be calling him at four in the morning.

"Nate, it's me at the door. Is Jenny with you? Let me in," he gasped, as the fear in his voice penetrated the door like a knife.

Nate opened the door and Hans flew past him like a blur. "Shut the door," he croaked. He had never known Hans to fear anything. The publisher had always been the one in control, very calm, and never in a hurry. Roused by the commotion, Jenny had gotten up and was sitting in her bathrobe on the foot of the bed. She gave Nate a perplexed look, but she caught herself in the middle of a "what the heck is going on?" look and started for the bathroom.

"I don't know where to begin Nate, but it started before I sent Karl to Delaware to ask you to come back. That was the day after Omar al-Douri called us at Karl's number. A man we now know to be Umar Badawi came to the office and introduced himself as a Saudi businessman doing business with al-Douri. He knew enough details to be credible," he said.

"This explained how these terrorists knew details of their travels," Nate thought. "When we learned of the incident in London's train station, we knew we had been duped," he added.

"Why the visit in the middle of the night Hans," he asked. "Omar called an hour ago and told me that I had been declared a 'special enemy of the Jihad' and anyone that killed me by decapitation would be paid one million dollars in American currency," Hans blurted, his voice trembling. His whole body was shaking convulsively at intervals as he babbled the details.

Jenny, who had just returned from the bathroom, and Nate were stunned, but they should have seen this coming. The Jihadists only successful tactic was the use of terror, intimidation, indoctrination and deception as a means to an end.

Nate and Jenny didn't doubt for a minute that their names were probably on this infamous list too. Obviously, Al-Qaeda didn't like losing one of their coveted tactical nuclear weapons that they probably had paid so very dearly for. This could mean that their timeline for an attack could be changed or advanced.

"This is Jenny's area of expertise. They probably felt that *Global News Weekly* is responsible for their loss and issued a fatal fatwa, directing all "true believers" to kill the messenger. That could mean the same for me, but they've already tried and missed once," Nate told him. "Get your wits about you, Hans or you'll be easy prey," he added.

Hans seemed to be calming down. Nate went to the refrigerator and got him a bottle of ale. He looked at him appreciatively as he quaffed half the bottle in five seconds.

"Feel a little better Hans," Nate asked him. After Hans finished the ale, he sat in a chair and visibly started to relax. "Maybe there's room for you at the ranch Omar is staying at in Montana," Nate said, speculatively. His face changed expressions as he considered the possibility.

"Maybe I could use a long vacation to the American Northwest," Hans said, reflectively.

"The safest place for you to stay tonight is right here. With all the publicity, they won't try to take three of us," Nate told him.

The rest of the night passed in relative quiet. Nate grabbed a fold up bed out of the closet for Hans and he was fast asleep as soon as his head hit the pillow.

"It looks like my new flat is becoming a crash pad," Nate thought.

Hans packed a few of his things and Christine drove him to the airport the following afternoon. Hans had turned the over reins to Global into Christine's capable hands in the meantime. "It was probably for the best," Nate thought, as the first trace of the predawn light of the New Global era appeared on the corporate horizon. "Sooner or later, she would eventually get the magazine anyway."

With Hans safely on his way to America, Nate and Jenny sat in Christine's office, finishing the details of the proposed trip to Madrid. If Badawi were there, they would find him, he was sure of that.

"They may move the timetable up for their attack," Nate said.

Christine's face changed expressions as she considered this new scenario. "That would certainly put pressure on the entire Western and European communities, wouldn't it," she stated. The terrorists would be hard to figure. They were in a position to change their strategy as the circumstances permitted.

Jenny's cell phone rang, "Hello, this is Fatima," she said. She stepped out of the office into the hallway to take the call.

"Badawi has been spotted boarding the Euro Star in Paris bound for Madrid," she said, as she re-entered the office. "There were two of them. The other one must be al-Mashad. We have two undercover agents on the train with orders to follow them." Nate smiled, hoping the two guys following these two were not as obvious as the others he had seen.

His thoughts turned to Abbey despite all the busyness of the moment. He realized that she would probably be arriving at the Swissotel before he could think the situation through.

Nate had told her to call first, but he knew how much women liked to surprise their lovers. Now that Greta had entered the picture, Nate was uncomfortable with the idea of the two of them sharing information and he wasn't good at games.

Although Greta and Nate had made no commitments, she seemed to be a little possessive and he didn't need any tensions or complications in the office just now.

Jenny's voice broke into his thoughts, "A penny for your thoughts Nate," she probed, gently nudging him in the side with her elbow. "I think I've worked myself into a corner with these women Jenny," he confessed.

She gave a slight chuckle and said, "Just like a man to worry about a problem when there isn't one." Greta hasn't asked for or demanded anything other than what you've had together," she said. Nate had to admit, she was right, but he was still a little uneasy with Abbey showing up so unexpectedly.

Jenny was able to get the room next to his suite with the connecting door. He felt a lot better about her being in the room next door instead of another floor.

As Nate and Jenny walked to the elevator Abbey and Julie strolled into the lobby entrance looking as American as possible.

When she spotted Nate by the elevators, she immediately smiled and ran to him, hugging his neck so tightly that it was hard to breathe.

The elevator was crowded and silent and Nate caught Jenny sizing up both Abbey and Julie as they ascended to the third floor. When they exited the elevator, Jenny smiled "Not bad," she quipped.

"It's not like you think, Jen. Julie is Karl's friend," he said, trying to defend him.

"Nate and I are just friends," Abbey said to Jenny.

"I'm sorry I've been so rude, Abbey. Nate and I just work together on this case," Jenny said. Nate detected just a bit of defensives in her voice.

"I've seen your pictures on cable news with Nate. I guessed as much," Abbey said in an attempt at friendliness. Jenny smiled and nodded as she disappeared into her room through the connecting door, leaving Julie, Abbey, and Nate in the suite.

Abbey was dressed in a mauve colored sundress that showed every curve of her ample figure. She sat on his bed with her legs crossed, her beautiful blue eyes sparkling with energy and a touch of a smile on her lips. She looked radiant, her captivating eyes teasing and reminding him of their night in Dewey Beach. Suddenly, all the pressure was gone and he was glad she was here.

There was a knock at the door, "The ladies' luggage sir," the bellhop said with a heavy Swiss accent. After tipping him five Euros for his trouble, Nate's mind returned to Abbey. He realized that he really didn't know anything about her. They had only spent one night together at his home in Delaware. He wasn't sure how she would fit in his life, but he didn't want her to leave.

There was another rapping at the door with Karl's voice booming in the hallway. "Nate, you in there," he asked.

"Just a minute Karl, I've got a surprise for you," he replied, as he opened the door. Karl spotted Julie and Abbey and his whole face brightened and broke into one of his famous smiles.

"I'm famished, are you guys ready to go to the café and get something to eat," Abbey asked.

The connecting door opened and Jenny stepped into the suite, "Not without me," she said. She had changed her clothes, into a beautiful floral sundress with a matching ribbon, setting off her luxurious black hair.

The five of them sat in the café eating a light dinner, while chatting about anything and everything. Nate's mind was wandering as he thought about Karl and Julie. He wondered if Karl would take her off his hands and take her back to his apartment.

Nate wanted to speak with Abbey and find out what her plans were. Karl and Nate began talking about the case, just browsing the surface, without speculating on their next move.

"I think it's pretty obvious, Karl. We're going to Madrid the day after tomorrow after the two agents gather some information for us," Nate informed him. "You're the lead journalist on this one, Nate. I've been in the back seat on this one ever since you came back," he conceded.

"We got some new information. Badawi and al-Mashad were spotted boarding a train in Paris bound for Madrid. How they managed to get across the Channel is anybody's guess. There are a couple of CIA agents on them right now and they should have more information when we get there, including the location of a new Al-Qaeda cell in Madrid," Nate told him, as the girls chatted about shopping for clothes in Zurich.

"Karl, I need to speak with you privately," he said. They got up and went into the lobby of the hotel.

"It's about Julie and Abbey, isn't it Nate," he asked.

"You asked them to come, didn't you Karl," Nate said accusingly. "How long are they planning to stay?"

Karl was quiet for a few seconds before answering. "All summer, they want to get jobs here," he finally said. "You could've at least told me they were coming Karl," Nate replied. Karl gave him one of his famous winning smiles of helplessness and shucked his shoulders.

Abbey understood just how important and dangerous this assignment was. When he told her that he would be leaving the day after tomorrow for Madrid, she didn't ask any questions. He tried very hard to give the impression that she and Julie were not invited to follow.

"This could be very dangerous … these people play for keeps," he told her. Abbey just smiled and said, "I'll be good, Nate. I know you're working."

Abbey and Nate were the last two to leave the lounge. Back in the suite, they were alone at last. She let the sundress slip to the floor. It's amazing how little a woman can wear under a dress. She melted into his arms, her full lips finding his like two magnets of opposite polarity meeting and drawing together as if they were meant for one another.

They were breathless as the heat of the moment and body chemistry overcame them as they fell onto the bed. Nate forgot about everything except her and didn't want to escape the situation, but instead was caught up in her passion as she clung to him with a fierceness he had never known. He had forgotten the softness of her skin and her scent, only now to be reminded as his senses whirled and everything else became inconsequential.

He awoke at five, his usual time, and his mind still filled with memories of the night and made coffee while writing the first of his notes for a follow-up story.

"We sure beat *Time* and **Newsweek** on this one," he thought. He looked over at Abbey sleeping, her light brown hair falling gently across her face. He imagined her sparkling blue eyes as if they were open, with their own unique chemistry and mystery. At six-thirty, he heard a gentle knock at the connecting door to Jenny's room.

She entered, knowing he was an early riser. "I knew you would have coffee ready," she said, while pouring herself a cup. I couldn't sleep and I knew you'd be up," she said, almost whispering. Jenny always looked radiant when she was fully rested; and as she sat at the breakfast nook on a high stool, her eyes radiated a sparkling energy of their own.

"If we have today, let's take it and make it a real day off," Nate told her. It didn't take much to convince her. She looked at him with an ever so slight Mona Lisa smile and nodded affirmatively as she slurped her hot coffee. "We should take it light today," she agreed.

He glanced at Abbey as she was sleeping easily. "God," he thought," I envy people that could shut everything out and sleep that soundly." She looked as beautiful sleeping as she did fully awake with her make-up on. He pointed towards the door and Jen nodded as they exited quietly.

Jen had not only rented another 480-SL Roadster, but the color of this Mercedes was a sharp deep metallic blue that made it distinctive. "My favorite color," he thought. "I hope they like it."

The metallic flakes seemed to dance in the sunlight, giving expression to the deep rich blue paint that surrounded them. With the top already down, he quickly slid into the comfortable passenger seat with a satisfied look. "This day already has promise," he thought, as Jenny pressed the accelerator and the car shot from the curb where the rental Agency had parked it.

The cool breeze of morning was comforting in the rapidly rising sun of Zurich's clear blue sky. Jenny's face beamed at the pleasure of driving the beautifully engineered machine. Her long black hair flapped wildly in the breeze creating a beautiful contrast to her beautiful brown face, as the quickly accelerating roadster picked up speed.

The countryside flew by as his concerns fell by the wayside. He was glad that Abbey and Julie had made their own plans for today, since he needed the opportunity to take this time to unwind from the sequence of events that had unraveled since his return to the world of international journalism and *Global News Weekly*. He felt the pressure flow from his body as the roadster careened around the mountainous curves, fulfilling its function as the high performance precision machine it was.

Jen seem to know where she was going as she maneuvered the Mercedes out of Zurich and into the countryside where a mixture of mountains, pastures and rolling meadows dominated the landscape.

Minutes that seemed like hours passed in silence, when suddenly Jen broke the silence. "What're you going to do about Abbey," she asked. Nate gave her a look that said, "Not now, please."

That didn't stop his persistent sidekick. "Look, you're going to have to deal with this sooner or later," she said. "Nothing like stating the obvious," he thought.

Nate didn't want anything to break the quiet soothing calmness of the Swiss countryside. She was right, body chemistry was not love and he didn't want a woman waiting around for him to come home, at least not just yet.

Jen suddenly slowed down and pulled into the small parking lot of a quaint distinctly Swiss chalet. There was an aroma wafting from it that gave the impression of breakfast being cooked. His stomach started to growl at the thought of a hearty breakfast.

Suddenly, a blonde giant with a full mustache burst through the front door of the chalet restaurant, immediately making a beeline for Jenny, who was getting out of the car. He lifted her high in the air like a rag doll while laughing the whole time.

"Olaf, put me down, you big oaf," she admonished him mischievously. Olaf gently lowered her to the ground, his face bursting into the broadest grin he'd ever seen on a man his size.

His attention suddenly turned to Nate as he walked toward him, speaking good English, "You must be that Nate guy I've been reading about," he said, offering his enormous right paw. His hand dwarfed Nate's and he shook it vigorously. Nate had to tilt his head to look him in the eye. The smile and the twinkle in this giant's eye revealed his good nature and friendliness.

He looked at the chalet and there was not a hint from the outside that this was a breakfast and lunch restaurant, except for the number of vehicles parked and the sense enticing aroma emanating from within. The rich smell of waffles and sausage wafted through the air, as they entered the front door with Olaf in the lead.

Jen quickly strode up to the only remaining empty table in the place. Within twenty minutes, two platters, brimming with waffles, sausage and eggs were placed before their appreciative eyes. Nate dove into the fresh Swiss sausage with relish, his stomach growling appreciatively as he eyed the waffles and eggs.

They finished eating, but Olaf wouldn't accept their money. He sat down to chat about their recent escapades throughout Europe. It was obvious from the detail that he displayed that he had watched their adventures on cable news television.

Jenny seemed to talk endlessly with Olaf about Brussels and London. The gargantuan meal had made Nate sleepy and he didn't want to discuss the last week's events. He wanted the day to be countryside and relaxation, driving through the Swiss farmland and rolling hills. Being born and living in the country as a child, he could never shake his fondness for nature.

Suddenly, Olaf was standing, offering Nate his hand and telling him what an honor it was to meet Nate Adams. After energetically pumping his hand one more time, he disappeared into the kitchen still wearing his huge grin.

Jenny accelerated quickly from the chalet. The car effortlessly picked up speed, while Nate noticed two cars pulling onto the roadway from the gas station next-door, as he glanced in the Roadster's side mirror.

"What're you thinking about Nate," she asked. "Nothing," he replied. "I'm just trying to enjoy a little bit of Switzerland," he replied.

They drove for a few minutes and when he looked in the side mirror, one of the cars had turned off, but the gray Volvo was still behind them.

"How long have they been following," she asked, indicating the two men in the Volvo behind them.

"Since the restaurant," he told her, as he reached down and felt the reassuring bulge of the Glock strapped to his lower leg beneath his pants. Jenny reached under her seat and put her weapon on her lap for easy access.

The Volvo suddenly sped up and decided to pass. They both reached for their weapons as the car sped by. He uttered a sigh of relief as he noticed it was two middle-aged European businessmen in a hurry to get somewhere.

"We're a little jumpy Jen," he said, in an attempt to laugh it off. However, they both knew that it was better to be jumpy than dead.

Things had changed for Nate and nothing seemed to be a coincidence anymore. He made a clear mental note of the two men. Sure, they were innocuous looking, but he had learned that the most successful agents or assassins never stood out in a crowd and he would not forget them. They were usually people, who could only be described vaguely, because they appeared to be so innocuous and mundane that they were rarely noticed. It was a real art to be able to blend in, while being hardly noticed, and it made an agent very valuable.

Jenny wheeled the blue Mercedes to the front of the Swissotel and came to an abrupt stop at the front doors with a slight smile of satisfaction on her face.

The doorman came around to Jenny's side of the car as she got out. "I'll park it in your regular spot, Mademoiselle Martinez," he said, in a heavy French accent.

One thing Nate liked about Europe and especially Switzerland is its exceptional diversity of people. Many people in Europe are multilingual and it worked well for them as well as for tourists.

They were famished when they entered the lobby and decided to eat dinner in the Swissotel's restaurant. The cool mountain air had given them a hearty appetite and they attacked their evening meal with relish.

The two men in the Volvo that had passed them in the countryside weighed heavy on his mind. "You've got that look again Nate, as if you're someplace else," Jenny said.

"I just can't get those characters that passed us in the Volvo out of my mind," he told her. "There was no reason for them to pass us. We were doing eighty and the suits they had on were American -- not European."

"You've become observant, Nate," Jenny remarked. Nate looked at her as he cut and shoved the last delicious bite of a porterhouse steak into his mouth and slowly chewed it, tasting the delicious meat covered with an exquisite steak sauce while savoring every bit of its culinary nuance.

Jenny's cell phone broke the silence, shattering the intensity of his thoughts. She looked at the display window on the phone and said, "I've got to take this," as she disappeared into the ladies room. Nate drank the remainder of his lager and observed the surroundings, noticing that people were discretely glancing at him. Appearing on European-wide television certainly removed one's privacy. At least the damned paparazzi weren't all over the place looking for a photo-op," he thought.

When Jenny stepped out of the ladies room, the skin of her beautiful light brown complexion had turned ashen. She sat and looked down at her plate with disinterest. He decided to let her speak when she was ready. Nate had never seen this side of Jenny. She was silent for what seemed like an eternity and then she spoke in a low voice that he had to strain and lean over to hear.

"That was my fiancé's father on the phone," she said barely audible. "Ahmed died about an hour ago."

"Let's get out of here Jenny," he said, placing the equivalent of about eighty dollars on the table. Nate took her hand and walked her to the elevator. She hadn't said another word. She needed space and he intended to give it to her. When they reached his room, she lay on the bed. He looked at her face and she was very exhausted, her usually light brown skin had lost its luster. After he covered her with a blanket, she was asleep within five minutes, tossing and turning as if she had somehow been forced into a bad nightmare. He watched her, but knew, what she needed now was to be alone with her thoughts and plenty of sleep.

Why the terrorists would choose Madrid as a target suddenly became clear to Nate. He knew that they were limited on targets with the five or six bombs they had available. Nobody came up with any more intelligence on the exact number of tactical nuclear weapons Al-Qaida had, but at this point, it didn't seem to matter. One was more than enough to send shock waves and chaos throughout the Western World.

Madrid was the third most populous city in Europe. For over a thousand years, it had been under an Islamic Caliphate. It was only when Christian forces pushed the last of the Islamic forces back into North Africa that Spain was totally free of the Crescent's imposed *dhimmitude*. The Hapsburg Dynasty of Charles I of Spain, the Holy Roman Emperor, took hold in the Early 1500's and Spain had maintained control of the Iberian Peninsula, shifting the balance of power in much of Europe.

If the new Jihadists and their terrorists could destroy Madrid and bring in enough armed maniacs to overcome the devastated inhabitants, Spain would once again become an Islamic Caliphate. Such a victory could ignite the whole of Islam, even the moderates to attack the West. In the event of a nuclear explosion, he was sure that an army would be massed just within reach of Spain with the intent of occupying the entire country. However, the NATO alliance stood in its way, so all hope was not lost in the multidimensional netherworld of asymmetrical warfare that was driven by religious fanaticism.

There was no doubt these people were organized and deadly serious. They intended to take the entire planet for Islam and make the world a theocratic dictatorship. The freedom of the entire Western World was at stake and the problem was that only a very few understood or realized what was happening.

There was a knock at the door and he opened it to find Christine standing there with a look of fatigue in her face. "Hi Nate," she said, as he stepped into the hallway and closed the door behind him. She handed him an envelope containing two tickets to Madrid.

"What time is the departure," he asked her without even looking at the tickets. "Ten in the morning," she replied. They decided to go to the hotel café to talk, but he was as tired as Jen.

Nate asked her how she was doing at the top job and noted that her vulnerable little girl look had been replaced with that of a competent professional woman. He was assured that *Global News Weekly* would run smoothly with her at its helm.

"How's your father doing," he asked her. "He's already in America and on his way to the ranch with Omar," she said. "He needed a vacation anyway and I think he wants to retire. He could see that with Christine at the controls, the publication might be on a different track. Who knows? Maybe, this is what the magazine ultimately needed if it was to reach the next level in the rarified world of international news journalism.

Chapter 6

They watched Zurich disappear as the plane gained the cruising altitude of about thirty thousand feet and turned southwest toward Madrid. Jenny's recuperative powers were amazing and she seemed to be her old self again. She disappeared into the bathroom as her phone rang and when she reappeared, she handed me a folded paper.

He opened it and she had scribbled, "Sorry, no fancy hotel this time. We're going to operate out of a safe house." Nate looked in her direction, fully understanding the gravity of the situation. Madrid had a large Muslim population and the terrorists now felt safe to operate with more ease, if not impunity. Nate and Jenny's faces were too well known by now and they had made serious enemies -- enemies that would not only be relentless, but also viciously attack their families as well.

Nate drifted into sleep and was startled by Jenny's voice, "Wake up, Nate! We're approaching Madrid." As he peered out of the window, his mind drifted to their two foes, Badawi and al-Mashad. "How many nukes were they able to acquire," he thought.

These two characters were not run-of-the-mill terrorists. They had sophisticated American educations and were both dedicated to weakening the west any way they could. They were devious and ruthlessly ambitious enough to take a leadership role with their people when the battle was finished.

Jenny was right; they needed to play this one very carefully and much more professionally.

Sam Baker met them at the terminal. "It's good to see you again Nate," he said, shaking his hand. "Thanks for requesting me on this one, Jenny."

"We needed another good man," she replied. Sam gave them directions to the safe house located in the Malasana district of Madrid and a number to call as well as his cell phone number. Sam was a good man and Nate was happy to have him on their team.

Madrid was hot and humid in June and this summer was no exception. When they stepped out of the terminal, the heat hit them like a blast furnace. "I must be getting spoiled," he thought. Jenny had already rented a car. Nate smiled when she looked disappointed as the attendant drove a Volvo up to the curb and handed her the keys.

"Don't worry Jen, without the Mercedes maybe we won't be so recognizable," he said. Cable news had begun to relate Jenny and her love for the famous roadsters. She impishly sneered at him as she pulled away from the curb. Fortunately, the Volvo had a great air conditioner and Nate immediately cranked it up. "We'll just have to rough it," he quipped.

The streets of Madrid were crowded and had a large immigrant population, many of which were Arab or North African. Nate knew he and Jenny would not have the home court advantage on this one. Madrid possessed the type of Islamic infrastructure a

The Lavapies neighborhood is one of the poorer areas of the city and houses many immigrant populations, including a large number of Arabs. It is in the area that they would probably find these two terrorists and in all likelihood, the tactical nukes.

There were many extremist underlings just waiting in the wings for leadership to be provided so they could wage Jihad in the name of Allah.

This area also attracted artists and musicians and was widely diverse in its immigrant population including Africans, Hindi, Chinese, Filipinos and Caribbean's as well as the large Arab population. It had been ten years since he'd been in Madrid and had enjoyed the area's cheap but great restaurants, serving a wide variety of international and local foods.

Their faces were far too well known on the streets for them to be seen in public in Madrid. From now on, they would operate as much as they could from behind the scenes letting others gather information for them.

Jenny drove the Volvo into Madrid's Malasana neighborhood where the safe house was located. Before going to the house she pulled into a little shop that served lunch; they chose to sit inside at a table that afforded them a view of the entire café and the front door. She had been uncharacteristically quiet and the silence made him wonder if she was still mourning for her fiancée.

The sound of her cell phone ringing broke the silence. She ignored the first ring and kept chewing a bite of food. When she glanced at the display screen, her mood instantly changed. "Hello," she said, "Yes sir, I understand. We're here now and we'll be at the safe house in about twenty minutes." She listened for another minute then put the phone down.

"Jim Hammel is thought to be in Madrid and I have orders to eliminate him if I can do so without causing an international incident," she said. Nate wasn't in the least surprised. He had wondered when and where Hammel would show up, and he understood why the Agency would want him eliminated. They wouldn't have to deal with the public embarrassment and major scandal of a trial of a despicable traitor and mole, who had killed one of its own.

Nate wasn't quite sure where Freedom of the Press ended and National Security began on this one. He decided he would follow his instincts and hope for the best

Sometimes a journalist needed to act in the best interests of the country, if not the world, instead of reporting every iota of the story no matter who got hurt in the process. "It was a line in the sand," he thought "and the line shifted as events unfolded."

He was starting to get the idea of how the Agency operated. They were a team, that when it benefited them, but they could also be as self-serving and corruptible as any other business or organization.

The game had become both deadly and serious very quickly. He wasn't just a journalist chasing a story any longer; he was now, like-it-or-not, a proactive frontline participant, honing the skills of an intelligence agent. He was in this for many of the same reasons as Jenny and wanted very badly to eliminate a nuclear threat in Europe before it could spread to America. Subtly, gradually and nearly without his knowledge, he had become a key player. Civilization, as they knew it, hung in the balance.

The attacks on the World Trade Center and the Pentagon on September 11, 2001 coupled with the increase in acts of terror around the world should have been an ominous call to arms in the mind of any rational person. Many if not most people instinctively feel that if they ignore the problem and don't provoke anybody, it will simply go away.

History has repeatedly proven that this is a wrong and a deadly assumption. It was George Santayana who said that "Those who forget history are condemned to relive it" and these philosophical words were applicable now more than ever.

"We've lost a lot of Freedom after 9-11 and we simply can't afford to lose any more," reflected Nate.

If the terrorists could orchestrate the annihilation of several of the world's cities, they could easily integrate most of Southeastern Europe into a new caliphate. Most people felt threatened, but couldn't quite envision the larger picture, beyond their daily lives.

They pulled up in front of an upscale dwelling that would be considered almost a palace in the states. "There's nobody home," said Jenny. "This is a very limited operation and the only agents except for Sam and I that will be on this case will be flying in tomorrow evening from the states. I don't know who they are. This one is a notch higher than Top Secret. Nate, you're the only non-Agency person that has access."

Once inside this veritable small palace, the details of the interior decorating was breathtakingly exquisite. The foyer floor was ornately laid out with Italian ceramic tile. The uniquely shaped windows were encased on the exterior with wrought iron encasements that looked anything but cheap.

Nate looked at the construction and could see that everything was a handcrafted one of a kind design. The builder had spared no expense on materials or labor and every detail looked to be the best available.

The kitchen was decked out, complete with the ornate tile countertops, ultra-modern appliances and copper overhanging hooks for cooking pots. Large glass double doors led to a rear courtyard with an outside dining area that was uniquely shaded but not covered, tiled with an Italian style Mediterranean aqua with thin lines of black running through it showing no particular pattern.

An elegantly tiled swimming pool finished the effect that the perfect landscaping had only started. Nate wasn't astounded at the opulent lifestyle of the fabulously wealthy, but he certainly wouldn't mind taking advantage of it for the moment.

Nate was immersed in his thoughts, while Jenny had located a package that had been left for her "eyes only" by superiors in Washington. She started flipping pages of the document with a look of wonderment on her face. "What's up," he asked her.

"We've got problems," she replied, momentarily glancing in his direction. "Apparently, Umar Badawi's father was educated in America and during his four year stay at the university he had a relationship with an American woman named Martha Hammel. As it turns out, their relationship was a fruitful one. Martha bore him paternal twins, a boy and a girl."

"Would you like to take a wild guess at what the she named the boy after the elder Umar disappeared during her pregnancy," she asked.

"Well that explains the leak," he said sarcastically. "No wonder how Badawi had slipped through the CIA's background check. He didn't change sides. He was never on our side."

Hammel at six foot had dark brown hair and brown eyes. He had inherited his mother's fair skin and apparently his father's ideology. He could easily be considered as one of the worst threats in the world to western culture.

Hammel had ended the façade of functioning as a CIA operative by taking the life of the fellow agent he had befriended. He was highly trained and it would be very hard to locate him in the burgeoning Arab population in Madrid.

Jenny had taken a break from reading the extensive intelligence report and scavenged through the cupboards to come up with all the makings for a great cup of coffee. "Mind if I go through the report," he asked her. "Not at all," she replied, "two sets of eyes are better than one."

The details of Hammel's life, had been intricately compiled and were more complex and complete than any biography he had ever seen. Badawi must have sent Martha money for the boy's upbringing and kept in constant touch with her. Young Jim, had been taken to mosques by his mother for schooling, where he soon became fluent in Arabic. More importantly, the imams had obviously instilled in him an intense hatred of the West. They had schooled him in the radical right wing beliefs of Islam. Nate and Jenny knew that Jim Hammel would be a considerable foe and not one to be underestimated or trifled with and taken out with extreme prejudice.

They knew James Hammel's whereabouts and activities, but questions remained about his twin sister. Her mother had named her Angela. "A bit ironic," he thought, because the name "Angela" meant angel in more than one language.

Jenny and Nate had been ordered to keep off the streets until the reinforcements from the states arrived. For the first time since all this started, the CIA seemed to be playing this one cautiously.

"There was a lot at stake here," Nate thought. If Western and Southern Europe were taken down by terrorism, then America was certainly was at risk.

This new line of terrorists were sophisticated enough to figure out that using Spain as a launching pad to attack the United States was far easier than using the Middle East as a staging area, especially when this would put them in control of all of Spain's resources and its strategic position.

Nate's intuition was playing havoc in his mind. There was a missing piece of the puzzle concerning Badawi and he wouldn't feel right until he knew what it was.

He had an ominous premonition that all hell was about to break loose. "You've got that look on your face again Nate. What's wrong," Jenny asked. "I don't quite know, but I get the feeling that this place has been compromised.

Jenny didn't say anything right away, but she was deep in thought. After a couple of minutes she said, "Nate, this house was leased at the last minute from a very trusted person within the Agency."

"If I recall correctly, Hammel was a very trusted person within the Agency," he shot back at her. Jenny shifted uneasily in her seat and the look on her face told him she was thinking the situation through.

She rose to her feet without as much as a sigh and started making a meal from the well-stocked pantry. He peered at the ingredients and the bottle of dry white wine she had amassed on the countertop. Artichoke hearts, mushrooms, linguine and chicken. It looked like Tuscan chicken, with a white style Alfredo sauce over linguine with a bit of dry white wine, cooked in the sauce for good measure.

"She certainly had talent," he thought, as he watched her move around the kitchen as if she had been in one all her life. He had also seen Jenny in action. This girl seemed to be a complete package and she was good company.

After dinner, he decided they should look around the neighborhood. To hell with the Agency's orders to stay indoors until reinforcements came. He was never one to take those kinds of orders to heart blindly anyway. He wasn't employed by the Agency and couldn't be made to face any consequences for disobeying their bureaucratic rules.

Nate donned a *National Geographic Expeditions* ball cap that he had been given after a hike in the Grand Canyon, khaki shorts and a pair of sunglasses for a bit of a disguise and headed toward the front door. "Where are you going," she asked. "We've been told to stay on the property until the other two agents get here."

"I don't work for them, remember … anyway, I feel like a sitting duck here," he said.

"You could be right, Nate. If you'll wait a minute, I'll go with you," she said, sounding a bit impatient. He had always been a bit of a rebel and he disliked being told what to do by somebody who didn't sign his paycheck.

It was ninety-two degrees, sunny with eighty percent humidity when he stepped from the safe house into the driveway. When Jen was finally ready, he almost didn't recognize her. She had her hair covered with a red American style bandana and wore sunglasses. He didn't think that either of them would be easily recognizable unless someone was looking for them.

Malasana is an energetic neighborhood with numerous bars and an active nightclub life that the jetsetter could become inconspicuous in without much trouble. His mind was focused on finding the remaining four tactical nuclear weapons before they could be used to destroy four European cities and the way of life for more than a million people.

Jenny hopped in the driver's seat of the Volvo and backed out of the driveway. "Where to, Nate," she asked flippantly. "Let's just get a feel for the neighborhood," he replied.

The streets of Malasana were bustling and busy with people doing the everyday tasks of life in a lively city. Most were young and from virtually every ethnic background. Everyone seemed in a hurry to get somewhere. "It was similar to a cross section of any large American inner city," Nate thought.

They sat at an outdoor café that was equipped with contemporary oval shaped tables with large Italian style umbrellas to shade a patron from the intensity of the sultry summer Madrid sun. A waitress sauntered over to their table and said something very rapidly in Spanish that he couldn't decipher. She suddenly stopped in mid-sentence realizing that they didn't understand a word she had said and started again in heavily accented, but good English.

"Hola, my name is Lucia. We have great ice coffee. It will refresh you in this heat." The two nodded their ascent and she traipsed off to fill our order.

They sat sipping their iced coffee that more resembled a coffee flavored Icee, but it was refreshing and tasted great. The afternoon drifted by slowly and they left the café deciding instead to stroll down the street. The shops were filled with huge assortment of goods that were sure to entice passing window-shoppers to enter and browse. Jenny glanced at the watch on her right wrist almost as an afterthought and casually commented, "It's six o'clock, and their plane should be arriving about now." They drove the Volvo back to the house just before the arrival of their backup team.

"It would be complicated to trust the two new agents after the treachery of Jim Hammel," he thought. "Let's face it, if the CIA ranks were that easy to infiltrate, it brought doubt into the entire organization."

These terrorists meant bloody business and were willing to die for their cause. There is nothing more threatening than a religious zealot, especially one with a nuclear weapon.

He could sense her anger as she watched the two new agents step out of the rental car they had driven from the airport. He gazed at the expression on her face and realized that she knew both of these operatives or at least one of them. It was apparent that her opinion of them was unfavorable.

He had learned to trust her judgment just as she had learned to trust his uncanny intuition. They had become a good team in the short time they had known one another. Jenny had been great to work with in Zurich, Brussels and London and they had counted on each other for their very lives.

He had come to expect the unexpected from the Agency. "I'm relieved that *Global News Weekly* signs my paychecks and not the Agency, but Jenny isn't so lucky," he thought. "Well, with Christine in charge of Global, perhaps something could be done about that."

The two agents at the door were two more suits that had been cut from the same cloth. They appeared to be ex-military and still bore the crisp stamp of Government Issue. They wouldn't be hard to spot for any enterprising terrorist. Someday, the CIA would learn that the most effective operatives were the ones that didn't look the part. Perhaps they wanted high visibility on this one but for the life of him, he couldn't understand why.

Both men were in their early to mid-thirties with military haircuts and seemed like they could handle themselves.

He looked at Jen and was pleased that she had put on her friendly face. She knew the situation was far too serious to allow personal grudges intruding in their ability to work as a team.

"Nate, this is Art Winston, a senior operative with the Agency," Jenny said. "Hi Art," he said, "We'll be working closely and I hope effectively together."

It was obvious Jenny didn't know the other agent, so Nate broke a long silence by introducing himself. "My name is Nate Adams, Nate said offering his hand. "John Gainer," he said, while firmly shaking his hand, "It's good to meet you Nate."

Art carried what seemed to be a ream of papers enclosed in a large brown manila envelope, with him into the living room. "We need to get something straight Art," Jenny said with sharpness to her tone, "I'm the lead agent on this one. Winston bristled but said, "So I've been instructed by my superiors."

The packet of data that Winston was toting indicated that the Agency had at least one or two good sources in Madrid. By the looks of it, Jim Hammel had been linked up with Badawi and al-Mashad all along. "A dangerous trio," Nate thought, as he continued to scan the info.

Hammel had an American background and a working knowledge of how American intelligence operated along with the best training in the world. With his previous access to terrorism intelligence, sources and methods, he would be a formidable foe.

When Nate didn't come into eat diner, Jen sought him out, catching him in the act of reviewing the mountain of information that Art had delivered.

The intelligence packet was like a giant puzzle waiting to be deciphered and assembled into something coherent and Nate didn't want to wait. Somewhere in this pile of collected data was a lead and maybe an answer to stopping this madness.

He didn't have an answer and needed time to digest the data. One thing the Agency was good at was gathering information. They didn't have a clue at viable solutions but information, they could handle. They used the giant storehouses of money at their disposal, while they sat in the safety of their offices at Langley, taking no risk.

"Art doesn't like the idea of a civilian on the team, much less having access to classified information," Jenny commented, breaking Nate's concentration.

"He said that," Nate asked, his face betraying his dismay. "I told you he was an asshole," she said, through clenched teeth. "It wasn't good that a senior agent thought that having a journalist on the job would be dangerous," he thought.

"I am the lead agent on this case. I'll just call Langley and have him replaced," she said. "Don't let your personal feelings get in the way of this operation," Nate replied, "I can handle him," wondering just how he would handle the situation.

Art Winston didn't know what he was getting into with these terrorists, but he would soon learn and if he weren't a team player, it could and probably would cost him his life.

"I'm going to give Karl a call and get him in on this one Jen. What do you think," he asked.

After a brief silence, she smiled and said, "That's a great idea Nate and I'm all for it. We could use the help."

"Well, that could easily piss Art off," he said between chuckles. Jen shot back a "who cares?" look and smiled.

He dialed Karl's cell number, "Karl, you still in Zurich. Would you consider working with us in Madrid," he blurted out, in one breath.

Karl didn't hesitate, "I thought you'd never ask," he chuckled. "I just don't want to be left out of this one. It is the biggest story of the decade and it's unfolding daily."

"I'll fix it with Christine to have you on the operation permanently," he said, relieved in some unexplainable way to have another journalist on the job. "Get here as quick as you can," Nate said.

"I'll be on the next plane out of Zurich headed in that direction, Nate and that will be at two in the morning," he replied. "We'll meet you at the airport. Don't even call Christine. I'll take care of everything Karl," Nate said.

On the way to the airport, he studied the photographs of al-Mashad and Badawi. Both of them appeared as if they were cultured businessmen. Their eyes revealed educated intelligence. With their expensive haircuts and the sunglasses that were also part of their ensemble, they could probably be anybody they chose to be. These two in the company of Jim Hammel could easily blend into any western society. He studied them and made certain that their faces, were ingrained in his memory.

Karl spotted them immediately regardless of their attempts at dressing incognito as he walked through the gate with the multitude of incoming passengers.

They didn't linger in the terminal. Within a short time, Jenny had pulled the Volvo in front of the safe house. The ride home had been silent and as they pulled in front of the house, the hair at the nape of Nate's neck began to tingle.

"Jenny, there's something wrong here," Nate said. They exited the car with caution. An eerie silence hung in the air, where not even the normal sounds of chirping birds or other small animals was present. It was like the kind of dead silence that raised alarm in all other living forest creatures after a hunting kill.

Nate noticed that the front door was ajar and in a heartbeat his handgun was in his hand as he glanced at Jenny, but she had already beat him to the punch.

Karl wasn't far behind as Jen and Nate inched toward the door, one of them on each side. Karl positioned himself behind a tree with his weapon trained on the doorway.

Nate cautiously reached with his foot and kicked the door wide open. The only sound was the kick and sound of the door swinging open. The house was dark and an eerie feeling came over him as he looked down at the entryway and spotted a trail of blood leading out toward the driveway. Jenny swung herself into the house with her Glock trained on anything that might move. The silence was deafening and as Nate followed Jen into the house, a bad feeling came over him.

It became obvious that whatever conflict had taken place at the safe house had long been over with and everybody was gone, or so he thought. As he inched further into the house, he spotted a body lying on the floor just beyond the entryway of the kitchen. Jenny flipped on a light and saw John Gainer lying on the floor with several bullet wounds. It was obvious by the unnatural posture of his body that he was dead.

His intuition told him they were gone, by they, he meant the terrorists that had killed Gainer. The body had literally been riddled with bullets. It was as if he had been killed with extreme prejudice.

"No," he thought. "The word 'terrorist' didn't cover it. This was warfare, not terrorism."

He quickly started to walk through the kitchen to the door that led to the outside patio and pool area. Jen grabbed his arm but he told her, "They're gone, but they'll be back. It's you and I that they really wanted Jen. Their hatred must be inconceivable." He cleared the patio doors and immediately spotted Art Winston lying by the pool. There was so much blood splattered on the concrete around the pool that the place resembled the floor of a slaughterhouse.

As he neared his body, he noticed that Art had been shot several times, but none of the wounds looked fatal. Nate turned the body over and noticed that three of his fingers had been severed. Art had been tortured before he died. If he knew anything, he had spilled his guts.

"How much did Art know," he asked, "because he spilled his guts if he knew anything at all about the operation." Jen was already on the phone to headquarters and had moved away from the body by the pool. She had pulled out a camera and was snapping pictures of the entire scene.

"It looks like they've gotten serious," said Karl, as he turned away from Art's body. "They always have been. We're just catching up and I hope we're not too late," Nate told him.

Nate was aware that Karl had always been able to handle these types of scenarios better than him but this time Nate didn't feel nausea, just a feeling to succeed in their mission.

"Jen, did they give us a new safe house to stay at," Nate asked her.

"We need to leave immediately and leave the car so the terrorists think we're here. A car will be here for us in ten minutes so get all your stuff, Nate. When they arrive, they'll blink the headlights twice and honk the horn once. If the car fails the sequence we're to open fire," she replied.

Nate grabbed his suitcase and laptop and said, "You don't have to tell me twice Jen," as he turned toward the window facing the street

He caught sight of an SUV pulling over on their side of the street and turning its headlights off. In the absence of moonlight, the street scene instantly faded to pitch black. "Just our luck," he thought, "a new moon." His eyes never left the spot where the SUV had pulled up.

"That's odd," he thought, "nobody got out of the car." An interior light would have given them away immediately and if even one of the doors had been cracked, it would have been like a searchlight shining brightly.

"Jen, I think we've got company down the street, on our side of the road about hundred and fifty feet. An SUV pulled over and nobody has gotten out. Stay out of sight of the windows," he told her.

He checked his Glock and chambered a round. Nate listened, hearing Karl do the same. "Quite a party you've got going on here Nate," Karl said, stating the obvious.

"Damn, our friends will be showing up about now and it's too late to warn them," Jenny commented. Let's get out the patio door and come around the house so we can warn them," he suggested. "Good idea Nate," Karl said.

"Don't worry about our friends picking us up. They'll be expecting trouble after losing two agents," Jenny said, with one of the most serious looks on her face that Nate had ever seen.

They seemed to move as a team as they came around the house just in time to catch the headlights of the friendly car blink twice followed by a short honk of the horn. He looked down the street just in time to catch the interior light of the SUV shining brightly as all four doors opened simultaneously.

Automatic gunfire sounded down the street and the three of them returned fire striking the SUV from the cover of the bushes. The return fire must have caught the terrorists by surprise because the hail of lead from their direction halted momentarily. During the brief interruption of gunfire, two agents hurriedly jumped from the car onto the driveway.

Their car, had been riddled by the gunfire and one of the agents was hit. He crawled toward the bushes with his weapon drawn. "This way ... we'll cover you," Nate yelled. The fire intensified, but it couldn't last long. Nate could hear their rounds as they hit the SUV.

Jenny moved to the side of the house, as the four terrorists fanned out from their position by the now bullet-ridden SUV they had driven there.

A thought occurred to Nate. If one or more of them were wearing an explosive device, they needed to take them out -- not just evade them. He knew the terrorist's mission was to kill both Jen and him and they would settle for nothing less.

"They may be trying to get close enough to explode one of those body bombs they love so dearly," Nate said to Karl.

"That thought crossed my mind too," he shot back.

Jenny must have been on the same page because she spotted motion behind a tree about seventy feet away in the direction of the tree. She pumped two rounds in quick succession and he heard the distinct sound that a bullet makes when it strikes flesh followed by a grunt and low moan.

"Nice shooting Jen," Nate told her as a burst of automatic weapons fire opened up. Hot lead laced the house near Jen, creating a slight arc of a pattern above her head. Nate spotted the exact location of the flash from the barrel of the weapon and opened fire, emptying his seventeen-round magazine in the direction of the terrorist. This was one time that he was glad the Glock in his hand held seventeen rounds.

He heard the Jihadist's weapon clatter on the pavement and a dull groan as he recognized the thud of the body striking the asphalt. "There might be some hope if they could disable them before the two remaining terrorists could effectively use a body bomb," he thought.

Nate knew the police in Madrid would certainly be interested in apprehending these four. Memories of the train bomb that had slaughtered and maimed many of its civilians had certainly not faded. The horror of removing and cleaning up body parts after so many had died would have been difficult to erase from the minds of Europe's populace.

Now there was silence from the group of assassins, and in the pitch black of the night, they could see nothing.

Only an occasional moan from the wounded terrorist that Jenny had opened up on, was heard in the deadly silence.

After a bit of minor discussion, they decided to open up on the disabled vehicle, thus lighting up the street. They fired on the vehicle incessantly, finally causing it to explode, transforming the blackness of night into a cacophony of light and sound.

Almost immediately, he spotted one of their assailants creeping on the ground dangerously close. The trio spotted him simultaneously and gunfire erupted immediately. Several rounds struck the prone extremist and he ceased to move without uttering a sound. "That's two of them," Nate told Jenny, almost whispering, "We need to take one of them alive if we can." "I agree," she replied. "We need information desperately."

Without warning, one of them jumped from behind a parked car and sprinted toward their position at a dead run. Jen had just finished shoving in a fresh magazine and as it locked into placed with a distinctive click she fired once, striking the maniacal killer.

He lay motionless in the grass after turning head over heels about halfway to their position. Nate was on him in an instant, kicking his weapon, a Czech Skorpion, out of reach while Jen loosened and removed the bomb from around his waist. "He's still alive," Jenny said, after detecting movement from the unconscious Jihadist.

"You were right, Nate. This guy could have done some damage if he had reached us," Karl said.

When consciousness returned, the wounded extremist looked around hurriedly, grabbing at where the bomb had been. They took no chances as the uninjured agent and Nate dove on him, turned him over, pushed his face in the grass, and had him handcuffed in an instant.

"Mike," the agent said, offering him his hand. "You must be Nate," he said.

"Good to meet you, Mike," replied Nate. "Help me get this one into the van before the police arrive and break up our little party." Nate looked up to see the remaining terrorist running for his life, quickly losing himself in the densely populated neighborhood.

Chapter 7

The group had two wounded men in the van, one agent and one terrorist and they needed to find a doctor, pronto. Jenny was on the phone to headquarters, while Mike was chosen to drive.

"I've got a doctor we can go to Mike," she said, handing him a piece of paper with the address on it. Karl and Nate had placed a tourniquet on the upper right thigh of the captured terrorist and nearly managed to stop the bleeding. He looked up at them with fear in his eyes. "No telling what the guy had been told by his superiors to expect if he were captured," Nate thought.

The injured agent who introduced himself as Fred, appeared to have sustained a flesh wound on his upper arm and was applying pressure. He smiled and said, "It could've been a lot worse."

It was obvious that the nurse who appeared and started preparation to treat Fred's wound had been asleep minutes before. She looked tired and looked sleepy, but she was silent and moved competently.

The doctor was a tall man with dark brown hair combed straight back, his manner and appearance were both businesslike and somber and Nate wondered if he would even speak. Finally, he looked at Nate and said in a monotone voice, "I recognize you, Señor, from television. You are the Nate Adams that everyone is talking about."

Nate simply nodded, his weary eyes confirming the doctor's statement. Nate silently wished that the people who recognized him would find another line.

The doctor started working on the terrorist while Jen spoke to him in Arabic. His eyes grew wide at the American woman that spoke Arabic without a hint of an accent. He wasn't sure what the doctor's relationship was with the Agency, but he was silent and efficient. It was apparent that he had been briefed on the situation before their arrival.

Señor Adams, this man will need to rest and heal. This is a very serious wound," the doctor told him, without any further explanation. "We cannot leave him here, doctor. Do what you can to stabilize him and give us some written instructions and medication for his care and a number we can reach you at," he answered. The doctor nodded and said, "It will take about another three hours to do this correctly."

The new safe house was another palatial looking residence in a very affluent neighborhood. Its gated entrance, was supported by archaic stone columns and connected to walls that surrounded the estate. The house was covered in rolled reddish brown ceramic tiles that are reminiscent of the Mediterranean, and the Southwest region of America.

"I wonder if this safe house's location -- and I use the term lightly -- has been compromised," Karl asked sarcastically. Mike assured them that it was safe and secure, but Nate had his doubts. Everything was for sale for the right price.

Nate was tired and it had been a long night with no sleep. He told Karl with a slight edge to his voice, "Listen, my intuition tells me that this location hasn't been compromised -- at least not yet, or they would have had a crew out here to hit it," Karl shot back a doubtful look, but didn't say anything.

"Let's get busy on the intelligence while Jenny interrogates the prisoner. If he knows anything, she'll get it from him," he assured Karl.

They went into the kitchen and started to leaf through the relentless mound of papers that the Agency had provided. He knew that somewhere in this mountainous pile were clues that would lead them to the location of the other nukes.

Nate's eyes were having trouble focusing and he had trouble keeping them open. The last twenty-four hours of activity with no sleep had taken their toll on his energy level and his body was demanding sleep.

He put the papers down after his eyes started losing focus and sunk deeper into the couch, drifting into a deep sleep.

He was walking down a smothered path, overgrown with what seemed to be ivy and rich green underbrush, as he silently dreamt near an open window in the fresh air of Madrid's early summer, but the dream made no sense and was indiscernible to him. He seemed to drift down the path with little resistance despite the thick undergrowth, but some unknown force appeared to be blocking any progress he tried to make. Although the full moon radiated some light, the landscape was illuminated by some unknown source that gave the impression of never ending daylight.

He awoke abruptly, opening his eyes to Jenny's gentle nudging, "Wake up Nate, you're talking in your sleep. She strode toward the kitchen and was back in an instant with a steaming cup of coffee. He gratefully took it off her hands and sipped the rich steaming brown elixir. He looked down at his watch, it was six o'clock, and he had slept until late afternoon. "God," he thought, "he had slept on that couch eight hours.

After twenty minutes or so, the coffee started to work its caffeine magic and he was feeling vigorous once again.

He could hear Fred, Mike and Karl in the kitchen and by the friendly banter and laughter in progress; they seemed to getting along like football buddies at a tailgate party.

Jenny brought him back to reality, "He interrogated the terrorist while you were asleep Nate. He is barely twenty years old and from a town on the Israeli border in Lebanon. His parents and siblings were killed last year when an Israeli bomb destroyed his home and he is the only survivor. His name is Kamal Asaf and like most of them, once they lose their support network, they spill their guts.

Nate, they are planning to strike Rome as early as next week with one of those nukes. Do you know how much that would enrage the Christian world," she asked.

He thought about it for a moment and didn't say anything, but felt the gravity of the situation. Nate was aware that most of Islam felt that Christianity was a polytheistic religion. After speaking to many Arabs, he knew that they held the Catholic religion responsible and would strike at the heart of the "Great Satan." Just the name "Great Satan," had an overpowering and demonizing effect on all of Islam when describing Christianity.

Radical Muslims prided themselves on having faith in what they believed to be the one true religion that served only one god, Allah. Their hatred of Christianity went back to the time of the Crusades and they mention the crusades to this day when justifying Jihad.

After the loss of the tactical nuclear weapon at the train station, they probably decided to up the ante by enraging the Christian world. "Obliterating Rome would certainly accomplish that end," he thought.

When he called Christine, she wasn't quite willing to endorse an excursion to Italy, chasing a group of maniacs bent on destroying civilization, as they knew it.

"Remember, you're a journalist and it's not your responsibility to stop these guys," she chided. Just whose job is it then, Christine," he asked. After a long sigh, she conceded. Nate knew that if it had been anyone else, she would have told them, "absolutely not".

Christine was an idealist and had been educated at a very liberal university. No, Christine wouldn't care much for living in an Islamic world.

"As a matter of fact," he thought, "no sane woman in the western world would appreciate losing the hard won women's rights they had gained in the last hundred years."

Jenny walked slowly through the rear door onto the patio that led to a pristine swimming pool, as Nate finished his chat with Christine.

"Nate, they're headed for Valencia on the Mediterranean coast in a rented car and they've probably got the bomb with them. It's our best guess that they might have a boat waiting at the port to take them to Italy," Jenny said.

They knew that to head off the terrorists they had to charter a small plane to Valencia. Jim Hammel was on a mission to make a statement to the Western World and with his knowledge of the Agency and its machinery; he would be difficult to stop. He looked at Valencia on a map of Spain. It was a little more than two hundred miles from Madrid.

Hammel knew flying to Italy was impossible. They must have a boat waiting for them. It was the only option that he could see that made any sense if Rome was the target. Using a boat would avoid driving the entire distance around the coast of the Mediterranean to get to Italy and avoid possible checkpoints and roadblocks.

They poured over the map of the area between Valencia and the Italian coast. "Their first stop would probably take them to Palma on the Island of Mallorca,"

Nate loudly speculated and weighed the possibilities of heading them off with the possibility spooking them into detonating the device prematurely. They would definitely take out Valencia rather than lose another tactical nuclear weapon.

Jenny was preoccupied but nodded that she had heard. She realized that if they didn't allow the terrorists to board their boat with the device, they could detonate it right at the pier, obliterating a large portion of Valencia and killing nearly a million people. After the loss of one of their devices in London, they would guard the remaining nukes fiercely. They would almost certainly detonate it rather than risk losing it.

Nate had been to Valencia a couple of times and remembered that its architecture was as diverse as its past. Parts of the city contained buildings dating back to when this capital of the old Kingdom of Valencia was occupied by Romans, Visigoths or Arabs, depending on the period. Valencia was Spain's third largest city with over a million and a half people within the city itself, including its outside suburban areas. Like many of Europe's cities, Valencia was as diverse as they came, with many cultures mixing in a potpourri of humanity.

Apparently, Christine was willing to risk losing one correspondent but not two. She had called Karl, ordering him back to Zurich in the midst of their planning.

However, knowing Karl, he would squirm his way out of it. Having Karl's help would be great but perhaps Jenny and Nate would be a bit more inconspicuous. By the time that the Agency chartered a small plane to take the two of them to Valencia, Karl was on a flight to Zurich.

"With any luck, they would arrive in time to stop Hammel and his cohorts," he thought. Jen was constantly on the phone with Washington as new intelligence was being gathered and processed. When she finally turned to him, she didn't seem surprised at anything new that had happened.

"Washington has informed Spain of all the details. They will be assisting us in apprehending the terrorists and the bomb," she told me. This would be a joint venture of Spanish and American resources. Spain was an important ally and could play an integral part in stopping this attack within its borders.

The stifling heat coupled with the humidity made them appreciate the air-conditioning of the terminal in Valencia. This was one of the hottest summers the city had seen in decades. Not even an occasional cloud gave temporary respite from the sun's intensity. Even Jenny was wearing shorts and a blouse with a bare midriff.

When the pair entered the terminal, two Spanish agents met them and informed Jenny that this was their jurisdiction and that they would have to take a back seat as long as they were on Spanish soil. Jenny merely nodded and said nothing. "It didn't matter what these people said," he thought. They would do what they needed to do and let the governments figure it out later.

They headed right to the docks, where Washington had informed them they would find a forty-five foot yacht named the *Crescent Spear*. No one had seen hide or hair of Hammel and, although intelligence sources in Madrid had assured them that he would be with al-Mashad and Badawi leading this operation, they couldn't confirm that this information was accurate.

Nate figured that Hammel would be aboard the *Crescent Spear* and if they were lucky, they could nail him and al-Mashad in one swoop. He knew that Hammel was far too experienced in intelligence work to let that happen, but one could only hope.

The taller of the two Spaniards offered Nate his hand, "Carlos Hernandez," he said with a smile. "Mr. Adams, our government is inclined to permit the yacht to leave the city, if a nuclear weapon is indeed aboard," he said, speaking very good English with only a trace of an accent.

He studied Carlos as they drove toward the marina. He was only about five-foot eleven and his age was difficult to know but his craggy face told its own story. His face rarely showed emotion and his steely brown eyes indicated both intensity and intelligence. After sizing him up for a moment, Nate decided that this man might be formidable in a tight spot. He always seemed relaxed, but ready for action if it presented itself. Carlos gave the impression of a tautly strung trip line that could trigger a trap at any given moment if crossed.

"We have arrived, Señor," Carlos said, breaking his concentration. My superiors have informed me that no one matching the description your offices have provided has been seen yet."

"Good, we've beaten them here," he replied.

Nate stood on the first of the many docks in the marina and stared into the blue green water of the Gulf of Valencia, watching the shifting waves as they reflected the summer sun when the slight cool breeze whipped the water into gentle a gentle action.

Seagulls glided in a never-ending search for food scraps that were abundant along the inhabited coast. A few people walked along the water's edge, enjoying the cool breeze coming off the water in occasional gusts.

Nate was overwhelmed at the sight of the enormous variety of pleasure craft that the marina was capable of accommodating. A fifty-foot sailboat captured his attention and he scrutinized the beautiful craft as her skipper prepared to take her sailing to faraway exotic places. Her mast rose high into the air, begging for her sail to be unfurled, so that her bow might cut through the pristine waters of the Mediterranean.

He walked closer to the boat and noticed the name on her bow, *"Crescent Spear"* then something written in Arabic that he couldn't read. Nate turned nonchalantly and walked toward Jenny, quietly motioning her to the dock. She started walking in his direction with a questioning look on her face and he met her halfway.

"Jenny, I've found the *Crescent Spear.* Walk with me in the direction of that sailboat. They might be here any minute so let's make it quick," Nate told her in a barley audible whisper.

When they neared the beautiful sailboat, he could see that she was one of a kind. Her bow was long and sharp; the new paint glistened in the sunlight, casting shards of reflected sunrays from its beams. Every inch of this vessel was in pristine condition. Her bow lay silent in the murky water of the bay like a caged lion, waiting to be energized by seagoing hands.

Nate hoped they would not be recognized. "Well," he thought, "Washington had gotten it partly right. It was about forty-five foot, but it was a sailboat and not a yacht."

Nate was partly in disguise, wearing a tourist's fishing hat to hide his lighter colored hair. His sunglasses and dark tan hid his lighter complexion. Nate hoped to look like he belonged on the pier. He was aided by the fact that this area appeared to be an international tourist mixing pot and no one drew attention as long as they kept to themselves and their actions did not bring undue attention.

Jen glanced at the Arabic writing beneath the vessel's name and said nothing. They stopped at the end of the pier, pointed like tourists for a while and quickly got out of sight before making the return trip.

They had a great view from their vantage point behind some cargo crates. They were able to scrutinize the *Crescent Spear* without being seen from the sailboat. "The logo on the boat means, "Allah's Holy War," loosely translated, but to an Arab it means much more," Jen said. Nate decided to test his new camera while they were waiting. The zoom lens brought the *"Crescent Spear"* so close that he thought he might be able to reach out and touch her. He snapped a few pictures just for practice from his new camera and leaned back with Jenny to wait.

More than an hour had passed when a delivery truck pulled up to the pier and two men began to load nearly a truckload of supplies onto the boat. In a half-hour, they were gone. Nate glanced at the marina office just in time to catch sight of Carlos and his partner heading in their direction.

Even though they were on Spanish soil, this kind of terrorism knew no sovereignty. It had a life of its own and once started, the hatred seemed to feed on itself in a self-perpetuating blight of revulsion. Al-Qaeda had no sovereign country of its own and didn't respect any country's right to exist unless it was Islamic and sympathetic to its cause.

To Al-Qaeda, all non-Islamic countries were fair game. Hell! Everybody seemed to be fair game, Islamic or not with these guys. Nate knew that if it came down to a choice of losing the bomb or detonating it, the terrorists would not hesitate to choose the latter.

Carlos was nearly upon them and he smiled and said, "We must wait ... al-Mashad and Badawi must still be driving from Madrid." Nate said nothing, but instead handed him his field binoculars pointing toward the end of the pier. Carlos faced showed concern as he scrutinized the situation aboard the *"Crescent Spear."*

"You two have been busy Nate," Carlos exclaimed, "you're in the wrong trade, mi amigo."

Despite his hardened no-nonsense features, Carlos had an easy manner and worked well with others, it would be easy to call him a friend under different circumstances.

"We have an American destroyer off the coast in international waters to blow that boat out of the water," Jenny stated. "We will not let them reach the Italian coast under any circumstances."

As she finished talking, a dark blue van pulled up to the pier and three men got out. Badawi was in the lead carrying the large aluminum colored suitcase that was the trademark of a tactical nuclear weapon, followed by al-Mashad and Hammel.

Jen called Washington and received orders to stand clear while a naval destroyer stationed just off shore and out of direct sight of the coast coordinated the destruction of the *Crescent Spear* with the Spanish Navy.

The *Crescent Spear* left the pier under the power of her diesel engine. After a hundred yards, she began to unfurl her tall sails and picked up speed as the wind propelled her forward at a greater speed than her engine could.

Carlos looked in their direction, "Let's go," he said, "we have a Coast Guard cutter waiting and you're invited to come along, if you like."

He didn't have to ask Nate twice. They both started moving in their direction, jogging toward the third pier where the cutter was already casting off its lines and getting ready to head out. They jumped aboard just as she was cutting loose her last lines.

Nate could see the *Crescent Spear* about two or three miles into the gulf. She was easily distinguishable among the myriad pleasure craft that filled the gulf. Through his field glasses, he could see movement on the deck. He watched as three people lowered a motorized life raft into the water and sped toward shore.

Al-Mashad, Badawi, and Hammel were escaping and Nate and Jenny were powerless to stop them, only the bomb was priority now.

"What if they have the bomb and are headed back to Valencia," Nate asked Carlos who was now by his side. His eyes squinted with speculation and his hand dove into his pocket for his cell phone.

Although the sun was hot and the humidity drenched them like a sauna, the cutter picked up speed and the cool breeze bathed them in nature's air conditioning. A few cumulus clouds hung motionless above the gleaming water like giant cotton balls in a surrealistic painting.

Jenny stood close to him on the cutter's port side as they both scrutinized the sailboat. He handed her his field binoculars and she surveyed the growing image as the cutter fastidiously shortened the distance between them and the *Crescent Spear*. She handed the binoculars to him and he could see the landscape reflecting from her smooth dark sunglasses accentuating her jet-black hair trailing in the breeze as the cutter picked up speed.

A half hour passed and they were about eleven miles off the coast headed on a setting directly toward the Island of Mallorca. He wondered if the navy would allow the "*Crescent Spear*" to dock in Palma.

Christine who had been anxiously awaiting Nate's call, answered immediately. "Something significant is about to go down here Christine," he said. "I don't think the American Navy will let the *Crescent Spear* dock now that she's safely at sea and away from populated areas."

"Get pictures," she told him. "Damn, these terrorists were on their way to destroy Rome and all she could think of was pictures," he thought, smiling at the fact that

Global was in good hands and would become the major news source for Europe.

She had a professional record of recording newsworthy details as he recounted them and he talked nearly non-stop for ten minutes, while keeping a keen eye on the speck on the horizon, before he could get her to hang up.

Suddenly, the cutter picked up speed, seemingly flying through the water. Within minutes, the speck could be seen with the aid of the binoculars. "They are about fifteen kilometers from us," Carlos estimated, as he stood behind them. "They will be intercepted within the hour."

The destroyer appeared out of nowhere and it bore down upon the sailboat at tremendous speed, quickly closing the distance. Its bow sliced through the water with the sharpness of a hot knife shearing off a slice of butter. Two smaller Spanish naval vessels approached from the opposite direction, closing off any chance of escape.

The sailboat stopped dead in the water as if waiting to fulfill its destiny by luring the approaching craft closer to their trap.

With the military vessels approaching to within a mile, Nate and Jenny were still about five nautical miles away. Nate knew what would probably happen and hurried to Carlos to warn the American and Spanish vessel of an imminent detonation of the nuclear device.

It was already too late for any warning. Suddenly, a bright flash replaced the *"Crescent Spear"* and as time caught its breath, it came to a stop for Nate and Jenny. Nate took a deep breath and could not seem to release the air from his lungs.

The flash, momentarily brighter than a supernova, startled him. He quickly shut his eyes and simultaneously threw his hand over Jenny's sunglasses as the bomb detonated.

An eternity seemed to elapse, but in reality, it was only moments before they opened their eyes. Both of them realized that if they looked directly at the blast, they could be permanently blinded. He exhaled and took a deep breath after realizing he hadn't even dared to breathe since the detonation.

"Those bastards actually did it," Nate exclaimed. Moments later, a mushroom cloud slowly rose above the water and the shock wave moved quickly toward the two vessels within its range. The two Spanish military vessels were caught by the blast's shock wave. They rolled onto their sides, but slowly recovered, however, Nate knew that anyone aboard would probably be dead, if not from the blast, then certainly from the radiation. They were just too close and probably had received a lethal dose of radiation

Their cutter sat dead in the water while Jenny and Nate ran to an open hatch to escape the shock wave that would certainly hit the small cutter within a few moments. He knew that they were not in bomb's destructive zone. The relatively small nuclear blast was only capable of complete destruction for about a mile diameter of the blast, but he wasn't sure about the effects of radiation. He silently prayed that they were at a safe distance.

Nate breathed a sigh of relief that they were not any closer. He slammed the hatch door shut behind them while they waited for the shock wave to hit the cutter. "Let's stay below for a couple of minutes and wait," he whispered, as if someone was listening.

They waited for a shock wave that never really fully materialized and after what seemed an eternity; they felt the cutter roll a bit. He breathed a heavy sigh of relief and relaxed against the bulkhead. When they climbed topside, the captain was shouting orders to everyone in Spanish, while gesticulating wildly.

Sailors jumped to perform his will as the vessel retreated from the scene with hopes of putting a safe distance between the crew and any possible damaging radiation. Nate silently prayed that they would move quickly and would be spared a lethal dose of radiation.

He closed his eyes and remembered the documentaries of Hiroshima and Nagasaki, while thinking of the men and women on the American destroyer and Spanish vessels. He realized that casualties among those crews of the ships nearest to explosion would almost certainly be one hundred percent.

His hopes, were not dashed as captain and crew moved as fast as humanly possible and gave the cutter full throttle. The vessel felt as if it were turbo-charged, as it raced through the frothy turquoise green water casting a salty spray on the craft's superstructure and crew. He felt a feeling of calm come over him, as he watched the scene of the explosion move further and further away.

Nate pulled a camera from the pocket of his cargo shorts and began snapping pictures of everything in sight. The compact camera was a good one with a zoom lens and memory chip that could store over three hundred pictures. The trick was to take as many pictures as possible and let the office decide what to use.

He missed nothing including the crew aboard the cutter, who were not exhibiting their usual boisterous nature. The zoom lens brought the American warship into a reasonable range and he snapped an enormous number of pictures.

He looked back in the direction of the mushroom cloud as the cutter's bow gave the oncoming sea no respite while heading in the direction of the Spanish mainland. Nate had spotted the American destroyer that appeared to be of the *Arleigh Burke* class. It was dead in the water with severe damage.

Nate peered through the field glasses and could that see that the communication and radar equipment, were completely destroyed. The ship's paint had been blackened and peeled, obliterating its designation number; and he couldn't detect any movement on the deck.

The sight was haunting with bent metal and the scorched paint. The sight reminded him of a ghost ship in a haunted movie. Everything had changed in an instant of time. "That was the thing about destruction, or the taking of a human life," he thought. Once completed, it could not be taken back.

It seemed as if he was desecrating the memories of the crew by immortalizing their destruction with photographs, but he couldn't seem to stop taking pictures. The world needed to see this kind of destruction to understand the threat of global Jihad.

Jen had been able to raise a signal on her cell phone again and had dialed Washington. She, was crouched down behind a protected part of the bulkhead with one hand covering her other ear while shouting into her cell phone.

Reaching for the phone in his cargo shorts that had started ringing and vibrating, he whispered, "Christine."

"What's going on down there Nate," Christine's voice resonated in his ear.

"I was just about to call you, Christine. All hell has broken loose here," he said, trying to remain calm. "I have photos, probably fifty of the only ones I know to be in existence of this event," Nate blurted all in one breath.

"Photos of what," she asked, as if he were from another planet." "The terrorists just detonated a tactical nuclear weapon as the Spanish and U.S. Navy were closing in on their position in the Gulf of Valencia," he said, forcing out the sentence.

"You have photos of the mushroom cloud," she asked, incredulously.

"Yup," he told her. "I have photos of everything from about six miles out, using the telephoto lens and I'll e-mail everything as soon as the Spanish Coast Guard cutter that Jenny and I are on docks and I can get online. Look Christine, I don't know what their agenda is right now. There were two other ships approaching close to the sailboat when they detonated the bomb. I don't think anybody is left alive on either of those vessels and if they are, the radiation will soon kill them. They were just too close to the blast."

There was a deadening silence from her end of the line, as she struggled to process what he had just told her.

"How far were you from the blast when it first detonated," she finally asked.

"About five miles, I think. We should be all right. I don't know much about the dissipation of radiation as distance increases, but we barely felt the blast and we're moving toward Valencia as fast as this cutter will travel," he said.

The cutter had been recalled to the Port of Valencia. They both had responsibilities to their respective employers. Jenny was ominously quiet as she stared out over the stern railing at the blast site now becoming too distant to observe clearly. "This is only the beginning," he heard her mutter to no one in particular.

He started furiously jotting down notes and had no trouble finding details to add. The entire incident seemed to have happened so quickly that his mind acted like a movie camera, shooting an action adventure film in slow motion. The blast was as vivid as a surrealistic scene by an impressionist painter and would forever be etched in the synapses of his brain cells for exact recall.

He had little trouble describing the incident in the excruciatingly accurate panorama of detail from memory. He had just witnessed the death of the crews of three ships for nothing more than the fanatic ideas of a religious extremism at its worst.

They would be in port in about twenty minutes at this rate of speed. The cutter was built for speed and the shoreline looming in the distance was a welcome sight. Jenny put down her cell phone and looked at him blankly.

When she finally spoke, she said, "I've been ordered back to Zurich with you. The terrorists have hit the other safe house with another team and killed our two remaining agents in Madrid."

"My suspicions were true," thought Nate. "There was a leak in the Agency and it must be a mole planted deep within the office structure." The only person he would be trusting in the Agency from now on was Jenny."

Chapter 8

Christine sat comfortably waiting at the airport in Zurich when they arrived. Global News had been the first publication to print photographs of the nuclear explosion in the Gulf of Valencia and Christine was beaming from ear to ear. As they walked into the terminal from the arrival ramp, they were greeted by hundreds of camera flashes. Nate was tired, not in good humor and thought it was in bad taste to be happy at this time for any reason.

"Lighten up," he thought. "She's only trying to be lighthearted."

They were both dog-tired and Christine drove them straight to Nate's apartment at the Swissotel.

"You're on the world stage now Nate," Christine commented as she closed the door to the Suite.

"I hope you don't mind, but I had Karl help write the story that accompanied those great photos."

He nodded that it was all right and she gave him a hug and closed the door behind her as she left. He was secretly happy that Karl had written the piece for him. With all the detail he provided on the phone, they probably had the best exclusive in the world.

Christine was the kind of woman who took control easily. It wasn't only her good looks or her Ivy League education. She had the ability to make people feel comfortable with who they were simply, because she displayed that quality herself. She had taken control of the corporation when her father decided not to return from his forced vacation to America, and Zurich was never the wiser. She took her place at the top of the publishing world as if she were destined to lead.

Jenny had already claimed the spare bed and was nearly asleep so he decided not to bother her. He pulled a dark lager from the refrigerator and sat down to unwind. The new that Hammel would be coming after him along with his two dangerous cohorts. Nate felt no fear and even welcomed Jim Hammel's avarice. He welcomed the opportunity to take him down and didn't much care what condition the man was in when it was finished.

Nate thought about Abbey and the fact that she had come all the way from the states. Was it him, or was she just seeking adventure? She hadn't been any trouble but they didn't have any history and not much of a relationship. He knew he would have to break it off. "How the hell do I get myself into these situations," he thought cynically.

The morning sun broke through the scattered clouds of the Swiss sky spraying the bed with sunlight, the glass acting like a prism, distributing its colors across the suites interior. He awoke to the smell of eggs, waffles, and bacon wafting toward his waiting nose like an airliner coming to a stop before the end of a runway.

He rolled over to the sight of Jenny in her usual panties and T-shirt attire. "Wake up sleepyhead, they just brought breakfast, compliments of the hotel," she said. On the dining room table, carefully placed was this morning's copy of *Global News Weekly*.

On the front page was picture of the nuclear explosion in the Gulf of Valencia. An American destroyer and a smaller Spanish Coast Guard cutter were visible, lying dead in the water. The editing department had done a great job of enlarging and editing the digital copy and bringing out an enormous amount of detail. Hell, he could even make out the melted and bent superstructure, communication antennas, and radar of the American destroyer.

Jenny was in a cheery mood and she scampered around the apartment, as Nate had come to refer to the suite, her dimpled smile and tanned looking cheeks shining in the morning Swiss sun flooding through the window. She had put on shorts with florid Hawaiian designs on them and looked every bit a tourist.

Nate thought about the remaining bombs and silently prayed that they were still in one place. They still had no intelligence on the exact number of bombs the terrorists possessed.

If Jenny received instructions from Washington then, off they would go again. Nate looked at her as she continued to inhale her breakfast like a homeless bag lady at a shelter. It was good to see her happy.

He wondered about his changing role in this caper. He had recently been acting more like an agent than a journalist. He finally decided that it all came with the job. Job descriptions were not easily defined and nobody seemed eager to define Nate's role in this particular venture. He decided that he enjoyed his new role and the excitement and adventure it brought.

Unless necessary, He would stay away from the office today. He was in his comfort zone here at the hotel. Security was heavy around them and they were probably safer here than in the office. Nate had been informed that a Swiss National Security detail was in place at various points throughout the complex working in plain clothes, with strict orders to avoid civilian casualties at all costs.

He flipped on the TV and was able to get both CNN and Fox News Channel. It was apparent that all of Europe as well as America were completely outraged and vulnerable. Every news agency was printing, broadcasting or posting, one or more photos from his new digital camera and conspiracy theories were going already going viral on talk radio, tabloids and the Internet.

Christine had been the consummate businesswoman and publisher, by allowing in one masterstroke, the world's media access to the photos.

Europe finally realized that open and violent war had been declared on any country that was not Islamic. Hell, even Islamic sects as well as rival terrorist factions were fighting among themselves and did not feel immune. It reminded Nate of the Spanish Inquisition or a new style Salem witch-hunt. Everyone that didn't believe exactly as these extremists seemed to be fair game in their twisted worldview as it was all sanctioned by Allah.

Despite the incessant drumbeat of the "politically correct" progressive left, one couldn't be "just nice" to these extremists and become impervious to attack. The extremists were playing a high stakes game and they were playing for keeps, regardless of their toll on human life. In the growing social tensions following terrorist attacks in the USA, many Americans grew suspicious of a "fifth column" in their midst.

It had become obvious that a deeply imbedded mole in the Agency was wreaking havoc. He expected that the terrorists already had knowledge of Jenny's movements and they might again attempt to eliminate them.

"I believe we've got them on the defensive Jenny," he commented while chewing on a piece of toast.

"They know we're on to them but it doesn't seem to be slowing them down," she replied. She had a point. The terrorists had an immutable, "til death do us part" pact with the West and would exact their toll in blood, until they were eliminated.

As the last drops of orange juice rolled down his throat filling his stomach completely, there was a knock at the door followed by Abbey's familiar voice breaking the silence. Jenny rolled her eyes and he gave her a disapproving look as she returned to her breakfast.

Abbey flew into his arms, kissing him wildly until she looked over his shoulder and spotted Jenny. "Hi Jenny," she quipped, "I didn't know you guys were sharing a room."

"We're not. We got in late and it was more convenient to stay here than rent a room," Jen shot back, with a slight edge to her voice.

The sunlight pouring into the room caught Abbey's dark hair enhancing the sparkle in her beautiful blue eyes. She unabashedly sat on the edge of the bed as if she belonged there. "If she had been a cat, she'd be purring," he thought.

She had chosen a sun dress with a sharp mauve color that engaged her hair and creamy white skin making her look more like a Greek goddess than a real estate agent from Delaware. She rolled her head back shaking the mane of her hair, while giving Nate the sultry look of greater things to come.

Jenny finished up, winked at him, and boldly changed her clothes close to the spare bed she had slept in. Abbey seemed not to notice and gave him a glance that spoke volumes. The chemistry she radiated was irresistible and drew him to her as the petals of a rose attract sunlight.

He heard the door closing behind Jen and Abbey was in his arms, her clothes lay on the carpet were she had hastily cast them. Her breath was sweet elixir as she kissed his face and neck. He silently hoped Jenny wouldn't return soon. The day drifted by quickly while the two forgot everything except their breathless embraces and unquenchable passion.

"This was no way to break the relationship," he thought.

The morning came early and Nate was awakened by the ringing of the phone on the bed stand, "Hello, oh… Hi Karl, sorry you missed the fireworks in the Mediterranean," he told him.

That didn't seem to bother Karl one bit. There was something far more important on his mind.

"Omar called from Montana. Apparently he's been in contact with some of his people in Saudi Arabia and he has it on good authority that the hit on the Vatican is still on," Karl said sounding serious. "This time I'm going to be there."

"All right Karl, I'll speak to Christine. I could use your help. Why don't we all meet for dinner at seven and nail down the details," Nate said. "Let's eat here at the

Swissotel where the security is tight and we're in a more controlled environment."

Nate had never had a relationship as low maintenance as the one with Abbey. She demanded nothing other than his presence when she could get it and he had given her no depth to his character in the time they spent together. He wondered how long it would last and exactly what she wanted out of the relationship.

He tried to drift off to sleep but Abbey's soft breasts were gently pressing against his back with her breath steady and soft on his neck. He rolled over in bed and looked at her face as she slept. She looked angelic, with the reassurance of safety and complete confidence. He gently pushed her luxuriant auburn hair from her face as she let out a soft sigh.

His hand reached over the side of the bed to reach into his pants pocket for the cell phone that he now depended upon so dearly. He found it and dialed Omar's cell number.

"Hello Nate," Omar's voice reached his ear from halfway around the world. "You've been all over the news. CNN even interviewed the editor you used to work for in Delaware."

"Omar just how reliable is this information on the Vatican hit," Nate asked, while trying to brush the sleep out of his eyes.

"Nate, according to my friend in Riyadh, Al-Qaeda is not only hell-bent on assassinating you and Jenny, but they want to take down the most important symbol of

Christianity in the world. Watch yourself very carefully, my friend. There are rumors that a spy acting on behalf the Saudi Royal Family has infiltrated Al-Qaeda's tactical commander Jafar Khadduri's camp. That means this information is very reliable."

He had rarely heard Omar sound as serious and it caught his attention. He remembered that he hadn't even thought to ask about him and his family's well-being.

When he finally asked, Omar sounded and acted comfortable as he was settling in to Montana ranch life with ease. If the terrorists didn't locate them, they could take it easy on the ranch for a very long time. His family loved the American Northwest and the uncomplicated way of life, relative to their previous situation.

"If they locate me, they will strike without warning and kill everyone here," he said without any emotion.

"You watch your back, my friend," Nate told him before breaking the connection.

While Abbey still slept soundly, Jenny quietly knocked and entered, looking a bit windswept. We walked to the small kitchen area where strands of filtered light from the late afternoon sun cast an orange glow upon the glass dining table that was heaped by a pile of intelligence reports in disarray. He sat while Jenny busied herself making coffee, humming a tune known only to her.

The coffee was rich and aromatic with a hint of hazelnut. The stimulating elixir felt good going down and brought him slowly into focus as he recited to her what

Omar had told him. Jen informed him that *Global News Weekly* was also a prime target and in extreme danger of being attacked. She had just spoken to her superiors in Washington and was being suspiciously silent and uncharacteristically stingy with disclosing information.

Abbey's head peeked from beneath the blanket. "The smell of this coffee would raise the dead," Nate thought. She headed for the bathroom wrapped in a sheet and within seconds, the telltale hiss from the shower could be heard in the kitchen.

"You should send her back to Delaware Nate," Jenny told him with genuine concern. "If they can't get to you, they always go for the people you love most."

He hadn't thought of Abbey being a target, but Jenny was right, these people were animals and revenge was their motive for existence. There was long bloody history in the Middle Eastern countries of eliminating the entire family of opponents and enemies.

Abbey grabbed her purse, gave him a kiss, and walked out the door with a smile and a promise to return later that night. Her radiance was overwhelming and although he didn't feel like now was the time to fall in love; he didn't want to send her home either. He was getting used to her being around. It was like a snowflake, you didn't know when it was going to melt and disappear, but eventually it would be gone. She had revealed very little of her past.

"I don't want to review the past," she had so sweetly told him, while lying comfortably in his arms. Nate had a bad habit of falling for women with a past. "What the hell," he thought, "everybody has a past."

Nate's sixth sense started to sound off like a firehouse siren during a three-alarm fire. "My god, Abbey," he thought. He knew she'd be driving her rental car and it wasn't often when his sixth sense kicked in like this, but when it did, it was never wrong.

"Let's put her in a cab," he said to Jenny as he raced toward the door. They sprinted to the elevator and into the lobby. He hit the front glass doors of the hotel entrance like a hammer striking an anvil and looked across to the parking lot just in time to catch sight of Abbey getting into the rental car.

Nate raced towards her like a relay runner picking up speed to pass the baton to the next runner, quickly closing the hundred yards distance between the lobby door and her car.

"Abbey," he yelled his voice barely audible between the gasps of air that his oxygen starved lungs demanded.

Nate had closed the distance to about twenty-five meters when an explosion engulfed Abbey's car. The shock wave hit him, propelling him violently backward then casting him brutally onto the asphalt. He struck the asphalt viciously, turning end over end, finally coming to a stop.

Time moved as if he was watching a movie in slow motion. Nothing seemed real, he gasped to regain the breath that had been forced from his lungs by the shock wave as he lay on the asphalt. He had the same shocking feeling when he saw the nuclear bomb detonate. It was a prison of complete helplessness and he wasn't comfortable with something he couldn't control.

He felt something stinging his cheek and felt the warmth of his own blood as he removed a shard of glass. He tried to focus his eyes and squinted to look where Abbey's car had been and viewed only twisted metal and still burning tires.

The top of the car had been ripped upwards and away from its body. It hung to the car by a thin strand of steel as the interior upholstery burned. He tried to stand but his legs felt like rubber, buckling at the knees. He fought to remain on his feet as he moved closer to the burning hulk. His vision blurred and he felt his knees giving way to gravity as he once again fell to the asphalt.

People came running from every direction but he couldn't move to get up. It was as if every bit of strength had been drained from his body and he felt like an empty battery that needed to be recharged before anything would work. He could hear German, French and even some Italian being spoken, while sirens loomed, still sounding distant, but approaching. He thought about Abbey but was powerless to help her now and he certainly did not like or wanted to become accustomed to the feeling

Jenny leaned over him, wiping the blood from his forehead before it made its way into his eyes. "Stay awake, Nate," she said, her voice quivering. Tiredness swept over him and it became laborious to remain conscious.

When he opened his eyes, a bright light glared in his eyes like a giant Cyclops, blinding him, causing him to turn away. The antiseptic smell gave his location away and the darkness outside the window on his left gave indication that some time had passed. "Jenny, are you there," he asked.

"Nate, Nate, you're awake! They told me that you're fine, just a little shaken up with a few cuts," Jenny exclaimed. "How's Abbey," he queried, interrupting her and already knowing the answer.

"Maybe a miracle had spared her life," he thought; but he knew that it couldn't possibly be true. Jenny's eyes told the sad truth but she never said a word. Abbey had been a breath of fresh air in his life, and he knew that was over and he never knew anything about her or her life.

He would never again put anyone that he cared for in danger unnecessarily. Tomorrow, they would make arrangements to ship what was left of Abbey's body to her only living relative, her brother in Philadelphia.

He vowed to find Jim Hammel and make him pay, if it was the last thing he ever did. Although he couldn't excuse the actions of the terrorists, he understood their motives. They thought they were fighting a Holy War, but Jim Hammel was American, even though his father was an Arab. Nate considered him a traitor and would pursue and hunt him to the ends of the earth. Complete exhaustion came over him and he drifted into the deep sleep that his body needed to heal.

Chapter 9

Karl, Jenny, and Nate arrived in Rome in their rented sedan on June 30. It was the last Saturday in June and the atmosphere with the local officials was almost festive. They arrived with broad smiles on their faces to greet them. Neither Nate nor Jenny was accustomed to such fanfare and it made Nate a little uncomfortable.

Police Commissioner Armand Gucci quickly briefed them on the situation as the Italian authorities viewed it. By his tone, Nate quickly concluded that they would be largely on our own on this one. The Italian authorities would back them up, however, they had no intelligence reports of their own on this situation that amounted to anything, but he thought their good will, knowledge and logistical support of the area would be invaluable.

With the terrorist's deadly attack in Zurich, on an innocent civilian, the trio was intent on taking these lowlives out with extreme prejudice. They would give no quarter and would expect to receive none.

Television stations played and replayed photos of the nuclear explosion in the Gulf of Valencia, commenting endlessly until people quit watching, sickened by the thought of a possible nuclear explosion on Italian soil. News had leaked that Rome was the original target of the terrorists and the city's population was gripped with fear.

City officials were both generous and lavish with supplying their accommodations. They provided a suite at the Hotel Albergo del Sole al Pantheon in the Piazza ella Rotunda.

"It doesn't get any better than this," he thought, "City officials must be very concerned about what happened in the Bay of Valencia and were sparing no expense to assure themselves that the same thing didn't occur here in Rome."

The hotel had five hundred years of history and was considered one the most exclusive four-star hotels in Rome. At the height of the tourist season, this hotel could command almost any price.

The concierge known to them only as Carlo offered a three-bedroom suite that was luxuriously furnished. Carlo, a distinctly aristocratic classic Italian looking man close to six-foot with a wiry frame and wire-rimmed glasses gave Nate a glance that would stop a charged bull when he offered him a credit card for payment. "Please Mr. Adams, your accommodations have been more than paid for," he said in perfect unaccented English.

"We insist Carlo. We will pay for the room," Nate told him, handing him a sheaf of currency. Carlo had an unpleasant look on his face but took the money, "Very will sir, if you insist." he replied curtly.

The three of them settled in and Jenny broke out another one of those large brown document envelopes that the Agency was so fond of using when they handed her intelligence data. She began scanning the reports and stated, "Hopefully, we have more information on Al-Qaeda in Italy than they gave us for Madrid".

He knew from reading the previous reports that Hammel was a master of disguise and had access to resources that gave him a distinct advantage. He was also methodical, creative, and independent; which was probably the reason the Agency had hired and trained him.

Nate was tired and didn't think well when physical exhaustion was upon him. After laying his suitcase and laptop on the bed, removing his Glock with its two spare magazines and checking it for smoothness of operation and cleanliness, he lay down on the bed.

"That's odd," he thought, "in the past his first duty was to check his laptop." He stopped and thought about his change of priorities and dismissed the change as necessity. There was a time when the story would have been his first priority, but everything had changed.

He wasn't sure if the change was instantaneous when they decided to kill Abbey or if it had happened gradually since May when he had returned to *Global News Weekly* but it was definitely there.

Karl looked exhausted and he could see that Abbey's death had hit close to home. "Julie is devastated," he said, "I don't know if she will stay in Zurich."

Karl noticed that Nate's face had taken on a serious and dangerous look that he had never before noticed on his mostly cheerful good-natured friend. Karl said nothing. He knew his friend would talk about her death when he was ready.

"Karl, the rules are not the same for these terrorist low-lives. They have a tradition of brutally eliminating their opponents, their families, relatives and friends. That vengeful tradition goes back to the Babylonian, Persian and Assyrian Empires and it hasn't seemed to have changed," Nate said.

Karl's recognized the physical and emotional exhaustion that Nate was experiencing. He would need him in mint condition for what was to come. The last couple of days had been hard on everybody. The local television station in Zurich had related Abbey's death to terrorism and security had been stepped up throughout Switzerland.

"Get some sleep, Jenny and I will take the next watch," Nate said, trying to mask the stress in his own voice. He could see as Karl eyed the comfort of his bed that he wouldn't get any fight from him on the idea of sleep tonight.

Jenny entered Nate's bedroom, with a bounce in her step, beaming ear to ear just when he was thinking of taking a shower.

"They've got a read on Hammel's location. The bloody idiot actually used his cell phone. He's in Milan just to the north of here, headed this way," she blurted excitedly.

He could only hope they had the nuclear device with them. Maybe they were getting tired or perhaps this was a deception. Everything he had read in the reports of Hammel's behavior indicated that he would never make a mistake of this magnitude. He was probably already in the area and another one of their operatives had made the call on his cell phone from Milan.

"Jenny, I think he's already here and stalking us. Our arrival was not exactly low key and he could be planning to take us out. Hell, he might even explode the nuclear bomb next to the hotel," he said. Her eyes grew concerned and her smooth forehead was now wrinkled in thought. Karl would think that nailing Nate and Jenny along with Rome was just an added bonus.

"I think we should get away from here as quickly as possible.

"I think you're right," she said nervously.

When Karl woke, they told him of their suspicions. He wasted no time getting his stuff together. Nate's intuition was raising hairs on the back of his neck by the time they made it to the car.

Nate was on the phone with Armand Gucci, before Jenny turned the key in the car's ignition. "If I were you, Commissioner; I would start searching right now. I have a feeling that the detonation will be somewhere around the Pantheon. Listen, this guy wants to cause the most damage to the Christian world possible with this blast." Nate told him.

On the way out, they had told Carlo that they were taking a short trip down the coast before starting work tomorrow. The sedan sped quickly away from the city, with Jenny at the wheel, putting as much distance between the Hotel by the Pantheon and them as rapidly as they could.

The pleasant Italian countryside flew past the windows of their speeding car. Olive groves in neat rows adorned the scenery and the sweet smell of the Mediterranean entered the car as they continued to drive south toward Naples.

Jen pulled over into a small restaurant and gas station in the small town of Mondragone on the Golfo di Gaeta, just north of Naples. Nate went inside to get some snacks and pay for gas and Jenny was already on the phone to headquarters. Before going into the market, Nate heard her relay his suspicions to her boss who immediately put her on speakerphone. Karl was on the phone with Christine when he returned with snacks. Nate hoped that the police commissioner had taken what he told him to heart.

He glanced out into the Golfo di Gaeta with longing, where several small fishing vessels and sailboats lazily made their way in different directions in the calm green water of the gulf, while he munched on a banana from the store.

Total fatigue had finally hit him, but adrenalin had taken over delaying total exhaustion. When he looked in Jenny's direction, she was walking toward him at the choice spot that he had chosen to observe the beautiful bay.

A cool breeze flowed through his hair evaporating the beads of perspiration on his forehead, bringing refreshment to an otherwise hot muggy day. "It was a good day for dawdling," he thought. He knew they were now out of danger if Hammel detonated the nuclear device and he prayed that the Italian authorities would locate it before it was too late.

He looked north toward Rome, now far in the distance and saw what he thought was a mushroom cloud rising into the air and ran to the car to get his field glasses, snapping a few quick photos on the way.

"Jenny, look toward Rome with the binoculars and tell me what you can make out," he asked her. She grabbed them from his hand and wasted no time scrutinizing the north. "My god Nate, they've done it… they've finally done it," she managed to choke out.

Nate was on the phone to Christine, while Jenny was talking rapidly to Washington. Nate felt guilty at the relief he felt at being a safe distance from Rome, but they could not have done anything to prevent it. There had been no time and the weapon was virtually impossible to find without the help of the local authorities, but still he felt guilty.

When they left the market by the sea, Jenny was still peering through the binoculars and Karl was on the phone talking as fast as he could to Christine who was surely was recording every juicy detail.

Disbelief struck Nate like a brick wall falling on him from a collapsing building. "Did that really just happen," he asked Jenny. Her stony face confirmed what they had all just witnessed. "Why," she asked. "Still in shocked at the reality that Rome had been attacked with a tactical nuclear weapon by Islamic Jihadists."

Karl sat stolidly, just thinking. Nate had never seen this expression on his face as long as he had known Karl. His eyes were fixed on the spot of the explosion and he said nothing.

Nate knew the answer to the question, "Why?" He had seen too much of the same thing in Africa and the Middle East. Here, a good distance south of Rome, in Mondragone by the calm waters of the sea, no one knew that what had just happened would change their lives immeasurably in the next few days and the change would last for the rest of their lives. What had just happened here was far worse than what had happened on September 11, 2001 in America.

It was far too complicated to attempt to fix the world's hate and anger, impossible to understand, and important only to know that it existed.

Nate took over driving to find them a room for the night. He reached into his right front pocket and felt the reassuring bulge of five thousand Euros, left from the money that Christine had given him, while Jenny was on the phone to Washington. He was glad to have cash on him. There would be no credit card trail and cash in hand made everybody happy.

Driving south toward Naples, he spotted saw a small nondescript motel with perhaps thirty rooms in the entire complex, he pulled in the freshly asphalted parking lot in front of the office and switched off the car's ignition. He knew that the news of Rome's demise would have spread throughout the world and he was cautious as he peered in the window.

Nate entered the small clean office containing an ancient man, with meticulously groomed white hair, wearing old-fashioned spectacles, sitting behind the front desk by a window adorned with beaded curtains, that swayed as the breeze from the open door caught them, causing them to make a clacking sound, while dancing to the wind.

He sat motionless, with only his eyes moving, sizing Nate up with a look of ancient wisdom in his wrinkled eyes. The man possessed a timeless quality that made it difficult for Nate to guess his age.

Karl walked in behind him and spoke something in Italian that Nate didn't understand. The ancient one said nothing for a time and when he finally spoke, he said, "I speak English just fine and your Italian is atrocious. How can I help you?"

After renting a room for the night for the three of them and paying him in Euros, he handed Nate a set of keys. He surveyed the parking lot through the window and quickly ascertained that the motel had only two other guests. That suited him just fine, as they didn't need a crowd of people hanging around.

The room was as ancient looking as the clerk who had rented it to them. It must have been built in the early 1900's and the building sported Mediterranean style red ceramic roof tiles. The windows were bordered with trim that gave the impression of being hand-carved. The bathroom was large, with an antique bathtub that stood on four feet, shaped like tiger's paws. The fixtures on the sink and bathtub had been around since the turn of the twentieth century. The three beds resembled cots more than beds and there was a back door leading to a grove of olive trees and locked doors giving entry to the rooms on either side of theirs.

The walls were made of plaster that had been patched many times, but the cot-like beds were clean and the sheets had the fresh smell of drying on a clothesline.

His senses were telling him that the clerk who appeared to be in his eighties and spoke perfect English with a slight Brooklyn accent was probably not trustworthy and had an agenda of his own. He decided to stay awake for a while, hoping to prove his suspicions wrong and took a chair by the window, keeping the curtains closed.

"You'd better get some sleep Nate," Jenny whispered, while nodding in the direction of Karl, who was already sleeping.

Nate suspected that a tracking device had been placed on their vehicle and he couldn't shake the nagging feeling that they were being stalked. He knew that their arrival in Rome was no secret, the city's media and police department had made sure of that. He walked out to their rental car and checked the entire outside of the car for a GPS tracking device. "The damn thing must be inside the car," he thought.

He sat in the passenger side and opened the glove compartment and found that, taped on the right wall of the compartment, was what appeared to be a the tracking device. It was crudely held by duct tape and he easily ripped it free.

Across the street from the motel was a small gas station and store selling a few tourist items that always seemed to be in demand. Nate ran across the road to a gas station and taped it to the side of a soda machine outside the building, facing the road to the north and wiped off his fingerprints with hand sanitizer and tissues left over from his stay at the Swissotel.

"Jenny, Karl ... Wake up! We're going to have company, I found a tracking device in our rental," Nate whispered gently shaking her. "I've taped it to a soda machine across the road at the gas station. Now that we've got the hook baited, let's wait and see who bites," he chuckled.

"That's a stroke of genius," Jen laughed. "We'll make an agent out of you yet. I'll move the car out of sight and we'll see who shows up."

"It's more likely we'll make a journalist out of you," he replied with a slight grin.

They turned out the lights while midnight came and went, they stayed out of site and waited. They checked to verify that the back door actually opened and broke out some snacks. One of them constantly peered out the corner of the window with an eye on the gas station.

It was a twenty-four hour station, with a sleepy-eyed young man as its night clerk. He appeared to be studying and his glasses slid down to the end of his nose with his head buried in the book. He looked no more than eighteen. "Probably a student," Nate thought.

None of them could sleep and someone was on watch at the window at all times. Jenny had called headquarters to see if they could get back up in this area.

Jenny busied herself on her cell phone, explaining the situation while Karl kept a close eye on the gas station across the highway.

"Absolutely," her boss in Washington in charge of this operation, Stuart Owings told her. "My assistant is arranging it as we speak. What is your exact location?"

Jenny gave it to him and she was assured of backup arriving in a half-hour. "Tell them to park around back, we have the gas station across the street where we placed the tracking device staked out," she told them before severing the connection.

It was a black muggy night, with rain just over the horizon and the moon behind thick clouds, with only the dim yellowish light of motel casting its long shadows across the gravel of the parking lot. The occasional passing of a vehicle coming from or going to Naples was the only interruption breaking the eerie silence of early morning.

Nate knew now why police often laid in a supply of coffee and donuts, while staking out possible suspects. It was tiring and tedious work at best.

It was after one o'clock when their backup arrived, the van pulled around back and four men silently got out and opened the back door to their room, after a faint knock on the wooden door. They were dressed in dark camouflage with military style combat boots, their faces painted in grease paint for a combat style firefight. Except for the leader, they remained silent, keeping only to themselves and acknowledging only Jenny as one of their own. The four men took positions in the two adjoining rooms, after breaking out sophisticated automatic weapons that Nate couldn't quite identify.

Nate studied the men's actions and mentally noted that these four were real spec-ops professionals, not just run-of-the-mill agents. They would simply do their jobs efficiently and quickly. Every movement accomplished a goal with nothing wasted.

The lighted exterior of the parking lot easily reflected the steely deep bluish tinge of their gun barrels. Even in the darkness of the motel room, the light glinted from their weapons as the men shifted positions in the darkness of the room.

"Their firepower would be welcome," he thought, as he sat, while appraising their situation.

He silently hoped that Hammel would be coming. He wanted him alive if possible, dead if necessary. He would take no pleasure in killing him, but secretly hoped that Hammel would force him to. Revenge for Abbey's murder had been far removed, but had been replaced by hate for the ideas Hammel held.

There was no telling how far the Agency would go to retrieve the information that Hammel had in his treacherous brain. Badawi and al-Mashad would be opportune eliminations, but Hammel had insider information and was familiar with the inner workings of American intelligence and he would be targeted for elimination. Nate had a hunch that all three would surrender rather than die.

A little after three o'clock, a long van pulled slowly into the gas station. The clerk's head was still buried into a book as he studied and the van didn't concern him. From their vantage point, three pairs of eyes scrutinized every detail of the van. He watched as the four backup agents exited through the back door, crossing the road just north and out of sight of the van. They moved in a military manner, like a Navy SEAL Team, using only hand signals to convey their intentions within the unit. Nate didn't know where the men were trained, but he instantly recognized the precise movements of a professional military kill team.

"Jen, I hope they have orders to take them alive if possible," he said, fishing for information. "I don't know what their orders are, Nate. They aren't Agency, probably military spec-ops, Delta or an A-Team and they aren't very communicative," she said, not taking her eyes off the van.

There had been no movement from inside the van. Whoever was inside was checking out the situation and Nate was sure they were confused. It wouldn't be long before they figured out that it was neatly set trap. They waited in the dark silence of the motel room for the van's occupants to make the first move.

He watched, as a silent shadowy figure from the strike team seemed to flow from behind a tree towards the van on his stomach with a knife in his hand. He neatly sliced the two rear tires of the van with such precision that it seemed as if it was done in one motion. Another figure moved from the shadows, joining the first. Each now had an automatic weapon resembling an Israeli-made Uzi.

Looking through his binoculars, Nate spotted the two remaining figures from the strike force at the other corner of the station. The clerk became aware that the van in his parking lot was just sitting there and wasn't moving, he slowly got up and started for the front door. Caution got the better of him and he stopped and grabbed for the phone, probably to call the station manager. After the call, he promptly locked the front doors and disappeared into the rear of the shop.

Without warning, the two front doors of the van flew open and the two men occupying the front seats rolled onto the ground with weapons drawn. They were not quick enough and the strike team was upon them before they stopped rolling. After a brief struggle with no shots fired, the two were subdued, their hands behind their backs, secured tightly with plastic handcuff ties.

Jenny, Karl and Nate came around the back of the building just as the two remaining members of the strike team converged on the vehicle.

"If there was anyone remaining in the van, they would surely surrender," Nate thought. The thought hadn't even registered when the side door burst open with a ripping sound, as if blown open by a hurricane. A distinctly Middle Eastern looking young man hit the ground firing. He didn't have a chance and was dead before he could get to his feet, after three shots from an Uzi nearly ripped him in half.

Seconds clicked by in complete silence while two men from the strike force approached the open door. An automatic weapon and a knife were suddenly thrown out onto the pavement as a sign of submission.

The team took no chances. A soon as the man appeared in the open side door of the vehicle, he was violently yanked out and slammed to the ground near the dead terrorist. His hands were cuffed in the same fashion as the first two.

Jenny ran quickly to the van and spotted al-Mashad and Badawi. Neither Jenny nor he recognized the dead man, or the other terrorist that was handcuffed in plastic ties. "Damn," Karl said, "where the hell is Hammel?"

"Don't worry about it Karl," Jenny said. "Al-Mashad and Badawi are now officially off the street." The strike team worked with a precision that Nate had never before witnessed. It appeared that they worked in unison with no communication, both silent and deadly.

The leader of the strike force was on the phone to his superior, "The objective has been accomplished, sir. Three of the assailants are unharmed and in custody and one has been terminated," he stated, in a matter-of-fact monotone. He listened for a couple of minutes and replied with a curt, "yes sir," and broke the connection.

"The local police are aware of the problem will and not show up," the team leader told Jenny. "A clean-up crew will be here momentarily to take care of the body and the van. The three of you are to come with us to a safe house that is located south of Naples, about fifteen minutes from here."

There was to be no discussion. It was expected that they would follow orders. "Ok, we'll get our things in the car and will be waiting," Jenny answered.

The three terrorists were on their feet, being herded across the highway behind the motel to the team's waiting van. They retrieved everything from the room, hurried to their car and waited.

⋏

Commissioner Gucci flipped the cover down on his cell phone after talking to Nate Adams. His responsibility as he saw it was to protect Rome's citizens from harm. It's not that he didn't believe this popular American, Nate Adams; however, a general warning of a nuclear threat in the area of the Pantheon would cause absolute panic.

The commissioner decided to call a meeting of the city's top officials, thus spreading the responsibility if suspicions were true. They met at a city official's house about three kilometers from the Pantheon, where he related the conversation with Adams to five other men who were responsible for Rome's well-being.

They decided that Adams was a loose cannon and the information had not been verified by the American Government and adopted a "wait and see attitude" until this threat was further evaluated. After all, the Americans were their allies and they would surely apprise them of a situation as dire as what Adams told them about, earlier.

Ten minutes later, Commissioner Gucci stepped out from the front door of councilman Barlucci's house just in time to witness a bright flash coming from the general direction of the Pantheon. The six men gasped in horror at what they knew they must have been witnessing.

The mushroom cloud rose high above the city accompanied by a shock wave that moved along the ground, causing cataclysmic damage for a one-mile radius from the epicenter of the explosion. The heat of the explosion melted metal and incinerated everything within the blast zone. People in that area were the luckiest ones; they died instantly, probably never realizing what had happened.

The unlucky ones were caught outside the immediate lethal area and they would die a much slower death. Some would die more rapidly from the radiation that would be lethal over a longer period and some would linger on a while from serious burns over their entire body. Their deaths would be slow and agonizing.

The commissioner and five councilmen were at a safe distance and hid in the basement of Councilman Barlucci's house, hoping to avoid a lethal dose of radiation. All communications and electricity in the city were out. The pumps that supplied the water were not operating and radiation was spreading, making the entire city unlivable for any animal life.

Angelina Gucci, the commissioner's wife was not one of the lucky ones, living two kilometers from the epicenter. She had been working in her garden when she saw the bright flash and stared at it unblinkingly wondering what it could possibly be. All but one of her children were at school when she had just nursed her newborn infant and put her in her crib for an afternoon nap.

Angelina's eyes started burning and slowly her eyesight faded and then heard the explosion. The heat from the blast knocked her to the ground, "Mi bambino, mi bambino," she moaned, as she lay on the ground in her garden unable to get up.

Chapter 10

When Nate arrived at the safe house, he was lost. The van they had been following made so many turns traveling down the tiny streets that he did not even attempt to remember. He had always felt uncomfortable about not knowing his exact location, as it made him feel that he had no control in a given situation.

They stopped in front of a two-story house. Everything was dark inside and the stone exterior indicated ancient architecture. The house had been taken care of, but it must have been at least three hundred years old. It was a large two-story house in an older area of South Naples on a narrow street lined with similar structures. The neighborhood was well kept and neat even in the dark of night. It was about four-thirty and the faint light of dawn would touch the night sky in about a half hour.

A slight drizzling rain had started to dampen everything as they followed one of the team members to the front door.

The rest of the troop followed them inside within minutes. If eyes were watching their movements, they never knew. Nothing broke the silence or darkness of the night.

Al-Mashad had a sneer on his face as he seethed hatred in Nate's direction through eyes that were little more than slits. Nate immediately recognized him from the picture in the intelligence reports and confirmed it by the red burn mark on the left side of his face.

"It's good to see to see you Muntasir. You don't mind if I call you by your first name, do you," he asked. "You'd better tell us where those other bombs are. These guys won't play around with you," he told him pointing in the direction of the strike team.

He walked over to the leader of the strike team and offered his hand, "Nate," he said, waiting for a response. He looked at Nate and paused.

"Randy," he replied, shaking his hand.

How many people do they estimate died in the Rome explosion," asked Nate.

"Right now it stands at about forty five thousand people and growing," he answered. "There won't be any way of knowing an exact number for several weeks."

"Look, we're not sure about the number of tactical nuclear weapons that the terrorists have their hands on, but we're just sure they have more of them. I've assumed that if they had the money to buy the three that we're reasonably sure of, they could have bought any number of them," Nate told him.

"Well, we're about to find out what they know. We have two people coming that are experts at extracting information from hostiles, if you know what I mean," Randy said.

"Yeah, I get the drift," Nate shot back.

The bright Naples sun shone through the window, waking him from a sound sleep. He glanced at his watch. It was one thirty; he had been asleep for seven hours. Jenny was already awake and toweling off her hair after showering, but he could hear Karl snoring softly in the other bed.

"Hey Jen, have you talked to Owings in Washington recently," he asked. "I think you should be in on the interrogation. You speak their language and know the cultural differences."

Karl was still in the shower when they went downstairs. Randy had taken the three terrorists down to the cellar and handcuffed them to securely welded iron grates. Nate didn't feel sorry for them. It's more than they would have done for them if the tables had been turned.

"When will the interrogation team arrive, Randy," he asked the team leader. "They're on their way, they'll arrive when they get here," he said, sounding edgy. Randy appeared to be a quiet intense man of about thirty, he was not in intelligence, but with a highly trained military group. His group talked only amongst themselves and Randy spoke to them only when asked a question they cared to answer. They had easily taken the team of terrorists out and obtained their objective without casualties and had earned his respect.

Every channel was broadcasting coverage of the nuclear explosion in Rome. Brave photographers wearing what they hoped were radiation proof clothing came up with horrifying pictures that regurgitated memories of Hiroshima and Nagasaki. Nate wondered how something so small that it could be contained in an aluminum suitcase could cause so much devastation.

Even the government of the Peoples Republic of China was officially shocked beyond belief. It was as if the whole world, except for some of the more militant Arab Countries, Iran and North Korea had embraced the plight of the Italian People. Even the more conservative Arab States were paying the obligatory lip service by condemning the act of terrorism as unacceptable.

He was able to find CNN broadcasting in English with Italian subtitles. It seemed that no other news was being broadcast in the world. Rome dominated every station in every country. In America, paranoia was running rampant with even the most rational pundits and commentators. Everybody had an opinion and wanted to express it over the airways.

The entire world was fully conscious of the unimaginable maelstrom of catastrophe that had befallen Rome and was continuing to unfold on an innocent people.

The blast in the Gulf of Valencia had brought the world to attention, but had caused much less damage because of its location. The effect of the blast was taken much more personally when the target wasn't military, but instead a large urban center, with an innocent civilian population.

A blast in the heart of Rome, next to the Pantheon, killing forty-five thousand people instantly had made the world gasp. This one event brought the reality of sudden extinction of part of an ancient city to the attention of every rational being on the planet.

Very little was left of what was once one of the glorious achievements of this ancient but modern civilization. Radiation would recede, people would return, and with the passing of a generation or two, the wounds would be but a memory for our decedents and only history would remain. The precious relics of our predecessors would still be gone forever. However, a dangerous precedent had been set that any group that had enough could declare war on society and cause untold destruction in the name of religion.

Nate looked at Jenny's face as she watched the coverage. Her face was one of stoic belief that this had happened, with a mixture of unbelief that it could happen. The enormity of suffering that blind religious hatred could cause was now a reality that was deeply ingrained in the minds and hearts of the world.

The dust hadn't yet settled in Rome, when the European Union began spouting rhetoric indicating retaliatory strikes against the home countries of these terrorists.

"Hell, perhaps the EU was right," he thought, "These terrorists were receiving support, both financial and moral from somewhere. Without that support, they never could've pulled off a nuclear strike. Maybe it was time for the world to hold the terrorist's home countries responsible

Nate wanted to keep his face out of the news. He imagined they weren't too popular with the Italians right about now since bombing of Rome, despite his early warning. This one heartless act would change how diplomacy operated in the world forever.

Karl was up and writing the story for *Global News Weekly*. "Hey Nate, Christine wants us to write one article for the feature story for this week's issue and they already have enough photos of the blast and aftermath," Karl said.

"Alright," he told him, reaching for his laptop. He needed something to occupy his time and he didn't have any research on this one, but they had been there. They had just lived the story. "It would be great to get the perspective of a person who had lost family in the blast," he thought.

"Hello Christine," he said, after glancing at the number on the display window of his cell phone. "Nate, you two get back here as soon as you get everything wrapped up. There's nothing else you can accomplish there. You can go back for a follow up when things calm down." Christine told him.

"We'll wrap things and leave before the sun sets late this afternoon," he replied.

Karl and Nate wrote the next feature article for Global in the following two hours, while Jenny searched for alternative routes north that would avoid the radiation.

"Too bad," Nate thought, "I would like to tell the story of the aftermath." He was sure he would get that chance but now Italy was in turmoil. People were terrified and there were many homeless and nearly dying trying to flee from the radiation, rubble and chaos.

To avoid Rome, they traveled backcountry roads. Although the countryside of central Italy was beautiful, they found it difficult to enjoy anything. They drove mostly in silence, each of their thoughts racing, while Karl used his cell phone and laptop to e-mail the feature to Global while they were driving.

The world was radically different since Rome had been attacked. As hard as he tried to imagine, he couldn't picture forty-five thousand people lined up and then just disappearing as if they had never lived. The world had been given a new set of rules. No war had been declared but people, innocent people were being preyed upon by an entity with no sovereignty and no legal authority to wage war. There was nobody to negotiate with, to make peace with, surrender to or even care.

The Geneva Convention itself was confined to earlier conventional military conflicts of sovereign states in an industrial age and it never anticipated unconventional and asymmetrical warfare in an information age with its added dimensions of cyberspace, mass psychology and cultural conditioning.

They arrived two days later in Zurich and went directly to the Swissotel, virtually exhausted. "Mr. Adams," a young blond hotel clerk whom he recognized as Marguerite said, as they entered the front entrance. "Christine would like you to call her on her cell as soon as possible." "Thank you Marguerite," he answered.

He dialed Christine's cell, not really wanting to talk to anyone right now. "Hi Nate," she answered, "I received your story … Great stuff."

What's up Christine," he asked, figuring that something must be happening.

"The word on the street is that you and Jenny have price on your heads," she told him.

"I'm sure Jenny will be overjoyed," he chuckled. "Seriously Christine, nothing has changed. They're just using their tried and tested fear tactics. They tried to kill me just after I arrived in Zurich at the Bierhalle Kropf. Either I'm lucky or they need to recruit better people. I'll be in the office tomorrow."

Karl had decided to hail a cab and get back to his condominium just a short distance away. Nate had tried to convince him to stay at the Swissotel where security was good but he had been unusually quiet since the devastation of Rome. Nate knew he had some close friends in the city. They were all shocked about what happened, but it was a little more personal with Karl.

Jenny was lost in thought, lines of concern, on her forehead so distinct that they appeared to have been etched in with a carving knife. She had her Glock apart on the foot of her bed as she sat cross-legged in dark green silky shorts and a T-shirt, cleaning and lightly oiling it.

Nate walked over to the fridge and reached inside for a cold lager and heard Jenny's voice, "Grab one for me, would you Nate?" He handed her the beer and she took a long cool drink before placing it on the nightstand.

Chapter 11

The fact that they hadn't apprehended Jim Hammel with the other three terrorists probably meant that he was in possession of or knew the location of any remaining tactical nuclear devices.

Nate knew that it was now imperative that Hammel be found and eliminated after locating the remaining weapon or weapons.

He wondered just how reliable the information was that the Agency was feeding Jenny. In a world of intrigue and hatred, where money was the bottom line, life had become increasingly cheap and it was best to trust very few. He knew that these extremists would settle for nothing less than the genocide of everyone who refused to accept Islam as their religion. He would do everything within his power to prevent the world from becoming an Islamic theocratic dictatorship.

The office was in turmoil. Stories and priorities were changing by the minute. Copy editors made unreasonable demands to reach deadlines for the next issue of the magazine. He spotted Christine directing people on her staff like a cop directing traffic at a busy intersection. Editors were making minor changes in the copy and the staff jumped at their commands. She had changed things quite a bit since taking charge from her father and the job suited her.

It wasn't until now that Nate realized his priorities had changed. He had come to realize that stopping these terrorists from destroying western civilization, as he knew it might be a little more important than getting the story.

Christine peered at them while Nate was sitting at his desk and halted what she was doing instantly, her eyes scanning him to make sure that radiation hadn't affected him. She grabbed him solidly around the neck as if he might escape, planting moist kisses on his cheek. She glanced at Jenny, "Good job," she said.

"You two please come in my office," she asked, shaking Jen's hand. She closed the door solidly behind them and sat down behind her father's old desk. That desk must weigh five hundred pounds. It was made of solid oak with many areas that were hand carved. There were dates carved into the oak to commemorate important events in Hans' life and that of the company. This desk was very much a history of *Global News Weekly* and Christine looked great sitting at the helm. She had admired the desk since her early teens and now it was hers.

"Jenny would you like a job," she asked suddenly with no hesitation in her voice.

"The question took Jenny by surprise but she took it in stride. She opened her mouth but no sound came out.

"Give Jen time to think about it," Nate said.

"No, No, I don't need time," Jenny blurted. "I want the job, I'm sure of it. What would I do? I'm not a writer."

"That's easy," said Christine," you would be a special consultant on Middle Eastern affairs and special operations. You would accompany our correspondents on special assignments. In short, you would get to do exactly what you are doing now, only doing it for Global. Let me know what your salary requirements are and we'll have personnel take care of you."

Christine walked around the oak desk and offered her hand, "Welcome aboard Jenny. I don't know whether to call you Fatima or Jenny," she laughed. "I'll have to think about that. I'm kind of getting used to Jenny," she said, smiling.

"You two take a couple of days off. You've certainly earned them." She turned and looked seriously at him, "try not to get shot, either of you. The rhetoric in the Arab world against you is unbelievable and your names have become household curse words. It is worse against you, Jenny because they know you are of Arab decent, even though you are American."

They walked out to the new Mercedes Roadster rental that had been delivered to Jenny at the front entrance of the hotel earlier this morning. It was good to feel the cool breeze of Zurich's slightly cooler climate, evaporating the beads of sweat on his brow as the sports car picked up speed.

This was a pivotal moment. With Jenny aboard, the mainstream media could expose the cataclysmic behavior of the terrorists. She would no longer be hobbled by the fact that she was working for the CIA, but she would lose the benefit of receiving classified intelligence reports.

"It's only a start," Nate thought," but a good one."

They decided to catch lunch at the Bierhalle Kropf. Frederick was behind the bar. When he spotted Nate, he ducked quickly as if dodging an oncoming bullet. When he reappeared, he had his hand out in a warm greeting. "Welcome home," he said, handing him two dark lagers.

A fresh copy of *Global News Weekly* was brought to their table. On the cover, there was a photo of the small mushroom cloud that a suitcase bomb would generate, with the headline,"Hatred and Mass Murder in Rome."

Although the blast had leveled a diameter of one mile from its epicenter, the death toll in Rome's heavily populated area was nearing fifty thousand souls and rising. He gasped at the horror of the magazine's cover.

They ate their lunch in silence, savoring the tasty meal when Karl walked in and headed directly to their table. "Congratulations and welcome aboard," he said, offering her his hand, "I can't think of a better addition to our staff."

"Thanks Karl, it means a lot coming from you. Have some lunch with us," she mumbled, between mouthfuls.

The café was crowded with the hotel's guests, and people were discretely looking in their direction, trying hard not to be caught staring. Karl accepted their invitation to dine and ordered the lunch special. They had two days off and decided to get out of the hotel if possible.

After much deliberation, they decided to take a drive in the country and the convertible was the perfect vehicle to let the top down and take in the refreshing summer mountain air. Jenny stopped at a small store that sold sundry items and bought two canvas chairs; the kind that fold up and fit into their own bag, with a strap for carrying. The owner recognized them and smiled, but she didn't speak English and their conversation was short and limited.

It was good to have a day off and collect one's thoughts, he thought to himself as he watched Jenny negotiate the curves in the road, handling the Roadster like a NASCAR driver. Her face had a look of ease for the first time since he had met her and he wondered if it was because she had released herself from the swamp of intrigue that the CIA had become.

She pulled onto a road leading to the mountains. There wasn't much traffic and people were much more subdued and not as friendly as usual. He couldn't blame them, with these types of bombs, it was difficult to defend against an attack and death was instantaneous. People were just scared. Their country bordered Italy and they knew that the Italians had not been able to defend themselves against this devastating kind of a terrorist attack.

"I know a place that has sports, drinks and American style sub sandwiches, "she yelled while the wind was whipping her face and jet black hair wildly. The day was warm, but not hot and they reached the mountains in no time. The Alpine air was fresh to breathe, refreshing him with its crispness.

"The world has changed, you know," Nate said. "We just haven't caught up with the changes yet, Jenny."

"Maybe we never will, Nate. Maybe catching up with those changes means that, in a small way, we accept them and I'm not ready to accept those kinds of changes."

"Nate had to admit that she had a point. Once a person accepts terrorism as legitimate diplomacy or the 'new normal,' it is in place and acceptable forever," he thought.

Jenny slowed down and turned onto a small dirt road that was no more than a trail that led to a small clear water stream. The cobalt-blue sky was peppered with small puffy clouds that hung in the sky like white balls of cotton candy, seeming not to move if you watched them, but imperceptibly moved across the sky, unhindered by anything that happened around them.

They carried their chairs to the stream, setting them up with their faces to the wind, watching the water bubble over rocks as it moved down the mountain.

Several children of various ages were playing across the stream, in a green meadow, sprinkled with multicolored early summer wildflowers. Their two dogs were running after them, nipping at their heels, causing the children to squeal with delight. Their giggles of laughter while chasing one another gave proof of their innocence and their sense of security in their surroundings.

"I'm going to the Mercedes and check it for a tracking device," he said, getting out of the comfortable chair. Jenny didn't reply, only waving her hand goodbye, her dark sunglasses hiding her eyes as she relaxed, sinking deeply into the canvas chair.

"It just seems that I would learn to do this before we start, instead of halfway through the day," he thought, mentally scolding himself.

After reproving himself for not checking the car at the hotel, he walked back up the small hill to get to the stream. The car had been out of his direct line of sight of the stream.

He walked as silently as he could until he could see the roadster peaking over the ridge just as a blue Mercedes sedan pulled up behind it.

"Well," he thought audibly, "that answers my question about the tracking device."

Speed-dialing Jenny's cell from his prone position in the grass, he rolled back out of sight. "We've got company," he whispered into the mouthpiece as soon as she picked up.

Three men exited the vehicle carrying what appeared to be Uzis. Within seconds, he could feel Jenny by his side in the grass, with her handgun at the ready.

They watched as the three turned in the direction of the stream. By their movements, it was evident that they were not aware of the pair's presence lying in the grass just out of their sight.

"You take the one in the red shirt and I'll nail the one in white," she whispered, confidently. He aimed carefully for the chest of Mr. Red Shirt and waited. They would be in full view of them within seconds. They approached cautiously in a half-crouched position, their weapons scanning the area like binoculars, sweeping to the left and right, searching for their prey.

Nate and Jenny fired simultaneously. Mr. Red shirt lurched backwards as if a giant fist had struck him in the chest as the 9mm slug pounded into him. The guy in the white T-shirt was on the ground and not moving.

The third man raised his Uzi and started firing randomly as if hoping to locate his deadly target. Rounds chewed up the grass, tearing holes in the topsoil a few feet to Nate's right.

Nate fired one round. The gunman, was hit low in the stomach and thrown violently to the ground, caught in mid-stride by two rounds. He laid still, his chest heaving with the exertion of breathing. Nate knew from the placement of the rounds that the terrorist would never live to see a hospital.

Silence once again filled the quiet peaceful looking meadow. They ran to the downed men and kicked the weapons from their hands. One man was left alive and his face radiated fear as his eyes followed their progress to his position. He had been hit high in the chest and was having trouble breathing. "Ask him about Hammel while he's still breathing," he told her.

Jenny knelt by his side, "God," she thought, "he couldn't be any older than eighteen." She started speaking to him gently in Arabic, while Nate rifled through the pockets of the other two terrorists.

The boy died a short time after talking to Jenny. "These three kids were only after the two million dollars reward for our deaths. Incidentally Nate, that reward is only to be paid when they return with our severed heads," she said.

"I wouldn't call the Agency and quit until we have the information from the interrogation of Badawi and al-Mashad," he suggested.

"I've thought about that," she replied.

He dialed Christine and informed her of the situation. She didn't sound surprised and told him the police were on their way. "By the way Nate, make sure you get plenty of photos with the story," she said. He chuckled. He knew he could always count on her to put the interests of the magazine first.

Nate had gotten plenty of information from the bodies. He left the identification and passports on the bodies after copying the information. Jenny started checking the bodies in a far more professional manner, while he snapped photographs of everything in sight. As Nate wrapped up his work, he could hear sirens in the distance.

Police and paramedic units came to a halt close behind a pair of parked Mercedes. A tall man with an angular face and shock of blond hair, wearing a cheap ill-fitting suit, strode toward their position.

Following close behind was a much shorter competent looking woman in her early thirties, dressed in a light blue summer suit. The distinctive bulge of her handgun gave indication of her need of further instruction for carrying a concealed weapon. Her hair was dark brown, cut in the short European style of most professional women. Her confident stride and body language spoke of a no nonsense attitude that would allow no place for trivial pettiness.

The pair stopped directly in front of them. The tall man stood over Nate by a full three inches. "Albert Schwambach," he offered." "Nate Adams, with *Global News Weekly*," he said offering his hand.

"All of Europe knows who you are, Mr. Adams," he said a bit sarcastically. "Ms. Martinez," he said politely, nodding in her direction. "You've brought a lot of trouble to this area, Mr. Adams," he accused, finally accepting Nate's proffered hand.

"The trouble was already here when I came. You just preferred not to acknowledge it Mr. Schwambach," Nate shot back. "Let's not get off to a bad start here. This is the fault of the terrorists, not you or me."

"Do you know who they are," the detective asked a bit more pleasantly. "They didn't take the time to introduce themselves. They just pulled up and got out with Uzis in their hands, he replied.

"If you've got everything you need, detective, we should be getting back to the office," Nate said. Jenny was silent but gave him a sly wink as they turned and walked to the roadster.

They got away from the scene of the triple shooting quickly, and were back at the office within an hour. They stopped on the way at a gas station and searched for the GPS tracking device that had given their location away to those three young bounty hunter wannabes. They found it easily enough in the right front wheel well. Nate removed it, threw it to the asphalt and smashed it, striking a swift heavy blow with the heel of his right shoe.

When they got in the office, he went directly to his desk, while Jenny busied herself with a phone call to the Agency.

Nate started on the tedious job of putting together the story and within minutes, he had finished downloading the digital photographs into the system and started writing the article from memory of the incident.

"Can't you take a day off and stay at the hotel where security has been beefed up," Christine said laughingly, as she walked to his desk. Nate wasn't in any mood for jokes, he had just witnessed a boy breath his last choking breath for hatred and greed.

"We only have one more day off anyway, Christine. I'm starting to think we're safer out chasing terrorists than we are here in Zurich taking time off," he joked tiredly, tousling her hair with his free hand.

"I need to talk when we get to the hotel Nate," Jenny told him in a low voice. She learned quickly and knew enough not to say anything in the newsroom that she didn't want everyone to know.

Two hours later, he forwarded the article to the editor's in-basket and told her, "Let's go, I can finish this later, Jenny. We'll get some lunch on the way back. The car was right where they left it. They had parked it by the parking lot guard and had given him instructions to keep an eye out for anybody around it, with a tip of twenty Euros.

The day was bright and clear with an azure sky, and just a few high cirrus clouds, with not a hint of a breeze left in the air. It seemed to Nate as if the world was trying to catch its breath after the events of the last few days. The day threatened to be a hot and sultry one and he could already feel the mugginess of high humidity on his skin. Already beads of salty perspiration threatened to turn to streaming rivulets on his brow.

"Quite a change from this morning when it was cool and breezy," he commented to nobody in particular.

"I called the Agency and quit Nate," she said in a subdued tone. He didn't say anything for a while. An answer didn't seem appropriate, so he just nodded and smiled his approval.

"Well maybe, honesty is the best policy in this case Jenny," he finally told her. She remained silent while they drove directly back to the hotel to diminish the chances of any further attacks on their lives.

Jenny finally broke her silence abruptly. "Nate, the interrogators broke al-Mashad. There are many tactical nuclear weapons in the hands of Al-Qaeda. More than they thought in the beginning," Jenny said pensively. How many are they talking about here," he asked.

Jenny just shrugged, "No one knows for sure Nate, except Al-Qaeda, but they guess it could be as many as perhaps six."

He sat on the edge of his bed pouring over the enormous stack of intelligence that Jenny had received from the Agency before her resignation.

There had to be something in these stacks. Nobody was perfect and somewhere Hammel must have screwed up. He picked up an outdated list of cell phone call records from agents that were assigned to this case.

"These guys were so organized," he thought, as he peered at the records. They were listed in alphabetical order and Hammel's name was there.

"Jenny, I've found the list of Hammel's, calls since he's been on the case. Let's see if there are any numbers that will give us a lead," he said thinking there might be a chance he was on to something.

Nate poured over the list and felt his heart skip a beat as he passed a number he immediately recognized.

Jenny was looking over his shoulder and noticed the surprise on his face, as she watched his body involuntarily stiffen.

"What's wrong Nate, you look like you've seen a ghost. The date of the call was June 10. "Whose number is that," she asked him. "It seemed like an eternity before he could speak, "Greta's," he answered almost inaudibly.

"We've got to tell Christine," Jenny said, as if reading his thoughts.

She was right. If Greta was a mole, Christine had to know. That would explain how Al-Qaeda knew every move they had made. It would also explain why she had been so distant and not wanting a relationship, only the overnight stays.

"I'm surprised we aren't dead by now," he thought. Jenny walked over to her suitcase and removed an object he didn't recognize.

"What's that," he asked. "Just a device to check for bugs in the suite. After I make a sweep of this one, I'll go next door and do mine," she told him, as she started turning buttons on the face of the device.

"She walked over to the table by the refrigerator and started scanning around the area, stopping by one of the chairs, flipping it over, and removing a small object from the bottom of the seat.

She held it in the air for him to see with a smile on her face, "Got it," she said. "This one will only transmit about a mile," she stated.

"That's great, Greta only lives a half mile from here," he told her. If she's listening, she will know we found it," he said, after smashing it with the handle of his Glock.

Jenny made a complete sweep of both suites with the device and found nothing else. As soon as she was finished, he called Christine and told her of the situation. "Meet us here Christine, there might be one in your office too," She told him she would be right over and hung up

Chapter 12

Christine sat in one of the chairs while he showed her the intelligence and the disabled transmitter. Nate could see by the look in her eyes that she didn't want to believe it.

"It was hard for me to believe Christine, but these records don't lie and the Agency had no reason to feed us false information on this. Besides, we almost missed it," he told her.

Christine stared odiously at the list of calls made by Hammel, then turned and looked at the crushed transmitter. "The evidence is damning," she said. "Greta has a key to this suite because of her position."

"There isn't any doubt in my mind Christine. The terrorists knew exactly where we would be, whenever Greta knew. It's just too much of a coincidence," he muttered.

"Call her and ask her to come over Nate," Jenny said questioningly.

"No, I doubt if she's in this alone Jen. We should nail her accomplice and I have a good idea just who that might be," he said.

Her eyes denoted a sudden grasp of the situation. She smiled. "What do you have in mind," she asked.

"Why don't you go back to Global with Christine and do a sweep of the office. If you find a transmitter, leave it operational. It will be a great way to feed them false information and find Hammel," Nate said, failing to conceal his excitement.

"If this is Greta's doing, I'm sure you will find one in Christine's office," he said.

Nate just needed to be sure it was Greta. There was a place in the depths of his brain that just wouldn't allow him to believe that he had been duped by a woman he'd slept with. "Oh Well," he thought. It wasn't the first time he'd been sandbagged by someone he had trusted.

He had never even thought of deliberately setting out to kill a man. When he shut his eyes and envisioned nearly fifty thousand human beings, instantly massacred in Italy, it became a distinct possibility.

Not that Hammel was solely responsible for this evil, but he was a traitor to his country and they hadn't expected this from him. He had been one of a trusted team and this is what had made it so unacceptable.

"Well, a mole in an organization is usually the last person you would think it would be," he thought.

He locked the door to his suite and the adjoining door to Jenny's suite and drifted off to sleep.

When he awoke, it was to the sound of his cell phone ringing. "Hi Nate," Jenny's voice piped into his ear. "We found a bug in Christine's office and she's pissed, but I talked her out of hauling Greta in and firing her."

"Good girl, now get back here. From now on, we only travel together. It's too dangerous for either of us to be alone, with a price on our heads," he told her.

"You learn fast Nate," she replied.

He had almost hoped that it wasn't Greta, that they had been mistaken all along. The more he thought about it the more angry he got, especially when he thought about Abbey.

Nate realized as he lay back on the bed that they had only scratched the surface of this plot. It ran throughout the Islamic world. A frenzy driven by right wing religious extremists would dominate the more moderate factions of Islam. Their maniacal drive to dominate the world with an Islamic theocratic dictatorship would change and mutate, as their circumstances and priorities shifted.

They must change priorities just a quickly if they were to have a reasonable chance of stopping them. Their priority had blurred and perceptibly changed to getting the nukes off the street rather than getting the story. Nate realized at that point that once they had eliminated the nukes, the story would take care of itself.

Power hungry politicians of the Western World, were far too occupied to focus on one task for long, and remained focused on short-term goals only when it was to their advantage or profit. Politics played a part of every country's commitment to fight terrorism, but with this new unprovoked attack in Italy the world would rally, fueled by public opinion and fear.

Nate and Jenny realized they would be largely on their own. One thing was certain. Greta and Jim Hammel would pay dearly for their role in Abbey's senseless death and the slaughter in Rome if they were caught. The court of public opinion was an unforgiving one and it would exact its vengeance in the end.

Nate checked his Glock and after a thorough inspection, was satisfied that it wouldn't malfunction in a pinch, when he heard Jenny's distinctive knock at the door. First, two raps in quick succession, then after two full seconds two more raps evenly spaced out.

Satisfied, he opened the door. She quickly entered, shut and locked the door behind her. Jenny grabbed a dark lager from the refrigerator and sat at a high seat in the breakfast nook. She was tired and it showed in her eyes, but there was no time for rest and relaxation.

"We're going to interrogate Greta and scare the living daylights out of her. The money she received for helping them will seem small in comparison to the consequences she will have to pay if she's prosecuted for conspiring to commit terror in her own country. The authorities will not deal lightly with her," he told Jenny.

"It won't take much to make her spill everything, Nate. Beneath that exterior is a real softie," Jenny replied tiredly. "For now let's sleep."

"She sure didn't know Greta," Nate thought cynically.

Jenny stripped down on the other side of the bed to her T-shirt and panties and without another thought, climbed in. Nate watched as she placed her Glock under the pillow and closed her eyes. He smiled to himself, pleased with the new arrangement, but not quite knowing what that arrangement was.

He thought about this "comfort zone" between them and it didn't upset him. After all, they were friends and a certain amount of trust and familiarity had grown between them.

Women always took relationships with men for granted. "Hell, this wasn't even a relationship," he thought, attempting to remove the idea from his mind. "Too much to think about now and I'm tired," he concluded, drifting into a slumber.

He wasn't sure of the working relationship they had, or what the future would bring, but the one thing he knew was that she was welcome in his bed anytime.

He didn't go to sleep right away, but instead watched her for a long time, until her breathing became soft and even. Her face eventually softened in sleep, from the hard lines it had taken on from the last few days' horrors. She settled into the pattern of deep sleep and he could see by her fluttering eyelids that she was dreaming.

He would be spending much time with her now that she was working for Global full-time. She was an intricate woman, not easy to figure out, but she was faithful and loyal when she believed in something. He was fortunate to have her on his side. He looked down at the foot of the bed where her clothes lay on the floor, where she had cast them in a pile.

Tomorrow was another day and Greta would be told in the morning to report to them at Nate's suite in the hotel. Greta might know that they found the transmitter, but she had no way of knowing that they had possession of a list of Hammel's cell phone calls or that they had found the transmitter in Christine's office.

He was reasonably sure they could scare her into spilling her guts once they presented her with the evidence.

Jenny was up and humming a tune when he awoke. The sun was high in the sky on a cloudless day and Nate could hear the traffic on the busy street below. She was wearing the same deep green T-shirt and mauve panties, but he barely noticed, having become familiar with her lounging habits; and his mind was preoccupied with how best to handle Greta.

The rich aroma of coffee wafted through the air, tantalizing his senses. Jenny prepared a cup for him with just enough half-and-half. He had never been able to drink coffee the way most Europeans liked it. It was far too strong for his taste. Just a touch of half-and-half did the trick for him.

He stretched out on a comfortable armchair facing the balcony, sipping his morning coffee, while contemplating the meeting with Greta. The sun was already an hour into the eastern sky on a cloudless day and he knew the day would be a hot one.

"Greta is coming over at ten," Jenny said, as Nate sipped his coffee. "She was told she would work with us today doing research. Nate, it would be best to let me handle the interrogation. I'm trained at it and you've had a relationship with her," she reminded him.

It was okay with him. He knew this was her forte and he was comfortable with that.

He remembered the extended conversation with Christine from the day before. The intelligence report had infuriated her. There would be no explanation. Hammel had already killed his partner and defected well before he had called Greta. Greta had just become another pawn in his plan.

"I don't want her back in the office," she had told him. "While she is at your suite we'll pack all her stuff and deliver it to her house."

He had never seen Christine so angry. She had trusted Greta completely with every aspect of her business, as her father before her had.

He realized that she had the grit to run Global with a stern hand and could make the quick difficult decisions in bad situations. It took a person with very tough skin coupled with diplomacy to head a major news agency. It wasn't like running a corner store. A large news magazine like Global had widespread influence and was a major force in international journalism. The person at the top had to be tough and unwilling to cave in at the first sign of a rumble. Christine had that kind of grit.

Jenny was right. It would be best for her to handle the situation. He was in a vulnerable spot having had a relationship with Greta, if that's what it had been. He didn't count just sex as a "relationship," but was overjoyed when Jenny offered to take care of Greta, leaving him out of the equation.

Greta was punctual as usual. She entered wearing low cut blouse of light blue silk that radiated against her milky white skin and a chic mauve skirt cut two inches above the knee.

Nate had decided to go to the café for coffee and leave the two women to their own devices. He walked to the elevator. When the door opened on the first floor lobby, Karl was looking directly into his eyes. Standing at his side, wearing a beautiful summer dress, was Julie. Her statuesque beauty had an essence of its own. "Karl has great taste," Nate thought.

"Karl, let's go to the coffee shop. I need to talk to you," he said, noticing the somber look about him. Nate perceived, by the look of consternation on Karl's face that Christine might have spoken with him already.

After ordering a cappuccino and bringing Karl up to speed on their speculations concerning Greta's behavior, the entire table bore a pregnant silence. Nate could see then by the look in Karl's eyes, that he didn't have a clue. Julie sipped her coffee in silence, deeply immersed in her own thoughts, but saying nothing. Since the loss of Abbey, she was aware of the seriousness of the situation and was well aware that her own life might be in jeopardy.

"I thought that Christine might have told you some of this," he queried.

"No, but it makes sense now. They seemed to know our every move Nate," he muttered, almost under his breath.

"I still find it hard to believe. I've worked with her all these years. Is there any chance you're wrong," he asked. Nate simply looked at him and shook his head.

After two hours, his cell phone rang, "Come on up Nate. We need to talk," Jenny's voice had seriousness written all over it.

Karl sent Julie home and got in the elevator with him. Greta looked disheveled, handcuffed behind her back to the bedpost.

Jenny told us the whole story while Greta looked subdued and beaten. She had been hustled by Hammel in the same way a pimp hustles a whore. She had fallen for his rap hook, line and sinker. Under Jenny's skilled interrogation, she admitted placing both the bug in his suite and the one in Christine's office.

"She had agreed to act as a decoy if we didn't report her to the Swiss police for prosecution," Jenny explained. "She's going to call Hammel and set us up for one million dollars of the reward for our deaths. That's half of the take and he should go for it."

"That's cute," Nate said. He looked at Greta and said, "If you cross us, I'll kill you myself."

She gave him a baleful look, but her face looked like a deflated hot air balloon. She could see that he wasn't in the mood for any small talk and hung her head, wishing this would soon be over.

She didn't seem to know anything of importance about his plans, but she could get in touch with Hammel and that in itself was more than anyone in the Agency or here at Global could accomplish.

Jenny monitored both ends of the conversation between Hammel and Greta. "Damn, it was great to have a partner that was fully trained by the Agency," he thought. "Hell, she had the whole conversation on tape. They would be able to play and replay for those nuances of intelligence they had missed and it was damning evidence for the prosecution, if he were captured alive."

The mountainous countryside flew by as the gunmetal blue Roadster sped down the highway cutting through the air with aerodynamic precision. The thin clear Alpine air whistled past them as their Mercedes cut through the pleasant Swiss scenery.

The sun was high in the sky, pouring down its energy on the hungry verdant landscape. Multitudinous shades of green filled their eyes and senses with their richness and splendor as they sped by. The cooler mountain air tasted fresh and sweet to his senses as he laid his head back and took it in.

Nate and Jenny were caught up in the intense machinations of their own thoughts, each driven with a new desire to stop these insane maniacs before they could devastate another European city.

Rome had been at a standstill the last few days and the world community was just now starting to respond with financial and physical aid and compassion for its people to a level and extent that was unlike any other seen before.

He silently rested his head on the roadster's headrest, wondering if Greta had even more secrets beneath that serene veneer of her malevolence. "In a way, she had been a victim of this madness too, he thought" then rejected that idea.

He doubted that Hammel knew where the remaining nukes were. Being only a half-breed as they called him, Nate doubted that he knew anything of importance. It made sense that if he would turn on his own country, Al-Qaeda would be hesitant to trust him with that information, but if they could get their hands on him, he would no doubt be a great source of new leads.

Jenny had called her former Agency superior, Stuart Owings, to call in a favor. They needed a safe place to stay and gain the impetus to decipher the information and they would appreciate the support of Randy's strike force if possible.

Stuart was more than willing to offer any assistance they might need. Nate realized that the Agency would have more control over the situation than he was willing to give -- not that they couldn't use the help when the bullets started flying their way.

They had been given the strike force's safe house as a haven and base of operations. Now, they headed toward the location in Naples, where the interrogation of al-Mashad and Badawi had taken place.

The house was unexpectedly empty of both the strike team and their prisoners al- Mashad and Badawi when they arrived. The key had been placed exactly where Owens had told Jenny it would be and they let themselves in.

Jenny's cell phone rang within seconds of their arrival. She put the receiver to her ear, "Yeah Randy," she said to the leader of the strike team. She listened intently for a minute and replied, "Alright, I understand."

The house had been left immaculately clean with nothing out of place. "They want us to act like we're down here on a story for Global," she said. "I don't trust anybody at this point," Nate replied. "Every place I go, I will be armed."

"Well heck," he thought. Actually, they were down here chasing a story for Global, unless their priorities had completely changed and they were now just drawing a paycheck from the magazine. There was no doubt about it; journalism was fast becoming a dangerous and less glamorous job and being armed just made good sense.

The Province of Campania is a beautiful area where the lush verdant plains to the north sweep down to Santa Maria Capua Vetere, just north of Naples.

The safe house was actually located south of Naples on the Almalfi coast in a breathtakingly beautiful village called Positano.

This rustic village is built on a steep small mountainside with houses built in rows from the top of a steep mountainous grade and ending only at the water's edge. This area is known as a top spot for global jet setters and he had hoped that they could catch the hydrofoil to the Island of Capri while they were here.

The morning started in a surreal fashion. It started to drizzle over the beach, while far to the eastern horizon the sun broke over the water coloring the underside of the rain-laden deep gray clouds with orange and reddish hues. A short time later, the rain continued upon the beach as the sun rose above the clouds in the distance creating a rainbow on the horizon just above the water, its arc disappearing halfway through its journey into the sky.

When Nate looked a short time later, the clouds had swiftly moved to the east revealing what would be a sunny day. Out the window from where the house was located about halfway up the steep grade and into the northern shores of the Gulf of Salerno's sensuous blue waters, he spotted windsurfers skirting the waves and a few pleasure craft already dancing lightly on the swells just off shore. He could see an adolescent boy fishing from the surf for anything that might come his way.

Chapter 13

Jim Hammel had figured out from experience that the best place to hide was out in the open. What he didn't know was that while he sat in his beach chair on the Isle of Capri sipping an exotic drink that he was far more vulnerable than he thought. He had chosen this location because it wasn't that far from Switzerland and was visited by vacationers from every part of the world, and blending in wouldn't be a problem.

The entire population of Capri, except for a few locals, was transient and seasonal.

From his advantageous perch on the beach, he could hear at least three different languages being spoken. It disgusted him that these people seemed to care nothing about the demise of Rome or at least it didn't seem to be the main topic of conversation.

Hammel's cell phone rang disturbing his peaceful moment in the sun. It was Greta wanting to sell more information. She told him that Nate Adams and Fatima al-Zaida, using the name Jenny Martinez were staying at a safe house in Positano. Before breaking the connection, she demanded half of the bounty money for their deaths and an additional twenty-five thousand dollars for the information, be deposited in her numbered account in Switzerland.

"She's got a lot of nerve," Hammel thought sardonically. No matter, she would be eliminated as soon as her usefulness was complete. It was standard procedure to eliminate these kind people as soon as their usefulness was complete and he wouldn't think twice about it.

Badawi and al-Mashad had disappeared and he could only assume they had either been killed or captured. Knowing the CIA as he did, he must assume that any information they possessed would be compromised. When it came to interrogation concerning something this important, they would be ruthless.

He dialed his superior, Jafar Khadduri, in Riyadh. Khadduri was another western educated Al-Qaeda soldier. In the last eight years, the organization had become extremely sophisticated. Khadduri, was believed to be the best war strategist that Al-Qaeda had. He was known to be completely ruthless and rarely made a mistake or bad decision. He also had the reputation of being merciless with his own men, demanding perfection. With this man, there was no second chance and the penalty for a severe failure was death after torture.

Hammel had never met Khadduri in person and knew very little about him except what the terrorists assigned with him had sparingly told him.

Today, Khadduri was in a particularly foul mood. He had realized that two of his best field leaders, Badawi and al-Mashad, had been lost and would ultimately meet their end in the American military prison camp in Guantanamo Bay, Cuba.

He didn't fully trust Jim Hammel, not only because he was half infidel, but also because he trusted no one who sold out his own people. He listened and spoke cautiously with him, revealing nothing of the master plan.

"I will send four men to your location. They are highly trained soldiers of Allah," Khadduri said. "Hassim is my nephew and he will take command. Is that clear?"

Hammel was shocked, but knew better than to say anything. "As you say," he replied, doing his best to sound pleasant. He heard a sharp click as Khadduri broke the connection without further comment.

Cold chills started at the nape of his neck and raised goose bumps lower on his spine. His analytical mind calculated instantly the ramifications of such an insult to him. He had kept calm and he knew his life could be in danger and would further assess the situation when the four men arrived.

He knew that he had far more training than the men Khadduri was sending and he would be on the lookout for an on attempt on his life. Khadduri had limited resources outside of his sphere of influence and could not control the situation from afar with any reasonable accuracy. In short, their operation would only proceed as well as the people he sent

Nate and Jenny walked down the winding trail that was bordered on either side by pink, red, and purple azaleas in full bloom. The smell of the salt air mixed fragrantly together with the smell of bountiful blooming flowers titillated their senses as they followed the meandering trail down to the sea. The trail pitched steeply, demanding that they carefully negotiate the trek to the sea.

The morning was quiet with only a few locals hawking their wares to tourists out for a morning stroll and Nate enjoyed the free time they had. He inhaled the salty fresh sea air, filling his lungs, taking in the breathtaking panorama before him as he descended the gravely path.

When they arrived at the beach, a familiar face appeared out of nowhere. "Good morning. It's good to see you out already," Randy said. "Hi Randy, we weren't sure that your team was in the area," Nate said.

"These guys were good," Nate thought. "Well trained and ever vigilant."

"Wouldn't miss a good fight for the world," Randy chuckled.

He walked beside them, speaking with Jenny, "Look, somebody from the team will always be in eyesight of you all of the time. Most of the time you won't be able to spot us, but we will see you."

Nate turned, "It's good to know you guys are close Randy," he said, shaking his hand.

"Hey Randy, we're thinking of catching the hydrofoil to Capri later. Want to come along for the ride," Nate asked.

"We'll be there, but right now I have to attend to some details of the mission," he said, before disappearing around the corner of a small ancient boat shed. Nate thought, "these guys were much better at undercover than the CIA agents that he'd met."

Later in the day, they departed from the port at Naples on the hydrofoil for the Isle of Capri. It was a little more than an hour ride to the island by hydrofoil. It was the first time he had been on a hydrofoil and couldn't believe the exhilaration of the ride. The water appeared close as he looked down watching it go by as the craft picked up speed.

Glancing over the railing on the port side of the boat, he watched as the diminishing shoreline recede into the distance, as the boat accelerated. The foils, attached to the bottom of the boat like two giant water skis, lifted the hull of the craft out of the water as it gained speed. When enough speed had been attained, the boat was actually out of the water and able to move at an incredible rate.

He looked for Jenny and found her on the starboard side scrutinizing the same phenomenon that he had just witnessed. The water that apparently sped by the hydrofoil had a pleasant turquoise flavor to its coloring.

Turquoise was always his favorite color. As a child, he and his younger brother had walked in New Mexico's "Four Corners" area not far from where they lived in Aztec, filling bag upon bag with turquoise that they had found laying on the ground by ancient Indian ruins. Some had a strikingly blue tone with black lines delineating the stone and adding its own character to each piece. Some had a more greenish tinge and those he had considered of lesser quality were placed in a separate bag.

Now, years later he glanced at the ring on his finger made of silver and turquoise that had been specially handcrafted by the father of a Navajo boy his own age that he had befriended. He and William sat in their very modest hut and watched while William's father used the beautiful blue piece of bluish turquoise he had selected from his treasure of stones and painstakingly hand-crafted the beautiful one of a kind ring for Nate.

He had given him only twenty dollars, which was an enormous amount of money for a twelve year-old boy, at the time. It had been the best spent twenty dollars of his life. He had had the ring resized many times as he had grown to manhood, but still wore it to this day.

Aztec, New Mexico faded from his memory of boyhood thoughts as the boat came to a stop in the Grande Marina at the port of Capri where they disembarked. This was not really a pleasure cruise, but they couldn't really resist the urge to visit the island.

Jenny looked longingly at the beach beyond the marina and the village shops within walking distance of the hydrofoil and said, "This is the kind of place I could get used to."

"I've got no argument with that," Nate replied.

Nate looked behind him briefly and spotted what he thought was one of the Strike Team following, but he couldn't be sure. "These guys were elusive," he thought. He knew they weren't far.

The terrorists were not as brazen now as they were in Zurich. After several losses, they must have evolved in their craft of murder or at least become a bit more wary. It would be much more difficult to ferret them out as they attempted to collect the bounty on Nate and Jenny's heads

Capri was one of the most beautiful islands he'd ever seen. He knew why the Roman Caesars had chosen this place to build palaces on. The shores were lined with steep granite cliffs that plunged into the sea, broken every so often by breathtakingly white sandy beaches, many of which were the private beaches of the rich and famous. The interior of the island was mountainous and the verdant vegetation was lush and plentiful. The weather was mild and pleasant most of the year, but if you weren't a local, you needed a lot of money to live there.

"How do you measure a miracle," Nate thought, when they stepped onto the dock. He knew the place was the destination on many global jet setters agenda, "but, how does one prepare for such beauty," he wondered.

He could see it in Jenny's face. She was as overwhelmed as he was. They walked on the beach not wanting to go into any shops until they absorbed the ambiance of the salty sea air.

Within ten minutes of walking on the plush fine white sand, he could distinguish at least four different languages being spoken. Europe had its own flavor that only its rich history could provide. Many people were bilingual and many spoke three or four languages fluently.

He heard their voices as he sat on a beach chair in front of a small open-air café talking with some Americans from Kansas City he had just met. He wore tinted sunglasses, kaki cargo shorts, a white T-shirt with a "New York Yankees," logo in broad flaring red letters and a baseball hat, boldly printed "***National Geographic Expedition***" baseball cap. He laughed at the joke an American accountant from Kansas City just told him, but hadn't heard the punch line. His thoughts were focused on Khadduri's insult and he knew his time was limited here in Capri.

He was sitting with his back to the water facing the front of the café when he distinctly heard Fatima's voice.

There was no mistaking it; he had worked with her too many times in the past.

Jim Hammel heard their voices fade as they walked down the sand just a few yards from where was sitting. He turned and saw them both, when they stopped by a window at one of the shops, laden with tourist curios.

Nate was not aware of anything around him at the moment, but he knew Fatima would not be caught off guard. He looked around, aware that he was being watched, figuring that it was probably one of Randy's men.

What he didn't know was that Jenny's eyes caught everything around her as a matter of habit. Her training had been so intense that those habits would follow her for the rest of her life.

"Cute disguise Jim," she thought. She gave absolutely no indication that she had recognized Hammel as she and Nate strolled with no particular destination in mind. She was careful not to look back.

She stopped after a few shops, stood by a magazine rack and told Nate, "We just passed Hammel. Don't do anything rash. We have the advantage. He spotted us, but he doesn't think we saw him."

He reached down, felt the reassuring bulge of the Glock and fought the urge to walk back to where he was sitting and put one through his left ear. "Jenny was right," he thought, "we needed him alive to glean every iota of information he possessed."

"It's the nukes we want Nate," she said. "He's nothing compared to getting the nukes off the street. Let's concentrate on the big picture."

Jenny was in the corner of the shop, speaking into her cell phone while Nate browsed European magazines with false interest, occasionally glancing in Hammel's direction, his eyes shifting under his sunglasses without moving his head. He had learned that little piece of acquired ability from Jenny after she had grown tired of him being conspicuous just one too many times.

He was sure that the strike team shadowing them had already spotted them and Jenny's call was probably unnecessary, but it comforted him that they had covered their bases.

The couple Hammel had befriended looked like they had just flown in from somewhere in the Midwest and if Jenny hadn't spotted him they would had given him perfect cover. They had no idea as they sat taking pictures of the hydrofoil at the dock that they were in dangerous company.

When Nate looked from the dock, to the open-air table of the café where Jim had been sitting, his seat was empty. He was strolling toward the hydrofoil nonchalantly. On the railing where the boat was tied off toward the bow, Randy was standing in full undercover tourist attire reading a newspaper. Randy's Old Navy T-shirt, cut-off blue jeans, and Dallas Cowboys ball cap fit him to a tee.

Hammel knew that they wanted to keep him on the island at all costs. He was no fool, very well trained and he considered there was a good chance that Jenny had spotted him. Jim caught Randy's military athletic movements and knew there was a good chance he was under surveillance. After a short time of acting like a bored tourist, he returned to the table with the couple.

Randy knew he had been made by Hammel, but was certain that his crew hadn't. He noticed the slight change in the former agent's body language. He decided to keep him under surveillance as long as he didn't try to leave the island.

Nate and Jenny finally returned to Positano the middle of the night. As soon as the door of the house closed behind them, she said, "I wanted to take him out too, but we need him alive."

There was no comment for her conclusion that Nate deemed appropriate. Hammel, so far had been able to slip through the arms of justice, but he would see to it that the good fortune he had been enjoying for the moment wouldn't become a permanent lifestyle of discomfort for him.

Nate stood in the window of the safe house and looked down the steep mountainous grade that this quaint ancient village was built on. He caught the reflection of the moon upon the water of the gulf. The stars shone brightly in the clear Mediterranean sky, adding to the surreal effect of a postcard photo.

⋏

Jim Hammel didn't know how they had found him and was too much of a realist to believe it was just plain luck on the part of trouble, Nate's mind returned to Nate, who had never been to Capri and didn't want to miss the opportunity.

"I must be getting slack," he thought. Fatima had recognized him just as he had instinctively spotted her, as she and Nate had passed by. He spotted one guy working with them over by the dock reading a newspaper. He was sure there were more. This man had a military smell oozing out of the very pores of his skin. Hammel had been trained to spot them by their body language.

He had known they wouldn't make a move on him right then, hoping to gain more information before they took him down. These guys were amateurs and he could easily ditch them on the island, with his connections on the inner island's mountains.

He watched as Nate and Fatima walked aboard the hydrofoil on its next run back to Naples, then slipped through the back door of one of the shops on the strip and quickly eluded the men trailing him.

He would be careful to keep his head down and avoid any contact until the other four from Riyadh arrived. Nate Adams had proved a versatile and formidable adversary with Fatima at his side and he would not underestimate this man as others had done before him. He didn't believe in blind luck and this made him very wary of Adams and his comdrades.

The four men arrived at nightfall the next day. He estimated Hassim to be about thirty. The other three were barely out of their teens but had the maniacal appearance of martyrs about to strap a bomb to their waist.

It was obvious by his demeanor that Hassim was the educated one of the group and had been in a leadership position of some sort in Riyadh. He saw Hassim evaluating him and knew instantly that this man had been ordered to eliminate him as soon as any usefulness to Al-Qaeda was terminated. He smiled inwardly at Khadduri's pitiful presumptuous thoughts to eliminate him.

"This puppy wasn't yet dry enough behind the ears to perform that function," he thought, a little amused that Khadduri would send such a novice as Hassim with those orders.

Chapter 14

Since the day Jenny's fiancé had been killed in Iraq, she had shown no interest in forming a relationship of any kind. Nate had been content to sit and watch, as she mended. His own relationship had only just begun when Abbey had been killed and it had not yet taken on any depth. Although painful, her death was not as devastating as what Jenny was experiencing, but her relationship had a tone of permanence to it.

He looked across the room to the table where she was bent over double, pouring over the tons of intelligence reports. "Find anything interesting," he queried thoughtfully. She just shook her head, her long shiny black hair flipping gently following the motion of her head. She just shook her head and never took her eyes from the mountainous stack of papers. After an hour, she tired of searching the endless piles of paper and said, "C'mon, Nate, let's take a walk."

The afternoon sun was hot and sultry and they walked the fifteen-minute trek to the beach finding, two unoccupied reclining beach chairs. There were surprisingly few people on the beach and they sat back and relaxed. They were ever vigilant and never went anywhere unarmed. Both handguns wrapped in the towels like suntan lotion and were ready to use at the slightest hint at trouble. Nate was especially wary because his intuition told him that Hammel had spotted them on the island.

Jenny sat in the chair with her head back not moving, her breasts moving only so slightly with each breath she took. Dark sunglasses hid her eyes and emotions, betraying her inability to be considered as anything but a working partner. Beads of perspiration broke out on both her forehead and the rise of her breasts as the sun did its work.

Jenny had become a master at concealing what she was really thinking. He had been able to draw her out simply because of the closeness of their working relationship and right now, he knew she could use a friend. They had become dependent on one another for the little things that made up their everyday lives along with watching each other's back when the going got tough.

"She needs to work through this alone," he thought, in a sudden impulse of inadequacy.

The sun had started to bake them and they decided to walk along the stretch of beach near some small boats that were pulled up on the sand in the calm bay. The sand felt coarse and grainy to their feet and a gentle breeze caressed their bodies, evaporating the perspiration as they strolled casually, nearing their beach chairs.

The day had been too calm and perfect to remain undisturbed. Nothing seemed to move or disturb the calm. Then in an instant of time, the calm façade that masked the coming danger revealed its ugly head. A man wearing a windbreaker on a hot windless day moved past them with great speed, his breathing heavy with exertion.

Everything seemed to move in slow motion or was it just Nate's mind interpreting it that way. The picture unfolded before him like a surrealistic scene from Shakespeare's *Titus Andronicus*. He watched as a Middle Eastern man reached beneath his aqua and tan windbreaker, revealing a Russian-made AKS-74 "Skladnoy" underfolder assault rifle. With a maximum firing range 3,440 yards and firing rate of 650 rounds per minute, it was a dangerous little weapon. The "Skladnoy" sported a stock that would fold under the barrel, making it easy to conceal. It could easily be fitted with a grenade launcher and was also available in a submersible version.

His mind jumped before his body had a chance to follow. His instincts ordered him to dive for cover. Before hitting the ground behind one of the many rowboats that were beached, his Glock 9mm was in hand with a round already chambered. He realized even before the sound of gunshots began that they were heavily outgunned.

Jenny's natural reactions were even quicker. He heard the distinctive crack of her weapon and knew she had one round in the air already. Nate fired twice and the terrorist released a spate of bullets in his general direction.

The terrorist had made a drastic mistake by underestimating Jenny simply because she was a woman. "It was a mistake that most Arab men had been prone to. It was inherent to the nature of a male dominated society," he thought, as he caught a glimpse of blood forming on the terrorist's chest even before he hit the ground.

The explosive punch of the 9mm had flung their attacker backwards as if he had been punched in the chest by heavyweight boxer. The string of bullets from the AK-74 ripped into the sand kicking spray into his face and ended with a trail into the sky as he fell to his back. Before he hit the ground, one of Nate's rounds caught him in the stomach, sealing his fate.

He quickly turned to check on the terrorist's cohorts that he knew must be close, Nate spotted three others bearing down upon them with the same AK-74 underfolder weapons that it seemed were standard issue for terrorists these days, or at least this group of terrorists.

Randy was suddenly by his side. "We'll take it from here," he said, "Keep your head down." He told him.

"What, and let you have all the fun ... not on your life," Nate said smiling broadly. He secretly hoped that his bravado was not misplaced. He was overjoyed to have Randy's expertise at this particular moment.

Randy gave hand signals to three other members of his team that he had not yet spotted. The three terrorists coming toward them with their weapons in the ready position gave no indication that they were facing anyone other than a journalist and a woman.

Randy carefully aimed at the lead terrorist and fired. The man dropped instantly and the other two started firing at the sound of the shot, thinking Nate had fired it. All hell broke loose as the air filled with gunfire. After a quick ten seconds that seemed like an eternity, deafening silence infiltrated the air.

Four terrorists were dead and Jim Hammel was nowhere in sight, but Nate knew that he was in the area. Hammel was smart and knew better than to engage in this particular firefight. His training probably told him this was a setup. He would be a formidable foe in the end and Nate knew that only one of them would live.

"You two get out of here, we'll deal with the authorities," Randy ordered with a no nonsense look on his face. He got no argument from either of them, as they would happily let the government pick up the pieces and deal with the casualties. It hadn't been one of Nate's favorite duties to deal with the authorities and Randy was working for powerful people that would handle these matters far better than he could.

Asked to provide a reason for this madness, Nate probably couldn't have given a short answer or a long one for that matter. At this point, he didn't care about an answer. He had been drawn into a timeless conflict, with an adversary that concentrated on countless generations of revenge-motivated desire to wipe out the Jews, Christians, homosexuals as well as other non-believers with a goal of recapturing lost territory.

The answer was no longer relevant as it had become a conflict, where reasons didn't matter and only winning was important. They used a nuclear weapon on an innocent heavily populated city. The line of infamy was crossed in a single definable act that was unacceptable in any modern culture on the planet. It was WAR!

It was not a conventional war, fought by sovereign nations using rules fabricated at a convention in Geneva, but a real bloody and horrific war, nevertheless. It was a protracted, paradoxical multidimensional and asymmetric war without national boundaries or heart; wherein only total hate of the enemy dictated the rules of engagement. The war would never end as long as the ideology of the Islamic Jihad remained unchanged in the hearts of extremists and future converts.

They were overjoyed to leave the scene without their pictures being placed on the front page of every newspaper and television screen in Europe. He figured that Randy had this already covered and could have the U.S. Government deal with this one on an embassy level.

Nate sorted out the details in his mind and called Christine, and advised her to record the conversation. After giving her a long and detailed account of what had just happened and assuring her, both Jenny and he were no worse for the wear, he hung up and collapsed on the couch.

"Not so fast Nate, Hammel is still in the area and we should stay on alert," Jenny told him, as he spotted a long shadow coming from the kitchen. Neither of them had heard a thing and only the shadow had given them any indication that an intruder was in the house.

Nate rolled off the couch and softly hit the floor with his handgun out and a round chambered. The shadow quickened its pace and before he could get to his feet, the back door had swung open, with a slam into the wall and the sound of running footsteps were heard drumming into the soft dirt outside.

It was Hammel. He would never forget him whether he was facing him or whether he running from him, he would recognize him immediately. Nate ran after him with Jenny close on his heels, but the traitor had planned his exit expertly.

Hammel had been hoping to surprise them and hadn't expected the sun to give him away. They were either extremely lucky or destiny had given them a large break. "He must have ducked into somebody's house," Nate thought. If he knew Hammel, he also knew this guy had prepared for just such a scenario.

Nate got back down the hill just in time to watch Randy as he handled the last details with the Italian authorities. Ambulances had already loaded the four bodies, while grim looking attendants were finishing last minute details.

The location where the last three terrorists were taken down resembled a slaughterhouse. Each assailant had been shot several times and the amount of blood on the ground and spattered across several small beached motorized craft was enormous. Boat owners had gathered expressing dismay at the damage to their boats by gunfire and blood.

Nate approached Randy just in time to overhear the lead detective tell him, while handing him his business card. "If I can help you in any way, please don't hesitate to call."

Randy caught sight of him from the corner of his eye and motioned him over. He listened quietly while Nate related the events that had just happened at the safe house with Jim Hammel.

When he had finished he grabbed his field radio and alerted his men to the developing situation. "We've got some ideas on his mode of operation and we're going to start a sweep of the area. "Nate, if you have to shoot him, try for a non-fatal wound. We want him alive if possible," he said. "By the way, you and Jenny did some pretty nice work here; just don't get yourself killed while I'm responsible for you two."

"Geez Randy, I didn't know you cared," he shot back, as he turned to walk away; Nate thought he caught a slight smile on Randy's tan weather beaten taciturn face.

Jenny, still winded from running down the hill, walked up just as Randy joined his men to give instructions for a sweep of the area.

"Let's get something to eat Nate," she said. "I don't want to go back to the safe house just now." "That's a joke," he thought. "The word 'safe' implied the idea that we would be secure there and could let our guard down, at least to sleep". In this new world of terror and intrigue, where everything was for sale for the right price, there were no safe areas.

Nate hadn't caught the name of the place, but the diner was a pleasant small family place with a squat elderly Italian man in his fifties, with thinning hair directing a staff of five young girls as they waited on customers. The café had the smell of home cooked down to earth Italian food with the kind of sauce that had been simmered for hours for the right consistency and taste, with all the right herbs and spices.

A young olive skinned girl with long black hair reaching down just below her shoulders came to their table in the open-air front of the café. She stopped abruptly as she recognized Jenny with a new look of hero worship in her eyes. "Jenny," she said excitedly. Then she looked over to me and immediately screamed, "Nate Adams," in the cutest Italian accent he had heard to date.

"Don't look so bothered, Nate. Our faces have been over every form of media in the world ever since you went back to work for Global," she told me, exasperatedly. "I know but I'll never get used to it and I'm not sure I want to," he replied.

The girl's name was Lydia and she never left them alone. She spoke enough passable English just to use the pair for practice dummies. She appeared to be about sixteen and still had the innocence that only the young possess. It seemed as if the tragedy in Rome hadn't taken its toll on her refreshing youthfulness.

By the time he had finished his plate of linguine, the girl, who by this time had became a minor local hero of sorts, had alerted a small crowd of onlookers.

"Don't be so uptight Nate, these people usually only get the normal type of celebrities," Jenny said chuckling, trying to hold back the mirth in her voice.

Chapter 15

It was at this precise moment, sitting on the couch at the safe house that Nate decided to phone his friend Omar, who was still holed up in the comfort of a Montana ranch. Omar knew the mechanics of this entire operation and understood the players better than anyone he knew. They needed logistical help on this one and Omar was the man.

Nate anticipated that it would take a little coaxing to entice Omar from his forced vacation. The straw that would break the camel's back and sway him to come aboard would be his compelling lust for adventure. If he knew Omar, the guy would be bored to death and ready to join the fray by now.

Nate smiled as he punched in the numbers to Omar's cell phone, knowing he would catch him at breakfast in Montana. "Hello, Nate" he answered as if expecting the call. "Just a minute, I'm going to walk outside so we can have some privacy."

"I've been meaning to call you," Nate told him, "but things have been moving a bit quickly here. I need your help to get at the bottom of this before they can nuke any more cities Omar," he managed to get out, in one breath.

"Whoa, slow down Nate, you don't have to talk me into anything. I'm bored as hell here and my family is safe. They have enough security here to form a battalion. When do you want me there," Omar said excitedly.

Hell, he didn't think it would be this easy. Omar sounded as if he were on the verge of calling him and convincing him to become a part of the operation. It would be great to have Omar along and his knowledge would be invaluable.

"I'll call Christine at Global and have tickets waiting at the airport in Billings. We'll get you directly into Naples by tomorrow evening. Is that too soon," he asked hopefully.

"The tickets should be at the airport waiting within an hour," Nate told him. "It won't take long to pack," Omar replied.

Christine was a bit apprehensive with Omar entering the game, but after Nate explained that Omar would be a great consultant and after a little sweet-talking, she relented and her replacement for Greta called the airline in Billings, Montana and arranged for first class tickets.

Omar arrived at ten the next evening with one suitcase. They met him at the end of the arrival ramp and hustled him out of the airport before any reporters recognized them.

Once Al-Qaeda realized al-Douri was helping them in their day-to-day operations, it wouldn't be long before he had an additional reward on his head, but Omar already knew that and he knew they could only kill him once, so he might as well help Nate. Omar didn't seem to mind, and he joked and laughed all the way to the safe house.

Although Al-Qaeda loathed him with the vile hatred that is extended to all infidels, they would hate Omar and Jenny with the special hatred they reserved for traitors of Islam. They required all Arabs to be sympathetic to their cause. If caught, they would eliminate both of them and anybody in their entire bloodline they could get their hands on.

The three of them didn't get back to Positano until after midnight. They found an all night café in one of the hotels and ordered breakfast American style.

"Thanks for calling me Nate," he said. "I had to get in on this one way or the other. I'm not sure that I'll ever be able to go back to Saudi Arabia, but my family will adjust."

He smiled a tired smile and handed Omar an envelope with two thousand Euros in it for expenses. "This will help until Christine gives you an advance. You're on the payroll as a consultant."

He looked inside the envelope and smiled gratefully. "Still the same old Nate, taking care of your friends," he quipped.

Jenny's phone rang and she walked into the lobby and talked intently for a couple of minutes.

Once seated, she told him, Randy and his team had tracked Hammel back to Capri. "He must have some reason to go back to the island," Nate thought. "Maybe he has one of the nukes secured on Capri. Now, that was a wild thought. Why would they trust Hammel with one of their nukes? No, there was something else in the wind," he reasoned.

Jenny and Omar were speaking their more comfortable language of Arabic he when broke into their conversation and told them of his suspicions concerning Hammel's return to the island. Jenny peered at him thoughtfully, "Makes sense. The island is a trap for him. It leaves him little room for escape, so there must be an important reason for his return."

Jenny went to an old looking valise she was fond of, and pulled a Glock from a compartment in the bottom and handed it to Omar. "You'll need this," she said.

Nate looked inquisitively at her, coming to full realization that there was much to be learned from Miss Zaidi. She had surprised him more than once in the short time he'd known her.

There was no doubt that they would be returning to Capri tomorrow. That's where Hammel had obviously returned. Although technically working for Global, they were given wide latitude in their actions and they could expect the same treatment in the future. The three of them and Randy's team shared the common goal of getting the nukes off the street and into the hands of someone who would disassemble them for good.

The cobalt blue sky glared at him through the window as his eyes popped open from the deep dreamless sleep that had overtaken him. His two friends were still talking in the kitchen and he could hear the crackling of something frying. The smell of cooking eggs, home fires and toast filled his senses, reminding him that he had a stomach.

"Hello gang," he said, hoping they had cooked enough for everybody. Within minutes, Jenny placed a plateful of food complete with a glass of milk in front of him. "You're a godsend," he told her appreciatively.

He inhaled the food gratefully, stopping only occasionally to breathe. When at last he finished, he looked at them and said, "Let's rent a boat and head to Capri." They were out the door at a marina in Naples within the hour.

The dock disappeared as they sped into the bay standing at the helm of the beautiful thirty-two foot cabin cruiser, *Sophia*. He relaxed on a beach chair while their expert navigator Omar set a course for Marina Grande on Capri. Finding a boat to lease had been just pure luck and they felt fortunate.

The *Sophia* was sleek, with new engines, painted white with Mediterranean blue trim. She was built for comfort with a well-stocked galley and sleeping quarters for all. Her engines purred as her bow cut through the calm water for the trip to the island.

The humid late morning sun made the ninety-four degree temperature even more unbearable. Heat drenched through the thin misty clouds that had risen from evaporated seawater causing their clothing to hang, clinging to their sweat soaked bodies. Nate's arms and legs clung to the plastic straps of the beach chair pulling his skin each time he changed positions.

They gave up sitting and decided to stand with Omar at the pilot's position as they picked up speed moving toward the island. The effect of the air rushing past was the only relief from the heat that drenched them like a sauna. The air rushing off the water provided natural air conditioning effect and Nate tilted his head back enjoying the cool breeze running through his hair, evaporating the sweat from his face.

The *Sophia* looked good docked at Marina Grande. They walked to the central piazetta and found it lined with high-end boutiques, expensive cafes, and restaurants.

Jenny and Omar managed to find a business with Arabic writing on the storefront and crossed the street, making a direct beeline for it. Nate busied himself with looking as much like a tourist as possible, sitting at an outside café sipping iced tea with lemon. He kept his attention on the front door of the little Arab-owned shop that stocked many Near East Asian items and curios. A mixture of the world's well heeled, seeking to be inconspicuous, strolled along the street admiring the many curios offered at inflated prices.

From the vantage point at a table where he was sitting facing the docks, Abud Abdul Raman handed the waitress twenty Euros for his bill and waved her off. Abdul Raman was a tall man at six foot one, and his eyes indicated intelligence. He had donned western clothes for this mission and had taken great care to appear as a tourist. In the melting pot of Capri, money was the only currency that counted and everything was expensive. He had been provided with the credentials of a Saudi businessman and was given the best accommodations that money could provide.

He was in peak physical condition and at the very cutting edge of his game. Abdul Raman surveyed the landscape of this tourist trap and was confident that nobody knew of his existence. His one major weakness appeared to be his brash overconfidence. "That might be his undoing," Nate thought, while scanning the entire area.

Not many people in Al-Qaeda were aware of his existence and he had been sitting next to Jafar Khadduri when Jim Hammel called to report in. Khadduri informed him of the situation unfolding in Capri with this half-breed. He hated a traitor more than an infidel and this man fit neatly into both categories. In Abdul Raman's mind, there were no shades of gray. Reality was neatly packaged into black and white. That's why he was called in on the tough cases.

He was born in Saudi Arabia in 1972 to a fairly wealthy merchant family and he spent the first ten years of his life being taught the secrets of the Koran. He believed it was Islam's destiny to rule the world. Yes, he believed in Manifest Destiny, but from his point of view, Islam would sweep the world of lesser religions with the truth and those that refused to believe, would die.

At twelve, he killed his first American. As he thought back and remembered, there had been no honor in this extermination. He remembered the dank whorehouse filled with the lowest women in all of Arabia and the rich foreign infidels that frequented these brothels. He had taken pleasure as he pulled the trigger. It had been as the trainers had told him and his country was cleaner and more holy without this "enemy of Islam."

The woman had stared at him in horror as he turned the weapon on her. He had quietly told her as she begged for her life, "You must ask for Allah's forgiveness." He had left without harming her and slipped away into the night.

His father sent him to a camp for young soldiers to be specially trained to fight in the coming Jihad. He slipped out of sight for six years and while training with crack Pakistani Special Forces, before he fought Indian troops in their wars for possession of the disputed province of Kashmir.

The Pakistani Army specially trained him for Al-Qaeda as an expert marksman and sniper. He led a small squad of trained assassins in Afghanistan to eliminate those who opposed the Taliban.

Now, with the sun and humidity causing perspiration to form rivulets of sweat, stinging his eyes, he watched as the *Sophia* docked and two men and one woman walked onto the pressure treated lumber of the dock. He had only expected two, a man and a woman. He quickly sized up the other individual and dismissed him as little threat. He had learned to evaluate men by their body language and apparent state of readiness. He had not often been wrong when sizing up an adversary, while always searching for a weakness.

Abud Abdul Raman followed them to the central piazetta in town with his mind focused on the three targets. He would eliminate them when the time was right and attempt to make their deaths appear as an accident. He would receive further instructions concerning the half-breed, Hammel later from his wing leader, Khadduri.

He had no feeling, one-way or the other about killing anyone as long as the greater goal of Allah and Islam, were being served. He had trained his entire life to become the ultimate soldier for this cause. Abdul Raman was a machine trained to do the work of Allah, a role that he was well suited to perform. He considered death the final glory and noble end of servitude to the cause of Islam and Allah.

Abdul Raman surveyed the couple intently as they split from Adams and entered an Arab shop filled with overpriced knick-knacks from various Middle Eastern countries.

He watched Nate Adams and wondered if this man was just the luckiest man in the world or far more talented than he appeared to be. "No matter, the end would be the same and Islam would be one step closer to world domination," he thought.

He would reconnoiter the situation for a couple of days, watching them closely. There would be no mistakes. He was well aware of his reputation and value to Al-Qaeda and would do nothing to jeopardize his position. He also knew that his position was temporal and he was considered expendable. He knew of several that would be eager to fill his shoes, should he falter or show any weakness.

Nate had the distinct indication of being watched and it was strong gut feeling that raised the hair on the back of his neck. He didn't get this type of uneasy feeling often, but when he did, he learned from experience to trust his intuition. His senses became keen, giving only a slight change to his body language.

Finally, Omar and Jenny's forms darkened the entrance of the front door of the shop as they exited. Nate watched them crossing the street but could not shake the feeling of the extreme danger that now coursed through his body.

He checked the roll of money that Christine had given him before they left Zurich. With the stack of twelve thousand Euros was a note, "You're worth it," the note said in feminine handwriting. He knew that Christine had been destined to run Global since he had met her as a child. It was second nature to her and she was a natural in the position.

They checked into a suite at Casa Morgano, one of the five star resort hotels located along the Via Tragara, one of the most beautiful walking streets in Capri. Looking out on the islands beauty, he knew why it had been a favorite destination for relaxation, since the days of the early Roman Empire.

Nate could see from the look on his face that the concierge recognized them. He smiled and assured him there would be no trouble. "We're here only for a vacation," he told him, pressing two hundred Euros into his palm. The man merely smiled and assured him that they were used to celebrities and there should be no problem.

The uneasy feeling persisted and when they had shut the door to the luxury suite behind them, he related his sense of danger to Omar and Jenny. Omar knew about Nate's instincts from the old days in America and he needed no convincing. Jenny just nodded and asked, "What do you think Nate?"

He wasn't sure of anything but that they must stay on high alert and act as a group. If somebody were here for the reward on their heads, they would try to split them up and weaken the group as a whole.

Jenny and Omar had been successful in obtaining information on Jim Hammel from some shop owners from Egypt. It seemed that he had been in there and bought several souvenirs for gifts, and the shop owners had noticed a room key from the Hotel a Piazella, just around the corner.

He knew that Hammel would never purposely make a mistake of that magnitude. It would be like telling the world where he was staying. "My guess is that he took the key from a hapless tourist just to throw us off," Nate told them. Hammel was a traitor, not an idiot and had been in the game too long to make mistakes of that magnitude.

"Yeah, that was our first instinct too," Jenny replied.

⁂

Nate went to the refrigerator and pulled out a bottle of local beer, "Not bad for a local brew," he thought. Omar shouted from across the room, "Hey Nate, crack one open for me, would you?" It was good to have him around and it brought back memories of younger carefree days.

He sat on the balcony sipping the cold beer, taking in the view that led to the mountainous interior of the island. The distinctly Mediterranean vegetation with alternating bare rock of these volcanically formed islands gave the sultry salty air a definitive aura all its own and was unique to this area. Fresh summer wildflowers speckled the landscape with multiple colors adding flavor to the scenery.

A knock at the door brought Nate back to reality and kept him from drifting into a deep sleep in the humid afternoon. He heard the satisfying spray of the shower and heard Jenny humming an unfamiliar tune, while she finished up. Omar hadn't stirred. Jet lag, along with the salty ride to the island had exhausted him. Nate felt the danger they were in and it energized his very core being, sharpening his senses.

The door to the suite didn't have a peephole and Nate slowly cracked the door with the gun at the ready, but out of sight.

"Jesus," he thought, 'these guys are good." Randy stood there looking like anything but a Special Forces team leader. It took Nate just a second to realize Randy wouldn't be at the suite if something weren't in the air. "What's up," Nate asked glibly, attempting to minimize the danger in his own mind.

Randy's fishing hat completely covered his hair and forehead to the point where his reflective mirror-like sunglasses took over. His button down short-sleeved shirt was more reminiscent of a tourist in Hawaii rather than someone visiting Italy. The effect was genuine. Only an American tourist would wear such a getup. Nate couldn't suppress a slight chuckle, "Good disguise Randy," he chortled, with genuine mirth in his eyes.

"Glad you like it, Nate. I swiped the idea from a tourist from Nebraska," he said.

Jenny bounced into the kitchen with a towel wrapped around her luxuriant black hair, wearing shorts and an aqua top that revealed her midriff, still humming that same unfamiliar tune. Her skin glowed from the fresh shower. "I never got a chance to thank you for the help Randy," she said smiling sweetly.

Randy's looked shy and his swarthy weather beaten face took on a boyish look as he stammered for a reply. Nate perceived at that point that despite his training and toughness, Randy was probably a nice guy.

"I need to talk to you guys," he said, and his face took on a more serious businesslike appearance. Randy was a complex man well suited to his vocation. His face exuded the inner strength that he portrayed to his men. His unit was a well-tuned machine, ready for action. These four had been handpicked for their personalities as well as their effectiveness as a unit.

"We have word on the street from operatives inside of Saudi Arabia that a specially trained killer has been sent to eliminate problems in the area and clear the path for their nukes to be deployed," Randy said. "I don't know the name of this operative, but we know he has been effective for Al-Qaeda in other operations. Nobody from intelligence has ever seen his face, so we have no idea what he looks like."

"I know of this man and if he has been sent by the Wing Leader, Jafar Khadduri, he is indeed dangerous and not many people know what he looks like," said Omar. "If he is on the island we will need your help. It is believed that his name is Abud Abdul Raman but only few know for a certainty." Randy gave Omar an appreciative nod, mentally noting this important information for further reference.

Nate stepped forward, "Excuse my ignorance, Randy. This is my friend, Omar al-Douri, from Saudi Arabia." Randy was all business, "I've been briefed on the entire situation, but it is good to meet you Omar," Randy replied. "I've been told that this man is highly trained and very dangerous."

"This explains the uneasy feeling of danger I've been having all day," Nate thought. He caught Jenny glancing at him, breaking into his thoughts with her mahogany colored eyes that sparkled with mystery and mirth.

⋏

Walking to the piazetta for a bite to eat, Omar and Nate had changed into slacks, shirts and ties with sports coats for dinner. Nate looked at Jenny with admiration, proving the age-old adage that "It's not the dress that makes the woman; it's the woman who wears it". He watched as heads turned discretely as she entered, seemingly unaware of their glances.

She strode smoothly in her aqua cocktail dress, with its slight hint of interwoven floral design that fitted her like a second skin. Her jet-black hair flowed to her shoulders, covering the spaghetti thin straps on her shoulders that held the garment in place. Placed in her hair, an aqua ribbon matched her dress exactly, starkly contrasting and accenting her black glowing locks. Her thick dark lashes curled upwards from her mahogany colored almond eyes. Jenny knew how to make an entrance. They were about to cross the street to enter the Villa Verde, one of the finest restaurants on an island of great eateries only a few meters from the piazetta, when a long black Mercedes limousine slowed down and stopped in front of the restaurant.

The limo's windows were black, reflecting light and giving the impression of mirrors making nothing inside distinguishable, including the driver. Seconds passed with nothing happening, finally the driver got out and opened the rear door revealing a Middle Eastern looking man, who when standing appeared to be well over six feet tall.

His tuxedo fit him as if an Italian master craftsman had hand sewn it. It fit his broad shoulders so well that the bulge of the gun in his shoulder holster was only discernible to the keenest of eyes.

The woman that followed him from the vehicle resembled a Persian princess and wore the finest of silk dresses, cut low in the front to show just enough of her ample cleavage. The cream-colored dress was offset by a deep green sash that accented her dark beauty.

As she turned to walk into the restaurant, Nate noticed that the back of her dress plunged to the small of her back revealing only a hint of what lay beneath. Her hair swayed gently as her hips rolled with each step. She walked with a confidence not usually found in Arab women. Her eyes were the same dark mahogany as Jenny's, but they were cold and hard, radiating an unbridled anger of their own.

"I know that guy," Omar said to me, almost whispering. "I played with him in the streets of Riyadh as a child. His entire adult family members are merchants, and even then, they were radical Islamists. They hated not only everything western but everything non-Islamic. They were in the vanguard of the modern radical element that gave birth to Al-Qaeda. They made many contacts by traveling to various countries, gaining contracts to sell their wares."

"Are you sure," Nate asked. "No mistake about it. We played in the streets of Riyadh. It's him, Abud Abdul Raman."

There was a feeling of intense dislike emanating from his friend and Nate noticed the expression on Omar's face that the tall stranger in the elegant tuxedo was stirring deep memories from his past, with many unwelcome nuances best left in the past.

Nate surveyed the couple as they drank their Chianti and nibbled at their amuse bouche. Their body language warned of danger and revealed that they were not a romantically involved couple. It was obvious that they worked together as a team only.

Years of professional reporting and interviewing people had sharpened his perception of people and body language. Nate's trained eye revealed that their relationship was a professional one. Their body language was one of professional courtesy and not one of intimacy.

He caught the stranger glancing at Omar for the first time and instantly caught a hint of recognition in his eyes before it was hurriedly masked by the façade of his profession.

It became obvious that this could be the Abdul Raman, who Randy had warned them about. This man was considered one of the most dangerous assassins that Al-Qaeda possessed. He was a man dedicated to his work, a cold calculating killer who cared only for Islamic world domination. Abdul Raman was trained by the best that his world had to offer and it was obvious to Nate that he knew he had been spotted. This made him twice as dangerous. Randy had said nothing of the woman. The Agency had expected only Raman to show up for the festivities at hand.

The Persian princess rose with her purse on her shoulder and strode toward the ladies room. She was tall for a woman, nearly six foot and her stride was long, exaggerated by the high-heeled shoes she was wearing. Jenny waited a few seconds and decided to follow her. Nate put a hand on her arm to stop her, but a cool glance from her midnight eyes stopped him.

He mentally held his breath as seconds passed and grew into minutes. Nothing escaped the attention of the tall stranger in the tux. After a few moments, the Persian princess exited the ladies room and within a few seconds, Jenny strode boldly to our table with a smug look.

"The woman is carrying a handgun in her handbag. We must assume they are working together and that we are probably their targets," Jenny intoned. "She's a cool one."

Dinner was elegant. Nate ordered one of his favorites, Tuscan chicken, which was a finely sautéed combination of chicken, artichoke hearts, mushrooms, onions and whatever else the chef felt was good, in a type of white Alfredo sauce that made one's mouth water. This combination was served over linguine. He know that red wine was the appropriate selection with this meal but, his taste demanded a dry white wine to sip between bites of the delicious entrée.

Once back at Casa Morgano, they sat down to plan strategy. It was obvious that Raman wasn't about to attack them in the open, but Nate was certain he wanted that reward as well as the next terrorist.

It didn't matter how religious idealism had warped him, in the end, he would take the two million dollars when it was placed on the table in front of him.

Randy's familiar knock sounded at the door to the suite, while he was steeped in conversation with Christine on her cell phone at home. Randy strode in as if in command and his face was a portrait of seriousness. He looked like anything but what he was, except to the trained eye.

"I've got more news from headquarters about Abdul Raman and the woman. Nobody knows her name except her superiors. It seems everybody knows of her, but nobody knows her and she keeps it that way," Randy stated bluntly.

"Abdul Raman has been well trained in the martial arts and small arms. The people that know him consider him the most lethal man that Al-Qaeda has. We've been ordered to take the both of them out at the first opportunity and with extreme prejudice," he said in conclusion.

"We're in complete agreement with your headquarters on that one," Jenny agreed. She handed him a cold beer from the fridge. He smiled and sat.

It was the first time that Nate had seen him relax, as he sunk into a plush chair and took a hearty drink of the cold lager. He tossed his head back, draining half the bottle without stopping. "Kinda hot out there," he said. "It's been a long hot day keeping tabs on those two."

"We have to take them out or my family will never be safe," Omar said. Nate looked at him. He had been unusually quiet and that was out of character for Omar. He knew that the truth was far more complex than his last statement.

The truth was no matter how many of Al-Qaeda they took out, Omar and his family would probably be in danger if they returned to Saudi Arabia. The Arabs had a long history of holding grudges. "Just ask the Israelis," Nate thought.

Randy glanced in his direction and nodded agreement before finishing the beer off and heading for the door. "Call me if anything changes. Remember we're in this together and have the same goal in mind," subtly reminding Nate, that he was in charge of this operation.

The *Sophia*'s thirty-two feet of elegance floated comfortably at the dock at Marina Grande as Abdul Raman eyed it casually from an open-air café facing the marina. His eyes scanned the area looking, to find the best opportunity for the specialists to wire an explosive charge that could take all three targets out.

Abdul Raman felt a tinge of disappointment that his old childhood friend, Omar had become a traitor to his people, but perhaps Allah would heap more rewards in Paradise on him when he killed Omar. He knew from his superior, Khadduri, that Omar's family was in hiding somewhere in America.

He knew they had spotted him with the woman they had burdened him with. Fatima al-Zaidi had even entered the bathroom at the restaurant with her. The woman had been secretive from the beginning and her Arabic had a Syrian sound to it. She insisted on being called Anna and was fluent in English as well.

The explosives Khadduri was sending would arrive today on a private yacht from Lebanon and the *Sophia* would cease to exist along with the three infidels aboard. With the explosives would come two specialists, unknown to the targets, who would set the charges that would be detonated by a cell phone from a safe distance.

This reporter Adams had caused problems since his arrival from America in May and his unusual run of luck would be ended forever. In more favorable circumstances, he would take more time to dispose of such an infidel, but now time was of the great importance and he would be paid two million dollars for Adams and the woman's deaths.

While the specialists were planting the explosives, he and Anna would dispose of the men that had killed Khadduri's nephew Hassim and the other three.

Chapter 16

The night passed in a moment of time, Nate was awakened at 8:00 a.m. by the ringing of the phone. Refreshed, he hopped out of bed only to find that Jenny had beaten him to it. The rich smell of newly made gourmet coffee wafted from the kitchen along with the smell of breakfast being made. Jenny could have easily called and had breakfast delivered to the room, but she was an early riser with plenty of energy to burn and she loved to cook and Nate loved to eat.

Nate dined on the scrumptious breakfast, savoring each bite. Breakfast was his best meal. It started his day and he would use the time to map out the details of his plan of action. He shut out everything around him as the sun rose in the Mediterranean sky.

The sun was a giant yellow orb in the clear blue sky of early morning and was already casting its warmth on early birds walking the beach. In mid-June, the sun was already up at 6:00 a.m. and by eight, it had shaken the haze of early morning dew.

"After the incident with the car bomb in Zurich, we should check the *Sophia* before we take it out," Omar speculated.

"Yeah, you're right Omar, I wouldn't try to start the engine without thoroughly checking it out," Nate said, as his mind raced back to the day Abbey had become an innocent victim in a game she didn't understand, like so many others in Rome.

The space where the *Sophia* was docked was alive with foot traffic. Nate was wary while walking toward her as she rocked gently following the gentle waves as they came into shore.

Seagulls floated on the gentle breeze, their keen eyes constantly searching for any morsel that might be offered or escape the attention of its owner. They darted anxiously, floating on the breeze, playing the consummate role of well-trained food thieves, their eyes laughing as they gulped down tidbits cast by passing tourists.

After a thorough search of every nook and cranny on the boat that might contain an explosive device, they found no indication she had been tampered with and cautiously started *Sophia*'s engines.

Nate felt the craft's engine throb to life as he turned the key. The *Sophia* pulsed with power as he backed her out of her berth. "She was truly fulfilling her destiny only when she was in open water with a crew that loved the ocean," Nate thought.

⋏

Abud Abdul Raman surveyed the marina through binoculars aboard a smaller cabin cruiser he had leased. He watched as the *Sophia* backed out of her slip, turned and headed for the open water of the bay. He secretly wished that Khadduri had been able to provide the explosives and experts earlier.

Anna took the binoculars as Nate backed the boat and followed their craft with her eyes at a distance. She could see the black hair of the woman Fatima who had followed her into the bathroom of the restaurant. She handled herself well and Anna had a guarded respect for her. The other one she would relish killing. Omar al-Douri had betrayed his country and Allah, and deserved to die slowly.

She didn't care for working with Raman, but she was far too professional to register any indication of her displeasure with Khadduri's decision. Part of her training had been in the West, where women could rise to virtually any position. With her people, she would gain some respect, but would always be considered the chattel of the man she would eventually marry. This left a bad taste in Anna's mouth. She had been born into a rigidly traditional culture, in which she could not foresee any progressive change for women ever happening.

Randy and his three men rented a twenty-eight foot cabin cruiser of their own and followed behind Raman's craft at a distance. His three men, Mike, Seth and Jim were below deck checking the readiness of the weapons. They carried the Israeli made Uzis because of their compact size and dependability.

"Hey Randy, let's take these two out as soon as they get into open water," Seth said excitedly. Randy said nothing, but instead kept his eyes focused on their target. Randy was a well-considered leader and he would wait until he knew that he had the advantage and the best chance of success.

"We'll get our chance at these clowns. For now, just be patient," Randy finally replied. Mark was quiet, but went about checking each weapon methodically not missing even the tiniest detail.

When he finished, he sat back and lit a cigarette, drawing in smoothly and easily shutting his eyes, concentrating on the task ahead. He would not underestimate these two adversaries in the boat ahead. He knew the woman was dangerous, even more so if underestimated. He would take her out first.

Nate gave the *Sophia* a little more throttle as they started to get past the traffic in the marina and into open water and asked Omar to take the helm for a while. "Thought you would never ask," he replied, smiling at the opportunity to operate the craft. "It's a sweet little cabin cruiser," he said, with a wide-open grin.

Nate looked at Jenny while she removed the AK-74 assault weapons from a blue carry-on bag. He stared at them in sheer awe. "Where the hell did you find those," he blurted, while she continued unfazed by his tone.

She handled the weapons as if she had been using them all her life. Her actions were quick, smooth and sure. Beads of sweat broke out on her brow as she worked, checking the weapons.

"C'mon over here, Nate and I'll show you how they operate. I'm tired of being outgunned by these maniacs," she said angrily. Nate took the one she had just finished checking. "It feels surprisingly light," he thought. "No wonder the terrorists preferred it to the more bulky AK-47."

"We picked them up in that small Arab shop when we arrived at the island," she said nonchalantly. "They are incredibly easy to use and deadly. That's why terrorists like them so much. The price was reasonable and no questions were asked."

The most profitable criminal activities in the world were black market arms dealing, illegal drugs and human trafficking in that order. Nobody seemed to care much about either one unless they were victims of their violence.

"The world had changed, and in a global setting, there were more than enough clientele for arms, narcotics or slaves," Nate thought.

As soon as Omar cleared the remaining marina traffic, he turned to port, heading east about five miles distant from the coast. The day was sunny and from this distance, they could make out the beautiful inner terrain of the island, including its rocky mountainous interior.

Capri seemed to plunge from the sea like a monstrous rock that refused to stay submerged, demanding life. High cliffs that disappeared into the sea appeared between the sparse beautiful beaches.

"Somebody's following us at about two kilometers back," said Omar, still looking through his binoculars. Nate grabbed his binoculars lying on the seat and hastily scrutinized the craft following to see if it was just coincidence.

His eyes followed the craft. The man at the helm had on a white Panama Jack hat and sunglasses. From this distance, it was hard to make certain of his height but he appeared to be a big man, in good shape. He kept his eyes trained on the helm, when a woman with the jet-black hair of the Persian princess joined him. There was no mistaking the pair at this point. This was no coincidence. They were being followed.

Nate watched as the woman picked up a pair of binoculars and trained them on the *Sophia*. He knew that she had spotted them. Within seconds of being discovered, Abdul Raman and the woman turned their boat sharply and headed back to the marina to await a better opportunity where the advantage would be more favorable to them.

After another couple of miles, they stopped dead in the water to eat lunch and have a beer. While the *Sophia* lay drifted slightly, another boat came into view from the direction of the marina. The blue cabin cruiser appeared to be the same size as Raman's boat, but four men were arrayed at different positions. Nate studied the craft intensely for about two minutes when he recognized Randy's tourist disguise and let out a chuckle. "I knew they wouldn't be far behind," he said.

"Randy's right on time," Nate chortled, as Jenny gulped down a bite of a tuna sandwich, washing it down with a healthy gulp of beer. "Damn, this will be a day we can probably just relax a little." Omar piped in.

Nate thought about it. "Christina had put the *Sophia* on an open account with Global. Hell, he hadn't sent her a thing for a while," he thought. Global had the breaking news on the biggest story of the century and advertising sales were skyrocketing, so he wasn't feeling that guilty.

They pulled up beside the *Sophia* with the engine idling. Randy was smiling and it was good to see him and his men relaxing.

"Hey, Nate," Randy said, his face already getting a little sun burnt from the intense Mediterranean sun. "We followed you when we saw this guy's boat following you. Hope you don't mind." he said, with his face already taking on a wind burnt appearance.

No, he didn't mind and these guys looked like they needed a break. They had saved Nate's bacon, at the Amalfi Coast and he would not forget it. It's been good to take a day off and relax. No one knew when the next time such a day would present itself and they would take advantage of it.

"Raman wasn't stupid, he knew when the time wasn't right," Nate thought. The SOB would probably be a formidable opponent, unlike the others they had sent. Al-Qaeda had brought out the big guns.

"They passed us on the way back to the marina," Randy said, as he gulped the fresh cold beer they had passed him. "Damn! It's hot out here," he gasped, as he finished swallowing nearly the whole bottle. His men drained their beer and Nate promptly handed them another.

They passed over some lunch and a twelve pack of cold beer to Randy and his team. "Thanks," a tall thin six-footer with sandy blonde hair said, as he popped a cold one open.

"We're going to keep an eye on the *Sophia*, Nate. I figure that this guy Raman has reinforcements on the way," Randy speculated. "One thing we know for sure about Al-Qaeda is, that they are good with explosives."

"Thanks Randy, we all appreciate what you and your men are doing for us," Nate replied. "We have to get a line on their next move and if we're lucky where the nukes are located. Washington has decided that Italy has enough to deal with now and should be kept out of the loop on this one. If we capture these guys alive, we'll hand them over to Italian authorities for prosecution. They may not even survive to get to trial"

"That will give them some consolation," Nate thought. The Italians had taken the brunt of what the terrorists had to dish out and Nate felt a little guilty that he and Jenny hadn't been able to prevent the catastrophe. They had felt fortunate to get out with their own lives.

Raman and Anna knew they were outgunned and there was nothing more to be gained today when they turned the boat and headed back to Grande Marina. "It might be best to attack them on land," he thought. He knew they would be on guard now and would prepare themselves.

He had spoken to Khadduri and apprized him of the situation and the extra force of highly trained men that he had spotted. "Stay in place and keep low," Khadduri told him.

'Six men are on their way as we speak," he added. The two explosive experts and four more battle-hardened men would be arriving tomorrow evening.

Anna said nothing as she thought through the mounting pressure. The expression on her face revealed nothing of her thoughts. "She was trained and battle hardened," he thought, a little saddened by her cool detachment. He was from the old school where women did not take on these new roles in society. Western ways had already bled into his traditional society and he bitterly resented it.

Khadduri had told him, the team would come with explosives, but they would be delivering another one of the remaining nuclear bombs in a large aluminum colored suitcase. He would take possession of the precious weapon and guard it with his life. The half-breed Hammel was to know nothing of its arrival.

The target for the nuclear device would only be revealed to Raman when Adams and the woman going by the name of Jenny were eliminated.

Abdul Raman smiled. He had arranged for another boat with four men to meet them east of the marina at ten o'clock. He would leave early the next morning before the enemy came to the marina and force them to follow. They would have the tactical advantage.

⚔

Randy and his team decided to take the rest of the day on the water while keeping the *Sophia* within their sight and reach. Nate knew that they were the bait on the hook that kept these terrorists occupied and he would troll for all he was worth to intercept the next nuclear weapon. Randy was a good man. They would use the terrorist's hatred for Nate, Jenny, and Omar to draw them in and defeat them.

Nate's role for Global had become clouded and entangled in his mind with the added impetus to stop these maniacs from taking Europe and transforming it into a caliphate. The nuclear explosion in Rome had shocked him into the reality that this was more than a story. There were human beings and human lives being snuffed out by the hatred of a false ideology.

Nate's unclear role didn't seem to upset Christine, who was enjoying being a celebrity as Global's owner and after all, Nate worked for her. She was young, talented, and attractive and Zurich's latest hero.

In a time of crisis, people needed their heroes. It made them feel secure in situations they could not control. The magazine's popularity was skyrocketing and there wasn't enough space in the magazine to fill the demand for advertising.

"Nate, you're burning up. Here, put some sunscreen on," Jenny said, with a strange wifely look on her face.

Nate looked at his arms and legs. She was right. If he didn't put sunscreen on soon he would begin to resemble a freshly cooked lobster in another half hour.

Jenny left to get him another beer as he began to bathe himself in sunscreen. He heard metal noises and sounds coming from the aft area of the boat and looked in the direction of the noise, spotting Omar familiarizing himself with the AK-74 underfolders they had purchased on the black market. He caught the glint of new gunmetal as the bright sun reflected off the new firearm, alluding to its deadly presence.

Back at the piazetta, they stopped at one of the many eateries on the strip for a snack and something to drink. The sun had exhausted their energy and they were glad to be back at their temporary home away from home.

Nate's phone rang. "Hey Randy, what's up," he said, looking at the number on his display screen. "Nate, a forty-foot cabin cruiser just pulled up at the marina with six Arabs aboard. They were met by Raman and the woman," he replied, not wasting any time."

"I think the party is about to begin," Nate said, a bit sardonically and a little relieved. He had begun to feel like a tightly stretched rubber band needing to be released.

"Yeah, I guess that's one way of putting it. These guys are dangerous Nate," Randy said. "Yeah, I've come to realize that," Nate answered. The Roman Tragedy made the entire world realize that this was not a game.

"It's about time the world came to their collective senses," Nate thought.

"What was that all about," Jenny asked.

"We've got company. Another six Arabs pulled up to the marina in a large boat and met with our friend Raman," Nate told her, trying his best to sound lighthearted about it.

Jenny nodded but didn't reply. She was deep in her own thoughts and knew exactly just how dangerous this situation had become.

Morning came early in June and they were up at the crack of dawn, ready for anything the day would bring. The usual cheerful banter was replaced with the calm seriousness of the moment. Nate thought about the serious cheerfulness that permeated the air and knew they would be up to the task, thanks to Randy and his team of professionals. Every person on the team had taken stock of the situation and accepted all consequences that they would face in the event of failure – and failure was not an option.

Jenny used her time to clean her weapon, while Omar called his wife and children to assure them he was fine. Nate called Christine and checked in. This would be a busy day and he knew it.

Randy had called during the early morning. He had posted a guard at a distance, watching the terrorist's boat through binoculars. There had been activity the whole night and they knew that that they were facing at least eight heavily armed and well-trained guerilla fighters. Randy and Nate both realized that the large cabin cruiser was probably well stocked with weapons.

The three of them met Randy's team at the dock. All four of Randy's team were dressed in battle fatigues and looked like they could chew the heart out of a grizzly bear. "Oo-rah! ... Let's kick some terrorist ass," said the tall lanky one with the sandy blonde hair, who Nate had found out was Seth. Seth had energy to go along with the personality and the makings of a natural leader among the enlisted men. He exuded that energy and the men around him soaked it in like sponges.

"You guys are as ready as you will ever be," Nate told Randy. "This is the real thing, Nate." I noticed that you're one weapon short. Don't go into this with just a handgun," he said, handing Nate a polyester blue zip-up bag. He grabbed it and it was unexpectedly heavy. Nate looked at him quizzically.

"An AK-74 underfolder with extra clips," he said, smiling. "The terrorists aren't the only ones that can get their hands on them. Familiarize yourself with its operation."

"Did you notify the Italian authorities," Nate asked.

"No. Headquarters told us this was our operation and since you would only get in the way if you weren't made part of it, to make you three part of the team, today only," he emphasized.

Nate glanced in amazement at the empty berth at the dock that had held the terrorist's boat. "They left early according to the boat owner docked next to them," Randy said, as he came up behind Nate, putting his hand on his shoulder. "They carried supplies and plenty of water on board and headed east, the way they went yesterday."

Nate walked with Randy to the team's boat. Below in the cabin, he watched as Seth unpacked four rocket-propelled grenades. The skill with which he handled his weapons would make anyone hesitant to go up against him. This man was not a novice by any means. His hands moved over the weapons with the accustomed familiarity of a professional.

Seth sat with the others to apply camouflage grease paint to their faces while Nate watched. "It's just part of the hype to scare them," he said. It's not going to hide anything."

Nate remembered that the Celts did much the same thing in the Middle Ages, painting their faces blue and screaming their battle charge as they charged into the enemy ranks slaughtering them with broadswords and axes.

"Scary indeed," he thought. "If it caused these extremists to waver even a second in a crucial moment, they would be dead."

After fueling the boats and clearing the marina, they headed out of the small bay to find their prey. "It seemed great to be the hunter and not the hunted," he thought as the breeze whipped his hair and evaporated the perspiration already developing on his face. He couldn't believe it was ninety degrees already.

Their small task force headed west along the southern coast of the island in the direction they had taken yesterday. It was much muggier and as they moved further from the marina, Nate felt the excitement rising. The adrenalin pumped through his body, giving him new awareness and energy.

Humidity set in with the extreme heat. Omar took the helm and Nate decided to familiarize himself with his new toy, the AK-74 underfolder. He was amazed at its weight compared to an M-16 or an AK-47. He understood immediately after handling the weapon exactly why urban guerilla fighters would prefer it rather than the more traditional firearm.

Unexpectedly, the alarms went off in Nate's head. He wasn't sure what triggered it. He never was with his instinct, but it had never proved wrong.

He went topside to find Jenny. She saw him coming and said, "You've got that look again Nate. What's wrong?"

"I feel we're being led into a trap and it may be right around that outcropping of rocks a couple of miles up the coast," Nate told her.

He studied the outcropping of rocks that appeared to be harboring a small cove, raising his binoculars, he could discern the end of the white sand beach in the cove, but the deeper water on the blind side of the granite cliff was hidden from their view.

Jenny was already in communication with Randy on her cell phone. Nate watched as their boat slowed and began to stop, eventually lying dead in the water, with the engine idling. Being vigilant, Omar slowed and pulled up beside them.

He watched as Randy's crew prepared their weapons. Seth brought a rocket-propelled grenade to bear on the starboard side of their craft from a kneeling position.

Nate dove into the cabin grabbing his AK-74 underfolder, along with the extra clips Randy had given him. When he appeared on deck, Omar and Jenny were similarly armed.

Randy decided that the best tactic would be to head south in a wide arc and come in with their bows facing the beach on the other side of the hidden cove providing less of a target to their enemy.

Yes, the terrorists would be lying in wait. They had no other business in these waters and they would want the advantage of surprise. They had lost good men by underestimating Nate and he was sure that Raman would not make that mistake again.

"I'd lay odds he has gathered another boat from somewhere. Al-Qaeda must have supporters in the area just waiting to get their hands on any part of that two million dollar reward," Nate thought.

They completed their wide arc and were headed directly toward the gray mottled granite cliffs that hid the small cove that held a beautiful white sand beach. They would be in view momentarily, if Raman and his henchmen were lying in wait.

Nate watched as Omar and Jenny checked their weapons for the third time. The tension was as thick as a steel cable pulled taut and stretched to its limits before snapping.

Randy's team was already prepared and sat motionless in their places. The entire crew could feel the tension like static electricity in the air charging their bodies with an extra boost of adrenalin.

They slowly edged toward full view of the entire cove with Randy's boat in the lead. Suddenly, live fire sounded like the crack of lightning in the still morning air.

The sea danced to a staccato beat, as rounds hitting the water appeared to walk in a rhythmic cadence as the terrorists opened fire, seeking to find the correct range to the two vessels.

The heavy fifty-caliber machine gun aboard Randy's vessel returned fire on the terrorist's forty-two footer as it came into view. Steady fire from the three aboard the *Sophia* gave off the acrid stench of gunfire pervading the salty air, with the wind catching the smoke, filling their senses with the smell of battle.

The fifty caliber rounds reached the forty-two foot boat, hitting it just above the water line on the starboard aft side of the boat. The line of rounds advanced from the heavy gun advancing to the terrorists who were raking their boat with rounds from an AK-74. Two rounds caught the terrorist in the chest as if almost by accident and flung him from the boat with his weapon still spewing its death into the empty sky.

Two more cabin cruisers about the size of the *Sophia* came into view and opened fire with small arms. They returned fire vigorously.

It took only seconds for Nate to find the weapon's capability and become effective in the fight. He caught Seth out of the corner of his eye, as he balanced the grenade launcher on the railing, taking careful aim at the first of the two boats following the lead boat from behind the rocky coast.

His aim was true. The rocket propelled grenade struck the boat aft, exploding violently, throwing shredded fiberglass and wood into the air, killing the two men firing from that position. The aft end of the boat above the waterline disintegrated into pieces of flotsam, moving on the calm of the sea that had been ripped apart by men seeking to destroy one another.

Three other terrorists were on the boat but at the periphery of the explosion and were thrown to the deck, but otherwise appeared unharmed. The boat had caught fire and was beginning to sink while the remaining men donned life jackets and grabbed their weapons.

The gas tank burst, covering the water and the sea behind the stricken craft was ablaze, as the fuel from the ruptured tank spread into the water.

The craft was quickly sinking while men were jumping into the water wearing life jackets, still holding their weapons. "They were dangerous men indeed and they continued firing even from the water. They did not realize they were beaten and easy targets in the water. Nate watched as the strike team eliminated them one by one while they were firing from their disadvantaged positions.

Raman's boat backed off about a five hundred yards, as the element of surprise had been taken from him. He could smell disaster and was evaluating the situation as it changed moment by moment.

Raman watched as both of their vessels advanced, smiling and giving orders to his men. They started firing at Randy's craft with renewed vigor even at their range.

Nate saw one of the Special Forces team take a round to the chest and keep on firing after just a brief pause. He realized Randy's team was wearing body armor. They were giving chase to Raman's boat trying to get an accurate shot with their rocket-propelled grenades.

Nate saw the third terrorist vessel being cagey and circling their position to get a better advantage. The terrorist vessel was in a bad position with the cliffs and beach at their back with had no place to run if things didn't go their way.

"We can't give them the tactical advantage," Nate thought while opening fire ripping on their boat, hitting it amidships in an arcing pattern, using the bullet pattern to guide him. Everyone aboard was lying prone on the deck as his pattern of rounds flew above their heads tearing up the boat.

"These guys were recently acquired recruits and not the battle hardened men on Raman's boat," he thought.

These men were just out for the reward and didn't want anything to do with death, except for his, he reasoned. They were probably told that it would be easy money and a fine day of boating. Well, if they wanted Nate and Jenny's heads on a platter, it would cost them dearly. He had no intention of following John the Baptist's lead by having his head served up on a platter to Al-Qaeda.

Ominous clouds were now rising on the eastern horizon. Their bottoms were dark gray as if a Renaissance impressionist painter had brushed broad strokes of myriad shades of gray and black on them, while their high tops were lighter shades of grays, turning to a billowy white.

They were heavily laden with moisture and were fast approaching, but had not yet covered the sun. It was common in the summer for sudden storms to materialize from the sea's warm waters and now they approached with such ferocity that Nate knew the winds with this unexpected storm would change the sea from calmness to gale force winds in a matter of minutes.

A dark dot on the eastern horizon had taken the unmistakable shape of an American destroyer looming with its distinctive U.S. Navy gray outline. Nate watched as it approached their position with great speed moving ever closer to their miniature sea battle.

The terrorists had also spotted the American destroyer, called in by Randy and they were starting to maneuver for an escape route.

Randy moved in position to block any such move on Raman's part with his heavy mounted machine gun opening up on their boat, the rounds tearing into the bridge tearing and splintering both fiberglass and wood.

Omar guided the *Sophia* to block Raman's boat from escaping the now approaching destroyer that appeared to grow in size in each passing second.

Nate slipped his small digital camera back into his the pocket of his cargo shorts after taking multiple photos of everything in sight including the American destroyer and grabbed the underfolder to begin firing at the fleeing craft. He aimed directly at a swarthy-skinned man who was on the stern of the boat with Nate in his sights. He let loose with a burst and watched as the trail of bullets led to the terrorist, catching him in the midsection, casting him violently backwards and over the railing into the still calm sea.

The clouds had finally caught up with them. The billowy white tops of the clouds were now hidden, revealing only their dark stormy bottoms, turning the once calm sea into a grayish green. The temperature dropped at least ten degrees and the wind was whistling past them at thirty knots to make the ten-degree drop even more recognizable.

Both boats were desperately outmatched, but ran the gauntlet of fire that Nate and Randy's boats constantly streamed in their direction.

Nate concentrated his fire aft where the engine compartment was located; emptying two entire clips before any results were apparent. The boat slowed and eventually lay dead in the water, its engine spent.

Another terrorist, bleeding profusely from a wound to his right leg, knowing the end was near, laid down his weapon and raised his hands.

He was a small man of five-foot eight inches tall, thin, with black hair and almost Somali in his appearance. His eyes were wide with fear and he looked directly at Nate with a begging expression that had the look of defeat.

Nate watched in disgust as another terrorist came from behind him and fired a handgun into the back of his head. Blood spattered forward and the terrorist stood for a brief second before collapsing into a lifeless heap on the deck. He stood and screamed what only could have been obscenities at the inert form lying on the deck before casting him into the water.

Nate was very lucky. He had been given a special East German variant of the AK-74 with a precision Zeiss optical scope. He quickly switched to single shot mode, drew a bead on his target, fired and took out the "executioner" with a clean head shot.

The destroyer had slowed to a stop further off shore assuring it of not running aground. Three small Zodiac boats had been lowered full of armed marines, fully armed with everything they would need for enough of a show of force to halt all hostilities.

Raman knew this was his last chance to escape as the marines advanced toward them. Their camouflaged faces showed determination and resolve to their task. Their eyes were hard and these devil dogs were intent on fully accomplishing every detail of their mission. Raman and his crew were nearly completely boxed in and he gave full power to the forty-two foot pleasure craft to escape the gauntlet of approaching marines. The marines opened up on Raman's boat with M-16's, raking the boat without even issuing a warning shot across the bow.

The dark turbulent clouds of the storm threw sheets of rain from their midst along with forty-knot winds that drove the rain along a horizontal plane. The rain struck Nate's face and arms as if they were shots from a pellet gun. His hair plastered to his head and whipped around in his face as the gale force winds threatened to throw him off balance.

Raman's boat was slowing as she took on water taking on a deeper draft. The marines, with their weapons at the ready, waiting for the command to finish these maniacs off, circled the sinking craft.

Raman turned facing directly into the gale, rain pelting his face, defiantly swinging his AK-74 underfolder with a sweeping motion shooting at a boatload of marines. They responded with a fusillade of firepower, ripping through him like a welding torch through soft solder. He was dead before he fell to the deck.

"That maniac was defiant to the last," Nate said to Jenny. Her long black hair, whipped by the savage wind, was being thrown furiously to and fro with a steady stream of water dripping from her chin.

Yes, Jenny was happy to see Abdul Raman fall under U.S. Marine firepower. He had been a talented assassin and a leader for Al-Qaeda. He was a "shining example" to many young Arab boys aspiring to become Al-Qaeda soldiers. They would replace him and call him a martyr for the cause of Jihad. The world would be a little safer without him, at least for a little while.

With Raman gone, the spirits of the others evaporated into nothingness. The remaining men aboard threw their weapons to the deck and raised their hands.

"Cease fire," a young marine captain yelled. The sound of gunfire ended immediately leaving a vacuum along with the acrid smell of gunfire, rain and wind in the air of silence.

"We need to keep her afloat and search her," the young captain ordered. Five marines boarded her with the precision of men who had been highly trained. Their eyes were gleaming with deadly intent through the painted faces of war, giving no quarter.

The memories of the Twin Towers and more recently, the bombing of Rome were a stark reality in their minds as they looked for any sign of resistance.

Randy boarded the cabin cruiser along with the marine captain and five battle-hardened marines, while the *Sophia* pulled along the port side.

The marines rapidly frisked, shackled and loaded the four surviving Arab terrorists into Zodiac boats for transport to the destroyer by the time Nate and Jenny boarded the stricken craft.

"Look what we found hiding in a closet," one of the marines chortled, while dragging the Persian princess Anna by the arm. He beamed from ear to ear as if he'd been given the spoils of war. "Claims that her name is Anna and she just came along for the ride," he said, incredulously as Nate snapped photos.

She spotted Jenny and Nate and knew that her story would never hold water. Anna was disheveled, but no worse for the wear. She held her chin high and still wore a regal appearance in captivity.

Nate heard them tearing the boat up in their search. He knew then that they were looking for something specific. "They'd better be quick about whatever they were searching for, she's taking on water," Nate thought.

"I've found it," a marine yelled as he came bounding out of the cabin with a large aluminum case that looked like an odd suitcase in his hand that could only be a tactical nuclear weapon.

The young captain grabbed the radio two-way radio from a belt around his waist, "Captain, we've got the package and have it secured." "Have you opened it yet Captain Williams," he shot back. "If you haven't, I would suggest that you do. Don't worry, it won't go off, it hasn't been armed."

He was hesitant, but slowly released the catches that held the top in place and opened it. "Does anybody know what this should look like," he asked. He still looked like he was holding a live grenade and had pulled the pin out, while wondering in which direction to throw it.

"Yeah, that's what it looks like," Nate said, looking at the Russian markings on the controls. "You've got the nuke. Don't worry, the captain's right. It won't go off until it's armed."

"Captain Ripkin, we have confirmation on the device. It is a Soviet era tactical nuclear weapon," Williams said into the hand-held radio, after taking Nate's word for it.

"Good job, Captain. Once you have all prisoners secured and on their way, send the device back on a different boat with your best man guarding it. That means it will be on its way within five minutes Captain Williams, is that clear," commanded Captain Ripkin.

"Aye, aye sir… Will do," he replied, clicking the radio off and attaching it to his belt.

Coming from the west horizon were two Italian naval ships about the size of U.S. Coast Guard vessels and several smaller private pleasure craft following in their wake.

"Go now and get out of here. At this point, the higher ups will handle everything at the diplomatic level. When the Italians learn all the circumstances, they will be glad that there wasn't another nuclear explosion in their territory. Those damn reporters are another thing," Randy chuckled. "You'd better get going before they get here."

Rain fell steadily, but the wind had dropped off and sunlight peeked from between the clouds just to east of us. The freak storm had nearly run its course and was rapidly moving in an easterly direction.

Chapter 17

She lay in the sunlight like a panther basking in the noonday sun, her milk coffee skin glistening with beads of perspiration as the late morning rays caused the humidity to rise drenching the air with moisture. The midnight blackness of her hair shone with reflected light casting glints of deep purples that were only ephemerally discernible like chasing the fleeting ground shadow of a bird swiftly skirting overhead in the sun.

The silky light green bikini contrasted brightly against her latte colored skin, complimenting her Middle Eastern complexion. Jenny's mahogany almond shaped eyes hidden by deep grayish sunglasses revealed no trace of anyone being present. She was locked in her world, giving no indication of any other existence.

Nate approached stealthily silent from behind as not to disturb her peace. "Put some lotion on my back Nate," she asked, without registering any expression of his presence.

He pulled up a beach chair next to her prone tanning beach chair and picked up the tanning oil.

They were the only people on their end of the beach. She had chosen a solitary place away from the crowd and he was somehow pleased for this time alone with her. He had brought a cooler with a few cold dark lagers that she had developed a taste for and offered her one.

There was calmness and new resolve about her that drew Nate closer. Her chemistry became overpowering and he fought to keep his senses from reeling out of control. He touched her shoulder, feeling sparks run through his entire body, something he had never felt with any other woman.

She removed her sunglasses and looked at him through half closed eyes starting at his eyes and slowly running down his entire body. It gave him the pleasant but uneasy feeling of being closely examined with no detail excluded.

Saying nothing, she sat up on the beach chair, put her hand gently on the back of his head and pulled his head firmly toward hers. She moved forward kissing him with a burning passion he had never before felt.

When he felt the softness of her lips for the first time, emotion overcame his senses inflaming the desire within his loins with a passion he had never known. His mouth opened to her probing tongue and his hands sought her waist. The kiss went on forever, only ending when she broke free, gasping for breath.

"Still want that tanning lotion," he asked tauntingly.

"Only if you'll do my front, too," she taunted back. Nate rubbed her entire body with oil and put the container on the towel. "Aren't you going to do my breasts, too," she smiled. She reached around her back and pulled the tied string that held her ample breasts in place. They immediately burst free of their confinement as if expressing their desire for receiving their fair share of open sunlight.

His hand inched involuntarily forward until it had fully cupped her left breast, tweaking her turgid hard nipple with his fingertips. She let out a gasp and pulled his head toward her, giving him the most passionate kiss that he had ever received.

At that moment, no one else but them existed. They had sculpted their own private world in the universe with their consuming passion, to which public entry was strictly prohibited. He fought to maintain his composure, but felt like a giddy schoolboy. He fought to maintain control of his senses as her body chemistry slowly stripped away what was left.

"You would have never taken the initiative Nate," she cooed, softly in his ear. "I've seen how you look at me when you think I'm not watching."

Nate had to admit she was right. He was afraid to change their relationship from professional to personal. He had had strong feelings for her ever since the death of her fiancé and maybe even before that, though he did not want to admit it.

He looked around for a while and nobody had noticed. He liked that about Europe; it was a lover's paradise, where nobody noticed and couples were usually given privacy. The closest persons were fifty yards away -- a young couple too much in love to notice anything except each other.

Timing was always perfect for young lovers on Capri. Nate had to admit, the ambiance of the island was perfectly suited for the business and pleasure of love. He would remember this small piece of real estate with fond memories. They spent the rest of the day on their private spot on the beach, speaking about nothing and everything, while the sun journeyed on it slow arc across the light blue sky.

"Hi Christine, I'm e-mailing you about twenty photos of the encounter and a four thousand word feature story of the account on the south side of the Isle of Capri. I've got a couple of good photos of Captain Williams carrying the Nuke for delivery to the American destroyer," he said.

He clicked "Send" from his high-speed connection in the room. "You should be receiving just in time for this week's copy," he told her. "Thanks Nate, you're always right on time," she said, gratefully.

"I'm not trying to change the subject Christine, but it's nice down here and this one was worth some time off," he said, inquiringly. "If you didn't ask, I was going to force you to take at least ten days if you can stay still that long," she said

"Check your account. There is a nice bonus in there. I hope it covers a ten-day vacation. You've earned it and that goes for Jenny and Omar too," she said. "I just got your e-mail, Nate. Have a good vacation."

That's what he liked about Christine. She always was willing to share the wealth with healthy bonuses for those who she felt deserved them. Accordingly, she would be wildly successful in every venture she undertook.

"We're on vacation," he told Jenny. "Check your account. There is a nice bonus for you in there from Christine."

▲

Jim Hammel stared at the headlines: *America Saves Italy From Another Nuclear Explosion*. The photo on the front page showed a young marine captain holding an aluminum suitcase containing a tactical nuclear weapon and a sinking sensation came over him. The story made heroes of Nate Adams, Jenny Martinez and the American Navy.

He picked up a copy of the English version of *Global News Weekly*. Their pictures were everywhere. He had failed and he knew that Khadduri would not accept failure from him. He knew that he had been excluded from the attack on the two with the reward on their heads. He was out of favor and marked for extermination; of that fact he had no doubt. He had played the game and lost. There was a sinking feeling in the pit of his stomach that would not go away and for the first time in his life, a feeling of loneliness that was unrelenting.

This was the first time in his life that he experienced the complete fear of total emptiness and abandonment. He had burned his bridges at every crossing. Nobody trusted a traitor. He was fair game for anybody on either side of the coin and he knew it. Accordingly, he had signed his own death warrant upon changing allegiance.

He had three quarters of a million dollars in a numbered Swiss account that he could use to disappear in Central America, most likely Costa Rica. Just a flight tonight from Naples to Paris and he would be in Costa Rica by tomorrow night.

During his years with the CIA, he had obtained a genuine passport with the name of John M. Ledger along with a birth certificate and social security card. "It was easy when you knew the tricks of the trade," he thought. Although John M. Ledger had died five days after being born in 1975, a certificate of live birth existed as well as a social security number.

He knew he had nothing except money and he would have to be careful with that, perhaps enter into a venture that would yield an income, but he could never surface in America again.

They got back to Casa Morgano late in the afternoon after strolling slowly through the shops like tourists on vacation. Tourists and some locals who recognized them from pictures of them on television were after autographs or just wanted to say "hello" or "thank you", but nothing could ruin the moment and they took it in stride.

The two lovers ate pizza at an open-air café of the kind that were so popular in the Mediterranean, while Nate sipped a dry white wine, and Jenny preferred a sweeter red wine. Jenny reached under the table with her foot and grabbed his ankle with her toes.

"You're pretty dexterous with your feet," he joked, enjoying every moment with her.

"That's not all I'm dexterous with," she countered, looking directly into my eyes promising better things to come.

"We have Omar in the room," he warned her.

"Oh really, he can get his own room," she said. "Don't be so old fashioned, I'm not Abbey," she said. Her head came across the table, her lips almost touching his. He could feel the heat of her lips from this distance. It was a challenge and Nate wasn't used to being challenged by women.

He instinctively grabbed her head and kissed her with an overwhelming passion that he had never known. She gasped at the suddenness of his passion but didn't pull back.

Flashes from cameras filled the air. "The paparazzi must be on our heels. Shit," he exclaimed. "They'll make money on those photos."

"It the price of fame or notoriety," she joked back. Nate wasn't quite sure he was ready for that kind of fame or notoriety and just wanted to be alone with her and learn her secret desires. He really didn't want any interference, at least not just yet.

He didn't want anything to break the mood. The mystic magic of body chemistry coupled with the enchantment of Capri's ambiance, was doing double duty but flashes from the photo-hounds' cameras became insignificant. Nate was happier than he been in his life; a life that he now wanted to share with Jenny.

"It was inevitable, I guess," Omar said smiling. "You two have been working together for almost three months,"

"Nate, I've booked a flight back to the states tonight to spend some time with my family. The money from Christine will come in handy. I haven't been able to do the usual business and my income has stopped," he said, while packing his suitcase. Omar had been a friend he could talk to and there was no use of putting him in further danger. His place was back in Montana with his family.

"I'm happy for you Omar, but I'm sure we'll be seeing you in the near future," Nate said, giving his friend a bear hug.

Jenny gave him a hug, too. She and Omar had become fast friends and had shared much in the short time he was here. "Omar, I'll be praying for you and your family. Call me if anything happens with the cover that the CIA has provided," Nate told him.

With Omar gone, he knew it was still too much to hope for the privacy they both sought, but they could take the *Sophia* out to a private beach and spend time together just hanging out.

Nate sipped his favorite dry white wine while eating rock lobster with a side order of linguine smothered in a white lobster sauce. Just then, his cell phone rang.

"Hello Christine, we're on vacation, remember," he said, while still chewing on a piece of lobster he had just soaked in drawn butter.

"C'mon Nate," she chided. He could almost see the smile on her face from this distance. "We've decided to buy the *Sophia* from her owner. It was cheaper than paying what they wanted to repair the damage from all the bullet holes caused by your little sea battle."

"Before you return to Zurich, take the *Sophia* to the Ernesto's Boat repair shop in Naples," she told him.

"That's a nice surprise. It's a nice boat," he replied, before breaking the connection.

It had been so long since he had felt this kind of emotion and chemistry for a woman that the fear of doing or saying the wrong thing caused him to slow down and change his normal impulsive behavior.

He had learned not to lower his radar, as he was constantly vigilant and mindful that they were targets and had a price on their heads. They indeed had at least as many enemies as friends. He recalled what Randy had told him. "Remember it is the enemy you don't see that kills you."

The first week of their vacation burned away as quickly as a Kansas prairie wildfire in a drought. They took the

Sophia to the private beach beyond the plunging granite cliffs where the sea battle had taken place. The seclusion was complete as they lay in each other's arms not thinking of anything beyond the moment.

Chapter 18

Nightfall had just only obliterated the grayness of dusk when they retrieved Jenny's roadster for the journey to Zurich. The pair traveled north of Naples on Italy's west coast. The smooth engine of the high performance roadster purred as it sliced through the thin mountainous air, guiding them toward the alpine border with Switzerland.

They had taken the top down and the wind was cool and refreshing as it whipped Nate's hair wildly. Jenny's hair shone dark as obsidian as the light of the full moon glinted from it. She tossed her head teasing the strands from her face, as her eyes concentrated to negotiate the sharp curves in the road.

They were relaxed after ten days in Capri and felt the sudden release of pressure as they sped north. The dry coolness of the high-pressure area had settled over the region enhancing the brightness of the stars. They shown like diamonds on a blackboard, begging not to be disturbed, as the pair sped along the deserted highway,

His mind traveled back to reality for a moment. It was then that he realized that this twisted terrorism scenario must be dealt with at its source. They would travel to Saudi Arabia to find and root out the insidious head of the snake of terrorism.

He knew in the depths of his soul that this snake had many heads like a Hydra. Also like a Phoenix, when one was destroyed it would not die, but instead rise once again from the temporary death out of its own ashes and lash out once again at its enemies until it could be sure it had won. He knew the fight between the extreme wing of Islam, moderate Islam and the rest of humanity would be a difficult and never-ending bloody cataclysmic clash of two irreconcilable cultures.

Nate did not know what the "final solution" would be. Perhaps there could never be an acceptable solution. He just did not have the answer and maybe there just wasn't a permanent answer. The clash between the two ideologies and cultures had spanned millennia and had come no closer to a workable solution. Even the word "assassin" had old Arabic origins.

Terrorism, as an insidious mechanism used to control people rather than lead them, had its ancient roots of success and extolled nothing more than a horizon of fear and that fear was the root of all evil.

⋏

The office was ablaze with the chatter of their much reported sea battle and the captured nuke. Nate and Jenny entered the office just as the phone on his desk started ringing. He picked up to a voice identifying himself as an American Associated Press reporter, requesting an interview. "Bring Jenny," he said. Nate chuckled as he agreed to meet him in the café at five o'clock.

"She was the one who was photogenic and sold copy," he thought, sardonically.

His cell phone rang. "Hello Omar," he said. They talked for a half an hour while Nate revealed all his plans to tackle the problem at its heart, in Riyadh. "I want the first shot at Khadduri," Omar told him. "My family will never be safe while Al-Qaeda is in business."

"None of us will ever be safe regardless," he thought. The world had become a much more dangerous place because of Al-Qaeda -- not that it was much safer before. Terrorism would always be around now that Al-Qaeda had proven how easy it was to attack without even being a sovereign entity, with formal power to declare war.

Christine happened by his desk as he was catching up with Omar. "When were you going to include me in your grand plans," she asked curiously and exclaimed, sounding a little miffed.

"I was going to tell you at lunch. Are you ready to eat," he replied, looking nonplussed at her attempted chastisement.

The café at the Swissotel was crowded, but they found a table in the back corner facing the door. Christine looked a little worried.

"Nate, there's a difference between snake hunting and jumping directly in the snake pit, you know," she almost whispered. He could appreciate the analogy, but according to Omar, they could look forward to receiving a large amount of support from the Saudi government.

Christine stared at the stark steadfast blueness of his eyes and realized that the final decisions had already been made. She knew of Nate's resolve when she was a young girl flitting around his desk, wanting to know more about the business of journalism.

"We'll be in town another five days or so. Omar is going to put together details for our entry into Riyadh and we plan to work heavily with the Saudi government on this one," he said. "You can keep him on the payroll as a consultant, can't you Christine," Nate asked. She said nothing and just nodded her assent.

"Let's eat and I'll fill you in on details as we put them together," Nate told her amicably, obviously wanting to drop the subject for now.

The afternoon was sunny with a few high feathery clouds whisking around in the stratosphere. The air in Zurich was a refreshing difference from the humidity of the Mediterranean and he had decided to get in touch with Randy to arrange a covert entry into Riyadh. "Randy could get the Americans involved again and they needed the firepower that he and his top-notch spec-ops team could provide," he thought.

Their table in the rear corner facing the entrance of the crowded café was tailor made for their purpose. He had learned to sit with his back to the wall with a trained eye on the entrance, especially here in Zurich.

"I can't complain about the news copy you've been providing and the photos are all exclusives beyond my expectations; and we've decided to move forward and publish the magazine twice weekly," she said.

He handed the waitress fifty Euros and thanked her as Christine prepared to leave. "Just stay alive," she said, not smiling. Nate could see that Christine was not pleased with this one decision.

Two days later, Nate and Jenny had taken all of their newly acquired AK-74's, cleaned and oiled them and prepared alternative documentation along with passports and visas for the three of them. Their reliable 9mm handguns were still their staple weapons and they always had counted on them in a pinch, as their recent tactical history repeatedly proved.

Omar would be returning to Zurich in three days and Jenny detailed their plans to Randy who had passed it on to his superiors for approval.

Randy returned his call and offered his help only if he and his team could participate in their bold plan. "You don't expect me and my team to let you three have all the fun and glory do you," he had quipped, and Nate had almost been able see his rugged broad smile even over the phone.

"We're closer than you think." said Randy. "We'll be there to pick you up in five days. Be prepared to leave Zurich at midnight."

Nate felt comfortable with the knowledge that they had the backing of the U.S. Government and would be transported via a military aircraft directly to King Khalid Airport in Riyadh. "A first class ride," he thought, "and we'll have no problem with transporting our weapons."

Randy informed them the Saudis were too happy to help as they were brought into the loop on this one. It was common knowledge in the intelligence community that Al-Qaeda wanted to eliminate the present monarchy and grab power.

They would be wearing the uniforms of army officers for this venture and would have the full support of both Saudi and American forces.

Nate spent the time with Jenny in the countryside around Zurich, taking in secluded places and dining on great food. Frederick had completely healed from his wound and often chided Nate about being a dangerous friend. His natural sense of humor filled the Bierhalle Kropf with his effervescent smile.

⁂

The C-130 left from Zurich at 1:30 a.m. on a covert flight plan that took it directly to Riyadh. Nate wore the uniform of an army major, while Jenny and Omar were both captains. He had no idea or clue of how army protocol operated, but was overjoyed that they were not wearing enlisted uniforms. This would preclude just anyone questioning them and asking for copies of their orders.

Randy settled in and remained silent for the ride over, occupying their time with personal concerns. Jenny's eyes caught his, their dark almond pools smiling a special message in the dimly lit interior of the cargo plane. She rose from her seat and walked back to the rear section of the hold motioning him with her eyes. He rose and followed, with little attempt at discretion

He walked back into the darkness that disappeared among stacked crates and supplies, losing her among the small corridors that the stacks had created. A hand reached from behind a stack of crates and pulled him neatly around and into her arms.

Her mouth was instantly on his, her tongue searching his mouth demanding attention. After a half of a minute, he broke free with a gasp. Just then, they hit a turbulence pocket and were driven into a sitting position on the floor by the crates. Her eyes smiled their mahogany sheen, laughing and dancing their invitation to him like a siren, beckoning him into her chambers. He felt powerless to resist her lustful invitation and gave in to all his innermost desires, his breath quickening and his heart racing. This woman was not only exciting, but had a mind of her own. She would not be refused, but then, why would he even want to refuse.

Nate felt alive and became lost in her excitement as their hands explored each other with an intensity he had never known before. Her breath, like a blowtorch on his neck, had an urgency that could not be ignored, as his hand dropped to the buckle of her army fatigues.

He reached for one of the packing blankets lying around in piles and rolled onto it as he fumbled with her army fatigues, his lips glued to hers. They were probably over Israel by then at thirty thousand feet and that would make them both members of "the mile-high club". They struggled to get their clothes off, during the continued turbulence. Her skin exuded a sensual sheen in the dim light as he finished removing her camouflage pants and panties. He kissed her breasts with the fervor of an adolescent on his first date as she arched her body inviting his ardent advances.

Jenny always knew she would have to be the aggressor in the sexual end of the relationship but she didn't mind. She knew that Nate was tightly wrapped, like a volcano ready to erupt. She encouraged him and returned his fervor with equal intensity, knowing that their first sexual encounter would be the start of a long romantic relationship that would bond them irrevocably to one another. She was right, Jenny was always right and she knew exactly what she wanted and went after it.

⊥

Jafar Khadduri gazed out of the window from an unobtrusive dwelling located approximately fifteen miles west of the last civilization that made Riyadh, Saudi Arabia the sprawling modern city it had become in the last twenty years.

He fumed at the loss of Anna and his nephew at the hands of this stinking infidel Nate Adams and the shameless traitor, Fatima al-Zaida. "I must put this blinding hatred aside and keep the mission first in my mind. Allah will avenge me," he thought. He knew those around him waited for his leadership. Now, he must provide Al-Qaeda with impregnable security for the two remaining former Soviet tactical nuclear devices, soon to be turned against the West as the bold new fiery Sword of Islam.

There was nothing out here far from the city and the fifteen miles that separated them might as well have been five hundred miles. The desert was hot and dry and far beyond the comfort of Riyadh water and even electricity was at a premium.

He had chosen this place because he could see his enemies coming from a great distance. In the silence that was the desert, he could hear helicopters or American fighter jets in time to seek safe shelter. There were only four small houses in this small un-named area and loyal Al-Qaeda fighters inhabited each dwelling.

He mentally noted the remaining two suitcase bombs as he grinned to himself, knowing that if they were well placed, they would be enough to strike a major wound "deep in the belly of the Infidel" for Allah and Islam. Jafar's jaw gaped in wonderment at how much destruction something so small could cause and still be carried in a suitcase. Word had purposely filtered down from his leadership that no further failures on his part would be tolerated.

He had always known of his expendability, but to be so brutally reminded had been a shock that he wasn't expecting. It had been like an arctic blast cutting through the desert heat, striking his face with an appalling frigid force. He didn't mind dying for Allah, but he would not be a hapless victim of failure, assassinated by his own people.

Bin Laden and his top leadership, were securely hidden in the Safēd Kōh, the White Mountains of eastern Afghanistan at Tora Bora near the Pakistan border, with local tribes that were fiercely loyal to him and his strict and narrow brand of Islam. Bin Laden had long ago delegated authority for almost all operations to qualified specialists like Khadurri, but he still wielded tremendous power and influence as the founding figurehead, for his role in starting the Jihad against America and the West.

He had only met Osama bin Laden one time. The Al-Qaeda leader had been severely injured when the Americans had invaded Afghanistan, using their giant bunker buster bombs on Al-Qaeda's caves and fortified places. Many seasoned and fierce fighters were killed, but bin Laden had survived to fight and lead. Jafar had seen the fierceness in his eyes when talking about the Americans and knew that Islam had found a true leader, a leader who would not buckle, but stay the course no matter what advanced weaponry the West had at its command.

He was comfortable in his position and wanted to strike the very heart of the infidel's power, but it had become increasingly difficult as America and Europe had become more organized and banded together to share intelligence. Their security had tightened and obtaining donations to carry on their struggle progressively became more difficult. He must become increasingly more inventive if he was to lead Al-Qaeda into the next phase of their operation.

The malignant tumor of extreme Jihadism subsequently metastasized into thousands of offshoots, each with its own name and leadership and the ideological virus even spread across the Internet, infecting youth and adults alike with a penchant for worldwide death and destruction.

The Al-Qaeda leadership had their eyes set on taking Southern Europe and forming a new Islamic Caliphate that would last forever. They had visions of solidifying their hold on the south of Europe, negating longstanding borders and surging forward like a flood into the rest of Europe.

Khadduri's intelligence network had lost track of Adams and the woman and, as far as he knew, al-Douri had returned to America into hiding with his family. He would deal with them later, after he put the two remaining nukes to good use.

Jafar didn't believe in luck and he left nothing to chance. He was a logical and pragmatic man and he believed in Allah and destiny as prophesized in the Holy Koran. He believed beyond any doubt that Islam would rule the world as immutable *mesh 'Allah*, the Will of God.

"If the infidels ever show up," he thought. "We will kill them once and for all. They would not escape one more time."

The door to the dwelling opened breaking the solitude of his thoughts. "Jafar, we have word from our military sources in the Royal Saudi Air Force that Adams, al-Douri and the woman will come to Riyadh in one of the American cargo planes," said Abdul.

Abdul was a young college educated man and had been a close personal assistant and lately a friend. His aquiline features appeared Caucasian, but his skin was the light brown of his people and his brown eyes burned fiercely with the struggle of Jihad. "They will arrive late tonight," he articulated.

He had chosen Abdul Hussein for precisely this reason. Abdul was detail minded and had contacts in every walk of life, including the Royal Family. He, like bin Laden, came from a well-respected family in the upper class of Riyadh, had grown up in wealth and privilege and formed well-rounded leadership abilities. Jafar had come to trust Abdul with all the inner workings of his tactical command.

Abdul had his doubts about Khadduri's leadership abilities and viewed failure as an unforgivable weakness. Even though he liked him, Abdul knew his time was limited. He knew what the nuclear weapons had cost Al-Qaeda in resources and two of them had been captured because of the intervention of Adams and the woman. These losses were unacceptable and wouldn't have occurred if it had been his command. Abdul did not want that command. His family was loyal to the Royal Family and he would do what his father wanted.

Abdul's loyalties did not lie solely with Al-Qaeda. He had his educational ties in the West and desired the material niceties that his well-placed family's money and western education could provide. The Royal Family was advised that Khadduri's intentions also included the overthrow of the Saudi Royal House.

⋏

The hot wind caught Nate's face as he stepped from the C-130 transport plane that had taken them from Zurich. Even at midnight, King Khalid Airport was lit up like a Christmas tree. It was unusual for the desert to be this hot at midnight. It was at least ninety degrees, with the wind having the effect of a blast furnace as it blew across the hot sand that it had already roasted in the scorching sunlight of day.

Nate remembered the Arizona Desert always cooled down at night, but that was a half a world away and this desert was nothing like the Northern Sonoran Desert of Arizona or the Mojave Desert of California and Arizona.

"It was good to be back," Nate thought, even though this was not a pleasure trip. The last time he had been here was many years ago to visit his friend Omar on the birth of his first child. It had been a joyous time, but now, as Omar and Jenny followed him, that initial feeling of joy was quickly transformed into stark realization the seriousness of the situation.

Jenny followed him in the night air and it felt sweet to her senses, "It's been too long," she thought, as she drew her first breath of desert air in three years. The air smelled sweet and dry to her senses and she felt the familiar grains of caramel colored desert sand in the wind racing from the desert across the runway carrying its cargo with it.

She stood beside Nate, her fingers intertwined with his, taking time to relish the warm desert night air as if it were precious nectar, the blood of many generations of desert dwellers running hotly in her veins. She was at home here in the arid lands of her ancestors and Nate wondered if he could ever become a full part of her life.

Nate glanced at her face, the color of the fine desert sand that rolled off the desert and on to the tarmac occupying every crevice that wasn't shielded from its insistent presence. Her head leaned back naturally and her eyes closed and relaxed as she breathed deeply. His hand still touching hers in a slight caressing touch, he wondered if the relationship would mature as he watched the gentle rising of her breasts with each breath she took

He could feel the intensity of her passion for him here in the arid land that her ancestors had occupied for millennia. For the first time in his life, Nate felt as if he was secure, whole and complete. She was at home in her mind and he felt the fierce bond she had with the land.

This was also home to Omar and he was wearing traditional Arabian robes in lieu of the U.S. Army Captain's desert tan battle dress uniform that Randy had given him. He looked regal, standing with his robes gently flowing in the wind.

Nate studied the area with Randy by his side. "We have a mole very close to Khadduri," Randy said with a Mona Lisa smile faintly etched on his lips. "We know where he is, but it will be difficult to get to him."

Nate mulled this new information a bit and knew why the Saudi and U.S. governments were being cautious.

"It figured," Nate thought. "Al-Qaeda hated the Royal Family of Saudi Arabia almost as much as they hated America. Both governments realized the grave danger of tactical nuclear weapons in the hands of terrorists."

Nate realized that the bigger picture involved more than he had initially considered. He looked at Randy's weather-beaten face and knew that he and his team were true professionals that gave willingly of themselves and asked nothing in return.

Two hundred yards distant, inside a hanger, Randy walked directly to a man dressed in a crisp white traditional Arabic *bhist*, a long flowing white garment that covers the entire body. Completing the ensemble was a *galupieh* held in place by an *aghal*, the double cord worn on top of the cloth headdress. Nate caught immediate recognition in Omar's eyes.

"He is a prince of the Royal Family," Omar whispered. "His position is equal to your Secretary of Defense."

Gesturing invitingly in our direction, the prince motioned them forward, smiling broadly, proffering his hand to Randy for the western custom of a handshake. "I am Prince Faisal, The Minister of Defense," he said. "I have heard much of your recent activities, Nate Adams."

He turned his attention to Jenny, "Miss al-Zaidi, it is not often that I am able to greet a woman warrior of such accomplishment. Your family must be very proud of you. If time permits, you must dine with me." If the prince noticed, there was no indication on his face about her lack of traditional dress concerning the covering of her head and face. Out of necessity, he had accepted her western style of dress. The prince's education and gentlemanly manners spoke volumes for his country.

Nate studied the prince as he was speaking and although they were perspiring heavily, there was not a drop of sweat on the prince's face. He was in his own element and had grown accustomed to the elements of the desert as well as its insistent heat.

"Mr. Adams," he said turning his attention to Nate. "We are honored to have a man such as you with us. Our government will of course extend you every courtesy. You have only to ask."

Faisal was a fine example of Saudi royalty. His eyes, the color of deep brown chocolate, spoke with the authority of command and his gestures indicated the familiarity of leadership. He spoke English with an easy American accent, giving the impression of the finest of American university educations.

The Defense Minister quickly changed to his native tongue when approaching Omar, who was attired similarly to the prince. Omar dropped to one knee but Faisal raised him to his feet with one easy motion, smiling as he shook his hand.

Two young men appeared at Nate's side, one speaking passable English. "I will guide you to your accommodations, Mr. Adams," he said pleasantly. Their jeep drove to the outskirts of Riyadh and onto a private road to a palatial structure that could have been the King's palace. Everywhere a person looked oozed opulence to the eye of the beholder. The structure indicated extreme wealth and power from its very appearance.

Their guides led them inside to the kitchen area. Nate had noticed that Jenny had not touched him since they had disembarked from the plane. He knew the rules of behavior were much different here and she did not want to offend their hosts.

Nate had never seen anything coming even close to this magnificence in America. The kitchen alone was larger than most affluent houses in America. A full liquor bar stocked with the finest selection from around the world adorned the room that appeared to be an extension of the kitchen. An assortment of choice cold beers, ales and lagers from around the world was displayed from a refrigerator with a clear glass door beside the liquor cabinet.

The two young men politely excused themselves and were gone before they could thank them for their kindness.

Jenny had already collapsed into the lushness of the couch with a cool bottle of Budweiser in her hand, not even waiting for their hosts to leave. The bottle was at full tilt in an attempt to drain as much as she could. She relaxed and set the half-empty container on the stand beside her.

Nate's thoughts drifted between contemplating the seriousness of a full-time relationship along with all the responsibilities and trying to keep it light. He knew that Jenny was not a part time girl and would not accept anything but the real thing. At that instant, his mind gave in to the idea that they would always be together and they would meet life head on and confront each situation as it challenged them. He knew she was the woman, who would be in his future.

He contemplated long about going into dangerous situations, with her safety being the utmost concern. It was the timeworn protective syndrome of man when it came to 'his' woman" he thought. "It's ridiculous," he almost said aloud. "She's more qualified in a firefight than I am."

He smiled to himself and decided that thinking about how to form a relationship with this woman was utterly ridiculous. She had already decided those fine points, much to his satisfaction.

Nate wasn't quite sure how deeply he felt, but he knew that he wanted her by his side and he had never felt this way about any other woman.

He glanced at her as she lay on the sofa. She had drifted into a deep sleep, feeling completely safe in her surroundings. Nate went into the kitchen to talk with Omar about the situation and Jafar Khadduri. He knew very little about this man, so intent on destroying the western way of life.

He had never known Omar to be a drinker, even in his college days at American University. Omar had always been the perfect example of self-control. Two beers were strictly his limit and even then, when others felt the need to let off some steam, he was always in control.

"I've met Khadduri before, perhaps two years ago," he finally broke the silence, as if he knew what Nate was thinking.

"I knew that he had something on the Royal Family. That is the reason they are backing the Americans in their drive to eliminate him. He is cagey and very smart, Nate. If we are to find him and secure the remaining nukes, we will need all the resources Randy's team can give us," Omar said.

Nate was silent, occasionally glancing at Omar while he took another drink of the Japanese Kirin beer that he had selected from the palatial reserves. Kirin is a fine Japanese beer that he had acquired a taste for while visiting Japan. It was twelve percent alcohol, much stronger than most beers in the world, but it had a distinct taste he had grown to savor. It wasn't often that he had been able to find this fine brew since leaving America.

"The Royal Family fears him," he went on from where he had stopped a minute before. "He knows that one of Al-Qaeda's goals is to topple the Saudi government and eliminate the Royal Family from the face of the earth. The Royal Family feels they are in a precarious position with many of the country's population secretly supporting Al-Qaeda, while some of them are even openly in collaboration. You must understand that the Saudi government may abandon us at any time without giving a reason, if it is expedient for them to do so," Omar concluded.

"I don't know if I would do anything differently if I were in their situation," Nate replied. "We should take advantage of Prince Faisal's hospitality and any assistance he is willing to provide, while it is there. We're going to get this guy, Omar and make him pay for the mass murder and destruction he is responsible for in Rome."

Nate knew that the responsibility for what had happened in Rome lay far above Khadduri's authority. He knew that the structure within Al-Qaeda would be replenished after each loss by new young energetic extremists seeking glory and paradise.

"The Saudi's were right to fear Al-Qaeda," Nate thought. They were walking a tightrope collaborating with America. Most of the radical Muslim world condemned them for allowing American troops on their soil and the first chance that they had to back Al-Qaeda's quest for power in Saudi Arabia, they would.

There was a knock at the door and Nate knew before he opened it that Randy would be standing on the other side. Randy had cleaned up and changed into the only set of civilian clothes he had with him.

"I just wanted to reduce my visibility at a target," he said, noticing the look in Nate's eyes.

Nate laughed, "Well Randy, you didn't succeed. You still have the U.S. military look written all over you."

His team was with him, all dressed in 'civvies' as they called them. "Come in. There are six bedrooms in this palace and I haven't even looked at half of the place," Nate told them. "The kitchen's that way and it's fully stocked with anything you can imagine."

His team scurried for the kitchen, opening cabinets and the refrigerator that revealed delicacies from around the world, while Randy stayed behind to talk. Nate could hear sounds of food being prepared and beers being opened. "Those boys could sure eat," he thought.

"Nate, we haven't been able to get in touch with our mole and command is getting a little nervous," Randy said.

⁂

Jafar Khadduri was fairly certain he had a mole in his organization. Information from a private informant in Riyadh, unknown to anyone but himself, indicated that the American and Saudi governments knew far too much about the activities he was planning. He agonized over whether to believe his source, but being an extremely cautious and suspicious man, he knew that he had trusted only one person with the details of his strategies.

He would not act without proof and his mind would not accept that Abdul Hussein was a mole. He had taken the young man into his confidence as he had never done with anyone else and he didn't want to believe that his judgment was that faulty. If there were a mole in his tight little group, there would be an attack within the next few days. He would assign a trusted loyal soldier to monitor Abdul's actions and he was certain that all suspicions would evaporate, like a dish of water in the dry desert heat.

He prepared to move his camp. The three trucks were removed from their camouflaged locations after dusk and loaded with everything they would need for desert existence. They would travel to a location about 110 kilometers to the south where water was available.

Everything was dependent on water in this harsh environment. He knew the Bedouin leader of the small group that inhabited this oasis far from nowhere. He could use his satellite uplink for communication with his American made Dell computer.

"The infidel Americans manufactured fine computers and lived in the lap of luxury while holding the Third World in poverty," he thought, cynically.

Jafar never stopped to think about how much work the American's did to build such a diverse country that exuded such wealth. He was trained to hate everything America stood for. To him, the West was the Great Satan. He would enter the lands called Rub al-Khali, the Quarter of Emptiness and the Americans would not follow. Only the Bedouins were hearty enough to survive in this desolate inhospitable forgotten place – or so he thought.

The land area south of Riyadh called Rub al-Khali or the Empty Quarter is an arid desert wasteland with hand dug water wells from which the Bedouins water their camel and goat herds as well as themselves to sustain life, in an extreme environment on the edge of human habitation.

It was the Empty Quarter to which the al-Saud family had fled in 189,1 when they were overthrown by the Rasheed dynasty and Khadduri was well aware that the House of Saud still had strong connections with the Murrah tribe who occupied these desolate deserts and ranges.

The Bedouin leader was an ancient Sheikh by the name of Muhammad who had welcomed Jafar and other Al-Qaeda soldiers seeking refuge before them.

Khadduri had brought fresh supplies and coffee as a gift with new cooking utensils, which brought smiles to the Sheikh's wives as they peered discretely from behind the veils that completely hid their faces.

Khadduri sat with Muhammad in the goatskin tent while the women served refreshments and as the Arab manner was, the main topic that interested both men would wait until after the traditional pleasantries were finished. Courtesy must be observed at all costs. The breaking of bread between honorable men was an ancient custom that gave protection to the guest and formed a strong bond of friendship.

It was impossible to tell what the Sheikh's age was, for he moved quickly and without effort. His gray hair and the lines on his deep brown weather-beaten face told, of both extreme age and wisdom. He silently sipped the mixture of coffee and ground cardamom seeds as he had done since he was a young man, with much the same relish. Coffee was a luxury he would not do without and proudly served it to his guests.

The Sheikh was silent and the minutes became tortured in Khadduri's mind when the ancient man suddenly spoke. "This infidel, he will follow you," he said, with a slight inflection that made it a question.

"First he must find me, my honored host," Khadduri replied politely. "I have not made it easy for him." The nagging suspicion that he had a mole in his organization had remained a constant sliver of fear in his heart. He must not fail.

Had the Sheikh known that Khadduri had plans for the annihilation of the House of Saud, Khaduri knew that his throat would have been slit in his sleep that very night. Muhammad had much respect for the King and had known Abdul Aziz when he himself was very young. Abdul Aziz had taken back his kingdom from the Rasheed family, but had kept strong ties with his friend Muhammad.

"You may come and go in my lands as you please," the old man said without adding conditions of any kind.

Khadduri was well aware that the situation could change at any time. He knew that the Sheikh's men would appear out of the desert and slay him and his men almost without a fight if the old man or his sons were to discover his intentions.

Abdul Hussein was frantic about the sudden move to the Empty Quarter and checked the signal on his cell phone prior to making an attempt to phone his contact. He knew that Jafar suspected him because that cursed little Syrian, Kamal had not let Abdul out of his sight in the last three days. Abdul had noticed that after dark the signal was much stronger on his cell phone.

Abdul knew about Rub al-Khali. His father had taken him to this place when he was a boy. He had explained to Abdul that this place was the honored hiding place while the House of Saud was in exile and that Abdul Aziz had risen from the Empty Quarter and carved out his new empire known as Saudi Arabia.

He stood quietly now and smelled the dryness of the desert as midnight came early with the temperature dropping and moisture forming on the rocks. His father had taught him much about the desert.

Abdul stepped from the bathroom into the moonless starlight, feeling better having called his government contact. He heard a slight movement of a sandal scraping slightly on the cool sand. Silently, a shape floated from the blackness of the desert. The curved knife shone briefly in the moonlight, as it was lifted upwards in the dim starlight before disappearing into Abdul's lower chest, piercing his heart. His blood spurted like Saudi oil from a newly discovered reserve. He slipped to the desert sand that he had been born upon, without a sound, dead before he lay still.

The silent figure clothed in a white robe removed his hand from Abdul's mouth, wiped the bloody blade on the victim's robe and slid into the desert night from whence he came. Not even a sound was left to betray the intruder's presence, only the still horizontal form of Abdul's lifeless body.

Khadduri had witnessed the assassination from behind the flap of his tent. The phone call had been inevitable and he was relieved that he had discovered the leak in his organization. "They will not find me again in this Quarter of Emptiness," he thought, gleefully.

Nate absorbed the opulent surroundings with the Olympic size swimming pool placed at the rear of the house surrounded with Mediterranean style tile and palm trees. The caretakers of this virtual palace told him that this estate was primarily used to quarter visiting heads of state. "The ultimate safe house," he thought.

Randy and his men had wasted no time heading to the pool after stowing their gear and arms in three of the bedrooms on the opposite end of the house. All rooms were adorned with an excess of porcelain tile floors and furnishings that Nate never knew existed. Sounds from the pool indicated that Randy and his team were making good use of it.

Nate, Jenny and Omar grabbed fresh towels and headed out to the pool area, excited for the time they would have with one another, but breathlessly awaiting the adventure ahead. They spread their towels on a couple of beach chairs by a grove of three palms while Jenny began oiling her arms and torso.

Nate grabbed the oil from her and gently began massaging the soft skin of her back working the coconut-flavored oil into her mocha colored skin. "My turn," she said, as she reached for the oil. Every caress of her hand flowed with sexual chemistry.

Nate's mind skirted back to last night's passion filled embraces as her hands spread the oil over his chest, causing the curly hair to reflect the sunlight from its oily coating. He glanced at her eyes, but her sunglasses hid any indication of what she was thinking. There was a secret side to her, hidden so deeply that it only occasionally betrayed the guise in her dark eyes.

Randy's looming shadow and booming voice interrupted the intensity of the moment and the focus of Nate's thoughts. "Party's nearly over," he said with a slight chuckle. "They've got confirmation on a location for Khadduri. We're to be packed and ready for an excursion into the Empty Quarter far to the south of here. They don't call it the Empty Quarter for nothing. Only a few Bedouins are brave enough to call this place home."

Randy called a briefing shortly after everybody at the pool had enough sun for one day. "C'mon," he called to his men. You'll get more than enough sun where we're going."

"Tonight, we will pack as a team and each person will carry what is necessary for the success of the mission. The Empty Quarter will require special preparations and I intend to return with all of you alive." Randy looked serious when he glanced in Nate's direction. Omar and Jenny were standing directly beside him. "I will be completely in command if you wish to come. Is that understood," he said, with a new appearance of authority in his voice.

Chapter 19

They ate dinner in a silence that was eventually broken by the sound of two large desert camouflage painted Saudi military trucks pulling up in the circular drive that adorned the front of the house. Both trucks were loaded with survival, communications and special gear that would support an extended stay under extreme conditions in the Empty Quarter.

The group drove south from Riyadh for two hours on a dirt trail that passed for a highway in this part of the world, when the lead truck stopped behind a small outcropping of rocks that didn't completely hide their small caravan.

Randy held a global positioning device in his hand, while consulting the sergeant in his command and pointing to a map.

"Ok, this is where the free ride ends. We will camp here for the night and wait for an elite Saudi special team to rendezvous with us at this location in the morning," Randy stated, before walking to the rear of one of the trucks to unload equipment.

"When we make camp, Randy will brief us with the most recent information about the terrorist's operational plans," Seth said, while helping them unload their gear. He was assigned to help "square the group away" and thoroughly enjoyed his new role.

"Hey Seth, they'll give sergeant stripes to anyone, won't they? Congratulations, you've earned them." Nate chuckled, while admiring the fresh chevrons proudly pinned on the lapels of his fatigues.

The team worked fast, erecting a tent-like structure that would provide shade in this deadly heat. Nate looked at the temperature. It was already a hundred and ten degrees and rising and the heat felt like walking into a slow roasting oven with no escape.

Randy's team worked in unison, each man aware of the other's actions, providing support and help to complete each task. Although this was the first time for any of them except Omar in the Empty Quarter, they worked as if they were veterans that had been here a lifetime.

The extremely dry and intense heat was like a malevolent and merciless siphon, constantly sucking the moisture from the team's skin cells, virtually evaporating the very last drams of their life giving fluids.

Nate had spent part of his young life growing up in the deserts of Arizona and New Mexico. He knew the danger of not finding shade in the day and traveling at night and that danger, was only amplified and intensified here in Rub al-Khali.

Nate now understood why the people of this region wore long flowing white cotton robes that fully covered their bodies. Omar had known since childhood the dangers of the Arabian sun and had wisely chosen to wear the traditional *bhist* complete with the cloth headdress secured by the traditional double chorded *aghal*. Nate glanced at Omar as he sipped from a canteen of water looking comfortable in the heat. "You should try one on sometime," Omar said to Nate, as if reading his mind. "I'm twenty degrees cooler."

"He looked more than comfortable," Nate thought, "He appeared at peace and even content at being in the desert sand once again. Omar had a large stake in this venture. He was a Saudi citizen who had gone into exile because of the terrorist threat to his family. With his family safely secreted in America on a ranch in remote Montana, he felt safe to pursue the maniacs that sought to destroy the world he knew and loved.

Omar had come to realize that when this venture was over, even if they were successful, his family could never again live in Saudi Arabia. He understood only too plainly that his actions against Al-Qaeda would never be forgotten. There would always be an ardent young Jihadist to seek him out for the greater glory of Allah.

With the camp erected and evening rations meted out, Nate was glad he had left his laptop and other extra provisions at the palace. He would be able to carry only enough rations, water, weapons and ammunition for himself.

He had left Christine a message on her voicemail, stating he would be out of contact for quite a while. He didn't provide many details and the message was short and to the point.

"This would be the scoop of the century," he thought. Even though he was a journalist, he could feel the subtle, but inevitable change that was slowly shaping him into more of a warrior. He knew that three months before this, his primary concern would be the story at all costs.

Now, he was part of a national security team that could make a critical difference if they were successful and he was rapidly learning the craft of war. He would do nothing to jeopardize the safety of the team or the mission. The world might become a safer place, at least for a short while, if they were to succeed.

Randy's men divided the night into three watches without much ado, while Jenny and Nate started learning much about military life.

"Get some sleep. The Saudis will be here in the morning to join forces and we'll be on foot, packing our supplies with us," Randy suggested.

Nate watched Randy's team, as each man prepared his weapons and supplies with precision and speed, helping one another. They constructed small tents to protect them from the temperature drop and dew that would inevitably form on everything left uncovered.

Nate felt the temperature drop dramatically during the night. Although he had experienced it in the Sonoran Desert of Southern Arizona, here in the Empty Quarter the change in temperatures between day and night were greatly amplified and experiencing it put a sense of supreme reality and urgency in their mission.

The night slipped away quickly and before the orange tinge of dawn, he heard Randy and his men, up and cooking breakfast over a small stove, surrounded on all four sides by shields so as not to give any enemy scanning the area an indication of their location.

Seth's voice was heard distinctly above the din. He was a natural leader and the men liked him. Nate understood why Randy had promoted Seth to sergeant. Seth had an understanding of leadership and confidence that seemed to seep from the pores of his soul, and his men knew it.

Although the false dawn had not yet painted its orange hues on the eastern horizon, the time was not far in coming. The expectancy of another scorching day on the desert hung over the air like a twenty pound weight holding down a stack of heavy papers, daring a strong breeze to carry them away. Nate could hear the men joke easily while eating their field rations and drinking coffee.

When Nate approached the three men, expectation of a new adventure filled the air heavily cloaked by the façade of laughter and familiarity. These men, despite their age were seasoned veterans of many similar and dangerous campaigns and they realized the dire importance of this mission. They would function like a well-tuned and oiled machine that had performed without fail on many occasions and would continue without a hitch. Yes, they were a team that depended on everyone's abilities and had long ago become brothers as warriors.

Omar sat among the team, looking comfortable and joining the conversation while joking easily with his new acquaintances. The men realized that Omar would be a valued member in these arid wastelands and his fluent Arabic would come in handy to the group's versatility and ultimate effectiveness.

"Even if I were the most inept of enemies, I could hear your revelry from ten clicks," Nate joked as he approached the gathering. "Hey Nate, Jenny still out," Seth retorted easily.

"Didn't have the heart to wake her," Nate replied as Seth handed him coffee in a metal field cup. The men liked Jenny and grew to respect her. They had watched her in action and heard of her exploits from various media sources. They knew she could handle herself, but they still felt that protectiveness that men had felt since time began and that instinct would not change.

"Well," Nate thought. "Women's rights may change, but to these men, although she was no less of a warrior, she was still a woman and must be protected." Hard line women's rights groups might not like it, but these were good men that had come from grass roots America and there was no such thing as "women's liberation" in their world.

None of these three young men were married. Mike and Jim were both in their early twenties, easygoing but with a rough edge to them. Their behavior had changed considerably since Jenny had joined the expedition. Although she was considered an integral part of the team, she was still a beautiful woman and they treated her as such. Their rough talk and horseplay subsided when she was nearby, as a sign of respect.

"This is some of the toughest terrain in the world, Nate," Seth said with a serious look. I just want you to know that we're happy to have you along."

"Thank you Seth, you couldn't have left me out if you had tried. There is far too much at stake here. These people are maniacs and aren't afraid to die. In the United States, they would be treated like common criminals. They refuse to fight like real men. They hide behind homicide bombing, killing women and children in the name of Allah, requesting seventy-two virgins as a reward upon their deaths."

"They believe that they have honor, but they don't know the definition of the word. No, Seth. A team of wild horses couldn't have drug me away from this one," Nate told him.

"Hey, got any of that coffee left and a little of whatever that is you guys are eating," Jenny asked, with a little laugh.

The group of men hadn't heard her come in and turned in surprise, "Nate's right, an enemy could have heard this party for over a mile in this desert," she laughed.

"We haven't yet found a word for whatever this brew is, but it does have caffeine in it," Seth replied, "and you're welcome to some."

"We've all come to the conclusion that they feed us this awful stuff to keep us from getting fat." Seth said. The lighthearted joke received roars of laughter from everybody, including Nate.

"The Saudis should be getting here in about three hours. Oranges and pinks of various shades began to break the eastern sky, revealing the low craggy rocky ranges to the south starting at the northern edge of the Empty Quarter. In the desert sun, nothing seemed to move except in the shade. The animals that had evolved here each had their niche in the ecosystem and had survived for eons on the meager sustenance that this terrain provided. Most of them were nocturnal, hiding from the deadly heat of the daytime sun.

Randy joined them, his face somber as he pulled up a small canvas chair. An air of quiet expectation filled the air like a heavy thundercloud waiting to release its moisture.

"We had a mole inside the terrorist camp," Randy began. "He hasn't called and his GPS tracking device is no longer operational. We must assume that his cover has been blown and he is no longer alive."

"Khadduri is now aware that his location has been compromised and will go deeper into the Empty Quarter. The Saudis are sending Bedouin trackers and camels to carry supplies." He said. He looked around for comment and received none. His men sat stone faced, knowing they would be facing a difficult challenge against a determined enemy but their demeanor was one of a look of expectancy and eagerness on their faces.

These terrorists would not hesitate to detonate one of the nukes to avoid capture and each man knew it. They had previously proven that fact to be accurate off the coast of Spain, earlier in the summer.

By noon, the camels and Bedouin with supplies arrived, followed by a Saudi Special Forces detachment in two jeeps. They appeared to be well trained and their commanding officer, a young Saudi captain, greeted Randy with a salute then a handshake.

The officer was a member of the Royal Family, possibly a second or third son of one of the King's many wives. He had a sense of intelligence and keen awareness that indicated his competence. The Saudi team moved much like Randy's men. They had trained together and acted as one unit for a long period of time.

The Bedouins and the camels in their charge took a separate place about a hundred and fifty feet east of the main campsite, next to a high escarpment of craggy rocks. They had their campsite arranged with speedy precision within a half an hour. The three camels that would carry the extra water and supplies that would keep them alive as they tracked the terrorists through Rub al-Khali were indeed ugly slobbering beasts, but well adapted to their task.

Omar gazed at the group of Bedouins for a time then strode over to the group and began talking to one of the older members. It was apparent that the two knew one another and they sat and spoke after formalities were finished.

They unscrewed the caps from plastic fifty-gallon drums in the Jeep and inserted a hose, siphoning the water into a large container on the ground to water the camels for their journey. Bedouins were well known for the expert care of their animals. These wanderers highly prized both their camels and goatherds; their relationship was virtually symbiotic. Without their animals, they would find life nearly impossible in Rub al-Khali. There were two drums in each Jeep and the camels came first, for they would carry spare water for the entire crew.

"Hey Jen," Nate yelled. He had almost forgotten that her name was Fatima. He realized he had become so familiar with calling her Jenny, that at times he had even shortened Jenny to the more familiar Jen. She smiled at Nate's familiarity and had grown to like the sound of it.

"It looks as if Omar had found a familiar friend," Nate told her as she approached.

"Yes, I watched their greeting and they have known one another for some time from the looks of it," she replied.

An hour later, Omar's hand touched Nate's shoulder and he jumped. "You're a little jumpy, aren't you Nate," he joked. "Abdul Ibn Muhammad, a friend of my father and also much beloved by the House of Saud is on this expedition and bears gifts to the Bedouin tribe led by Sheikh

Muhammad from the King along with a private communication. It is a great honor for him to carry these gifts and message from the King. My father and this man were great friends before his death and now he looks upon me, the eldest son with the same friendship." The customs were new to Nate, but he had watched the subtle nuances of greeting and respect.

Preparations were being made for departure to the Bedouin camp, which Omar informed us, was a two-day walk with the camels.

⋏

Rub al-Khali -- even the name in Arabic sounded desolate and foreboding. The last two years had seen an influx of activity in the area as international oil companies arrived with drilling equipment. Oil and gas deposits are abundant in the Empty Quarter and there was no lack of companies willing to pay for the drilling rights as the area's vast crude petroleum reserves were being developed and exploited.

The local Bedouin tribes were not quite ready for the amount of new activity and interest in their formerly worthless region. They had existed and even flourished for thousands of years with little or no interference from the outside. They practiced a unique mixture of Islam with a fair amount of tribal custom. The new intrusion into their traditional homelands would bring much unwelcome change to their lifestyle in the next few years.

The Empty Quarter takes in not only a large quantity of Saudi Arabia, but overlaps into Oman, Yemen and the United Arab Emirates and it occupies more than two hundred thousand square miles. All of these governments respect the Bedouin's rights to wander this area freely.

The Bedouin trackers would be earning their pay and more if they located Khadduri and his band. In all probability, Khadduri had flown the coop from his last location after killing their informant and it was anybody's guess as to where they had gone.

Their joint force headed south toward Sheikh Mohammad's camp and the only known water in the three-day march south in to the Empty Quarter. Three hours into the trek, he realized that this desert was nothing like the Sahara of North Africa. Although there was much sand, the area that they covered was composed mostly of graveled low-lying areas and small rocky hills with low escarpments, with drifting sand dunes that appeared to be endless.

Nate and Jenny cast off their army camouflage hats and borrowed traditional white cotton headscarves from Omar to stave off the heat. They were much better off for the trade. By late afternoon, the Bedouin trackers called a halt and made camp within a half- hour.

"Well Nate, what do you think," Omar asked him, as he checked his Army issued M-16 for sand and grit. "As long as we get these maniacs before they can destroy another city, I'll be happy," Nate replied. He knew there would be more than an even chance, when the terrorists realized that there was no escape, they would detonate the nuclear weapon, killing everybody. This was the chance they had to take.

Randy's men had much the same resolve, with looks of determination on their faces as they had trod forward through the desert sand and gravel, each man lost in his private thoughts. They knew what they had signed up for, and for Randy's battle-hardened team, it was just another stroll in the park.

Jenny opened a chair under the flap of their tent and was relaxing in the shade. They had covered twenty-five miles of rough terrain and he failed to see one living thing, excluding their caravan, which braved the extreme danger of the sun in the daytime.

Omar informed him that in the time after sunset, when the temperature dropped below the dew point, the sounds of abundant life would burst forth, as various creatures appeared from their secret places in search of whatever food and moisture was available.

They ate army rations while the Saudis and Bedouins prepared their own dinners. Omar looked at the MREs, and then made his way over to the Bedouin encampment, where he was graciously invited to dinner. Nate studied his friend from afar, noticing how his friend was indistinguishable from the wasteland nomads.

The sun had sunk from sight and the temperature immediately plummeted. Even the camels appeared more comfortable, as they milled on tethers attached to their feet. The mood in the camp became jovial and carefree as the temperature dropped.

Nate could smell the coffee brewed by the Bedouins and the inviting aroma of fresh cardamom they added wafted across the sand, adding to the ancient custom they commonly shared.

Nate took the cue from Omar about how much water to consume. He knew they would refresh their supplies at the Bedouin encampment, but after that, it would be only the Empty Quarter and water in any form would quickly become scarce.

The next morning they set out, each group bunched together, the Bedouin trackers taking the lead, followed by Randy's crew. The Saudi team chose to follow up in the rear.

By eleven o'clock, the scorching sun began to take its toll and only the Bedouins and camels kept up the pace that quickly became unbearable. They walked at a slower pace after that, simply because there was no shade in which to stop and rest.

Two days later, their Bedouin trackers followed by the camels, led the caravan into Sheikh Muhammad's encampment by the hand-dug waterhole, sometime in the late afternoon. He looked at his GPS display and it appeared that they had traveled sixty-three miles into the relentless heat of the desert and the terrain looked no different from when they had started.

It was a modest encampment, with all the essentials required to eke out a basic existence. The goatherd was penned close to the water source, while the activities of maintaining the camp broke its pace and children stopped playing to gawk at the newcomers with caution as they strode into the camp.

The Saudi troops and Bedouins were talking excitedly when Omar joined them in a serious discussion. Jenny hung back according to Arab custom, knowing that she would not be welcomed in the discussion. They were close enough to overhear the conversation and a look of consternation, quickly replaced by anger, masked her usually benevolent features. She listened intently to the words of the Bedouins as the anger on the faces slowly turned to sadness.

"Khadduri has murdered the Sheikh and his son and has gone south in an attempt to reach Yemen," she said. "Abdul Hussein, who was an informant for the Saudi government was discovered and murdered, but not before he talked with the Sheikh about Khadduri's plan to murder the entire House of Saud, using one of the two remaining tactical nuclear weapons. The word of this spread across the desert and Khadduri will find no safe haven. The Sheikh was much beloved," Jenny translated for him.

Nate felt sorry for the good people who had shown hospitality to Khadduri. It appeared that the Sheikh had confronted Khadduri and the terrorist had simply gunned them down like dogs. The Bedouins had scimitars in their hands, an ancient weapon they still carried to this day and they were in a furor. The young Saudi captain spoke to them at length and they started to calm a bit, but a terrible angry silence had replaced the joviality they had known since the beginning of the trip. Omar spoke to his father's long time friend, but the tones were hushed and the conversation serious.

The young Saudi captain was on his radio to his superiors, but had moved to a private area. He spoke for a few minutes then returned to Randy.

"This man is to be captured alive," he said. "Your government may take possession of the nuclear devices. We will handle Khadduri according to our custom."

Khadduri had a two-day head start, but he had left his trucks at the encampment, camouflaged under netting. The Saudi troop quickly disabled the trucks to prevent them from doubling back and leaving the Empty Quarter to attack Riyadh.

⋏

Morning came early in the camp and the Bedouins didn't wait as usual but instead set a new pace in their eagerness to wreak vengeance on Khadduri. The Saudi captain would not be able to save Khadduri from his fate if the Bedouins captured him and he knew it.

The trackers hadn't taken Khadduri's murderous actions personally. He was one of them, one who clung to the old ways and they had known a bond of kinship with him. Nate knew, by the punishing pace they had set, that Khadduri would die a slow and very painful death if the Bedouins were the first to reach him.

Abdul Ibn Mohammad had told Omar that Khadduri's death would be slow one, if they could wrest him from the control of the Saudi captain. Nate didn't care what happened to Khadduri, as long as they got our hands on those two nukes and he knew that Omar didn't care either way.

The Bedouins followed Khadduri's spoor with ease even joking and commenting on his stupidity, laughing amongst themselves. After three days, the trek became easier for Omar, Jenny and Nate as they watched the Bedouins and learned from them. Nate started from each rest period with renewed energy. He knew that Khadduri would not be taken easily and he started to form a plan in his mind to obtain the nukes before the maniac could detonate them.

Randy and his men had been bringing up the rear and quickly caught up with Nate. "The Saudis have control of this operation Nate," Randy said, as he reached Nate's side. "They have decided to keep it low key and have the joint allied team track Khadduri's band of terrorists. They don't want any prisoners, except Khadduri and we get to keep the nukes. That's the unofficial version. Something different will be entered in my report to Washington. The Saudis don't want to alarm the populace with a large operation using helicopters."

"That confirmed it," Nate thought. The Saudi government wanted to sweep this one under the rug and not alarm their citizens of the danger of their tenuous position as heads of state.

He was certain that Global's story, when this was over would be vigorously denied and it didn't matter. Governments always put their own spin on details and the Saudis were no exception.

It didn't make sense to Nate, but if that's the way the Saudis wanted it, he didn't object. "I've been given orders directly from Washington to play it their way and bring those two nukes home," Randy said.

Nate felt no misgivings about hunting down the murderous scum and killing them, as he would exterminate a pack of rabid dogs. His intuition told him that the spoor they had been following had come far too easily.

⸺ ▲ ⸺

Khadduri had suspected that Abdul Hussein had spoken to the Sheikh about their intentions against the monarchy when he ordered him killed. The killing of the old man and his son had been a mistake and a bad one. He knew every Bedouin in Rub al-Khali would desire the honor of making his death a slow and painful one. He ordered his men to carry all the water they could and the salted meats and rations would be their only fare.

He knew he must go south to Yemen, where he had supporters that would get him into Pakistan, for any chance of escape. The way north, west, and east would be far too dangerous because they would face certain death. "Yes," he thought, "the only way lay to the south where the people hated Americans as badly as he did.

He knew they couldn't carry enough water to gain their objective and within three days of forced march, they would have to find a well. He looked into the cloudless sky at midday and the sun was already taking its toll on some of his men. He had assigned two men, whose sole responsibility were the nuclear weapons they carried.

His party, himself included, numbered nineteen and their water was dwindling faster than expected.

Khadduri raised his binoculars toward the south and searched for a place to rest. He spotted a low escarpment rising from the sandy gravel of the plain that would afford some shade for the afternoon. After resting until dusk, he would start once again and cover more ground in the light of a nearly full moon. Stooping momentarily to look at his compass, he knew it was at least a thousand kilometers journey to Adan, a port on the southern tip of Yemen where he could find safe sanctuary. A rapidly dwindling water supply was the only limiting factor that could hinder him on the completion of his mission.

The shade of the low rocky overhang gave the refreshing shade they desperately needed. Khadduri pulled a map from its case and measured the distance to the small village of As Sulayyil that lay on the road halfway to the western coast of Saudi Arabia, bordering the Red Sea. The village was about a hundred and fifty kilometers distant and with luck, if they traveled at night, they would have enough water for the journey.

He took a compass reading and realized there would only be a slight adjustment in direction. He must stay off the road where they would almost certainly be captured immediately. The authorities would have notified local officials to be on the lookout for Khadduri and had probably offered a reward for his capture or death.

Dusk was yet another hour away and they would rest and conserve water. The men were sleeping because they knew their only chance of survival was to travel at night. They had already wasted too much water traveling in the scorching heat, a mistake they would not repeat.

Khadduri instructed his Egyptian assistant Hassid, who had replaced Abdul, to wake him the very moment the sun dipped below the horizon. He was exhausted and a few hours rest would rejuvenate him to travel in the refreshing coolness of the nocturnal desert.

The nearly full moon was high in the sky at midnight when Khadduri peered at the florescent dial of his watch. This was much better and by his estimate, they had already covered more than fifteen kilometers and would probably triple that number by sunrise. "They had consumed less than half the water of daytime travel," he thought satisfyingly. His men had even shared a few jokes and light banter while hiking and they knew that As Sulayyil was an obtainable goal.

"Allah is with us," Khadduri thought, as the light of false dawn broke over the wasteland. Two hundred meters ahead, he spotted an outcropping, which would provide plentiful shade and perhaps the opportunity he sought to even the odds between the Bedouins and troops he knew would be tracking him. He knew they would have camels and plenty of supplies and surely would be making much better time than his own men who were raised with the easy life of the city.

They stopped by the high escarpment that various wanderers over the centuries had worked to excavate a large cave that extended back more than thirty meters. He and his men quickly set up camp and he explained that they would wait in hiding for their pursuers and ambush them in a surprise attack. He knew the camels would be carrying much extra water and rations. He sent four men to erase any tracks or spoor that would reveal their direction or location.

"The time must come to use his men to eliminate some of his pursuers or he would never reach his goal with the nukes," he thought. He considered every one of his men expendable and his priority was the future use of these weapons for the "good of Islam".

Nate looked up, wiping the rivulets of sweat running from his eyes, as he studied the arid emptiness of the desert. The Bedouins had eased up a bit, bracing down a couple of notches from their original exhausting pace. Even the face of their leader showed the strain of their forced march as he looked back to gauge the amount of stress that the fast pace had been exerting on the team.

"They are saying that we are still eight to ten hours behind Khadduri," Omar said, breathing hard, but obviously relieved at the slackened pace.

"We are rapidly shortening the distance between us and them," Nate replied.

"Khadduri knew for a certainty he would be followed, yet has done nothing to cover their spoor. I have a bad feeling that we're being led into a trap, Omar."

"Yeah Nate, that thought occurred to me also," Omar said thoughtfully, keeping his eyes dead ahead, scanning for any possible site for an ambush. Abdul Ibn Muhammad suspects as much. He has said that the spoor of Khadduri has been much too easy to follow and he suspects a trap, also.

The group stopped and the Bedouins appeared to be having a conference. Omar and the Saudi captain stood listening intently while their leader pointed toward the southwest. Nate looked into the sky and watched as the first clouds that he had seen on this empty sand and gravel plain appeared. Although they were high cirrus clouds, they were a familiar and welcome sight in this arid and inhospitable land.

Omar's voice broke into his concentration. "Khadduri's group has taken a new direction to the southwest. They believe that he's heading toward the village of As Sulayyil, a little more than one hundred and seventy kilometers away, to refresh their water and supplies. The Bedouins think that he will then travel to Yemen's port of Adan where he has friends and contacts."

"They are probably correct, but if he suspects that he is being followed and he knows he can't beat the Bedouins to this village, then I smell a trap," Nate replied. Omar and Jenny had known Nate's intuition to be correct too many times to ignore this warning.

Abdul Ibn Muhammad decided to use this time for a break and had already erected an impromptu camp that would provide much needed shade.

"Khadduri is traveling at night, according to the Bedouins, to maximize his water, but we cannot do the same and read his spoor. It would be very easy for him to set a trap for us in the darkness," Omar stated.

The savory odor of coffee wafted through the still desert air, filling Jenny's nostrils with its rich flavor. One of the Bedouins came to Omar and spoke for a moment before returning to his group. "We have been invited for coffee. You won't want to miss this treat Nate," Omar told him.

Nate glanced at Jenny and she had already covered her face so that only her eyes and forehead were showing. She knew the traditional values these people shared and her modesty would go a long way in showing the proper respect they expected from an Arab woman.

They sat in silence sipping the coffee slightly spiced with cardamom. "A rare treat," Nate thought. Omar and Abdul Ibn Muhammad spoke with the familiarity of ancient friendship while they sipped their coffee.

"The men will travel for five hours more, until dusk after this rest. They also feel that Khadduri will lie in wait along the way, perhaps behind an outcropping of rocks they happen upon, but they say they are prepared and will wreak their revenge for the death of the Sheikh," Omar said.

Nate noticed that there was not an appearance of anticipation or fear on the faces of any of the Bedouins, only the firm resolve to avenge the death of their longtime friend. To them, Khadduri had no honor and was little more than a dog and they would show this in their actions when the time came.

Without a word, they broke camp and within ten minutes, they refilled their personal water supplies and were back to the same quick pace, only slightly adjusted to the southwest toward As Sulayyil. By dusk, they had covered forty kilometers and made camp.

A subtle and inexplicable transformation took place as they trekked in a southwesterly direction. The terrain changed and took on a rockier appearance with outcroppings and less sand and gravel plains, lending more opportunity for a guerilla style attack.

Jenny had started walking beside him on this new brisk pace and he watched the bounce in her step as she energetically smiled in his direction. Nate's mind traveled back to the special moments on the yacht with Jenny after the sea battle had ended south of Capri and wondered when it would ever be safe enough for them to relax again. The intense heat broke his concentration, bringing him back to the reality that was Rub al-Khali.

Nate reached into his backpack and retrieved his binoculars, scanning the trail ahead, keeping a special surveillance on any hiding places in the rocky outcrops. He would spot anything that the sun might reflect, like the face of a watch, binoculars or eyeglasses. He glanced at Randy's team and noticed that one of his men had already been assigned to the same task.

Dusk came at eight o'clock and the Bedouins called an abrupt halt. Omar was traveling with his Bedouin friend and would know their plans. They chose to set up camp near a small rock cliff that could easily be defended and they cooked from a small light smokeless stove. Within fifteen minutes, they had coffee brewing while Omar had a small amount of cardamom he had obtained from his friends and spiced each cup much to their delight.

The Saudi and American teams each offered a man on watch the entire night, switching shifts so there were two men constantly on watch. On a wild chance, Nate checked his cell phone for a signal while Jenny gave a slight chuckle. "I haven't seen a relay tower anywhere in this desert Nate," she laughed.

The terrain had changed dramatically, but with such slowness, that Nate had been unaware until the change became a blaring reality. They now were forced to walk around small outcroppings that were directly in their path, instead of the straight line they had traveled before.

Jenny sipped her coffee with deliberate slowness, succoring each sip, while Nate wondered why the West had not yet generally adopted the rich flavor of cardamom. America had taken the best foods and cuisine from all the peoples that had immigrated to its shores in the last two centuries and it was filled with ethnic restaurants of every kind.

Nate felt the first wisps of a cool breeze emanating from the cooling sands of the nocturnal desert. He removed the Arab traditional headdress he had donned and allowed the air to evaporate the perspiration of the day.

"My friend tells me we are about six hours behind, but there are many places to lay in wait for an opportunity to ambush. We will stay in the open tomorrow and keep well away from the rocky hills if we can. If we come within range of their weapons, they will kill the camels to slow us down," Omar said pensively.

"Is that coffee I smell," Randy asked with a cup in his hand. He sat and Jenny filled his cup with the steaming liquid. As Jenny reached to add their favorite spice, Randy covered the top, "No thanks, I take it straight and black. It's high test for me."

He sat for a few moments, savoring his precious brew. "I've been instructed by my superiors to radio in as soon as we find the terrorists," he said nonchalantly. "Frankly they don't trust the Saudis to hand over two suitcase nukes without a struggle. We figure a couple of Blackhawks will urge them to keep their word."

"Yeah, I guess that would do it," Nate speculated. "Don't worry about offending the Saudi's sense of honor, Randy. They are only our friends for convenience sake. If the situations in the Middle East were to change, they would side with whoever moved in to fill the vacuum."

Randy knew what Nate was saying was true, but at this instant in time they were allied with an elite Saudi strike team that had shown them every courtesy and he must support his superior's orders to the last detail.

Randy was a well-educated man with a degree in political science before he had decided to become an army officer. His father had not been happy with his decision, but Randy wanted to serve his country and make a difference. He was an only child and his father hoped he would enter politics and follow his footsteps. Randy did not find politics intriguing, but instead, rather boring and he really didn't have the patience to play the game. To him, everything was black and white and he didn't care for the endless rhetoric, duplicity and nuance that politics involved. He and his men were well suited to their chosen profession. Even though there was caution in their every move, Nate could not detect an iota of fear shown by any of these men.

Randy knew that he would be promoted to Major after the successful completion of this mission. Recovering that nuke off the coast of Capri had put him on the fast track to advancement in the eyes of his immediate superiors. "There's nothing like a little limelight to help the career a bit," he thought.

Nate looked at the M-16 he was issued and started checking it for the desert sand that inevitably would seep into any crevice left open or exposed. "Clean it very good," Randy advised. "They're better than they were in the sixties, but they still like to jam in the middle of a firefight. I heard that's the reason a lot of men in Vietnam took Russian AK-47's from the dead Vietcong to use," he said.

Dawn had not yet broken when Omar shook Nate. He had been awake about an hour and jammed a fresh cup of steaming coffee into Nate's hand while reminding him how fortunate he was to have an extra hour of sleep.

The three of them hurriedly packed up and loaded the extra supplies on the camels, refreshed the personal supplies they carried and each grabbed an extra canteen of water.

An eerie tension rang silently through the camp as everyone checked their weapons, including Jim who had been packing the team's only rocket propelled grenade launcher. "Everything looks great," he told Randy.

They struck out at a slower more cautious pace, keeping a sharp eye out for any flicker of reflected sunlight from the surrounding hills. "They have no pack animals and have only the water they were able to carry with them," Omar reminded them. "They must be near the end of their supply."

"The Bedouins have lost the spoor. There has been an apparent attempt by the terrorists to cover their spoor," Omar said. The entire force was on high alert, as expectation of an ambush increased tensions across the entire group. An eerie quiet ran though the men. Their nerves were pulled as tightly as the line on an eighty-pound recurve bow.

Randy was speaking quickly into the radio, obviously signaling for the launch of the two Blackhawks. His men took more widely dispersed positions to avoid the possibility of being taken out by a single rocket propelled grenade attack.

The ancient desert wanderers had decided that the camels would be the probable first target and in realization of the danger, they had stopped to make camp. They chose a place behind a small outcropping, not much taller than the camels, to make camp.

"They are convinced that these sons of unclean pigs lay in wait to attack just over that far rise of rocks and have camped in the cave beyond," Omar said. "They are probably right. They knew they could not outrun us with their dwindling water supply and their only option must be to attack."

The Bedouin's tent rose quickly, and they tethered their camels by their legs to stakes driven deeply into the sand and gravel. Nate caught a small flicker of reflected sunlight glancing off his sunglass-shielded eyes. He raised his binoculars in the direction the high ridge to the left of them, scanning each set of outcroppings continuously until the quick flash of light showed again.

"I saw it too," Randy said as Nate started to open his mouth. "They have laid their trap well. There is no way to approach without being seen. We'll have to stalk by night with infrared equipment. I don't believe they were able to carry much with them, so I'm guessing they don't have similar equipment.

They set camp and ate lunch under the shade. Nate glanced at the temperature gauge that he had placed in the shade of the tent flap earlier and it read a hundred and twenty-five degrees. Nate could not recall ever being in this kind of heat, even in the southern Arizona Sonoran Desert

The sand's blast furnace had worked its way through the soles of Nate's army issued combat boots, literally broiling his feet. He removed them with an anxious look and was surprised that his feet were not injured.

"Here's an extra couple of magazines each, for your weapons," Randy offered. Nate gladly took them. He had cleaned and oiled his Glock 9mm handgun and well as his M-16, while Jenny inspected the infrared night gear Randy had left.

⁂

During the blackness of night, Khadduri and his new default Aide-de-camp, Abdul Hussein, strode quickly over the rocky embankment carrying the two suitcase nukes to conceal them from capture at all costs.

The two of them would bury them safely under the desert sand, out of sight of the other men and they would be the only two to know their location. "It would do the infidels no good to torture any of his men for they would know nothing," he thought coldly.

They dug into the packed gravely sand until past midnight, their only respite being the coolness of the night-time desert. The two men finished working and leveled the ground, brushing away any indication that man had been present. It took both men to roll the large boulder over the spot where the nukes had been buried. They wrote the exact GPS location coordinates on a scrap of paper and forever locked the knowledge tightly into their memories.

Khadduri had known the Saudi Government would send troops and had watched, hidden behind a high ridge as they closed in on his position. He had spotted the cursed Nate Adams and the traitor Fatima al-Zaida with the force. Every time he had locked horns with these two he had come up short, but he would not let that happen again.

Back at the cave, he appointed a young firebrand with a fair amount of leadership ability to hold the attack force at bay for at least four hours while he and Hassim left for the Yemeni port of Adan.

Khadduri took most of the extra water, for he was certain that the remaining force would either be completely obliterated or badly decimated and captured by the Saudis and Bedouins and forced to talk. "They would never find

Allah's weapons of vengeance," he thought. "The desert was just too vast."

Khadduri had seen the Bedouins set their camp just out of small arms range. They must have known that he was using the ancient cave as a campsite. He had known that he wouldn't be able to outpace his enemies if they had Bedouin trackers and he had no choice but to attack the approaching force.

He set a grueling pace toward the Yemeni port of Adan. There was no sense in going to the small town to the southwest, he would be much safer and find secure allies in Aden and return for the nukes by helicopter when the coast was clear.

Jafar and Hassim hurried south in the moonlight at a very fast walk carrying all the water they could manage. Dried meats and fruit were their only fare. They had only one thing on their minds as the false dawn broke with its pale light on the eastern horizon. They had to find a place to rest and shield themselves from the oncoming sun and deadly heat of the day.

Khadduri spotted a rise of low hills that would provide such relief and broke into a light jog toward the low escarpment about a kilometer away. They reached the outcropping just as the sun's orange tip broke the plains transforming the sand and gravel into a brilliant reddish orange. They found a perfect niche in the side of a small cliff that would provide shade the entire daylight hours and decided to take turns sleeping while the other stood watch.

Jafar estimated they had covered at least forty kilometers and the moon would provide enough light for another few days' travel. They each took a ration of water and settled in for the day.

⋏

Wearing their night vision gear, the entire team advanced on the terrorist's position from relative safety. Nate, Jenny and Omar were with Randy's team abreast of the Saudi Strike Force, while the Bedouins stayed behind with the camels.

The whole area was naturally lit with an eerie light green glow that gave sufficient visibility to catch any movement in the rocks above. The entire team together numbered twenty-three and silence was the rule of the day. Each person was aware of the value of placing his or her feet correctly as not to disturb the rubble of the desert floor.

Nate caught movement on the rocky outcrop about sixty meters ahead. Randy's hand came up and the entire team stopped as if all were coupled like a train. After a few hand signals, the team spread out in an evenly spaced array without a word spoken.

The Saudi team sent six men to the left in a flanking movement around the low cliff to advance from behind the enemy position. They hoped to attack the terrorists from behind and force them to fight on two fronts. The Bedouins had already given them the exact location of the cave behind the escarpment.

These desert wanderers knew every inhabitable place and water well location in their territory, and were a wealth of knowledge when it came to the harsh terrain. The old Bedouin leader had known many skirmishes in his days and was familiar and knowledgeable about using his time and resources wisely.

Confidence ran high as a single shot from an AK-47 on the ridge above shattered the early morning silence, kicking sand and gravel from the desert floor a hundred and fifty feet in front of the approaching force. Nate was satisfied that they could not be seen by the terrorists. The moon had set and left a total blackness that the approaching sun would replace within an hour.

He glanced at Jenny and realized that none of the Saudi force had objected at the presence of a woman being among the strike force, or if they did, nobody said anything.

His face remained calm and he studied the woman he loved and now saw only the warrior in her. He knew instantly the reason he had fallen in love with her. There was no guile or guessing in their relationship. With Jenny, what you saw was what you got.

The dark silence was broken by a distant sound from the north. The familiar sound of the rotors of two approaching Blackhawks Randy had called for grew louder as they approached the group's position following the GPS coordinates that Randy had provided.

The Saudi commander radioed his team approaching on the right flank of the terrorists, advising them to pull back. The Blackhawks would be using heat imaging to spot the enemy and he didn't want to lose any of his men to friendly fire.

The sound of the Blackhawks became louder until it filled the air with its insistence, drowning out even their voices. "Dawn's an hour away," he heard Randy say into the radio. "Land a quarter mile north of our camp and we'll strike at dawn."

The camp became loud and busy. The reason for silence had evaporated with the rising sun. The strike was being coordinated to capture as many terrorists alive as possible. Information was crucial and the capture of Khadduri would strike a decisive blow to Al-Qaeda.

"We need those two nukes. It's our primary objective," Randy told the young captain commanding the Blackhawks. He nodded his head and said, "I understand, sir."

The choppers would lead the attack and break any resistance, while the allied forces mopped up any survivors.

Like two menacing birds of prey, the Blackhawks rose majestically in the heat of the morning air, kicking sand in all directions as they floated easily above the desert floor.

Automatic gunfire erupted from the ridge as the two dark shapes approached. Both choppers opened up with their automatic light arms to soften the enemy force. Within a few minutes, the terrorists broke into a full retreat into the cave while the allied ground force advanced toward the opening, passing bodies heavily mangled by automatic fire.

All fire from the terrorist's positions ceased and those remaining in the open threw down their weapons and raised their hands.

The Saudis extracted the five remaining terrorists from the cave in a severely dehydrated condition, learning that Khadduri and an Egyptian known only as Hassim had left the previous night taking most of the water, leaving the remaining force to give them a significant head start.

The nukes were nowhere to be found and information obtained from Khadduri's depleted surviving forces revealed that he had not taken the nukes with him. "Damn," Nate thought. "They would need equipment to find them, at least a metal detector and a radiation detector and there was no telling where he might have buried them. They could search for years and never find them."

Randy was thinking the same thing. Only Hassim and Khadduri knew the exact location of the nukes and if captured they would, in all probability take that information to the grave with them.

After water and food, Khadduri's deserted men indicated that their former leader had marched straight south to the Yemeni port of Adan, traveling at night to conserve water. The demoralized and dehydrated terrorists looked relieved that their ordeal was over and soon realized that Khadduri had thrown them to the wolves, to be discarded like so much garbage.

The Saudi government ordered their troops back to Riyadh. They broke camp in haste with the Bedouin trackers and prepared to travel at night at a relaxed pace.

"We've been ordered to remain on his trail south to Yemen, to capture him alive. We are to recover the nukes at all costs," Randy told Nate. "You three have the option of coming with us."

"Just try and get rid of us," Nate challenged him jokingly.

Omar knew there was no choice for him if he ever wanted to return to his native country with his family and live without fear and just nodded his assent. He would see that Khadduri was sent to hell where he belonged. Nate looked at his friend and knew that Omar had made his decision.

"I'm in, all the way," Jenny piped in.

"The decision has been made Randy. You have our full support," Nate told him decisively. The young captain just nodded his assent.

"We'll travel at night in the choppers and try to pick up their heat signatures from the cold nighttime desert, otherwise it will be like trying to find a needle in a haystack," Randy said. "The desert will be cool enough at seven. Be packed up and ready," he said, expecting the same from us as he did from his own men.

The temperature reached a hundred and twenty-five degrees at 3:00 p.m. and they spent the time in the shade while the two crews of the Blackhawks assessed just how far they could travel with the fuel they had been able to carry before turning back.

Their theory was a hundred and fifty or seventy-five miles before turning back to the air base in Riyadh. They could easily be refueled by another chopper if the need arose they had told Randy.

"The plan is to spot them by their heat signatures in the night and drop the team off a couple of miles behind them. There are seven of them and the plan is that we should be able to demand surrender, capturing both terrorists alive," Randy outlined for them.

"Things never go according to plan that easily," Nate thought. He knew that with water in short supply, Khadduri would be covering distance at night in a slow jog while holing up in the shade during the day. The choppers would cut the distance they would have to travel and put them on his heels fresh while Khadduri was spent, but extracting information from him might prove difficult.

Omar decided to help the Blackhawks' crews with preparation and left Jenny and Nate to their own devices. Hidden by the tent flap she flung her arms around him and buried her face in his neck. "I love you Nate," she said. Gradually, everything seemed like it would work out the way it was supposed to. In reality, Nate knew that life was not that easy, but the love of a woman made it seem that way. The three words, "I love you", honestly spoken by a woman were like a healing salve to the heart of any man.

"I love you too Jenny," he told her. "After this one we'll demand a long vacation. Try to get some rest. It's going to be long night. We'll take the new company yacht, to the Greek Isles."

"If we go to Greece we may never return," she joked.

"She might be right," he thought, smiling.

⯓

Khadduri and Hassim had rested the day beneath an outcropping they had found just before dawn and had watched eagerly as the sun had set. There had been little talk as each man steeled himself to cover the most ground they could once the sun had set.

They felt comfortable that they had enough water and dried meat and fruits to reach Adan if they were careful and Allah watched over them.

Both men were raised in the dry heat of the Middle East and were not strangers to the dangers it presented. They also knew the Bedouin culture and were certain they would indeed be lucky to outrun the trackers to Adan. They had been lucky to catch the moon while it was in the full phase and gave enough light for their sojourn to the coast. As the minutes turned into hours, they grew steadily in confidence.

For three hours, they were able to maintain the steady pace of a slow jog. Khadduri felt the reassuring bulge of his AK-47 strapped to his back although he knew that if the Special Forces caught them, it would be of little use.

Khadduri called a momentary halt, while he strained his senses detecting the faint distinctive sound coming in on a northern wind that could only be caused by the blades of an American Blackhawk helicopter. He reached for his military canteen to take a sip of his precious water reserve, while listening intently for the ominous sound and was about to dismiss it from his mind when he caught the familiar sound once again.

Khadduri instinctively knew why they were out in the night searching, using their heat sensors and that the Americans search would become incredibly easier when they were spotted by their cursed infrared detectors. He also knew that he could not escape.

Hassim also heard the rotors of the attack chopper and knew that the AK-47's they carried would be worse than no weapon at all and would bring instant death upon the both of them. They would need to shield their body heat behind an overhang of rocks to have any chance of survival. He frantically searched for such a place, but they were currently caught in a seemingly endless expanse of open desert plain.

⋏

The chopper covered ground quickly, slicing through the cloudless cool desert sky. The moon was still nearly full, providing its dim light breaking the blackness of night. The technician steadfastly kept his eyes glued to the Forward Looking Infra-Red heat sensor screen, looking for any sign of human life upon the now cool desert floor.

"We've got 'em," the sergeant said excitedly. He put down after another mile and Randy watched as the two shapes on the screen separated and ran in two different directions. One headed directly to the southwest, the other kept in a more southerly route.

Nate glanced at the FLIR's heat-sensing monitor, watching as it revealed two shapes that were much too large and moving quickly to be anything but men. "It was 10:30 and they had probably been traveling since about 7:30 or so," Nate calculated; and the terrorists would be spent and needing water, while their pursuers would be fresh.

Randy had convinced the pilot of the Blackhawk to wait and give them a ride back with their captured terrorists. He reasoned that they would use no more fuel and there was more than enough to return to Riyadh. The pilot readily agreed with his assessment.

"Okay, here's the deal gang," Randy said, addressing the whole group. "It appears that the terrorists have split up into two groups, thinking they would have a better chance of escape. I've divided the seven of us into two groups. Mike, you, Omar, and Nate will come with me and Seth, Jenny, and Jim, will trail to the southwest after the other one, who appears to be headed straight for this place called As Sulayyil. It looks like a small place, but it's reasonably close and he could make it."

Nate didn't like being separated from Jenny, but he understood the reasoning behind Randy's decision. He knew these men would look out for her as well as Nate could.

After disembarking, Seth, Jenny and Jim started toward the southwest after one of terrorists while Randy, Mike, Omar and Nate started directly south in hot pursuit of the other one.

Nate figured that the terrorist commander had about a one half-mile head start on them, but they should be able to overtake him easily enough.

"The air was cool and they were fresh with their ride back to Riyadh waiting in the wings," Nate thought. For a brief moment, he worried about Jenny, but soon realized that she was more than able to take care of herself and with Seth leading the other team, Jenny was in good hands.

Randy was in great shape and started at a medium jog. He had brought his infrared equipment and was now working hard to capture this band of sworn enemies of humanity, before the sun came up when they would lose the window of tactical advantage. Randy had been adamant in his insistence that there should be no reason to receive any casualties and Nate knew that he would use every advantage to reach that goal.

They jogged steadily and heard the chopper start and rise into the air far behind them. Randy's radio crackled and came to life, "Desert Fox, your target is about one half mile ahead and maintaining the same approximate speed as you. I'm coming up behind you and will land. We could do this until we tire him."

"I copy loud and clear. Over and out," Randy said, without breaking stride. The now constant breeze carried his words in their direction as the wind was broken slightly by frequent stronger gusts.

The wind picked up on the desert from a gentle breeze to a constant ten to fifteen miles per hour speed with some gusts reaching thirty-five miles per hour. Blowing sand had become a factor and the team had covered their faces by tying bandanas or any piece of cloth that was handy to keep sand out of their mouth and nose.

Nate shielded his eyes from the stinging sand that penetrated every crevice. Sand was an equal opportunity irritant, seeking to fill every pore, crevice and space that would permit it.

"This one could be bad Nate;" Omar yelled over the wind. "These windstorms come up without any warning and can kill before they are over. We need to find an escarpment or overhang quickly to wait this one out."

Randy heard him loud and clear, "You'll get no argument from me." He pointed to a rocky outcrop he had spotted using his infrared gear. "C'mon, it's about a hundred yards," he yelled.

The four men hastily scrambled toward their destination as the wind increased in its intensity to a fierce roar, all but blinding them as they stoically moved forward covering the last twenty yards. Sand and larger pieces of grainy desert debris struck their faces as if catapulted from a slingshot. They reached the cliff just in time.

Randy's tactical flashlight had just enough power to spot a shallow opening that had been gouged out over a period of time by the elements that would easily provide shelter for the four of them, with little room to spare

Nate sunk back into cleft of the escarpment, grateful for the protection it provided. The wind had taken on the effect of a sandblaster and it wouldn't take long for an unprotected traveler to succumb in this environment.

Nate knew that it was crucial that they capture these two alive if there were to be any chance of recovering the two nukes in this Quarter of Emptiness. A person could look for a lifetime and never find them.

Randy sat calmly checking his equipment, while Omar glanced at his wristwatch. "Not yet midnight," he said to anybody listening. "It's going to be a long night. At least Khadduri won't be going anywhere either," Nate thought.

The sand was like a blizzard, but with much worse ramifications. The sand would find its way into all electronic equipment and weapons. "Randy, wrap that radio," before the sand gets inside it," Nate said. He nodded his assent, giving Nate a silent, "thank you."

Randy decided to try the radio, "This is Desert Fox, over," he spoke into the microphone. After ten seconds of static, they heard only voices, indiscernible and broken by heavy static and radio frequency interference, giving proof of the storm's intensity. At the most, the chopper's location was not much more than four miles north of their position, but the sandstorm's intensity was too great for any local radio reception.

"You're right, Nate. I can't get a signal anyway. Randy said. "Alright men, wrap your weapons in anything you can find and hunker down to ride this one out."

Time seemed to stand still and at 3:30 a.m. contrary to all reason, the wind increased its ferocity with such intensity that a man would find it difficult to stand. Even though the four men were sheltered from the worst of the cyclonic winds, they still felt some of its effects as the sand unrelentingly crept onto their temporary shelter. It would have covered them if they hadn't constantly cleared it off.

Each man had covered his mouth and nose with bandanas to breathe air that was free of sand. They settled in for a long night, hoping the storm would let up.

Nate knew that unless Khadduri had found similar shelter, his chances of survival were slim and they desperately needed him alive to reveal the location of the nukes. They had purposely assigned each of their fluent Arabic speakers on separate teams to improve their chances of getting the information they needed, to get these nukes back into friendly hands.

Jenny peered out from the only place they had found that would provide them some protection. Although it wasn't big enough, it shielded them from the brunt of the flying sand. She desperately wished that Nate had come with her team, but Randy had thought it might be a bad idea. He had observed the chemistry between the two and thought it best to split them up for this excursion. They would make it through this sandstorm with little damage and be in hot pursuit first thing in the morning if the storm had cleared by then.

Before departing from the Bedouin encampment, she had been able to change into her army issue fatigues. She was as comfortable as could be expected and waited patiently for morning to arrive or the sandstorm to abate. They wrapped their weapons in anything they could find to prevent them from being totally inundated with sand. Although the crevice was small, the wind came at the back of the overhang, providing almost perfect protection from the sandstorm's ferocity.

At four in the morning, the wind gathered even more speed and violently shifted the sand until it had piled high, mounding only two feet in front of them.

She thought of Sheikh Muhammad and his son at the Bedouin encampment, where the Quarter of Emptiness began. Bedouins, many centuries ago, had dug the well that had sustained so many travelers over the millennia. The Sheikh was one of a dying breed, the last generation of his kind in the face of inevitable change.

With the discovery of massive oil and gas deposits in the Rub al-Khali, this enormous wasteland would never be the same. Developers would continue relentlessly drilling every producible well with the cries of the Bedouins dimming in the background.

Her mind raced back to her home in Virginia and her swing set in the back yard of the middle class home in Alexandria that her family lived in. Each time her father had left on a secret trip to Baghdad, she had cried, fearful that he would not return. She had known from the visitors and the whispering she had overheard, in the back yard that her father worked for the CIA. She had wanted so much to be like her father, but it had been difficult because of her Arab culture. She clung to the fact that she was an American and in America, anything was possible.

Now, as she sat in a cleft hiding from the most ferocious sandstorm she had ever known, her mind drifted back to reality from the memories of her childhood fears that were fading; and suddenly, she was dreadfully tired, more tired than she had been in her entire life.

She had Nate now and a feeling of vulnerability shrouded over her like a heavy winter blanket in a snowstorm. She knew that the men who were with her would protect her, but she also knew that her much-needed skill would suppress any feelings of vulnerability.

She looked at Seth and Jim nestled in the same crevice that protected her from the vicious sandstorm and envied them for being able to sleep at a moment's notice. The Special Forces warriors were good men and they had sought to protect her until she had shown them she could do her job with the best of them. Even now, they still looked at her as one to be protected. When she glanced at the florescent hands on her watch, she realized that dawn was less than an hour away and she drifted into desperately needed sleep.

The sun crept over the horizon in a burst of color, awakening Jenny from a sound sleep. Not a breath of air moved in the desert calm of Rub al-Khali.

Seth and Jim had quietly risen without disturbing her earlier and were surveying the surrounding terrain. Their voices were too distant for her to discern their conversation. Seth was pointing to the southwest and talking on his radio.

Jenny rose quickly, cleaned the sand from her body and clothing; and approached the two men. Seth had reached Randy and was preparing the tactical plans for their day, using their secure radio communications. It seemed that they would start at full march in a southeasterly direction while the helicopter scanned the area.

The table in the main room of the crudely built dwelling was rough and made from hand-hewn oak, complimented with four similarly made chairs. The Eastern style oil lamp placed at the table's center, cast a pale yellowish light that cast ominous shadows and reflected a pale amber tint from the two glass windows in the dwelling.

Rashid al-Jurnani and the Al-Qaeda leadership had chosen this remote region in Northeastern Pakistan for refuge for its closeness to the Afghan border and Kabul. The Northeast Tribal Areas were well known for their difficulty to be controlled and governed by the central government of Pervez Musharaf.

Al-Jurnani sat in the predawn darkness of the dwelling that was located less than a hundred yards from the Afghan border pondering the catastrophic results of Al-Qaeda's rhetorical attack of the Pakistani government. Their leadership had recently come close to declaring war on the Pakistani government after calling the regime "nothing more than a puppet of American interests".

"Autumn gave them a chilly start in this remote mountainous region and it would be bitterly cold this winter," he thought, as he pondered the growing problem of his tactical commander, Jafar Khadduri in Saudi Arabia. and he was entrusted with many responsibilities and resources

Khadduri was entrusted with five tactical nuclear weapons to attack southern Europe on a five-year plan to spread Islam to southern Europe and establish a new Caliphate. Khadduri had been the bright and rising star in the middle leadership of Al-Qaeda. If their plan was to be successful, their strategy would critically change the face of politics and the global balance of power.

He, Rashid al-Jurnani, was responsible to the men above him, he thought. He had chosen Khadduri for this special mission that would solidify Al-Qaeda as a world power. It would be the first time that a non-state actor, instead of a sovereign nation, would exhibit such power on the global stage.

He thought about how he was named "al-Shaitan," the devil by his men while fighting the Americans in Afghanistan a few years before and how the name had caught on and become a battle cry to the men who fought with him. He had become a minor legend to the Jihadi troops and "freedom fighters" still fighting the Americans in the hills.

He had intervened with his superiors on behalf of Khadduri, but the cost to their organization had been too great. The Cold War vintage Soviet portable tactical nuclear devices were acquired from unscrupulous Russian arms merchants at a cost of over twenty million dollars. Now, there were only two left and more would certainly be difficult to come by.

Khadduri had approached al-Jurnani with an alternate plan to take the country of Saudi Arabia, to use as a launching pad for the destruction of the West. Khadduri knew nothing of the negotiations that the Al-Qaeda leadership were having with Saudi Arabia. The King knew that eventually the American People would tire of this war and abandon the Iraqi people. When this happened, the Saudis would need the friendship of the Arab nations surrounding them to stay in power.

"Khadduri was attempting to conceal his failures and inadequacies with his bold new plan," al-Juranni thought.

As he sat pondering the situation, a team of ten lead by an Al-Qaeda captain was already penetrating Rub al-Khali from Yemen in the south with instructions to intercept Khadduri. They were to eliminate him at all costs and retrieve the two remaining tactical nuclear weapons, before they fell into the Infidel's hands. He knew that an

Army Special Forces team was to the same task. Personally, he didn't care who killed Khadduri, just as long as the job was completed and Al-Qaeda recovered the two remaining nuclear bombs.

Al-Jurnani had not been able to speak for Khadduri any longer and his effectiveness as a leader had evaporated. When he was eliminated, his death would be blamed on the Americans and Khadduri would be declared a martyr. The movement needed martyrs to fuel its engine of terrorism.

They were given strict secondary orders to torture and kill the infidel, Nate Adams and his traitorous ally, Fatima al-Zaidi. The young terrorist commander had orders to use any means necessary to reach Khadduri before the Americans could retrieve the tactical nuclear weapons and he meant to fulfill his orders, lest he be next on Al-Qaeda's hit list.

The eleven men were seasoned desert fighters and had grown up in northern Yemen near the Empty Quarter. The long trek to the north would be no stranger to them. They were as good on this hot desolate terrain as the local Bedouin.

Al-Jurnani watched as the dawn broke, while he stepped toward the old small wood stove that provided heat and cooking for the modest structure. He reached for the freshly brewed coffee before deciding to awaken the three men sleeping in the other room and send them on their way to retrieve intelligence from Afghanistan.

When the three men had left, al-Jurnani picked up the cell phone and dialed headquarters to report his activities and suspicions concerning Khadduri and request any further instructions.

He felt sorrow for Khadduri, but the cost of failure was too great and the cause of Islamic world domination must go forward at any cost. The thought came to him as to when it would be his turn, to be cast aside like a used plastic water bottle.

⊥

Randy watched with the freshly refueled Blackhawk touched ground less than a hundred yards from where the team had holed up from the sandstorm. He walked to the warrant officer who was piloting the chopper.

"We have intelligence reports that indicate that an Al-Qaeda team is coming our way from the south, Captain," the warrant officer told Randy.

"It figures … are you authorized to stay and provide support for us," Randy asked with a serious look on his face. He knew he would be outgunned, but a Blackhawk spec-ops variant would even the odds considerably.

"I am indeed, Captain and it will be my pleasure to aid you in any way possible," he replied. "I have been authorized to provide logistical support and use deadly force at my discretion, sir. What is your plan?"

"We should get a visual from the air, then disembark and engage. If an Al-Qaeda force from the south reaches this man first, our job will become much more difficult," Randy told him.

The chopper lifted with the four additional passengers, slowly flying in a southern direction. Randy had guessed his team was probably following Khadduri himself on the pair's original course, while he sent the other terrorist on a separate trail to the southwest, also dividing the American forces.

The chopper moved a hundred meters off the ground with four pairs of eyes scanning every nook and cranny of the oncoming surface.

Randy pointed to a small overhang and cliff three about hundred meters away, "Let's take a look at that crevice at the bottom for sign," he said. The pilot landed set down completed a circling maneuver landing about a thousand meters on a flat gravely surface. "Good luck, Captain," the warrant officer bid Randy.

They spread to about ten meters apart, approaching cautiously, wary that their prey may still be lurking. The crevice was more like a small cave that probably would provide shelter during a sandstorm.

The small force halted at Randy's hand signal, weapons trained on the small cave, while Randy motioned Mike forward to reconnoiter the cave. Mike gave an "all clear" sign and Nate hiked to the left of the cave about fifty meters where the cliff came to an end, looking for footprints or any spoor that would indicate human presence.

He scanned the ground as he looked to the south following a small rise and discovered fresh footprints in the harder surface of the gravel-laden ground. He whistled for the team and within seconds, Randy was looking in a southerly direction at the fading footprints that their quarry had left in his haste. "He's wasting no time. Look at the prints and spacing, he started jogging right here." Randy said, following the prints to the end of the rise and pointing to the ground.

"He has a two-hour head start," said Randy. "He probably left as soon as the sandstorm abated, trying to conserve water in the dark."

Two hours later, the spoor they were tracking turned a little to the west toward As Sulayyil. Randy stopped and studied the tracks. "He has been forced to travel during the day and doesn't have enough water for the trip to Adan," Randy told his team.

"Makes sense," Nate said. "They just split up to force us to split our forces." He probably has a two way radio and has been in contact with his friend who must be close to As Sulayyil." The NSA may even be able to give us an intercept, if he uses it too long."

"Let's go," Randy said. "We'll put the heat on and try to tire him."

⋏

Ali Hilala led his ten men to a warehouse on the outskirts of Aden, used mostly to store hordes of used military equipment and clandestine weaponry from the United States, Russia, China, North Korea et.al.; including some American shoulder-launched anti-aircraft Stinger missiles, originally missing from Afghanistan. The arms dealer who owned this warehouse was connected distantly to the Royal Family and was thereby above reproach or question in the community. His activities went unnoticed and unquestioned in Yemen's busy port of Adan.

Ali entered the warehouse at six in the morning. While the sun had not yet risen, he hoped to be well on his way northward by daylight. Walking in the direction of the large troop transport truck with Saudi military markings on the doors of the cab, he bid his men to follow.

A middle-aged man with ruddy skin and a balding pate emerged from the shadows behind. With little fanfare, he walked up to Ali and said, "Everything is as arranged," handing him the keys. He directed a flashlight inside the rear of the transport that was filled with a full range of weaponry, including American-made Stinger missiles that would bring down a Blackhawk helicopter or even take out a tank, if necessary.

"You understand that full payment is due now for all equipment," the man said, spewing the words as if they were a threat. Ali said nothing, and only handed him a package that he had not opened, but obviously contained the money that the little distasteful man desired. Ali disliked doing business with this kind of individual and it showed on his face.

The businessman was not insulted, but instead grabbed the money and turned, immediately dismissing them. The little man seemed to disappear within the shadows of the warehouse without making a sound and was gone, thinking Ali would change his mind.

Ali motioned his men to the rear of the truck, where they would sit along the built-in benches along each side. The entire front bed of the truck was loaded with sophisticated weaponry, familiar to Ali and his team.

They headed north along the isolated stretch of road that looked endless as it stretched four hundred and fifty kilometers to Najran, then another three hundred and fifty kilometers to As Sulayyil. The little fat man at the warehouse had also added six Jerry cans containing thirty additional gallons of gas. He smiled ironically that they had the original US Army "5 Gallons" label on the cans, boldly written in English. He didn't know how to compute that into liters, but it appeared to be sufficient gas until they could refuel.

He had chosen his team from the best and would tolerate no disobedience, he needed complete discipline form his men if this mission was to succeed.

He sensed that this American was not only lucky, but he possessed incredible skills of perception that must be overcome with Allah's blessing and an immaculate performance on his part. He would intercept Khadduri and lull him into a false sense of trust and when he had obtained the coordinates of the nukes; he would quickly eliminate this man, and then pray for his soul in the name of Islam.

Dawn began to streak orange on the high feathery clouds to the east as Ali eased the transport truck from the warehouse and left the northern outskirts of Aden to cover the fifty kilometers north to Najran.

In the greater Al-Qaeda scheme of things, Ali Hilala was a procurer and transporter, whose major task was to keep its multifaceted and ever-evolving machine of terror supplied with whatever it needed to wage Jihad against the Infidel, He was both ruthless and efficient, and more than willing to die in service to Allah and Islam.

The only way to win this game was to drive to As Sulayyil and embark into Rub al-Khali on foot as quickly as possible.

He knew that Khadduri would travel the entire night, pushing his men beyond endurance to succeed in his task. Ali would drive north all day and night, stopping in another hundred and fifty kilometers to top off the fuel tank at a gas station he was familiar with. He would hold the fuel in the bed of the truck, in their storage containers, in reserve until the last to reach the desert town in time to rendezvous with Khadduri.

His men were competent. He had fought alongside them many times and they would fight to the death without questioning his authority. Most of these men had grown up around Rub al-Khali and bragged that they had the endurance of a camel in this rugged wasteland. Ali secretly smiled, wondering if this were probably not true.

Ali's brother had taken a Saudi military flight from Riyadh to Adan and spotted an American UH-60L Blackhawk helicopter searching for Khadduri and the missing nukes. Flying at fifteen thousand feet, he had easily positioned the chopper's exact location east of As Sulayyil.

Khadduri should be in range of a relay tower for his cell phone by nightfall and he would know his position. They would travel as far in the transport vehicle as possible to gain time on the pursuing Americans.

He knew they would be far better armed than the Americans. If they could take out the Blackhawk with the Stinger, it would please his superiors when he reported the death of Nate Adams, the infidel that had thus far thwarted the greater plans of Allah.

Ali could almost taste the sweet flavors of success and knew he could perform as Al-Qaeda's new tactical commander, delivering the two nuclear bombs to their targets.

Khadduri had failed miserably and perhaps when he had recovered the hidden nukes, his superiors would know of his ability. When he learned the location of these weapons, he would kill Khadduri immediately, along with any remaining men he might command.

⋏

Randy sent the Blackhawk to pick up Seth, Jenny and Jim and when they had once again joined forces, it was Randy's guess that Khadduri had somehow caught up with his cohort. The team of seven once again sought to pick up Khadduri's spoor before they reached As Sulayyil and relative safety.

If the pair was able to reach the city, they could disappear within a population that was partially sympathetic to their cause and the nukes might be lost to them.

Nate and Jenny walked a hundred meters ahead of the remaining five. "The narrow pass between two low rocky ridges that formed a valley was the only way west from this point without walking miles out of their way. Nate was relatively sure that if the two had left a trail, it would be in this area.

After walking for ten minutes, he spotted two sets of clear footprints in the hard gravel plain. They were at the western edge of the Empty Quarter and the terrain had changed slightly. The fresh spoor was clearly visible, even to an amateur tracker like Nate. "We've got 'em Nate," Jenny said.

"Over here," he called to Randy. The five men broke into a jog to catch up to Nate's position. Randy studied the footprints quietly with Seth when they finally rose from their squatting positions. "It's them alright. They've paired up and they're moving at a light jog".

"They've managed to keep ahead of us," Randy said. "We have to stop them before they get to the town."

"Send the Blackhawk ahead and cut them off," Nate told him.

Randy decided to clear the small valley between the ridges where he could view the plains ahead, trying to get a visual with his binoculars and within ten minutes, they had a clear view of the plain ahead.

"No such luck," Randy said, after scanning the plain ahead for a few minutes. They might have hunkered down in the shade until dark, saving their water. It was less than fifty kilometers to As Sulayyil and they had to stop them tonight or it would be too late.

Khadduri was close enough to the relay tower in As Sulayyil to get a signal on his cell phone in the shaded overhang they had found to wait out the daylight hours. There was one message to call Ali Hilala. He knew this man and trusted his competence and determination to serve Allah and Al-Qaeda and he was in no position to balk.

The phone call was quick and brisk, far too much to the point for Khadduri's taste and it left a bad taste in his mouth. He felt the lack of camaraderie that Allah's soldiers had for one another. He needed this man's help, but would be on his guard for treachery. Khadduri knew from experience that when a person fell from favor with the top leadership, the verdict of death was a swift, painful and final result.

Ali Hilala and his team were ten kilometers east of the city and traveling in his direction on prearranged coordinates. The team leader had asked him about the coordinates for the location of the two remaining nukes, but he told him that he would not reveal them over a cell phone on open air as the infidels had the ability to listen to their words.

⚔

Nightfall came at 7:30 and the Blackhawks had moved up to their position after being refueled by another chopper from the airbase at Riyadh. The seven-member team rapidly boarded the attack chopper. As the door slid shut, Nate could hear the engines scream as the Blackhawk's rotors picked up speed and power, as she lifted into the air like a sleek bird of prey seeking its quarry.

Randy's men were silent, all with the somber faces of men calculating their fate. They knew that an Al-Qaeda team had been dispatched to help the pair they were pursuing, and they had known that circumstances change in an instant of time. These men knew the odds and how best to beat them. Even outnumbered and outgunned, they had been trained to adapt and overcome the odds.

Randy's eyes were glued to the FLIR heat seeking screen, looking for indications of human forms on the cool desert floor as they sped west toward the city fifty kilometers distant.

Jenny's hand slipped down to Nate's leg in the darkness of chopper's interior. The dim lights kept a dark shimmering glow mixed with high-pitched whine of the engine and whirling sound of the rotors. The interior gave off the pungent odor of many troopers, days from home in an inescapable war that had engulfed their lives.

This war, if it was a war, had taken many of America's best, and with American support waning at home, the warriors were getting weary of putting their lives on the line.

Jenny's hand gave Nate's right leg a slight squeeze just above the knee. It wasn't totally sexual in nature, but meant to reassure. Nate had been waiting for many years to feel this way about anyone and he would fight to keep what appeared to be so fleeting, in a world of confusion.

His conditioning and experience as a reporter had taught him to take nothing for granted, but instead, savor the moment. He smiled at her, knowing that whatever happened here, when it was over, he and Jenny would take a long vacation in the Mediterranean on the *Sophia*. He allowed his mind to wander to the luxury of the Mediterranean and the *Sophia*, thinking only of Jenny and their fleeting time together, without the concern of the nuclear weapons and the damage they could cause on many innocent people. Nate snapped out of his daydreaming with the sound of Randy's commanding voice.

"Look lively back there, men," shouted Randy. "We've got something on the screen. Randy and Seth were bent over the screen in heavy conversation trying to interpret the visual images they were receiving. Randy scratched his head and said, "There is way too much activity here for just two terrorists we thought were here," the co-pilot piped in," Captain, there are at least twelve to fifteen hostiles in the area you are targeting."

"Yeah, that's what I was afraid of. Set her down quickly," Randy told the pilot. The pilot started to set it down," We've got incoming and looks an awful lot like a Stinger," he shouted, as the chopper touched the ground. The side doors of the chopper flew open as soon as the chopper was down solidly.

Nate and Jenny flew out of the chopper with Omar almost landing on them still dressed in native Saudi garb with his M-16 in hand. Nate took a few steps dragging Jenny by the arm while Seth and his team seemed to be a bit more fleet-footed. The Stinger had flown a few feet too high as it sought the dying heat of the Blackhawk's extinguished engines. Only the pilot's quick reactions saved the crew and team from instant annihilation from the deadly missile.

"These bastards have American Stinger missiles," Randy spat, as he ran for cover with his men. The chopper's crew was already out and following Randy's team at a distance. Their first responsibility was the Blackhawk and they knew it.

"They're about five kilometers due west," Randy shouted to them. "Let's get over there and lay down some ground fire so we can get that chopper airborne again.

"It would be a long night," Nate thought, as he glanced at the luminous dial of his watch.

At 9:30, the moon hadn't yet risen enough to shed any light to the situation. Fortunately, the infrared detection system was fully operational but they were outgunned and outmanned by a force of perhaps fifteen heavily armed men.

The team moved forward with resolve. They were at their best when the odds were stacked against them. Nate glanced directly to his left at Seth as he moved forward and saw only a warrior. Any vestige of the fun loving guy by the palace pool was missing. He had the hard determined look of a warrior and Nate felt fortunate that Seth was on their side.

After two kilometers, the team stopped, "They're only two kilometers west of here and almost within range. Our objective is to lay down heavy ground fire that will prohibit their use of the Stinger missiles. Remember, we have the advantage. We can see them and they can't see us. The team took a few minutes to check the readiness of their weapons and extra magazines before moving forward.

"We don't know they can't see us for certain. The new unit may have more sophisticated gear. We know they have Stinger missiles," Nate said calmly, not wanting to challenge Randy's position.

"Thanks, Nate. It must be the time of night. I should've caught that," said Randy. "Alright men, be cautious. No casualties," Randy commanded.

"I like the way he commands," Nate thought. "He just simply gives an order that there will be no casualties and believes it will come to pass."

Nate checked his infrared gear and lowered it over his face checking for operational clarity as Jenny did the same. Randy and his men had taken up offensive stalking positions, but were moving swiftly toward the enemy positions. They cleared a small rise where they could view the vast plain ahead when Randy raised his arm to halt.

"The first objective is to ascertain whether or not they have night gear. Is that clear, men?" Randy looked at Jenny and muttered, "And women." There were nods and grunts of assent as the men moved forward.

Randy and his team dropped to a prone position with Nate, Jenny, and Omar following suit. The plan was to let the enemy advance to their position to reduce any chance of being detected.

They lay quietly in the desert sand, their eyes intently scanning the area of the advancing Al-Qaeda force. Minutes stretched into an eternity of time.

Nate checked his watch. Fifteen minutes had passed and he could distinguish the skirmish line of enemy soldiers advancing. Nobody would fire until Randy opened up. He wanted to spot the man carrying the Stinger missiles and take him out, possibly destroying the weapon in the process.

"Sir, they have no night gear," Seth told Randy. "Good. That will make things much easier," Randy replied, with a sigh of relief.

The engines of the Blackhawk had cooled and it was no longer in danger from a strike by a Stinger missile. Their crew was camped outside the chopper in the cool dry desert night air, anticipating their readiness to take the enemy force out.

The pilot was prepared to start the powerful engines the moment he was called upon but not a moment before, lest they become victim to an anti-aircraft missile built in their own country by American hands. If they had not been so close to the ground when he spotted the missile, they would not have been so lucky.

Nate felt the beads of sweat rise on his forehead. This was a waiting game and he could see, by the way the enemy team was advancing, that they were completely unaware they were being watched, as they inched closer.

Suddenly, Nate spotted the Stinger missile launcher, carried by a man that appeared a little larger than the other eleven men. He signaled Randy, but the team leader had already drawn a bead on the man from a sitting position leaning his elbow on his knee to steady his aim.

He knew from experience that there was a sequence of order on which man to take out according to your tactical position on the ground and he aimed for the third man in from his right side using the same technique Randy was using. The silence was deafening except for the occasional sound of enemy boots scraping along the desert floor.

From his position, he could see Randy's finger slowly tightening on the trigger until the shot rang out like thunder, breaking the silence and faux serenity of the cool night air. Except for Randy's shot, everything remained silent for an additional second before all hell broke loose. Nate's shot winged his target, but he went down with an audible groan and remained down.

He chose another target, but the remaining unwounded men dropped immediately to prone positions, realizing their predicament. Their leader had put them in a desperate position, from which there was no escape. They had no cover and could not accurately ascertain their attacker's positions to return fire. They started firing at random locations hoping to score a hit, but drew heavy fire in return. A man yelled something in Arabic and threw down his weapon.

"I think they've surrendered," Omar yelled to Randy.

Randy ordered a cease-fire and was on the radio to the crew of the Blackhawk. They heard the chopper's powerful turbines come to life as Randy scooted along the ground to Omar's position and asked him to tell the remaining men to stand with their hands in the air.

Omar spoke for a minute, informing the terrorists of what Randy had asked of them. There was silence and Nate hoped that Khadduri was not taken out at the onset of the engagement. The men rose to their feet slowly as if undecided and dropped quickly to retrieve their weapons. They began firing fiercely for a few moments, as their distant battle cries of "Allah 'u' Akbar, were barely audible in the desert air.

The sound of the approaching helicopter filled the air long before its lights became discernible. The lights on the approaching helicopter gave it the ominous appearance of a mythological bird of prey that would devour anything in its path.

The death-dealing machine hovered back two hundreds meters behind their position and zeroed in the enemy's position.

Rounds began to fly precisely where the gunner aimed them. A straight line of fire kicked up sand seventy-five meters from the enemy position as a warning that the next burst would show no mercy on them. The rounds were heavy, causing the earth to be riddled violently. A look of shear terror and defeat came across the faces of their foes as the Blackhawk's guns fell silent.

Ali Hilala knew when he was beaten. He slowly stood, with his hands in the air, followed by every man left, who could rise to his feet. "We surrender," he said in Arabic. Omar quickly translated for Randy, who instantly signaled a cease-fire.

Nate marveled at how disciplined the team was and how they had taken no casualties. They advanced slowly with their weapons aimed directly at the remaining enemy, watching carefully for any sign of treachery.

Jenny was silent but had taken aim on one of the prone terrorists. She had taken down her first target and he wasn't moving. "A good clean shot," thought Nate.

"Get Khadduri, if he's alive and isolate him immediately," Nate said to Randy. "We've got to get the location of those nukes before the Saudis."

Randy motioned to Omar to come with him. Omar started speaking to the leader of the group. After a minute, he turned to Randy and said, "Khadduri's been shot but fortunately he is still alive. We can't let him die if it can be avoided. The pilot had landed and a medic came running at Randy's call on the radio.

They walked to the man that Nate had shot. "I glad you weren't a better shot," Jenny chided him. "She was right," Nate thought, as he looked down at the moaning terrorist. "An inch more on target and there would be no location this man could provide."

"Ask them where the man that was with Khadduri is," Randy told Omar.

Within a few minutes of questioning, Ali Hilala walked to an inert body on the sand and pointed at Hassim. One of Randy's men had taken him out with a clean shot to the chest, his blood still flowing over the shifting desert sand.

"He'll live," the medic treating Khadduri said, after administering a saline drip into his right arm. The shot had taken him in the upper chest missing his lung completely. The medic staunched the flow of blood from the wound, but was concerned about the time it would take to get him to the hospital.

"This guy is responsible for the bombing of Rome. Do you really think I care about his life as long as I get the location of those other two nukes," Randy told the medic. "Just keep this loser alive until I get the coordinates." The medic studied him for a moment, looked down and worked intently.

The medic returned his attention to Randy and handed him a cell phone. "By the way, here's the cell phone I took off him," the medic said. "I hope it'll help."

"Omar," Randy yelled. Omar was at his side instantly. Randy handed him the cell phone. "We're looking for longitude and latitude coordinates stored in this phone. Can you check it," he asked. Omar took the phone, studied it for a couple of minutes and knew just where to look for any kind of information. He would scour its memory and if it was in there, he would find it.

Hilala's men were assigned to take care of their own dead and load them into the body bags that had been provided by the pilot of the Blackhawk. Khadduri was loaded into the chopper while Omar continued to work on the cell phone's memory. He'd lost a lot of blood and was slipping in and out of consciousness, but the medic claimed he would make it.

"I've got something here," Omar said to Randy, as he found what appeared to be MGRS coordinates in the message section of the phone.

"Wow! The dumb crazy bastards didn't even bother to encrypt it. Those are the coordinates where the other firefight took place and they are exact from an enhanced GPS device," Randy beamed. "I'm going to call these coordinates in to the airbase at Riyadh and we'll have a couple of choppers and a nuclear security team out there before morning."

"Next thing you know, they'll be using Roman numerals," cracked Nate sarcastically, in the joy of the moment.

Jenny looked at the coordinates and copied the numbers, while Nate strode toward Randy with a high five. Randy smiled, "This looks good," he said, as his face returned back to a more normal and somber leadership façade.

Randy didn't know it yet; but Omar, Jenny and Nate would be on that mission to find the remaining nukes. It was the best story anywhere on the planet and Nate would absolutely be there even if he had to walk. He wanted photos of those nukes being dug up. The world would know that America had meant it when they said it was a global war on terror.

Nate looked at the signal strength on his cell phone, "Voila!" he thought, as he dialed Christine.

Christine must have been waiting because the phone only rang once and he heard her questioning voice. "Nate, is that you?"

"Who else would it be," he said chuckling at her excitement. "I'm in a hurry and I won't have a signal very long, so listen." He related all the details of the last couple of days while she recorded and asked her if she could arrange for the three of them to be on the expedition to retrieve the nukes.

"I'll get right on it, Nate," she said. "Get all the pictures you can take, OK," The signal faded just in time for him to avoid being told by her, to take care of himself.

The pilot flew a quick mission to the airbase. There was excitement among the crew and Randy's men, and in the meantime, their joviality had returned. They had accomplished their mission with no causalities. There were a lot of high fives being given and received. Nate sat back until his head rested on the hard surface of the chopper's skin and drifted into an exhausted sleep.

Hilala and his four remaining men sat with their hands cuffed behind their backs, knowing they would face trial at the hands of the Saudi government after being tortured for any information they could give. Their eyes cast the same hollow defeated look that prisoners on death row for centuries had reflected.

Jenny had heard Nate ask Christine to handle the politics, for them to be on the mission to retrieve the nukes and smiled. She knew it was best to let Christine apply pressure at the top on this one, so she said nothing to Randy. The American Government owed Global and Christine, on this one and she was in a position to dictate some concessions on the nuke's retrieval.

Back at the hanger on the airfield, heavily armed crews were being prepared to board two Blackhawks. These men all had serious looks with camouflage painting on their faces. These tough and determined American warriors, who would get the job done and complete their mission, taking no crap from Al-Qaeda or anyone else that got in the way.

"We can't let you have all the fun," the captain of the reconnaissance team told Randy. "I'm afraid all the fun is over," Randy retorted. "You'll have to dig those nukes up by hand and you better bring some shovels and gloves."

They were in the air and Captain Mathews didn't look too pleased about the "extra baggage," as he called it. He didn't like the idea of journalists being embedded with the troops. "Don't worry about these three," Randy told Mathews. "They can take care of themselves and they carry their own weight. Mathews was silent at Randy's comment and just grimaced at the thought of journalists accompanying them on a mission this important.

They were on-site by daybreak. "It looks like it would be a hot day for digging," Nate thought, feeling sorry for these battle hardened troops who were dressed for combat instead of the hard labor ahead of them.

"They've got way too much gear on for digging in this heat," he told Jenny.

Nate leaned on a large boulder beside Jenny and watched as the soldiers dug holes in various spots around them. "Why don't we move this big rock and dig," Nate asked the sergeant who didn't look too happy at the prospect. Nate had the intuitive notion that these terrorists would certainly mark their spot and remember it with a landmark. "Why not a big rock that would take several men to move,"

"Let's Go ... This isn't an archaeological expedition!" said Randy. "Or, is it," thought Nate, in reference to the now-classic former Soviet nuclear relics of the old Cold War era.

"Careful!" It may be booby trapped," replied Jenny. "They were barely carrying enough food, water and ammo, so they probably didn't have time and didn't want to risk damaging the nukes," said the Captain, "but, there's really no telling with Al-Qaeda."

Nate, Jenny, Omar and some of the team gingerly pushed the giant boulder out of its spot and grabbed shovels that a couple of the exhausted soldiers had thrown down. After digging for a couple of minutes, Jenny's shovel hit something metallic.

"Nate! I think I've found them," she said excitedly.

"Careful!" Nate yelled. "Let's dig around it so we don't dent it," Nate said, taking as many pictures as he could, after gladly casting his shovel to the ground.

"We'll take it from here," Mathews said, with salty sweat running in rivulets from his forehead into his eyes.

"Be my guest," Nate said amicably, pointing to the shovels with obvious relish. Nate could see relief in Mathews' face that finally they could return to base and get his men out of the punishing heat.

Within five minutes, the soldiers had lifted the two aluminum colored large suitcases from the freshly dug earth. Nate walked from every angle, taking pictures of every phase of the recovery operation. The NBC Weapons Specialist's radiation monitor confirmed a nuclear footprint.

"Go ahead, open it. It won't go off," said Randy. He and Nate both read the original Russian Cyrillic characters, supplemented with improvised paper Arabic labels on the control surface. The original late '50s-early 60's period Soviet KGB model number "PA-115" hauntingly appeared top center, as if from a bygone era.

"That translates to RA-115," added Nate. "You know some Russian," said the Specialist, as Nate snapped a crowning detailed close-up photo.

With everything loaded, the entire team was not sad to leave Rub al-Khali once again to its own devices.

Mathews was on the satellite scrambler with the news of their successful mission and the Blackhawks were on their way back to the airbase in Riyadh. "Warehouse, Warehouse… This is Desert Fox … over. Affirmative, package recovered and en route … Out," he radioed. "Roger, Desert Fox. This is Warehouse … Acknowledged. Well Done, Desert Fox! … Out," crackled the reply.

Nate was relieved to return to the palatial accommodations, the Saudi government had afforded them; Omar went to his quarters to pack the rest of his gear and catch the first flight possible to America.

Randy and his men were detained at the American airbase for debriefing and would probably ship out immediately after, with orders for his team's new assignment.

The shower was long and hot. The tension of many days of extreme elements and stress washed away with the dirt and sweat of the desert would be left behind, but not forgotten.

Jenny came out of the shower with a towel wrapped around her midsection just barely covering the vital parts. Fresh drops of beaded water still glistened from her light brown shoulders. She came to where Nate was sitting and curled up in his lap with a look of mischievousness in her saucy eyes.

The towel dropped from her body as she twisted in his lap to give him a kiss that faded the recent memories of Rub al-Khali from his mind. All the tiredness and stress disappeared into nothingness and renewed energy flowed through his body as he felt her warmth and inhaled the scent of her skin.

Nate and Jenny lay back in one another's arms with Jenny folding gently into Nate's embrace. The sunburn, heat and dehydration were soon forgotten in the closeness and intimacy of their embrace. Nate's lips trailed from her lips to her neck while she gasped in pleasure at being nuzzled.

"Easy boy," Jenny joked. "We have all the time in the world." She was right, they could take the time they needed to relax and he fully intended to use the extra month the government had afforded them to use the estate.

Nate knew he wouldn't miss Rub al-Khali. He had never before beheld a desert so empty of life that only Bedouins could eke out a meager human existence. There had been a certain beauty in its emptiness, but he was glad their mission was accomplished and he eagerly welcomed returning to modern western civilization with all of its personal freedom and creature comforts.

"They sure had named this one correctly," he thought. The heat and dryness were so intense that a person not prepared, could die in the first day out.

Omar had already left and they had the house to themselves and the couple took full selfish advantage of it, whiling away the afternoon in each other's arms talking endlessly, foolishly and sometimes unrealistically of their dreams and desires.

At six, when the heat of the day started to abate, they moved to the pool with an ice-cold dark German lager. He lay in a beach chair next to an expensive glass end table. It wasn't just any glass end table. It was supported by fancy hand-made wrought iron that couldn't be found in any store he'd ever shopped in. He looked up, hearing her feet as they slid across the hand-painted Italian porcelain tile, lightly gliding toward him.

The pool was lined with tiles dashed with splashes of color that in any other setting would clash violently, but here they flowed with the naturalness of a Michelangelo painting. The entire landscaping was ringed with palm trees that looked like they each had their own personal caretaker. The back yard wasn't really a back yard. It just seemed to flow and merge into the desert at an indeterminable place.

"Jenny matched the setting," he thought. "Both exquisite and hard to come by and both well worth the effort." She lay back in the beach lounge chair with her arms languishing over the edge, touching the decorative tile that surrounded the pool.

Sitting next to him, she reached over with her hand and brushed though the hair on his chest while he leaned back, shutting his eyes to relax, blocking out the world, when his cell phone rang.

"Hello," he said, without even opening his eyes. This was a big mistake and now, he couldn't avoid talking to Christine. He figured that Global owed him at least a week off with no pressure.

"What do you mean, a month," she asked sweetly. "You'll lose your edge, Nate," she chuckled. "Look, those photos were great. We got the entire scoop and all the news agencies are calling us for information. Take the vacation, but write up the feature and send it to me by the end of business tomorrow for the next edition."

"That's a deal I can live with, Christine," Nate told her, flipping his cell phone closed.

He had never been good at bargaining, but Christine made it easy.

"I'll get busy on my laptop tonight," he thought. His best writing time was in the wee hours of the morning and he would have something good for her by noon.

The week was gone before they realized, it was Friday morning and they were scheduled to leave for Zurich on Saturday at 5:00 p.m. They had oiled their bodies and tanned all week, not allowing anything to break into their time. Nate was doing something he rarely had time for, but loved to do, read a book while Jenny tanned and wrote in her journal.

Armed guards had kept the world's media at bay outside the estate and, after two brutal days of braving the heat of the Arabian sun, they had given up, and scattered to the winds. When Nate looked to the front of the estate, there were only two brave souls left sitting in their air-conditioned cars waiting for opportunity to knock. Nate rewarded them with an interview for their patience.

⋏

Their plane landed in Zurich at 10:00p.m., Zurich time. When Nate and Jenny walked through the arrival gate, a throng of reporters, ranging the full gamut from print, broadcast and internet, were waiting like a school of hungry sharks after a single wounded tuna.

There was no escape that Nate could detect until he spotted Christine's friendly face behind the growing gaggle of reporters. The word was out, probably leaked by an airline employee, who was amply paid for such information.

Christine, flanked by two of Zurich's finest, cut through the swarm like a welding torch through a sheet of typing paper. She flew into Nate's arms, welcoming him back. She quickly recovered her composure as head of a major news organization and stepped back.

"We'll grant interviews at the Swissotel at 2:00 p.m. tomorrow," Nate yelled as they raced toward the door and a waiting car.

Someone jammed a local newspaper in his hand as he entered the vehicle. He nodded gratefully and folded it under his arm to read when he got the chance.

"Thank God were going to the Swissotel," Nate thought, wanting to relax and have some refreshments and maybe even some sleep. He always got jet lag and needed his rest after a long flight.

Christine parked and followed them up. "Nate, your next assignment is an important global issue," she said. "I've put together a package for you with all the details."

It was typical of Christine, "All business," he thought, "Perhaps that's why he would never make it as a managing editor or a publisher. There was much more to life than, just business. There was love, intrigue and adventure."

"Don't expect us before noon," he told her, with a tired smile. Christine turned around to Jenny, "Thank you, Jenny for the great job the both of you have accomplished," she said.

Jenny knew that her appreciation was sincere and was finally content with the fact that she had switched jobs from the CIA to Global. She wasn't so sure that this job would be any safer but, the money was good and she would always have Nate. The intrigue and inner workings of the Agency had always disturbed her. It had been as if everyone had their own personal agenda, with no room for error without serious consequences. It was far worse than politics.

Jenny relaxed while Nate showered, then moved around the kitchen humming to her, lost in thought. When he had finished, she moved silently behind him until her arms could encircle his waist. She nestled her head between the broadness of his shoulder blades, trailing kisses down the small off his back until the towel dropped to the floor.

Nate turned quickly, facing her. Passion exploded in his eyes like a bolt of lightning leaving a thundercloud. His hand reached behind her head, pulling her lips to his, almost crushing them with his passion.

She responded with equal passion, moving against his hard body. The softness of her breasts firmly molded into his chest.

Morning came early out of habit for the both them. Nate called down for coffee and breakfast to be delivered, while Jenny, already up at the veranda was watching the sunrise as it progressed from its place in the early morning mist moving higher into the sky.

Watching the sunrise here in Zurich had become one of Nate's favorite pastimes when he was in town. Over the years he had been here, he'd grown to like Switzerland and its mountainous countryside.

Jenny watched as Nate moved in the kitchen and noticed two brown manila envelopes that had been neatly placed on the breakfast bar with a small envelope strategically placed atop the larger envelope.

Jenny's black hair had fallen in disarray and the gentle morning wind with occasional gusts entering from the opened entrance of the veranda's glass caught stray strands, carrying and lifting them in various patterns as she turned to inspect the mysterious manila envelopes.

She reached for the small pastel aqua colored envelopes embossed in a feminine hand that simply stated "Nate and Jenny."

Nate watched as she opened the envelope and extracted an exquisite "Thank You" card. "This is our way of thanking you for the wonderful job that you both have done." The card was signed in Christine's feminine hand: "Christine and your friends and colleagues at Global."

The two manila envelopes were addressed individually, one to each of them. Nate grabbed his, looking to Jenny as if for approval as he slowly opened it. Inside was a recent picture of the newly restored "*Sophia.*" Neatly written and angled across the bottom of the right hand corner was, "Congratulations Nate, she's yours."

Nate was awestruck. For once in his life, he had no words to express how he felt. He glanced as Jenny opened her envelope and extracted a photo of the same size, this one containing the picture of a sparkling metallic blue Mercedes 480-SL Roadster. In the bottom of the envelope rattled keys on a fancy gold key chain, embossed with one word: "Jenny."

Nate heard her gasp. Until now, she had only been able to rent one every time she got the chance, but now it was hers and it was brand new.

Tears of joy ran down Jenny's cheeks as she flew into Nate's arms. "Oh, Nate," she said. "She sure knows how to keep her employees," she thought."

She ran to the front desk, where the concierge greeted her with a smile. "How can I help you, Miss Martinez," he asked. However, she had already looked outside the front doors of the lobby and spotted the exquisite machine.

She was in it before Nate could catch her. Nate opened the passenger door, taking in the new car smell and breathing deeply of it essence.

They arrived at the office in Jenny's new Roadster with the top down and the fall breeze racing past their faces with its dry coolness. "Nate, she even filled the tank," Jenny exclaimed.

They tried to sneak into the building, but their effort was useless. A throng of eight or ten journalists, who had been waiting for them at the back door, bolted from around the corner of the building. The young girl who was in the lead yelling, "They're going in the front door," caught them jamming a microphone in Nate's face; while the intern running behind her, winded from carrying the camera, caught up to them.

"Alright, alright, we'll talk to you now, "Nate said impatiently. The reporter put on her best broadcast-face and started speaking into the microphone. After a half hour of questioning, Christine flanked by two security guards came out and rescued them.

"We're sorry, Nate; but we didn't know you two were here until we saw you on the TV upstairs," she exclaimed, obviously out of breath.

Global's last two copies had been on newsstands around the world for a week now, with pictures of American military elite units digging up the remaining two nukes along with Randy's unit in their trek across Rub al-Khali to track Khadduri. Every conceivable picture from every angle that Nate had taken was published throughout Global's bi-weekly publications. The story had been written and re-written until it conveyed to the world that terrorism would no longer be tolerated by the civilized world.

The Saudis had handed Khadduri over to the Bedouin so justice could exact its toll to pay for the crime of killing the Sheikh and his son. The Bedouins would not be kind to him; and if he was lucky, death would come quickly if the *sayyāf* wielding the scimitar would be skilled and the blade sharp.

⁂

Nate entered the office. There were champagne and hors d'oeuvres spread out on a large table. Karl was there grinning, just back from a recent assignment in Greece. "He gets all the plush ones," Nate thought as they gave each other a hug.

"Isn't it a little early for champagne, Christine," Nate asked. "Don't be such a wet towel, Nate," she replied, leading him to his desk before he could thank her for the yacht.

She turned and smiled sweetly at Nate and Jenny, "the American government threw in most of the money for your expensive gifts, Nate. They're well deserved, but don't get too used to having as much free time." Christine laughed with merriment in her eyes, a little tipsy from the champagne.

Everybody in the office was sipping champagne. "Oh well," he thought, "they wouldn't get much work done today. The staff would be in on Saturday trying to catch up for the next issue."

Nate immediately spotted Christine's new trademark, the brown manila envelope on his desk. He turned and Jenny was at his side. She gave him a questioning glance as she peered at the envelope.

"Sit down, we'll open this together," Nate told her quietly. He had no idea what the new assignment would be as he plucked the envelope from the desk as if he were snatching a hot rock from a fire.

He opened the unsealed flap and drew the heavy batch of papers out in a single practiced motion. The top sheet was a cover letter summarizing the assignment and contents of the package.

The letter started, "Human trafficking is the scourge of the world. I want this blight on humankind tracked down and reported in full until we find the controlling agent that directs this insidious outrage on humanity. Try not to play hero on this one, Nate".

It was like Christine to joke a little at the end. Her personality had not changed much since she was a young girl hanging around the office, asking hundreds of questions.

Nate handed the cover letter to Jenny, while he leafed though the material that contained sources, photos and possible contacts.

"That is subject to change Nate, according to breaking news or more important issues," Christine said, with that winning smile she often used to her advantage.

"Take that package with you, take the week off and spend it on your new yacht Nate," Christine said. "Get good and rested. This one will keep you two busy for quite a while.

They stayed for a while after bargaining for a ten-day vacation from Christine. They planned to take full advantage of their vacation in Capri and Italy's Amalfi Coast aboard the repaired and refurbished *Sophia*.

Later that day, as dusk turned to darkness, they sped south in Jenny's new Roadster toward the border with Italy, where they fully intended to be on the yacht the next day. Only after their long needed rest, would they open the brown manila envelope and prepare for their next adventure.

Epilogue

ISIS has now called for a new Islamic Caliphate in Spain, after the last remnants of the Islamic Caliphate was defeated in Granada 1492. Isis has become increasingly relentless in raising the level of terrorism in both Europe and America and has no intention of relenting or negotiating. Although this is a fiction novel, many actual historical details have been included to portray the realism of an event similar to this novel, actually happening. Accordingly, the persistent threat of international terrorism is global in scope and concerns all of Humanity.

Made in the USA
Middletown, DE
30 January 2018